THE GUINEAMAN

When William Kite runs away to sea to escape a charge of murder, he finds himself aboard the *Enterprize*, a Liverpool Guineaman, or slave ship, destined for the Guinea coast of West Africa. Loaded with slaves, the ship then crosses the Atlantic, bound for the sugar plantations of the West Indies.

Despite the accusation hanging over him, Kite's compassion for the slaves' helplessness finds him serving as a surgeon on the ship, exposed to the dreaded yellow fever which decimates the *Enterprize*'s crew. Kite's subsequent adventures lead him into a world of corruption and love, of trade and friendship as the Seven Years' War breaks out.

THE GUINEAMAN

*'Until the lions have their own story-tellers,
tales of hunting will always glorify the hunter.'*
African Proverb

THE GUINEAMAN

by

Richard Woodman

Magna Large Print Books
Long Preston, North Yorkshire,
BD23 4ND, England.

British Library Cataloguing in Publication Data.

Woodman, Richard
   The guineaman.

26711350

A catalogue record of this book is
available from the British Library

ISBN 0-7505-1605-4

First published in Great Britain 2000
by Severn House Publishers Ltd.

Copyright © 2000 by Richard Woodman

Cover illustration © by G. B. Print Ltd.

The moral right of the author has been asserted

Published in Large Print 2000 by arrangement with
Severn House Publishers Ltd.

*All situations in this publication are fictitious and any
resemblance to living persons is purely coincidental.*

Magna Large Print is an imprint of Library Magna Books Ltd.

Printed and bound in Great Britain by
T.J. (International) Ltd., Cornwall, PL28 8RW

Part One

Blood

The Fugitive

His breath was rasping painfully in his throat now. The effort to run, to raise one foot after another, seemed too much for his failing strength, and still the ground continued to rise, a sharper incline it seemed to his numbed mind, for the sparse grass had given way to a treacherous scree and he sent stones tumbling down behind him. Instinct and a long familiarity with the wild countryside surrounding the lakes had brought him up on to the Black Fell. He began to slacken his pace, feeling his leg muscles trembling with the effort of escape, the thunderous pain of his beating heart and the fogging of his brain. Sweat poured into his eyes and soaked his clothes. He was close to fainting now, as he almost fell headlong, for he had no idea how long he had been running, only that his whole world had suddenly contracted in this effort of escaping his pursuers.

He slowed to a stumbling lope, gradually reclaiming the use of his faculties. He became aware, dimly at first, that night was coming on, and of a sharp chill in the air that presaged rain. He raised his eyes, and saw, at last, the summit of the fell. Now that it seemed attainable, it failed to bring him the security he hoped for. Breathing ponderously he stopped, trying to think. He bent over, gasping, hands on knees, his throat raw, his leg muscles cramped, the moisture on his exposed skin suddenly chilled.

Then he heard a shout and the baying of the dogs, and fear leapt again in his guts. Lifting his head with a strangled cry he began to run once more.

He knew his pursuers could see him against the sky as he crossed the ridge, but it was only as he felt the scree begin to fall away, treacherously inducing his exhausted legs to falter, that he realised how foolish he had been to expose himself. Had the effort of escape not dominated him, his normal ready intelligence would have prevented so foolish a mistake, but it was too late now. For perhaps another five minutes he blunered on, increasingly uncertain of his footing, his arms flailing, his will ebbing with his stamina. Then he slipped, the moment of lost control coinciding with a sharp declivity in the ground, and his shoulder glanced against a rocky outcrop. The impact spun him half round so that his left leg tripped over his right and he tumbled at the foot of the rock.

He fell full length, splashing into a cold

pool of water lying under the outcrop. Face down, he swallowed the brackish stuff, then, in a last reflex, he raised his head, gasped at the air and crawled, like a terrified child, along some ten yards of what felt like a magically soft landscape of green. Then he slowly subsided, lying down in the bed of the stream, his head to one side as he lapsed into complete unconsciousness. The water trickled into and out of his open mouth but the lush landscape of his imagination, which was in fact nothing more than tall flanking grasses and some patches of moss, concealed him in the twilight.

Some moments later, when his pursuers reached the rock, they had lost the trail. In the gathering darkness they stared down into the valley beyond, and one of them pointed to something bounding down a slope half a mile away. The two men bent, like their victim a little earlier, their hands on their knees, gasping for breath as they tried to make out their distant quarry. The hounds slumped on the ground, flanks heaving and tongues lolling from their slobbering chops as they panted like their masters. One lapped water from the pool, the other shook foam from its muzzle. Neither were good coursers, and both men and dogs were badly winded.

'Th' bugger always could run on the fells,' one of the men said to the other between

11

gulps of air, nodding at the dark shape still just visible below.

'He'll be back,' responded the other. 'Then we've got 'un.'

At that moment the rain began. A few tentative drops at first, followed by a sudden, sleeting downpour that hissed at them, bouncing off the scree as a squall drove it up the valley and over the brow of the open moorland. Twilight turned suddenly to the onset of night.

'Come on, Phil, time we got back home. We'll get the justice's men after 'im and have 'im in a noose in Carlisle by next quarter-day!'

The man called Phil did not follow his brother at once but continued to stare down into the valley. Rain streamed down his face. 'Billie Kite!' he roared into the wind. 'I haven't finished with you, you bastard!'

Then he turned, and was gone, following his brother back the way they had come, swallowed by the darkness and the torrential rain. Far down the side of the abandoned valley, the frightened goat ran in its sure-footed way.

The fugitive recovered consciousness a few minutes later. The cooling sweat of his exertion and the chill of the downpour woke him to a shivering cold. Slowly he raised his head, and for several long minutes he remained thus, listening with the keen attention of a hunted animal. All he could hear was the hiss of the rain on the stones and the low moan of the rising wind. The loom of the rock outcrop startled him for a moment, but then he realised not only what it was, but where he was. He had run near enough to five miles from the lake, up the steep incline of the Black Fell, far up beyond the trees and beyond even the high pasture where the flocks of sheep grazed. He had given the Hebblewhite brothers a good run for their money, to be sure! For a moment he thought it was time to return home and then the ghastly events of the early evening flooded back to him, along with the dark realisation that he was a damned soul.

By running away he had compromised his innocence. No one would now believe he had nothing to do with the girl's death.

Oh, God, that it should be his poor Susie…

The impact of this terrible realisation caused him to void his stomach in pure fear: he could never go home again. Never. He could only run on, away down the far valley after the goat.

One

The Whore

William Kite walked south by night, hiding up during daylight. He sheltered in a succession of barns, in a churchyard where the sexton had made a small bower to keep his pick, shovel, sickle and scythe, and, as he neared Liverpool, under the wreckage of an old boat he found on a beach on the southern shore of the River Ribble. At first he had been terrified, but once south of Lancaster, with no hue and cry obvious behind him, he began to feel more confident of escape. He was innocent of the charge the two brothers had screamed at him when they saw the body of their sister, but there was sufficient confusion and guilt attached to his relationship with the dead girl to prick his own conscience. That and the long-standing enmity of Susie's brothers goaded him with the very spurs of the devil himself.

All his fear and irresolution translated into the desire to put many miles between himself and the Hebblewhite farm and the bloody scene upon which he had stumbled that dreadful afternoon. Exhaustion induced sleep, but when he woke, cramped and cold, he sprang instantly to his feet and pressed on southwards. He drank from streams and scavenged what food he could. He caught and cooked a rabbit as he had often done in his carefree boyhood, a youth which now seemed an age away, golden in its fading insubstantiality. Yet, out of the conflicting conviction of innocence and guilt by association, he found the will to press on, to escape, to survive. And as time passed, and no one challenged him and there was no sound of bloodhounds borne on the wind, the eviscerating panic gradually faded. He found that he could think again.

As he walked, only hiding from another night traveller who rode north on a steaming horse with the fugitive air of a highwayman, Kite learned that the ability to think brought with it a train of terrors. The shadows of the gallows fell constantly across his path; the horror of execution, of the disgrace he knew capture, trial and execution would bring upon his father and sister; the impossibility of establishing innocence in an England lusty for death in this year of Grace 1755, spurred him ever southwards. His fear combined with a natural solitary disposition and the cunning born of a boyhood and youth amid the lakes and fells of Cumbria, to enable him to avoid other humans, and in due course he formulated a strategy, just as he had seen his father formulate a specific in the little workshop filled with the mysteries of the pharmacopoeia. It chilled him to think that he would never see his father again, nor his own sister, but the circumstantial evidence condemned him for ever. Only the dry logic of his father's profession of apothecary sustained him. Perhaps he could go for a soldier and lose himself in the ranks of a regular battalion sent on duty overseas … perhaps… But there were few opportunities that he could think of, although a thousand mad schemes came and went as he walked, burning his mind with the one searing certainty that somehow he must live to let his father know he was innocent.

And it was then that he thought of his cousin Francis, and the Liverpool merchant to whom he was apprenticed. Kite recalled the address on the letter his father had last written to Francis, for Kite's widowed father had brought up Francis as well as his own two children. Mr Kite had stretched his influence to the utmost to secure the young man employment which would remove the necessity of feeding him from the slender profits from the apothecary's trade.

During the fourth day, as Kite settled beneath the old boat on the bank of the Ribble, he spread out his coat and, having rinsed his shirt and hose in the sea, laid them to dry. If anyone saw them while he slept exhausted beneath the split tarred planking, nothing came of it and he felt better when he pulled them on again that night, for all the clamminess of the salt in his shirt. At the end of this fifth night's march he approached Liverpool. Intending to rest for only an hour or two, he fell deeply asleep, awaking towards evening in a state close to panic. He wandered utterly confused amid the crowded and noisy streets of the waterfront. Worn out with anxiety and exertion, he failed to locate his cousin's lodging. But on finding he had sufficient money to do so, he secured a night's sleep in a cheap lodging house near the river.

The landlord looked him up and down, shifted the quid of tobacco and remarked, 'You'll likely have to share before the night's out, but a young man of your quality'll have to get used to that if you lodge here.'

Kite was too tired to grasp to what the landlord alluded, aware only of the warmth of the alehouse and the smell of some sort of gruel or stew cooking within the tavern. An hour later, having removed his coat and shoes, he was stretched on a flea-ridden mattress, half covered by a stained blanket.

Some two hours later he woke suddenly, sitting up in bed with a start. The door to the room was open and in it loomed a man bearing a candle in one hand. His other was about the waist of a young woman. Her stays were loose and she and the man were obviously drunk.

'There's a young feller in the bed already, Jimmy. I didn't know youse was after having one of them nights–' and she broke off into a giggle, staring at Kite as he hurriedly reached for his coat and shoes, recalling the landlord's warning. He was confused. It was dark, he should have been marching; the young whore reminded him of Susie. The same wet and open mouth, the same dis-organisation of dress, the same damp stink of sexual intent.

He thought only of escape again, thrusting his feet into his shoes, grabbing his coat and making for the door, to shove past the swaying seaman and his hussy. The seaman reeled back with an oath as Kite pushed past. Kite stumbled on the stairs, recovered and then descended into the taproom. Behind him the seaman, having made an attempt to grab Kite, was drawn back into the bedroom by his whore and the door slammed.

The taproom was crowded now, the air thick with tobacco smoke and raucous con-versation. The variety of men, men of colour, men with red hair, men of sallow complexion and jet-black hair, even a Chinaman with narrow eyes that Kite had only ever heard of in a story, were interspersed with the shabbily gay dresses of the common drabs who sought to service them. Pots of ale and flip were borne hither and thither by the pot-boys and a lass or two and the whole thick atmosphere seemed instantly recognisable to a young man catechised from childhood. 'I am in hell,' he muttered, seeking the door to the street.

It was an ill-chosen and in the event a fateful moment for, as he made for the entrance and the cool night air beyond, two men rose in front of him. Already in heated argument over a smirking trollop who lolled back on the adjacent bench, one shoved at the other and he in turn, recovering, lunged back at his assailant. In an instant, they were fighting.

Kite recoiled from this further manifestation of devilment as the yelps of encouragement and amusement went up all around him. The crowd egged on the contestants until after only a few moments one fetched the other a heavy belt on the jaw and the luckless victim subsided with a crash against the bench.

The victor turned to the woman who was eyeing him with an excited gleam in her eye and held out his hand. 'C'mon, you!' he said, breathing heavily.

'You sure youse can manage her after all that fisticuffs, Tommy-boy?' someone called out and the excited company roared once more.

Tommy-boy ignored the ribaldry, tugged the girl to her feet and pulled her roughly to him, embracing her and planting a kiss upon her wet and ready mouth. The company lost interest and Kite made to pass the couple when suddenly the defeated man rose to his feet. Kite saw the flash of steel and shouted a warning, but he was too late. The knife, thrust upwards, was driven to the hilt into the woman's buttocks so that she screamed and arched her back, her would-be lover staggering under the impact. In the next second a bottle descended upon the head of the seaman with the knife and he fell a second time to the floor.

Kite's exit was now blocked as the other women screamed and gathered round. He caught a glimpse of stocking and a pink thigh pouring with blood and then, amid the wails and the screams and the shouts of the men now crowding about the wretched trollop, he reacted in a way that he could never quite explain. Perhaps it was the earnest desire to prove he was not capable of the murder of which, in distant Cumbria, he stood accused. Perhaps some unconscious urge drove him to prove his innate goodness, that he might, at some desperate future moment, call these low-born seafaring folk and their dockside whores to stand as witness to his character.

'Clear a table,' he said, his voice loud and commanding. He swept an arm and sent pots and bottles to the sawdusted floor, adding, 'Stretch her out here, and quick, for she loses blood.'

Amid the hubbub, a face or two turned towards him. It was clear from his coat and neckcloth that, modest though they were without any pretensions to fashion, he was not a man of the seafaring stock that filled the alehouse. His pallid complexion alone set him apart from them, but the impression of his being a gentleman was lent credibility by his assumption of authority.

'Lay her out upon the table,' he said again, eager to staunch the haemorrhage that reminded him so painfully of the bleeding Susie. Perhaps he sought to make amends, perhaps he accepted that this scene, with its terrible echoes of a late afternoon only a few days earlier, was a fatal repetition from which there was no escape. All he was aware of in that unpleasant moment was that from an unnerved young man intent on escape from a dockside alehouse, he had become again the youth who could set bones and stem the flow of blood. He had done it for Susie's pet rabbit after a fox had savaged it, he had done it for his sister's puppy after Philip Hebblewhite's hound had mauled it, and he had set the wings of birds caught in nets, including a beautiful peregrine falcon. He had been trying to help Susie herself when her brothers found him and raised the cry of 'murderer!'

'I can help her,' he said now, staring about him and dismissing the suspicion in the faces round him.

'Do as he says,' said the man Tommy suddenly, his face pale under his sunburn, the stink of liquor overlaying that of stale sweat. 'Get her up on the table!'

Kite turned, caught the eye of one of the serving girls and said, 'Get me some clean water and a clout... And a needle and thread...'

The wounded woman had fainted as Tommy lugged her unceremoniously on to the table. She lay face down, a large, buxom woman of some twenty-three or -four years of age, unlovely in her unconscious state. Kite carefully raised her filthy skirt and her soiled petticoats as the sailor's knife fell from her. He bent and retrieved it, regarding the wound as the crowd round about fell silent with an intent curiosity. The thrust had been upwards, and the blade had begun its incision in the upper portion of the thigh, reaching its greatest penetration in the subcutaneous fat covering her left buttock. If the cheated and would-be lover who stabbed her had been intending to wound her private parts, he had mercifully missed. The woman's ample figure had saved her from certain death. A momentary yet bitter reflection about the capricious nature of fate crossed Kite's mind: the drunken seaman had escaped a certain charge of murder while he himself, caught in a moment of extreme compromise, yet innocent of any harm to Susie, was sought as a murderer.

Kite shook off the thought and addressed the business in hand. The woman's wound was not as serious as it at first appeared from the steady flow of blood. She wore no drawers, but Kite used the knife to cut away a fold of her petticoat that had been driven into her flesh and then carefully withdrew it from the gash. A portion of muscular tissue obtruded in its wake and, calling again for water, Kite pushed it gently back and drew the two edges of the wound together.

The girl brought him water and he repeated his request for a needle and thread.

''Ere you are, love,' another trollop said, tugging the drawstring of a small cloth bag and withdrawing a rolled hussif. Kite swabbed the wound while the woman threaded the needle. A few moments later he had closed the gash with a half-dozen sutures. Cleaning the drying blood from round the neat stitches, he pulled the woman's petticoat back over her rear. Looking up at the man called Tommy he said,

24

'She needs to sleep quietly on her front. Can you see to that?'

'Aye, I think so, sir.' Tommy looked crestfallen. Someone in the crowd cheered as Kite rinsed his hands in the bowl and wiped them on a grubby towel the serving girl held out to him.

'You a surgeon, sir?' the woman with the hussif asked. Kite smiled. He was too tired to laugh at the ridiculous notion, and too tired to deny it. At their feet the wounded whore's felled assailant stirred, but no one took any notice of him. Then the landlord was shoving forward through the press.

'Let's be having your pots, damn you all! Get ye all off to your beds, and as for you, sir, please to follow me, I'll see to it you have a quiet night after all this botheration.'

Kite slept until late and woke to descend to the now stale air of the noxious taproom. A woman was swabbing the tables with a filthy clout and a pot-boy was eating what looked like oatmeal and water beside the fire. The woman looked round at the boy and nodded, whereupon the lad put down his bowl and scampered out, returning a moment later, followed by the landlord.

'You'll take some breakfast, sir?' the Landlord asked and Kite looked dubiously at the boy's bowl. A fierce hunger gnawed at him and he nodded.

'I'll see to it,' said the woman, bustling off to the kitchen while the landlord addressed the boy.

'You be off and tell the Cap'n, like I told yer, lad.' And again the boy disappeared, on a second errand.

Kite sat at the table which last night he had used to stitch up the slashed jade. Hot coffee and fresh bread were soon filling the taproom with a welcome and surprising aroma. In the chimney, the landlord eased himself on to a bench and lit a small clay pipe, eyeing his guest over the flame which leapt and subsided at the end of the spill.

He shook out the spill and blew a cloud of smoke from his mouth. 'We don't often get the gentry staying with us,' he said. 'I s'pose you'll be looking for a ship...'

Kite looked up with a start. The idea had never occurred to him, but it suddenly offered him a solution to his problem. He could write an affidavit, have it properly sworn and post it to his father. The time which would elapse during a voyage would allow the hue and cry to subside and the real cause of Susie's death to be determined by the magistrates. When he came home again, the whole affair would have blown over.

'You've the right trade for these parts and Captain Makepeace is hard pushed to find what he wants for the *Enterprize...*'

26

'Right trade?' quizzed Kite as it dawned upon him that he knew nothing of ships and therefore had nothing to recommend him as a potential seaman.

The landlord nodded. 'You're not the first barber's 'prentice we've seen here, familiar enough with lifting a doxy's skirts. Happen you've done it once to often and now there's a puddin' in the basin when all you wanted was to dip yer little wick, eh?' A leering wink and a chuckle that rumbled deep in the landlord's belly accompanied this comforting reassurance.

Kite, frowning, was in the process of working out what the landlord meant when the door flew open and a well-dressed man swept into the taproom, spun on his heel and, thumping the heels of both hands on the table in front of Kite, peered under the forecock of a silver-laced tricorne hat into Kite's eyes.

'I have heard you can suture a trollop's arse, Mister...'

'Kite, sir,' said the startled Kite, instantly regretting betraying his name, but rising slowly to his feet under the intimidating gaze of the stranger.

'I am Captain Makepeace of the *Enterprize*,' the stranger said, still leaning forward on his hands, but raising his head and following Kite's elevating figure. 'A Guineaman sir, perhaps the best in Liverpool, though I shall not claim it so myself.' He paused, regarding Kite with a cold eye. 'I want you to ship out with me as my surgeon.'

Kite suddenly made sense of the landlord's reference to his being a barber's apprentice, thinking Kite to be the indentured assistant to a barber-surgeon.

'Look, I have no–'

Makepeace drew himself up and stuck out his chin. Under the shadow of the hat, Kite saw him to be a man of some thirty years of age. The captain's features were handsome in a squared way, the skin swarthy and weather-beaten. Notwithstanding this, his jaw was already dark with the shadow of his beard, while his hair was his own and was drawn back into a clubbed queue. The captain's dark grey eyes bored into Kite's. He felt a sensation of unease so palpable that it silenced his protest, but this vanished as Makepeace clapped him on the shoulder with a charming smile.

'Come, Mr Kite, say you'll sign articles and I assure you of a profitable voyage which will set you up for life. A bounty of a hundred guineas on top of your pay will not displease you, eh? A man would be fool to pass up such an offer and stay an instant longer in a hell-hole like this.' Makepeace gestured at the tawdry surroundings, rapidly hurrying on, 'Well, then, the matter is settled.' He swung away, fished some coins from his waistcoat pocket and, flicking a copper penny to the boy and a gold half-sovereign to the landlord, concluded his business.

'Thank you, Young. I trust I am no longer in debt to you.' The landlord caught the coin and rose to his feet. 'Not at all, Cap'n. As usual, 'tis a pleasure to do business wid yer.'

Kite felt Makepeace's hand under his elbow. 'We shall find,' Makepeace dropped his voice to a confidential and intimate tone, 'a more congenial breakfast aboard the *Enterprize*.'

And having just time to seize his own hat, Kite felt himself propelled out into the street.

Two

The Journal

My Dear Helen, Kite wrote, his borrowed goose quill spluttering as he formed the letters in his quick hand,

I cannot Write without the Strongest Emotions almost Suffocating me with their Intensity. You will have heard, no doubt, of my now being a Murderer and that I was Responsible for the Death of Susan Hebblewhite. It is Not True, and I should be there to defend my Good Name had not the Two Brothers Hebblewhite Come Upon Me in the Most Difficult of Circumstances. I Write now that you may lay the Facts before Father and make him acquainted with them in the Most Emphatick manner possible, as you Love me.

I was, upon Friday last, coming through the Village from Mr Watkins' place, whither I had gone, you may recall upon an errand of Father's...

The normality of that quiet, late afternoon walk imposed itself upon Kite's imagination. He paused in his scribbling to recall the prelude to disaster. It seemed inconceivable that life should lurch round so abrupt and terrifying a corner, precipitating him into so desperate a situation and threatening his sanity. A sense of utter panic rose in him; he felt he was on the verge of madness as he attempted the task of letting his sister and father know what had happened. A cry almost choked him, but he recalled his present surroundings, that he was safe for the moment, and while the confinement of the cabin seemed like a cell, it was not so. After a moment, he grew calm and bent to his task again, once more resolute.

Watkins was a rich and retired old West India merchant who kept a rambling house just beyond the environs of the village and between which lay the Hebblewhites' farm. Kite had been in the act of passing the rickety gate of the mired farmyard when the scream that rent the quiet afternoon had so quickened his heartbeat that he scarcely remembered running from the lane, across the pebbled and muddy yard towards the whitewashed stone house. As the piercing shriek came again he swung aside, running full tilt into the adjacent barn.

Hearing a Scream from the Hebblewhites' barn, yet not seeing any Person about the yard, I gave a Shout that I was coming and Pulled aside the Barn Door. It was Dark inside and I heard a Rustling and Whimpering. Stumbling forward into the Gloom I came upon the most Hideous Sight. Susan, all uncovered, her Womb running Blood and Gore into the Straw and Filth, her Belly Pierced by a pitchfork which I withdrew Whereupon there went up a Great Shout, as of Joy, I thought in my hopeless Confusion, for I was so Shaking and Almost Weeping, when from Behind I felt Hands Laid upon me and turning, so Full of Fury was I Suddenly Infused that I wielded the Bloody Instrument of Death and Phil Hebblewhite and his brother Colin fell back and sent up the Cry. MURDERER! MURDERER! as if I had been caught in the very Act of Committing the Bloody Deed.

Instantly sensing that the Implication of Guilt was Strongly Laid Upon Me by the holding of the Pitchfork, I Stabbed Twice at the Brothers that they might Let me Pass and began to Run. Oh, Dearest Sister, how I now Regret this Impetuous Action and the Subsequent Flight. They Assumed Guilt lay Upon Me, and Knowing that I had some Affection for Their Sister thought the Worst – That I had got her with Child and was Intent upon Concealing my Crime with One more Heinous by Far. They set their Hounds upon me, but, As if the Devil

Himself possessed Me, I outran Them and so, after Many Days Trial, Came to this place and have now Taken Ship for the Coast of Africa.

My Only Object in Fleeing, was to Avoid the Murderous Intentions of Colin and Philip Hebblewhite who, You Know too well, Bear no Love for me. I durst not write to Father, but Plead with You that You will Lay these Desperate Circumstances before Him to Establish My Innocence. That this Matter May be Laid before the Justices is Something that I Devoutly Hope, but Whatever may befall I Affirm My Innocence...

Kite laid down the quill and buried his head in his hands. The headlong rush to express himself left him feeling drained. He wanted to write more, to express his stupefied gratitude to Captain Makepeace for his generosity in advancing sufficient funds for him to buy himself a few garments and necessaries, for his ready friendship in taking him up and his own guilt that, in his own eagerness to escape, he had so far obscured from the good captain the fact that he was not a surgeon. It had seemed that luck favoured his innocence as the day of departure arrived but then his anxiety had redoubled. Hardly had they warped out into the stream of the River Mersey than a blinding fog had descended and they had been trapped for two days.

The only merit in this delay was the opportunity to write home, an endeavour he had at first considered too risky until he recollected that no defence was tantamount to an admission of guilt. When he had casually, or as casually as his beating heart permitted, asked Makepeace, the *Enterprize's* commander had assured him the pilot would take the letter and post it, that being a part of his duty in seeing ships clear of the dangers of the estuary. As for the rest, Kite's anxiety, his need to acquire a few personal effects and the strangeness of his own confusing surroundings had swallowed the slow plod of time. He vacillated between periods of profound depression that led him to fearful and terrifying moments, but the instinct to survive and the strong restorative certainty of his own innocence pulled him back from the brink. He turned aside from contemplation of the dark river and its promise of eternal oblivion, thrusting himself into the business of the ship with a fervid activity. Apart from brief encounters, Captain Makepeace became an increasingly aloof, preoccupied or absent figure while, unfortunately, the society of his fellow officers had been denied him in the hurried preparations for departure and the apparent mayhem that prevailed. Any notion of matters on shipboard being well regulated seemed wildly inaccurate as stores, cargo and trade goods poured aboard the *Enterprize*. Kite, personally distracted, confused and neglected, had no hope of understanding the distinction between artefacts, consumables and goods of singular description that were salted away below, even had he had a mind to. All about him sounded an alien tongue, replete with lavish use of shipboard expressions and a proliferation of oaths. This was much conducted at the shout, so that he derived no information from it, other than a certainty that the crescendo in its general intensity seemed to rise as the moment of departure drew closer. When the decks were suddenly cleared and the teeming mass of seamen and longshoremen drew apart, a strange, almost silent order did in fact descend upon the *Enterprize's* decks. These were suddenly less cluttered, festooned instead by carefully coiled ropes, so that the business of their warping into the river, a shred of canvas dangling above their heads until the anchor was let go as the fog settled, seemed almost peaceful.

There had been some small duties thrust Kite's way. Makepeace, after his brief and generous solicitude in advancing him ten guineas, had hardly spoken to him. Another man, the ship's first officer, known not as a mate but as a lieutenant, as if he were a

King's officer, had introduced himself as Thomas Gerard. Gerard had shown him a small cubby-hole in the bottom of the ship. Where exactly this was in relation to those parts of the vessel with which Kite was better acquainted, it took him three days to determine. This cubby-hole was his store, in which lay several small wooden chests that contained his pills, tablets and other bottled specifics, a set of ghastly chirurgical tools, a pestle, a mortar and an assortment of dirty, glass-stoppered bottles. Having made a short trip ashore, constantly looking over his shoulder for fear of apprehension by constables, to fit himself out with some small clothes and a new pair of shoes, he occupied himself in a desultory attempt to make an inventory of his gear. He spent long hours at this task, reliving those dreadful moments in the Hebblewhite barn over and over again, suddenly coming to himself when some noisy oath obtruded and woke him with a start from his obsessive trance. Thus he filled his days and afterwards could remember little beyond the overwhelming confusion prior to departure. He slept but fitfully, disturbed by dreams of Susie and her torn belly, confusing reality and spectre so that he could scarce recall what he had really seen from the grotesque inventions of his fevered imagination. As is the way with nightmares, Susie's death agonies became confused with the stitching up of the whore's backside, the agony of pursuit and the slavering hounds of the Hebblewhite brothers.

The fog caused moisture on every rope and spar so that water dripped so persistently upon the ship's deck that it seemed like rain. As the *Enterprize* swung in the tideway, snubbing at her cable in this pervading damp, Kite completed his letter to Helen. Why he wrote to her in preference to her father, he was not certain, except that it seemed less likely that her correspondence would be suspect while he imagined every letter addressed to his father would be subject to scrutiny by the shadowy, yet persistent agents of the law. Despite the ease of his escape, his over-wrought imagination conjured up a constable or a sworn citizen skulking behind every cottage in the village, eager to pounce upon evidence leading to the location of his whereabouts, a tension heightened by their fog-bound delay. This seemed a cruel and fateful prolongation of his agony; a certain indicator that he would be caught, to dance at the end of the hangman's noose after due process in the Carlisle Assizes.

But it was not so, for on the ebb coming away that very afternoon, the fog vanished as quickly as it had appeared and the *Enterprize,* with equal speed, weighed her anchor. The stirring and the capstan shanty woke Kite, and he went on deck, to be first shoved out of the way by a stream of bawling men walking the bars of the capstan round, and then shouldered aside by cursing seamen as they manned the halliards and sent the yards aloft to another rousing and discordant song. He succeeded, however, in passing his letter and a half-sovereign to the pilot, lingering on deck long enough to wonder at the downright insolence of the words of the shanty. These blackened the name of the commander and his officers in an orgy of insubordination, but neither Makepeace, standing aft by the helmsman and pilot, nor Gerard, staring aloft at the ascending yards, seemed to take any notice, and when the lieutenant bawled 'Belay!' the words and rough tune ended abruptly, the men easing the ropes to the leading hauliers, who smartly turned them up on the pins and fell to coiling them neatly. The moment of near-mutiny had apparently passed. It took Kite some time before he understood this had been merely a ritual, a meaningless chanting to co-ordinate effort and only an expression of the crew's unity for a specific task; that of hoisting the heavy yards, not of over-throwing established order. With a half-comprehending shrug, he went below, resigning himself to fortune.

Here he hesitated a moment then, drawing out from one of the crude deal shelves that lined his nook a ledger left from a previous voyage, he tore out half a dozen pages of records and began a journal.

In my Extremity, he began under the date and making the only reference to his private misfortune,

I Commence this Journal of my Voyage to Sea in the *Enterprize,* Brig, of Liverpool, Captain Makepeace commanding. We are bound for the Coast of Guinea and I know not what Future Events shall befall us, but I am Determined that they shall find in these Pages a Faithful Recorder, that these Events, whatsoever they be, shall stand against my Good Intentions in This World.

He sat back; *against* his good intentions, or *towards* them? He thought of crossing the first word out and substituting the second; then he abandoned the idea. What did it matter? He was writing a journal for his own distraction. No one would ever read it; he would probably never read the words again himself, but it might prove a vehicle for his despair and help him bear the burden of his new life.

The wind, giving them a slant to the south and west, was light enough to rock the

Enterprize with a gentle motion and Kite slept soundly for the rest of that night. When he woke and went on deck the world seemed transformed and the moment suddenly lifted his spirits. By nature he was a cheerful, if thoughtful soul, not much given to fits of the blue devils, even during the most tedious days of his young manhood. Sunshine danced upon a sea which was thereby transformed into a bright and sparkling green. Gulls abounded, with black auks, their wings thrumming in a blur of effort, skimming the sea as they beat their way shorewards where the stacks of Holy Island rose on their larboard quarter. Beyond he could see the mountains of Carnarvon, upon which the winter snow still lay. The poignant sight of those distant summits, so like the pikes and fells of his native Cumbria, both cheered and depressed him. The notion of departure was born heavily in upon him, of an uncertain future and of what he was leaving for ever. Yet he took comfort from the sight, seeing in it a valediction, almost a blessing from fate, and he recalled again his innocence. Whatever perversion of the truth the Hebblewhites had peddled, and, he thought in the security of the outward-bound *Enterprize,* whatever fate held in store, he *knew* he was guiltless. At this point in his reflections he staggered, fetching up against the lee main pin-rail, feeling for the first time the growing discomfort of the ship's motion as she met a heavier swell rolling up from the south west.

'You've yet to get your sea-legs, Mr Kite,' a voice called, and he turned to see Captain Makepeace on his quarterdeck.

'Yes, sir,' Kite replied, making his way gingerly across the deck as a patter of spray swept aft from the weather bow.

'You will. In a day or so you will be rolling with the gait of a hardened sea-jack, as comfortable with the motion as the rest of these lubbers.' Makepeace paused, studying the *Enterprize's* newest officer, as if for the first time. 'Has Gerard told you of your duties as surgeon?'

'Well, Captain Makepeace, he has acquainted me with the fact that I am to attend the sick and to hold a daily meeting for those of the company wishing to consult me with their ills, but so far...' Kite felt a strange queasiness and a prickling sweat break out on his skin.

'Well, you'll be among the sick yourself for a while, I dare say,' Makepeace broke in, 'and then you will be called upon to provide mercury and potassium permanganate for the lues and clap.' Makepeace gestured forward. The men of the watch were hauling the foretack down to the weather bumpkin as Gerard supervised them trimming the yards to an alteration of course. 'Several of these wasters will have poxed themselves in Liverpool, Devil take it...'

'Captain Makepeace,' Kite broke in with a sudden urgency, 'you should know that I have no certificate ... I am not a proper surgeon...'

Makepeace stepped towards Kite and took his arm, turning him to leeward and propelling him none too gently to the rail, bending to his ear. 'Mr Kite, you should know that I am sufficiently persuaded that you can accomplish the duties of a surgeon well enough. A man who can stitch up a woman's backside and pop mercury into a sailor's gob will do the duty of a surgeon in a Guineaman tolerably well. Besides, I myself was once a surgeon – yes, yes, don't look so damned surprised, 'tis a necessary qualification, like that of sailing as mate, for a man to command a Guinea-bound ship. Providing you have sailed your two voyages as mate or sawbones, you may yourself become master. You will have papers enough then even if Surgeon's Hall has no present recollection of your existence. Besides, Mr Kite, a guinea or two will suffice to obtain the papers you seek and the Custom House in Liverpool is not aware that yours cost that sum.'

Kite frowned, comprehension dawning upon him slowly. 'You mean you have lodged false papers to the effect that I am a surgeon...'

'I would not put it quite that strongly, Mr Kite,' Makepeace said drily, 'you will be competent enough when this voyage is over, that is for sure. Provided you survive it, of course.'

Later, in the small lobby off which the cabins of the *Enterprize's* officers led and which served them as a wardroom, he quizzed Gerard. The first mate, or lieutenant as he was styled, for the *Enterprize* bore a dozen guns and had been a privateer during the last war, belched discreetly behind his fist, dabbed at his lips with a napkin and regarded his questioner over a glass. They had dined well on fresh provisions and Gerard was in an expansive mood. He was not prone to the megrims that bedevilled sea-officers just fresh from the shore where they had left the ordinary comforts of life which even the meanest cottager took for granted. On the contrary, he viewed the coming voyage with some relish, seeing in it both peril and opportunity. Of a somewhat mercurial temperament, Mr Gerard was, at that moment, inclined to be friendly.

'Well, Kite, you are a stranger among us indeed, I suppose you know what a Guineaman is?'

Kite shrugged. 'A vessel destined to trade upon the coast of Guinea, which I had supposed was somewhere in Africa.'

Gerard nodded. 'Well done. You are not a *complete* ignoramus. And what then?' The emphasis on the adjective suggested Gerard suspected Kite's phoney status and he faltered in his response.

'Well, er, we return home with the produce of the country. Elephant's teeth, I imagine, spices, jewels and, er, the skins of tigers. What else can net a humble surgeon the one hundred guineas that Captain Makepeace assured me? Come, sir, you are laughing at me! You have the advantage, damn it. Have I speculated foolishly?'

'Only moderately so,' Gerard said, leaning forward and refilling Kite's glass. 'There are no tigers in Africa, though you might stumble across a leopard should you prove unlucky, but the chief error is to suppose that we return home. First we go to Brazil or the Indies with the, er, the freight we take aboard on the coast...'

'That is the Guinea coast?'

'Just so.'

'And this freight consists not of elephant's teeth, but of something else?'

'Well, we shall almost certainly ship a quantity of tusks, but no, this is not the chief commodity from which your profit of one hundred guineas arises. Your principal task,

45

and hence the importance of every Guineaman carrying a surgeon, is not to minister to the lubbers forward who ship as seamen, though you will be expected to lose as few of the fellows as possible, but to act in behalf of the blackamoors who come aboard.'

'Blackamoors?' Kite frowned. 'You mean – slaves.' The truth dawned upon him. His preoccupation had prevented his enquiring the reason for the quantities of chains, shackles and leg-irons that he had seen about the ship, vaguely supposing them to be object of export, but now Gerard nodded.

'Blackamoors, Negroes, men as well as women–' Gerard leered unpleasantly – 'and their welfare, my dear Kite, will be your sole concern. Furthermore, may I be permitted to add, solicitude for the preservation of all of them is paramount. You will find them well treated aboard the *Enterprize,* not, as you may have heard happens in other bottoms, abused and beaten and thrown overboard. They are a most valuable commodity and the captain will have had to purchase them with a not inconsiderable laying out of money, trade goods and rum. Moreover, my dear Kite, and of the utmost significance to you as surgeon, the dues payable to the majority of our ship's company will be dependent upon the highest number reaching the markets in the Brazils or the Indies.'

'So the burden of this enterprise falls upon me?' Kite's pun was involuntary.

Gerard tossed off his glass and rose to his feet. 'Squarely, if not fairly, my dear Kite, though as you will discover Captain Make-peace takes a very great – no, a very *personal* interest in the welfare, if indeed that is the absolutely correct term, for the preservation of the blacks. And now forgive me, I have but three hours before being on deck and must get a little sleep.'

The following evening, somewhere to the north and west of the Isles of Scilly, the *Enterprize* ran into a gale. For Kite the experience was numbingly humiliating. The incipient queasiness, felt since the ship rounded the Skerries of Anglesey, now burgeoned into a violent succession of retching upheavals so persistent that his throat was rasped raw and the muscles of his gut seemed incapable of anything but a furious gagging. He was revolted by his own stench, yet was powerless to overcome his lassitude and lay prostrate as the motion of the ship made his head spin. In his lonely agony, he was reminded of once having been made drunk. He had been only ten years old when Colin Hebblewhite had forced ale on him and reduced him to an intoxicated stupor from which he took two days to recover. His father had been uncensorious, and treated him as though poisoned, remonstrating with old Hebblewhite to little avail.

''Twas but a prank, Maister Kite,' the farmer had laughed, 'boys will be boys, d'ye know.'

Mr Kite had told his son not to keep the company of the Hebblewhites, but it was they who constantly pressed themselves upon William Kite, seeing him as fit for guying and bullying. Kite had been of the same age as their own young sister Susan, and had sat beside her at the little dame school they were favoured with in the village. Susan was the first girl he had kissed and later, the first his questing and curious hands had fondled when she possessed growing breasts. They had other things in common. Both their mothers had died in childbirth, Susan's at her own and Kite's at Helen's birth. Kite and Susan were equally sensitive to this loss, but the subtle distinctions of class obtruded. Joseph Hebblewhite successfully farmed rented land, held learning cheap and needed his children, particularly his strapping lads, to work his land; Jaybez Kite practised his quasi-profession amid a small library of battered volumes, patiently acquired, some in payment for simples, others bought at Carlisle,

48

or Cockermouth. The Hebblewhites maintained a rough claim to social distinction, though it was the Kite children who played at the vicarage.

At puberty the lives of Susan and Kite had divided. He had gone to the grammar school at Cockermouth, she had continued her work in her father's dairy, where she had found her charms useful not merely to pleasure her old classmate. Jealous, but at the same time growing away from the narrow confinements of the village, Kite had sought a new purpose in life. Friendless and lacking invitations, he found himself unable to participate in the social life of Cockermouth. Cousin Frank, older and more cocksure, had done better, though he had not won any great distinction in the little town and, in any case, left the grammar school before William. In due course Kite returned to the village, content with is own company and interests, if somewhat introverted, and relatively untroubled by his solitary existence. The village had not changed in his absence, but it seemed to the metamorphosed Kite that it had. Susan was a comely and confident young woman, her brothers prospering boors who fell to their old ways of taunting the now lettered Kite. The bullying that he had forgotten or cast aside amid the remnant memories of childhood, was now insufferably insulting to him.

Wanting employment he had found himself a half-hearted unindentured apprentice to his father's trade, a runner of errands and messages, still living off his father's charity though it was assumed that in due course he would be as competent an apothecary as his parent.

Kite's lack of interest in his assumed career was well known to his father, but the older Kite was too conscientious and attentive a man not to fill his entire day with his own business, never quite understanding a son who seemed, to his well-ordered mind, more than a trifle wayward. The senior Kite was also unable to remonstrate with his son, for the youth possessed too disquieting a likeness to his dead mother for the widower to unleash anger in the empty house. Kite's father mourned ceaselessly, figuring the lad would come round in the end, while Kite himself suffered a long, if well-meant neglect.

Insofar as son was like father, the younger Kite's enthusiasm was for the natural world. But it was not the ground-foraging botanising of the apothecary's necessities that drew the young man to his native fells. He loved the open air of the uplands and the soaring flight of the buzzards. He loved the bottled screech of the moorland grouse and the upward whirr of the brown wings; he felt his heart thunder whenever he saw the lordly peregrine stoop like a Jovian bolt and shatter the fat bird into an explosion of feathers. He was a good shot too, with a long-barrelled musket of uncertain manufacture and had once sent a ball whistling damnably close to the head of Philip Hebblewhite whom he had met one day on the western slopes of Dander Pike. Kite's motive had been more than fury at the insults offered him by the lout; rather, a fierce objection to the oaf's presence in that high and lonely place. For the fells were where Kite sought solace, and he had tramped thither on an expedition that had lasted a week and had had a search-party trudging thought a night's mist after him when he learned of Susan's first unfaithfulness. Not that Kite had entertained any right to her fidelity, but the unspoken bond of their first trembling sexual questing had, it seemed to him, united them. He felt Susan's spurning with an acute pain.

Beyond the vague notion that he would succeed his father, Kite's life became aimless. Only his odd ability to bind up wounded animals was regarded with any wonder by the few people who witnessed it. For the most part, he was regarded as a disappointment, a feckless and idle waster, slowly but surely acquiring the reputation of being the young man who first turned

Susan Hebblewhite into the trollop she had since become.

Such rumours feed on bird seed in a small community and Kite knew that there would be those that would readily believe he had killed Susan. The incident when he had shot at Phil Hebblewhite would be adduced as evidence of a violent nature. That the young woman had been pregnant was beyond doubt, that she had been killed by a jealous lover was also likely. Circumstantially, William Kite was known to roam the moors for unrequited love of her, after he had received an education in Cockermouth and become too grand for the village. They had all heard how he had been seen tending her little dog, making calf's eyes at her all the while, though she was no better than the male members of her family, growing up without a mother. She had had it coming to her, of course, but that did not make the matter right, and someone should swing for it.

Kite had done it, no doubt about it. He had skidaddled, had he not? It had to be him; that it should be someone else, someone still at large in the village, was unthinkable.

But Kite had had no hand in the affair. He had fondled Susie, as she had him, but not for more months than it takes to make a child, and the tending of her dog almost a year earlier had been the last time they had spoken at length. Not quite, though; a week or so later, some ten months ago now, he had caught her in the churchyard with a man who had made off in the dusk.

She had laughed at him, reminding him that he too had played with her, though he had lacked the courage to fulfil matters – 'like,' she taunted him, 'a real man'. He had blushed foolishly. Susie had been the first and only woman to grasp his eager manhood and the first to hold the sticky results of her motions as she stirred him to uncontrollable passion. And though he had probed her in a reciprocal act, her ministrations to him, pleaded for for months afterwards, increased her power over him. Thus the wounding she had given him later in the churchyard stung him the more. It seemed she had matured and, where once she had been so unlike them, had grown up with the offensive character of her brothers. Angry, he had shunned her for months before that last, tragic encounter in her father's barn.

As he lay reeking in his cot, watching the deckhead and the beams swing about him and feeling the endless churning of his heaving gut, he remembered again the events of that dreadful afternoon. It was strangely as if he had never recalled it before with such precision, as though his earlier terrors had missed some details in the overwhelming inflammation of mental anguish. It was as if the images that now came back to him had in some strange way been withheld, frozen by the wild reflexes of action, of self-preservation and escape. He now knew that he had run not merely from a scene of brutal and bloody murder, but from a place of unimaginable horror.

Now, with perfect clarity, he recalled that between Susie's white thighs there had been something other than the blood of her apparent evisceration. The vertical pitchfork had not been planted in her voided belly or in her spread legs, but had transfixed the thing that lay between them.

Kite had run not so much from the bloodily bespattered and twitching corpse of the murdered woman, but from the monster she had given birth to.

Three

The Egyptians

It was three days before Kite made his renewed appearance on deck and then he endured a last humiliation, being told by Gerard, who popped his head into Kite's tiny cabin, that only a surgeon would have been suffered to lie in vile indolence for so long. Had he occupied any other station in the ship, Gerard explained with heavy emphasis, he would have been turned out to keep his watch.

Yet Kite, finding himself so much better, bore the jibe without protest. He was, after all, a neophyte and although the wind remained strong and the ship laboured with a creaking and a groaning, he now knew his condition was not fatal and he seemed to be as durable as the ship herself. The certainty overwhelmed him with relief. The very vastness of the heaving Atlantic, when he finally stared out over it, was too immense a thing to be affected by the hue and cry of a handful of Cumbrians. Even the notion of the island of Britain with its bewigged judges and slavering jurymen seemed faintly ridiculous, somehow so small as to be insubstantial amid this eternal, undulating greyness. He felt at last that the matter of Susan Hebblewhite's unhappy end belonged far astern, beyond the horizon in a world whose very existence was now doubtful. So full of the unknown was the foreseeable future that it too offered no identifiable threat to him. He was young enough not to be fearful of the thought of death and saw only boundless possible opportunities. He had run away to sea, and the security of that trite phrase now struck him with an accuracy that he had never before considered.

Bracing himself against the working of the brig, he clasped a rope that led upwards amid what appeared to him a tangle of other such ropes, to be lost against the grey and racing scud as the brig's two masts and their yards crossed and recrossed the sky in a dizzying series of arabesques. As he stood in his shirtsleeves, he muttered his triumph to himself. 'I have run away to sea.'

As if sensing this lightening of the surgeon's mood, though in fact merely reacting to his obvious recovery from seasickness and his appearance on deck, Captain Makepeace called out to him.

'Mr Kite!' Kite turned. Just for a moment he realised his escape was compromised by the fact that Makepeace knew his name and had presumably used it to obtain the false papers declaring him a surgeon. But the thought failed to dampen his mood as he crossed the deck, almost sure of his footing, to pay his respects to the master.

'Good morning, Captain,' he said, and recalling Gerard's remark, added, 'I apologise for failing in my duty–'

Makepeace cut him short. 'No matter, Mr Kite, there is little duty for you to attend to at the moment and that is why you may stand your watch on deck with Mr Gerard. 'Twill be useful for you to acquire a working knowledge of the ship,' Makepeace said, fixing his eyes on Kite and giving his next remark significance. 'You never know when you might find it expedient to become a proper sea-officer.'

If Makepeace guessed anything of Kite's predicament, and the gravity of his utterance suggested to the susceptible Kite that he not only guessed but could see into his very conscience, the captain's expression was not unsympathetic. Instead of holding over him the Damoclean sword of exposure, Makepeace seemed to offer a friendly, almost disinterested complicity. As if underwriting this unspoken bond, Makepeace went on, 'At sea, Mr Kite, one never knows what will happen. You have joined a fraternity whose fates are inextricably linked. We are, forgive the abject pun, all in the same boat.'

Makepeace was smiling with that charming air that Kite had first noticed in the Liverpool taproom. He smiled back. 'I take your point, sir, and will do my utmost to acquire some sea-sense, if that is what you call it.'

'Very well, Mr Kite. That will do splendidly.'

'As if to set its seal of approval upon this accommodation, the overcast broke and the sun suddenly shone down, transforming the world, turning the under-crests of the grey and breaking seas to a remarkable pellucid green. From one of these there suddenly leapt a pair of bottle-nosed dolphins, whose course for some moments lay parallel with that of the *Enterprize*.

That evening, after standing his first watch with Gerard, Kite wrote in his journal:

Today, thro' the Kindness of Captn Makepeace, I Kept the Deck with the First Lieutenant, Mr Gerard. He was civil enough to Inform me the Names of the Spars and Sails and of the Principal Ropes which Controul them. He also appraised me of the Difference between the Standing and the Running Rigging, and How the Helm Works, Promising, should circumstances permit, to advance my Knowledge by Degrees until I have a Perfect Understanding of Matters Nautical.

I found his Instruction Interesting and Diverting...

To those last words, Kite owed an untroubled night's sleep.

Not that it was what he would have called a full night, for the *Enterprize's* officers worked watch-and-watch, four hours on and four hours off duty. Having perhaps foolishly delayed climbing into his cot until he had made the entry into his journal, Kite found himself roused out again, after less than three hours' rest. But he rose willingly enough, and stumbled out on deck to be put on the wheel until daylight, an old seaman standing near him to admonish him every time he tried to correct the course by chasing the lubber's line.

'No, no, Mr Kite. That'll never do, sir. See–' the man took the helm and with a swift half turn stopped the brig from swerving out of her track and throwing all her sails aback – 'see, the lubber's line there, that marks the heading of the ship, and while it looks like the compass card swings in the bowl, 'tis really the ship that be swinging. Though in truth,' the man conceded, 'the motion of the ship does make the compass card turn about a bit.'

It took a moment for the laws of physics to

sink in at such a chilly, dark and unsociable hour, but when Kite grasped the fact that, despite appearances, the compass card effectively remained stationary and the ship revolved around it, he had little trouble holding the *Enterprize* on her headlong course to the south-westwards. That morning established a pattern for all the days they ran south. Kite quickly picked up the rudiments of sailing a ship and even began to tackle the greater challenge of understanding the art of navigation. By the time Makepeace backed *Enterprize's* main-topsail off Funchal and sent a boat thither for fresh fruit and some casks of Madeira wine, Kite could work a traverse, box the compass in quarter-points, join two ropes in a short splice and lay an eye splice, and he knew a dozen common knots and hitches. He had, moreover, taken his place on the yards when shortening down and knew the perils of passing gaskets. All this raised his status in the eyes of the crew so that they were less free with their comments and began to recognise that, while he remained a neophyte, he nevertheless possessed the qualities of a potential officer. Not that Kite appreciated any of this, he was far too self-conscious of his shortcomings and ignorance. But he was keen to learn and discovered for himself that here was something that, all unknowing, he had an aptitude for. However, while the crew might approve of him, they had yet to test him, and on the fifteenth night at sea, a few moments after he had gone below and was in the act of undressing, a soft knock came at his cabin door.

Opening it, Kite was confronted by a young able seaman named Thomas. He was a short, wiry man, not much older than Kite himself but with the sunburnt skin of an experienced sailor.

'Beg pardon, Mr Kite, but I've got a problem. Not the first time, but I've caught a dose of the clap.'

'Ah...' said Kite, conscious that he had been saved the ignominious task of attempting a diagnosis. 'You've had it before, then?'

'Scarce rid of it, sir, to be truthful, but a body can't pine for ever an' there always are them promptings by way of nature, sir.'

Kite frowned, caught between genuine interest, fear of the infection and of being exposed as a fraud. 'It is an, er, intractable condition,' he bluffed, aware only of the pertinacity of the infection. 'Er, what did the last surgeon prescribe for you?'

'That purple stuff...'

'Permanganate of potassium,' Kite said hurriedly, keeping his voice matter-of-fact as he grasped the passing straw. 'And you, er, did the application yourself?'

'Oh yes,' Thomas said leering, 'bit awkward to get another feller to do it, even aboard this bleeder, eh? But it works out all right when we get the blackamoors aboard...'

'You mean...'

'You know, Mr Kite,' Thomas confided with obvious relish, 'ask one them black wenches to get it up and you can pour the stuff down dandy-oh. We make a joke of it, telling them they'll all beget mulatto pickaninnies and the perm ... the purple stuff is white magic.'

Kite dismissed the disturbing image Thomas's words conjured up. 'What do you use – to apply the solution?'

'There's plenty of straw in the manger forrard...'

'You *must* clean it first,' said Kite with sharp authority, in his first original contribution to this one-sided medical discussion. It was a fundamental principle he had learned from his father, that no object should be introduced to any subcutaneous part, wound or orifice of the human body that had been in any contact with another such place. Using a straw from the filth of the live animals' manger as a pipette to insert drops of specific into the canal of the male member seemed a most disquieting method. 'Salt water will do, but don't neglect this precaution and neither use the straw twice, nor neglect this whenever you take up a piece of the stuff. I shall make you up a preparation in the morning. Now, you had better let me see...'

The tone of Kite's short lecture to Thomas obscured any early havering on the former's part, while Kite's inspection of the errant seaman's organ convinced Thomas of Kite's professional ability. Kite's own morbid fascination threatened to keep him awake after Thomas had gone. Terrible things, it seemed, lurked between the thighs of human beings. But he forbore commenting upon his first medical task and instead, as he lay back in his cot, he forced himself to enumerate the ropes that controlled the foretopsail. Before he had followed through the procedure for taking in a double reef, he was fast asleep.

Thus passed Kite's days as the *Enterprize* sailed southwards from Madeira. Passing the magnificent peak of Tenerife she skimmed before the north-east trade wind under a sky of unsurpassable blue. The puff-ball clouds that accompanied their passage were unthreatening, but a metaphorical cloud was growing in Kite's mind. The dominating terror of Susie's death and its aftermath had disposed him to imaginings of deep-seated worry. He had become an obsessive, and had had to develop tech-niques to divert his mind to prevent himself dwelling upon the horrors he associated with those terrible few moments in the Hebblewhite barn. Thus the trick of going over Gerard's lessons to superimpose his own memories had helped him manage this inclination to worry, but also acted as a maturing process, moulding the turn of his mind into deep ruts of preoccupation. Thus Thomas's crude reference to 'the blackamoors' and 'those black wenches' combined with certain oblique references of Gerard and others to prompt him to consider the next few weeks, when they would arrive 'on the coast' and take up their lading of slaves. The notion of slavery was one that he considered biblical, most naturally associating the state of enslavement with the Israelites. This historical plight seemed remote, so remote that it involved the active participation of the Jewish God who was, most emphatically, on the side of his unfortunate if occasionally wayward children. Jehovah's rescue of the Hebrew tribes was the triumph of good over evil and their delivery out of the hands of the Egyptians a satisfying confirmation of ultimate justice.

If we are to take on Board Numbers of Slaves, that they are Black seems not to be the Matter for Consideration, he wrote in his journal.

That they are not Free and are to be Sold into Servitude seems the Chief Concern in this Age of Enlightenment. That we Traffick in Them places Us in the like Case as that of the Egyptians who, for their Wickedness, were afflicted by Seven Plagues and Drowned in the Red Sea.

Life, it seemed then to him, had every prospect of being one long series of moral dilemmas compared to which the acquisition of a sea-officer's skills was a simple matter, and moreover a far more enjoyable one. Therefore he threw himself into an understanding of meridian altitudes, parallel sailing and stellar recognition. He learned how to determine the latitude by the elevation of Polaris and, it has to be said, entirely specious methods of determining the ship's longitude. Despite this progress, Makepeace made no attempt to share the secrets of command, to show Kite, or any of his officers, the *Enterprize's* progress on a chart. The descending value of the parallels of latitude therefore meant little to Kite, who could not relate them to their progress across the earth's sphere, no matter how much he longed to as he recalled the large globe in the grammar school at Cockermouth. Nor did Gerard or his colleague in the second lieutenant's berth evince the slightest curiosity in this regard. For them the swift progress of the ship was all that mattered, and while they took those observations that were necessary, they seemed to work the figures out as a matter of rote, handing them to Makepeace for inscription upon the chart in the privacy of the commander's cabin. Kite was somewhat confounded by this apparent secrecy; it was only long afterwards that he discovered that the chart, such as it was, was Makepeace's private property and bore all the secret notations of the captain's collected experience. Indeed, the printed chart was almost valueless without these superscriptions, bare of any but the most basic geographical information and produced speculatively by a company of self-styled cartographers in the city of London.

But these esoterica did not concern Kite in those last weeks of their outward passage to Guinea. Among a few sprains, bruises and one rupture, he dealt competently with a number of cases of venereal infection. His patients reported relief from the painful symptoms of the infliction by the lavish application of permanganate of potassium. Kite caught them once, a circle of half-ashamed, half-amused seamen, squatting by common consent within the amphitheatre of the coiled anchor cables on the orlop platform, their pipette-straws applied to their private parts. They had a guard, designed to keep out the mockery of their unaffected shipmates, though Kite himself was suffered to pass, as the *Enterprize's* medical officer. Despite this privilege, he beat a hasty retreat, musing on the willingness of the men to share their common misfortune in so public and demeaning a way.

Rather shocked, he mentioned this to Gerard, while they stood upon the quarterdeck that afternoon as the *Enterprize* doubled Cape Verde, distant somewhere far to the east. Gerard merely chuckled.

'There are few secrets in a ship, Kite, that is why we maintain the social distinctions of rank, or all would soon tumble down.' His face became serious and he turned towards his younger companion. 'You may find greater surprises in store for you. You should not judge us. Just as you will find the ways of the blackamoors curious because of the country in which they dwell and the tribal society in which they live, you must regard seamen in a similar fashion. We are, after all, circumscribed by the limits of our ship, cooped up upon the raging main and subject to all the powerful vicissitudes of nature... Well, you shall see and you are not now a man apart; you are now – well, almost–' Gerard grinned again – 'one of us.'

Kite only partially understood these oblique remarks, but he was pleasantly surprised by the acceptance of the *Enterprize's* second-in-command, who, despite his earlier sarcasm, had proved a willing instructor and an affable companion.

'Oh, by the way,' Gerard went on, 'are you much of a shot?'

For a second Kite was drawing imaginary sights on a lofting grouse rising above his native fells. 'I can shoot, yes,' he said.

'Good. Fencing is not required, but can you handle a blade?'

'Well, I was tolerably able with the single-stick.'

'A hack and slash man, eh?' grinned Gerard. 'That will do nicely, I dare say.'

The following day, at the change of watch at noon, Makepeace summoned all hands. By a process of elimination, with all the seamen shooting at empty wine bottles hauled out to the lee foretopgallant yard-arm, a platoon of 'marines' was enlisted from the most able shots. These were placed under the command of the second lieutenant, Francis Molloy, a heavily built Liverpool Irishman whose acquaintance Kite had hardly made, since he was on the opposite watch.

The officers too, including Kite, enjoyed a few shots by way of target practice. On completion, Makepeace told the mustered company that within a few days they would arrive off their destination, the coast of Guinea. 'We shall anchor off York Island,' he announced, 'in the mouth of the Sherbro

River, and determine the state of trade. It is not my intention to linger if we can complete our lading, though I must seek the best prices for the goods we have brought with us. In the meantime I shall not countenance any drunkenness among you. Most of you know well the native liking for liquor and most of you indulged yourselves to excess in Liverpool. Any man found half-seas-over runs a great risk from apprehension by the Negro chiefs, whose kings are not only important to themselves but to the prosperity of our trade. Therefore I consider any man among you who loses himself to drunkenness to be opposed to the profit of our voyage and he can expect little mercy from me. I can always ship mulattoes as seamen...' Makepeace paused to let the inference of abandonment sink in and the men shifted uncomfortably; Kite knew from his associating with Gerard and the men that Makepeace was both admired and feared.

'As for licentiousness,' Makepeace resumed, 'I cannot properly ask you to be continent, but I can advise you to be wise. As you indulge yourselves in liquor in Liverpool, you are best to whore in the Indies...'

'Where the dagos have poxed all the women?' a voice queried loudly from the crowd. 'Not me, Captain, nor you if I know your liking...'

A laugh passed through the old hands and it was Makepeace's turn to look discomfited as he braced himself and called for silence.

'Belay there! D'you mind my words!'

'Aye,' murmured someone behind to Kite, 'not thy deeds.'

Makepeace called out: 'Now dismiss!'

Kite turned and caught Molloy's eye as the men dispersed. The big Irishman was shaking his head. 'What did–?' Kite began, but Molloy cut his question short.

'He shouldn't moralise on *that* score,' Molloy muttered.

'The commander is a womaniser?' Kite asked, stealing a glance at the figure of Makepeace as he descended the companionway to his cabin.

'Womaniser, profligate, whore-master, bugger, but a most successful slaving commander withal. So, my friend, our Cap'n Makepeace is not altogether a bad fellow.'

This news shocked Kite. Up until this revelation he had assumed Makepeace to be a gentleman, if engaged in a trade of some moral dubiety. Exposed to the world beyond the lakes and valleys of his former life suggested to Kite that the extent of human activity and endeavour was almost incredibly diverse. Much might run contrary to one's private opinions, but that did not arm one with an incontrovertible righteousness. *Judgement and Vengeance*, Kite confided to his journal later, *are matters for the Divine Disposal of All Things.* It was not for him to do more than make the best of his circumstances. In the eyes of parts of the world, he recalled with a shudder, he was himself far beyond the moral pale. But Molloy's confidence deprived Captain Makepeace's invitation to dinner of any pleasurable anticipation.

It was difficult to square Molloy's evaluation of Makepeace's character with his host. The *Enterprize* was heading south-east, parallel with the Guinea coast, and the captain presided at his table with the westering sun gilding the heaving seas astern of the ship. Occasional twinkling points of light stabbed the incautious eye as it was drawn beyond the dark outline of the captain to the mighty ocean beyond the glass of the windows. The wake streamed out, a marbled roil of water given a curious personality. Kite thought inconsequentially, by the groaning of the rudder beneath them. It was odd that although the passage of the ship seemed stately from the vantage point of the quarterdeck, the escape of water running out from underneath the stern was surprisingly fast.

'Well, gentlemen,' Makepeace said, raising his glass to his guests, Kite and Gerard, 'to your continuing healths, I'm sure.'

The guests reciprocated and they fell to their meat with alacrity. The two capons had had their necks wrung only that morning, and were exceedingly tasty to Kite, who enjoyed a young man's appetite. After a short pause for assuaging their hunger, Makepeace said, 'So, Kite, Mr Gerard tells me you have taken to the business of a sea-officer with commendable alacrity, diligence and understanding.'

'That is generous of Mr Gerard, sir,' said Kite, smiling at the first lieutenant.

''Tis no more than the truth,' confirmed Gerard. 'You were like a fish to water, Kite.'

'It was not entirely disinterested tuition, Kite,' Makepeace went on, 'the dangers of the coast, due mainly to marsh ague, but with a score of subsidiary maladies, take any one of us at any moment, and sickness, or even death, may ensue. It is therefore prudent to ensure that as many of us as possible are competent to manage the ship.' Makepeace paused on this solemn note. 'Now to other matters,' he resumed cheerfully. 'When we arrive in the Sherbro I shall require your close attendance upon myself, Mr Kite. Both as surgeon, in which capacity you have not yet been overtaxed, and also as my assistant. In this capacity, you will assist me in the trafficking which will occupy me for a few days. As few days as I can possible contrive at a profit, of course, eh, Gerard?'

'Indeed, sir, only that which is commensurate with the satisfaction of your partners...'

'One of the advantages, Mr Kite,' Makepeace explained with a condescending air of confidence, 'of being no mere master, but a part-owner in the *Enterprize*.'

'I see, sir. Well, then, may I offer my best wishes for the voyage.' Kite politely raised his glass. Both Makepeace and Gerard joined the toast, but Kite was uncomfortable, feeling the captain's eyes upon him and with Molloy's words lingering in his ears.

As if divining Kite's train of thought, Makepeace asked with a disarming candour, 'Are you fond of women, Mr Kite?'

'Er, as, er fond as the next man, sir,' responded Kite quickly.

'But you are a young man...'

'Though well enough acquainted with the pox, I hear,' added Gerard.

'The clap, Mr Gerard. Mercifully I have not yet encountered a case of the pox.' Kite recalled an embarrassing evening in the serious company of his father when that worthy attempted a cautionary explanation of the diseases of Venus. Kite had most certainly not yet encountered the horrors, as taught to him by his parent, of the 'foreign disease', attributable it seemed to loathsome intercourse with the French and Spanish.

'But you have had a wench, or two, I dare say?' queried Makepeace with a disquieting persistence.

Kite faced his interlocutor, a little flushed with the captain's wine, and skilfully turned the question. 'Surely, Captain Makepeace, you will recall our introduction was occasioned by my familiarity with the parts beneath a woman's skirts.'

'So it was, my dear fellow,' said Makepeace smiling his charming smile and raising his glass, 'so it was.'

When he returned to his cabin, Kite was more than a little drunk. He drew his journal towards him, then rejected the idea of making an entry. He would be required on deck shortly and instead he lay down in his cot.

'I fear I am to become an Egyptian,' he murmured as he sank into sleep.

Four

The River

Across the entrance to the Sherbro River lay a bar which, even on a day of light winds, caused the Atlantic swell to rear up and roll over upon the shallows with a menacing and forbidding roar. To Kite's horror and, he noticed, to no little anxiety upon even the suave Gerard's experienced face, Makepeace held *Enterprize's* course boldly east, heading towards the line of roaring breakers, behind which the low, jungle-clad coast of Guinea could be seen. Makepeace stood beside the two helmsmen, from time to time raising his hand as if to restrain them from nervous or faulty movements of the helm, commanding them to keep their eyes upon the compass as he took *Enterprize* over the Sherbro bar. At that moment, Kite admired Makepeace's coolness, glimpsing the degree to which a man must cultivate nerve and command over himself before he was fitted to command a ship. The evidence of danger became suddenly obvious as the swell steepened and heaved beneath them, lifting the vessel and speeding her forwards, before dropping her in a hollow with such precipitation that Kite thought she surely must strike the bottom. Hardly had his conscious mind recognised the proximity of the sand beneath their keel from the thick sediment swirling about them, than the *Enterprize* was borne up on the succeeding swell. Propelled forward they now seemed to hurtle on the very crest of a toppling wave which broke with a roar, setting the ship down again and filling the clear warm air with a mist of spray. The breaking water rushed past them, disintegrating in a welter of white foam which slid ahead, over-running the blue-green surface of the shoal water beyond the obstruction of the sand-bar. Birds dipped into the turbulent shallows, picking off the bounty of the ocean, and then the *Enterprize* broke free, clear of the bar, breasting the seaward flow of the Sherbro itself.

The boatswain, standing in the starboard fore chains, swung the lead rhythmically, steadily calling out the soundings as Makepeace sought the deeper water of the river's channel. All about him Kite noticed the relaxation apparent in the men; the smiles and resumption of suspended tasks. A man who had paused in coiling down a rope finished it off with a twirl about its belaying pin; another, taking off the cover of the longboat, pulled the last lashing clear and withdrew the canvas, to roll it on the deck. Gerard looked at Makepeace and grinned, which the captain, unconsciously betraying his own anxiety, removed his hat and flicked a linen kerchief across his brow.

Beyond the confusion of the bar, the outward flowing Sherbro darkened the sea water with its brackishness and the random flotsam of the interior jungle of the great dark continent of Africa. Slowly they left the roar of the breakers behind them, the green line defined itself as dense and swampy jungle, and then the pale shallows also fell astern and they entered the river itself.

Instantly the fresh sweetness of the ocean wind left them, though a breeze still filled their upper sails. A heavy heat fell upon them like a blanket, palpable in its weight. The air filled with the harsh whirr of insects and the occasional screech of a bird; Africa embraced them as the men clewed up the courses and went aloft to furl them.

York Island lay some twenty miles upstream, a low place, clear of the denser vegetation, though covered with palms. At its inner extremity it subsided into a marsh, at its seaward end it bore the ruins of a fort which, built in the previous century, had for a score or more years been abandoned when the trade in slaves fell off. A recent revival had reinvigorated the place, so that as the *Enterprize* dropped her anchor, after a slow passage upstream against the green current of the river, she found herself in the company of four other Guineamen. Three of these ships were from Liverpool and all were swiftly recognised by the ship's company.

'There's the *Lutwidge*...'

'Aye, and the *Nancy* ... and the *Marquis of Lothian*...'

Hardly had the *Enterprize* brought to her anchor than Makepeace called away the longboat. Kite made ready to join him and, as the majority of her hands went aloft to put a harbour stow in her canvas, the grinning boat's crew began to ply their oars and drive the boat shorewards through the anchorage. It was blisteringly hot, and Kite felt his skin prickle with sweat. Though Makepeace and Kite were both in shirt-sleeves, their tight neckcloths felt uncomfortably like hangman's nooses.

Makepeace looked at the anchored Guineamen, raising his hat to one man on the stern of the *Lutwidge* as they passed. 'This is not a good sign,' he remarked to Kite, sitting beside him in the sternsheets of the boat. 'It argues delays in loading, which in turn means either the coastal chiefs have not brought down sufficient Negroes, or the damned lançados are asking too high a price for my fellow commanders to agree upon.'

'The lançados...?'

'Oh, men of mixed blood, mulattoes, quadroons, a very devil's brew of half-castes, fathered by seamen from the slaving vessels and born to women of the country. They all want to trade and act as go-betweens and agents. Most merely make fools of themselves, comic characters posing as self-styled white gentlemen who possess only the worst attributes of their fathers: they drink like fishes and whore like dogs.' Makepeace dismissed the human results of miscegenation and slapped at a mosquito that landed upon his bare wrist.

A few native canoes passed them, and Kite stared with unconcealed curiosity at the gleaming figures of the black men bending to their paddles. Their unfamiliar physiognomy struck him at once and Makepeace, noticing his fascination, chuckled. 'Ugly devils, ain't they? They're gromettos, free blacks who are useful to us here as we await our lading. You'll become used to them, even find their women capable of rousing your lust!' The captain exchanged a complicit grin with the seaman pulling stroke oar, a small, wiry Welshman. 'Eh, Jenkin. You love 'em, do you not?'

'Aye, sir.' Jenkin grinned back and winked at Kite; he was one of what Able Seaman Thomas had ironically named the Cable-Tier Rangers. Kite suppressed a shudder.

The broken-down ramparts of the ancient

fort fell astern and a low and sandy strand, backed by wooden buildings and grass-roofed hutments, came into view. 'Behold the true coast of Guinea...' murmured Makepeace, half to himself.

In the ensuing hours, for all that he kept Makepeace constant company, Kite had only the haziest notion of what was going on. In the largest house on York Island, a clapboard, daub and wattle structure roofed with long grass thatch, they sat and spoke with a strange white man whose name, Kite learned, was Thomas Lorimoor. He traded in all manner of goods and, in what Makepeace afterwards facetiously called a 'palaver', exchanged information with them about the availability of slaves and other commodities. Although born a Scotsman, Lorimoor used English mixed with a strange argot, a mishmash of English, Portuguese and native words taken from the languages of the Mandingo and Bulum tribes. Since Makepeace was familiar with this lingua franca, Kite could make little of the substance of the conference. He was left to bring himself to eat from a calabash of what appeared to be revolting worms, but which Lorimoor called *bul* and what Make-peace assured him were good eating. Indeed the commander endlessly picked at the contents of the calabash until it was emptied, whereupon a native woman suddenly appeared, silently barefoot upon the floor of beaten dirt to refill it. She was flat-faced and bore about her neck a thick silver ring that Kite at first took for a necklace but later knew for a thrall-ring. Her large body was ungainly under the loose, brightly coloured cotton wrap she wore about it. She seemed to be a sister, in all but colour, to the sad trulls that had inhabited the dark dockside tavern in which Makepeace had found him, except that she moved with a motion that Kite could only describe as dignified. That she was Lorimoor's native concubine was confirmed as they pulled back to the ship, an hour before sunset.

That evening Kite confided the day's events to his journal.

The Scotch trader Lorimoor lived with a Black Woman. He is a Sick Man, much taken with a Fever which, in the Season of Tornadoes, becomes Quotidian. His Pallor is Severe, his Eyes are Bloodshot and marked by Empurpled Shadows. Though having the Appearance of Age, his long Sojourn in this Countrie has Aged him far beyond his actual years which, I understand are about Forty. His Woman, whom he calls Elizabeth, Captain Makepeace Informed me, had lived with him a Slave for nigh Twenty Years and certainly All the Years that the Captain hath known Mister Lorimoor which is about half that time. Our Palaver lasted for five Hours in which we ate a Species of Worms of Disgusting Appearance but which Owned a taste not unlike Fresh Mutton and Quite Delicious after One has overcome a Natural Disinclination to Swallow them. We Drank also what I supposed to be Palm Wine which I was told is taken directly from the Bark of that Tree which grows well upon York Island. I am Disposed to suppose this some sort of Joke played against Persons without Experience in the Ways of the Countrie.

I was much Mystified as to All the Deliberations entered into by the Captn and Mister Lorimoor, but the Captn was solicitous enough to offer me a Full Explanation which I but imperfectly understood, not being Conversant with the Manner of Trading in this Countrie.

There is somewhat of a Currency which for Convenience is called a Barr. The Value of a Barr varies as to whether it be a Ship's Barr, or the Trader's Barr, thus a Quantity of Goods hath Two Values, a Matter of Speculation apparent to those familiar with it, but from which I could Derive no Satisfaction other than that it be a Method of Extracting a Profitt, at least upon invoice. This is more than Somewhat of a Mystery to Me. This Barr equates to the Value of Iron which is much Prized Hereabouts and which we have in Quantitie in the Hold.

There was also some Discussion of the Countrie which I better understood, Mr Lorimoor spoke of a Native Chieftain whose Name translated meant the Great Son of a Woman on Account of him being a Bastard. This Chieftain who is styled in the Place a King, is of the Mandingo Tribe, a Warlike and Mahomettan People who reside some Distance from the Sherbro River, but who Seek to Convert the Bulum Tribe to their Religion. Since the Bulum are Pagan, Lorimoor spake as though Their Society would derive some Benefit from this Civilising Influence, and though I suppose it Better than to be Bound to Superstition, I cannot pass up the Opinion that it would be more Desirable that they should know the Gospel of Christ than the Teachings of Mahomet.

This Mandingo King is waging War in the Interior of the Countrie and Delaying the Sending down to the Coast, of the Slaves. This Accounts for the Number of Guinea-men waiting at Anchor Here. But there is another Reason, Captn Makepeace Opines, and that Mr Lorimoor put into his Mind with the Rumoured News of a Greater War. This is said to have Broken Out between England and France and Spain, tho' how this is Known hereabouts but was not Known at the time of our Departure from

Liverpool, I am at a Loss to Comprehend, as is Captn Makepeace. Perhaps the Turbulence with the French in North America has Precipitated Hostilities.

But the Captn says with a Perfect Logick that, Mandingo War or Not, such Rumours, Whether or Not they become Proved by Time, are often Employed by the Traders, the Lanchadoes and Even the Native Chiefs, to Delay the Delivery of the Slaves to the Coast. This Raises the Price, Particularly as the Hurricane Season in the Indies Approaches and the Anxiety increases among the Commanders of the Various Ships to Depart. Such a Delay, in the Present Case, gives Time for the Enemy, if there be one, to Send down his Men-o'-War to Cruise in the Offing and to Trap Us in Leaving the Guinea Coast, whereby all our Endeavours may be Brought Swiftly to Disaster.

I am Not Certain but that Captn Makepeace is not going This Evening to Concert his Intentions with his Fellow Commanders, Most of Whom are Liverpool Men and can thus be Depended upon.

Kite set down his quill and slapped at the buzzing mosquito who flew about him. Sweat poured liberally from his body, and as he raised his left hand from the pages of his journal he left a damp stain upon the paper.

A score of flies and moths fluttered and buzzed around the candle flame. He went on deck. In leaving Lorimoor's house, he had caught sight of the trader's bed, a stout framework of camwood over which hung a tent of plain calico; he wished now he had some such thing to drape above his own cot to protect himself from the infernal pestilence of insects.

Molloy, a pale shape in the darkness, had the anchor watch and straightened up from where he had been leaning on the rail.

'Not asleep, then, Billy?' he asked.

No one had called Kite 'Billy' since he had been a boy and the familiarity caught him aback. Molloy seemed unaware of the impropriety.

'Too hot for you, I imagine. Still, you'll become accustomed to it.' A few lights showed on York Island, like small eyes piercing the blackness surrounding them. The chafing rasp of unnumbered cicadas filled the air, giving voice to the heavy oppression of the tropic night.

''Tis a little hellish,' Kite ventured, leaning on the rail beside Molloy. Both men stared out over the dark swirl of the river rushing by below them. Over the water wraiths of mist coiled, at once both sinister and yet unreal.

Molloy chuckled. 'Sure, you are a real Englishman, Billy. Tch, tch, a *little* hellish.

Now, how can that be? Yes, it's Hell, but put your conscience aside, Billy; see it as a little bit of God's good earth for you to profit from. Hasn't that stingy bastard Makepeace told you your interest?'

'My interest?'

'Your share; your dividend under the provisions of the articles. He might be a part-owner in the *Enterprize*, but surely you've seen the agreement?'

Kite had seen no agreement, though he did not like to admit it; all he had agreed, and that by word of mouth, was to sail with Captain Makepeace on the promise of a profit of a hundred pounds or so.

'I suppose you didn't read the damned thing and took it all on trust. How very *English* of you. Well, Billy, as the surgeon you're entitled to one shilling per head on the blacks that are discharged on two legs in the West Indies...'

Kite supposed that his profit of one hundred pounds derived from this source and, embarrassed he said quickly, 'Oh yes, yes, I knew of that.'

'But did you know of your right to ship a quantity of scrivelloes?' Molloy asked, mocking him.

'Er, no, I confess I did not, nor do I comprehend what scrivelloes are.'

'Well, then, let me tell you. They are the teeth of elephants. You will learn that elephant's teeth, which some call tusks like a boar's, are a commodity much beloved in London. You'll not be permitted to ship large tusks, since they hold the greatest value, but the smaller teeth which we call scrivelloes, may be traded by you an' me and Mr Gerard, God bless him.'

'I see.' Kite had no idea what profit might be made on these scrivelloes, nor how he might raise any credit to purchase them, let alone whether he would be permitted the liberty to sell them if he ever reached British shores again. As he put these disquieting riders aside, trading in elephant's teeth seemed to his conscience far less reprehensible than trading in human beings, notwithstanding the fact that they were black.

'But that isn't all, Billy-boy,' Molloy went on, 'the best is yet to come.'

'The best...'

'Oh, indeed it is. You are also allowed, on your own account, two slaves. If you're smart you'll pick strong ones, but the balance of all the private slaves chosen by Makepeace, Gerard, yourself, myself and the gunner, must be equally men as women. I don't, for the life of me, know why that regulation is insisted upon, unless it is to keep the breeding stock provided for, for if I had my way we'd trade only in hefty big fellers, but the captain'll insist upon it.'

'I see.' Kite's heart sank. While he could

reconcile receiving twelve pence per head on delivery, which he was content to see as an incentive to keep as many of the unfortunate blacks in good health, the thought of directly profiting from the seizure and sale of individual persons seemed a great and terrible sin. Whatever the world thought of his culpability in the matter of Susan Hebblewhite's death, he knew he was innocent. Fate, it seemed, would have him a mortal sinner by alternative means. For a moment a dark and terrible horror overhung him, then he threw it off with a question to Molloy.

'I, er, I was ashore with the captain, but I could not understand where the slaves come from and where they are now.'

Molloy gestured at the jungle, a gunshot away. 'Out there somewhere, in a stockadoe or a barracoon guarded by the warriors of the local chiefs...'

'Then blacks sell us blacks?'

'Oh, yes. Did you think we went into the countryside and stole them?' Molloy laughed. 'No, no, 'tis a very well-regulated trade, Billy, very well regulated. You'll see, you'll see.' Molloy straightened up and yawned. 'Enough of this! You can take over the watch, if you wish. It wants only a while until we turn the glass. Let the infernal mosquitoes dine off you for a few hours. I'm for my cot.'

Despite Makepeace's insistence that he had 'no intention of hanging about awaiting the convenience of a dying slave-dealer' and the delivery of several ultimata to the wasting Lorimoor by a deputation of all the masters of the Guineamen lying off York Island, a month passed and, to Gerard's frustration, species of grass grew on the white stuff payed upon the brig's bottom. The weed would slow them on their passage to the Antilles and, Kite learned, with the grass came the shipworm, an infestation of which could ruin a ship's hull in weeks.

The enforced idleness prompted the commanders of the vessels to adopt a practice of dining daily in each others' cabins, indulging in games of chance and once or twice quarrelling among themselves. Rumours circulated among the ships that, if matters were much delayed, they would sail upstream and bombard the barracoons until the recalcitrant chief's released a sufficiency of their prisoners to complete the Guineamen's landing. No one apparently believed Lorimoor's claim that the Mandingo war had choked the supply of slaves and the experienced men freely voiced the opinion that it was all a device to raise the price on them.

This has been done on Former Occasions, Kite confided to his journal, but the Masters are Reluctant to carry this matter to a Precipitate Conclusion owing to the Revenge taken upon those who come afterwards. Much Mischief has been Caused on sundry Occasions by Dishonest dealing by Various Commanders, their Abduction of slaves without Proper Payment and their Cheating of the Blackamoor Chiefs. The Science of Justice in this Countrie is based upon Revenge, so while the Blacks and Lanchadoes will not Trouble the Ships of a Another State, they will Wreak Vengeance upon a British Vessel if they Conceive their Previous Wrongs to have been Inflicted by a British Vessel, and Upon a Dutch, or a Portuguese Guineaman, & Co, & Co.

Moreover, it would not be Politick to Aggravate the Chiefs if War between England and France is Truly Imminent...

Kite was permanently relieved of his watch-keeping after a few days. His duties as surgeon now fully claimed him, for the first cases of fever began to appear aboard the *Enterprize*. Diagnosed by Makepeace and the other officers under the generic term 'marsh ague', two seamen named Noakes and Hughes were the first to die. They suffered an initial shivering fit and were sent to their hammocks, which, by

Makepeace's orders, were swung forward above the manger, in a kind of quarantine. The two men were soon running high fevers, with terrible pains in their backs and necks. Their arms and legs were also afflicted and they became, as Kite noted, *taken by a Great Lassitude accompanied by a Deep Depression of Spirits and sense of Mortality.* Retching, vomiting and an insatiable thirst provoked mixed feelings of disgust and compassion in Kite, who found himself isolated and left alone to care for the two wretches. After a few days he was pleased to notice an improvement and an abatement of the fever. He expected the men to mend, at least in the manner of Lorimoor, who though profoundly affected, seemed able to continue living. In the gloom of the forward 'tween deck, the inexperienced Kite failed to notice the yellowing of the eyes and the skin, nor did he see the first sign of final decline that followed. Soon, however, the men submitted to the terminal stage of their disease by sudden copious eructations of blood which brought on a sinister cooling of the body.

This morning, Kite scribbled hurriedly, aware that circumstances compelled him to observe and learn from the two invalids, but drowning a greater and personal horror by this bloody climax,

Hughes was as Cold as Death Itself and I noticed a Yellow Hue Suffusing his Skin. On Examination Noakes was the same, though to a lesser Extent. Both Men are Reconciled to their Fates

This evening, though Life was still discernible in Both Men, I could Determine no Heartbeat and Their Bodies are already Cold to the Touch...

By next morning both men were dead and were conveyed ashore for burial beneath the ruined ramparts of the fort. The following day three men from the *Marquis of Lothian* were laid to rest, followed in the subsequent ten days by eight more from among the crews of the waiting Guineamen. These sad events, though failing to surprise the experienced seamen in the combined company, nevertheless had a demoralising effect, prompting a restlessness and a desire among the assembled ship's companies to get away. In fear of their lives, they increasingly spoke among themselves of sailing upstream to bombard the Bulum townships and coerce the chiefs to trade. They resolved to urge their commanders to do this before more of them died, but before any deputation approached Makepeace and his colleagues, the *Cleveland* arrived. She was from Bristol and her master, Captain Burn, soon spread the news that the rumours of a European war were confirmed.

This further depressed the crews spread among the waiting ships but in fact acted as the spring for their release. For weeks Makepeace and his colleagues had advertised the wares they had brought to trade. The Manchester checks and Osnaburg cottons so beloved by the natives, the gin and so-called brandy, the musketoons, flints and gunpowder, the knives, soft iron bars and metal trinkets had all been shown to the lançados and the gromettos. But the inhabitants of the coast viewed these products with some disdain; they had satisfied their immediate wants and now craved novelties, aware that the musketoons they were sold were inferior to the muskets the white men kept for themselves. Moreover, the lançados, affecting the dress of white men, had created a desire among the envious chiefs for cocked hats and even boots of soft leather, such as the Arabs of the far distant desert interior sometimes, and these white interlopers of the coast often wore. Lorimoor had shaken his head and the palaver had descended into a complex and apparently irreconcilable variation between what Makepeace and his fellow commanders, and Lorimoor on behalf of the chiefs, regarded as a negotiable barr.

Captain Burn's news, however, spiced up this game of supply and demand. By good fortune Burn had a few tricornes, trimmed with silver braid that he had brought out to sell to a hatter in Antigua. Under pressure from his fellows, he agreed to trade these at once, enabling the deadlock to be broken. Makepeace also counselled his colleagues to threaten to withdraw without further delay, arguing that the presence of French cruisers in the chops of the Channel would deter other Guineamen from sailing and the slaves would be left in the stockades, an ever and increasingly hungry liability to the chiefs.

Humbert of the *Marquis of Lothian* thought that, on the contrary, a delay would bring down the price, but Makepeace poured scorn on 'so meanly Scottish a proceeding', arguing that a debilitated and ill-fed black would not survive the middle passage to the West Indies or the Brazils and what was saved in the initial purchase price would be lost to mortality on the voyage. Besides, Makepeace reasoned, their ships had already been affected with the dreaded yellow jack; as every master knew, if they cleared out promptly, the infection would likely subside and those not yet affected would escape with their lives.

'Once let the sickness take a hold and it will be crews we will all be wanting, not cargoes! Aye, and more, what crews are left may want commanders...'

Makepeace delivered this logic and stared about him. Humbert finally turned his palms upwards and shrugged. The difference of opinion being thus resolved, the masters agreed to send word of their resolve to Lorimoor and to make ostentatious preparations for departure; meanwhile the lançados were shown the silver-laced hats. The ruse worked. The following day Lorimoor passed word that the chiefs would send down the first canoes on the morrow and so *Enterprize,* with her sister Guineamen, prepared to receive her lading.

Five

The Cargo

The hands were turned up next morning as soon as the first canoes were sighted coming downstream. They gathered at the rails of all the assembled Guineamen like excited children as fortune and opportunity approached them in the form of abject misery and degradation. As he came on deck, Kite was immediately aware that changes had taken place about the ship. One of the *Enterprize's* six-pounder carriage guns had been run inboard, moved amidships and swung round. Now the breech was quoined up, so that the black muzzle pointed down into the waist through the rail, a deterrent to insurrection. The seamen designated marines were paraded with their muskets under Mr Molloy who, with a piratical air, bore two pistols in his belt and wore a hanger on his hip. Further aft, lounging on the taffrail, Makepeace and Gerard were similarly armed, while several of the crew bore whips or canes.

To the watching and waiting Kite, it was the smell that first turned his stomach, for although only a few dozen slaves arrived aboard the *Enterprize* from the initial consignment of twenty or so canoes which dispersed about the anchorage, it was clear that the distant barracoons were little better than overcrowded sties. Perceiving that the slaves' own ordure clung to their legs and their breechclouts, Kite was moved to approach Gerard and request that they were all soused down as they came aboard, and allowed to rinse out their flimsy clothing.

'You're not a prating Quaker, are you, Kite?' a high-spirited Gerard asked, with a leer.

'No, I am not, Mr Gerard, but you would not put a horse in a stable in so filthy a condition.' Kite, remembering his father's odd conviction that in dirt lay disease, a theory based largely on some observations that purulent infection and uncleanness were not uncommon neighbours, added, 'And we have so recently buried our ship-mates. We'd be damned stupid to admit another fever to the vessel.'

'Tut, tut, Kite, the heat hath made thee damned touchy.' Apeing the speech of the Quakers, Gerard turned with a grin to Makepeace who, surprisingly, nodded his approval. 'I concur. Let the men give them a wash down. It may ease their minds before we send them below.' Makepeace straightened up and called along the deck to where the boatswain, a man called Kerr, stood upon the rail.

'Mr Kerr, where the devil is my linguistier? Ask one of those damned gromettos if he has come down as arranged...'

A tall mulatto lançado, who bore a striking resemblance, Kite noted later in his journal, to pictures he had seen of Sir Francis Drake, came over the rail in response to Kerr's enquiry and walked insouciantly aft. The man wore an ancient red velvet jacket, frayed knee breeches and silk stockings from which the bottoms had been cut, leaving his feet bare. Stuck into his belt, like an old-fashioned rapier, was a long-handled whip, the tail of which was coiled neatly round the staff. As he approached Captain Makepeace he doffed a new silver-laced tricorne and, sweeping the deck with it, footed an elegant bow.

'Captain, my name is Golden-Opportunity Plantagenet and I am at your service. I bring you forty-two fine blackmen according to Sir Lorimoor's instruction'

Makepeace graciously inclined his head and responded in an ironic tone. 'Honoured, Mr Plantagenet, deeply honoured. I wish you to tell the forty-two fine blackmen that my surgeon will not examine them unless they wash their arses and their breeches. My surgeon is, you see, Mr Plantagenet, like yourself, a gentleman of refinement,' and turning to Kite, Makepeace added: 'You may concert with him, Mr Kite, he will act the interpreter for you.'

Plantagenet bowed to Kite who, embarrassed and awkward, scarce able to make out to what extent Makepeace was guying him, the interpreter, or both of them equally, followed the mulatto forward. As the first of the slaves clambered aboard, the whites of their eyes wide with terror, there began a pantomime of shouting and misunderstanding, of flung buckets of water, of moans and cries of humiliation and shock until, after about fifteen minutes, the seamen had grown fed up with inflicting this mild cruelty on their victims and the terrified slaves realised what was expected of them.

I am Surprised how Willingly They Acquiesce to being thus Treated, Kite wrote later that evening, after a second shipment of male slaves had arrived.

Indeed, left to Sit about on Deck until their Clouts dried under the Hot Sun, there Seemed nothing very Terrible about their Circumstances, tho' Molloy and his armed Mariners were in Continual Attendance. But then, at about Noon, more Canows Arrived and the First Party were taken below and Secured Between Decks. Here they were each Allocated a Space and

100

Compelled to Lie Down. Then the leg-irons were Placed about their Ankles, at which Terrible and Piteous Cries, which Rent the Breast, went up. This Stirred no Compassion among my Companions and I thus take it to be the Sad Manner of carrying on this Trade.

The Lanchadoe who brings the Unfortunate Blacks down the Sherbro from the Barracoons Rejoices under a Most Extravagant Name. Mr Gerard Informs me that it derives in part from the Ship on which his Father probably served, Thus is he Called Golden-Opportunity by way of a Christian Name. His Surname is Plantagenet, but his Mother cannot have known of the Plantagenets and Gerard says the lanchadoes often take a Name they Conceive to be of Noble Blood. Such Names are supplied by the Factors or the Commanders of the Vessels, who think it a Great Joke to thus saddle the Half-Castes with Pretentious Names. In this Manner we have a Mr Duke Attending the 'Lutwidge', and even a Mr Emperor aboard the 'Nancy'. Such Conceits, Vastly Amusing the Masters & Officers of the Various Ships, are carefully Observed in All Propriety. I took notice that the Factor, Mr Lorimoor, is Dignified hereabouts, with the Title of a Knight.

Kite paused, thinking of his own part in

the day's proceedings.

I hope my Examination did not much Distress the Slaves. I am Obliged to Establish they are All Sound in Wind and Limb, and Free from Infectious Disease.

He stopped writing again, unsure of whether or not to commit all his private sentiments to paper and then, with a shrug, bent again to the lamp-lit page.

At first, I supposed them all to be the same, finding in their Features a Similarity of Flattened Noses, Thickened Lips and Black Hair covering their heads in a close matting of Curls. The Deep Brown of their Skin admits no Differentiation, unlike our own Pallid Countenances with our Individual Colouring, and only the Whites of the Eyes seems to indicate a Lack of Spirits, while their Teeth betray Evidence of Age, as do other clear Differences. However, the Similarity soon Disappears and one can mark Distinctions in their Individual Appearance, Indications of Character that mark them as they would Ourselves. Some I hold to be Possessed of a Rebellious and Contrary Spirit, which is Unsurprising, while Others gave every Appearance of Submission to their Captivity. For the Main part, they were in Good Condition, if Tired and Hungry, and even the Boldest, not a little Affrighted.

It is very Hot Tonight, and it seems our Peace is Over, for the Moans of the Slaves in the Slave Rooms between decks are Terrible, accompanied as they are by the clink of their Fetters.

In five terribly similar days, as the hot sun beat down from a cloudless sky upon the ships anchored off York Island, the slaves arrived in canoes under the convoy of Mr Plantagenet and his fellow lançados. It was a grim business, but Kite became inured to it, even in that short period of time. Only once did he hear the treatment of the natives spoken of in any critical sense when Mr Kerr remarked that it was 'a brutal necessity'. Kerr's comment, propped up by assertions that Kite had already heard, assertions claiming the blackamoors would be far better treated by white masters in the Indies or the Brazils than ever they were under the native chiefs, was provoked chiefly by the arrival of the first women, which occurred on the third day of loading. In retrospect it sounded like an excuse for what was about to happen and which was anticipated by everyone except the inexperienced Kite. Perhaps Kite's acceptance of the fate of the blacks began at that same moment, when the women were sighted and the word passed through the waiting men like a gust of wind through dry grass, for he was not insensible to the prickle of expectant lust that the news provoked.

Like the men, the women were all young and strong, the oldest still capable of breeding. Although they climbed up on to the decks nimbly enough, once there they huddled in a group, heads together, occasionally turning in anticipation of torment: nor did they have to wait long. Mr Plantagenet strode in amongst them, his long whip in his hand, pulling the huddle apart and roaring instructions that they were to remove the loose, gaily coloured but now filthy cotton wraps from themselves. Here and there he gave a helpful indicator of his requirements by tearing garments off, exposing the women's bare backs. They screamed, the seamen cheered and from below there arose a howl of pain and rage from their fettered menfolk.

Intimidated by the muskets of the marines, the women stood and gasped as the remaining seamen plied their buckets and the sunlight sparkled on flashes of flung water. Hurriedly, the wretched women washed themselves down, a sight which infected Kite with an almost overwhelming lust. The sight of breasts and thighs, of the gleam of light upon wet skin and, most shocking of all, the feathery pudendae showing beneath the buttocks of the women as they squatted in the scuppers to pummel their besmirched clothing, sent a physical shock through him. It struck him that despite or perhaps because of their humiliation, their brown skin held a potence absent from the discomfited white flesh of the Liverpool whore. In his arousal, he shunned all thoughts of poor, bloody Susan Hebblewhite. He could not yet admire these Negro women as beautiful, for his sensibilities were suspended and his lust was tormentingly mixed with a self-loathing that he could even contemplate coupling with what, despite his natural compassion, he regarded as not fully as human as himself. This and his natural reserve held him back from any precipitate action, prompted by raw and primitive instinct, but in this he was almost alone.

As the first two boatloads of women finished their washing and hung their clothing in the rigging to dry, they squatted together, crying and wiping the tears from their faces with the palms of their hands, staring fearfully about them. Circling them, their jibes ended, the watching ring of seamen seemed poised for some act of violence. Then this momentary spell was broken. Mr Plantagenet's whip cracked in the air and he roared something in the native tongue. The women began to stand uncertainly when from the quarterdeck,

Makepeace's voice called out, 'Your examination, Mr Kite, and make it speedy, sir, make it speedy!'

The captain's impatient tone was reinforced by a murmur of anticipation from the men and a shuffling, instinctive recoiling from the women. Kite was suddenly confronted by the first woman, unaware of crossing the deck. He motioned her to stand and ran his eyes over her as the sweat poured from him and his lust lay half formed in his breeches. He twirled his hand and Plantagenet gave an order. The woman revolved and, at another barked command, she obediently opened her mouth. Kite peered at her teeth and looked into her eyes, touching her only to draw down the lower lid.

He was about to tap her shoulder and pass on to the next woman, when Makepeace said from just behind him, 'Look at her cunt, Mr Kite. We want no trouble from that source.'

Kite turned, his face pale beneath his tan. Makepeace was close beside him, his face flushed, and Kite could smell a sourness on his heavy breath. Kite thought of the 'trouble' the Cable-Tier Rangers would bring to the women.

'Captain Makepeace,' Kite began, but Makepeace cut him short.

'Do as I say, Mr Kite,' he said, his voice purposeful as a sword-blade.

Abashed, Kite looked at the woman as her eyes flickered from his own to Plantagenet's. The mulatto was saying something to her, at which she gasped and her gaze came back to Kite. He felt the hatred in their slight but telling contraction, saw the ripple of muscle settle along her jaw and then her hands drew his own eyes downwards. She parted herself, and he stooped to peer into her.

'Properly, man, properly!' Makepeace commanded. 'An examination, for God's sake! Not a damned sniff!' Kite hesitated, then felt himself shoved aside while Makepeace bent in his stead, handling the woman with his intrusive fingers, opening the red vulva with a coarse gesture, then standing, slapping her thigh and, moving to the next, to repeat the humiliating procedure. The first woman hurriedly squatted, her thighs so tightly pressed together that the muscles trembled and tears poured down her face as her whole body began to shake. Having examined the second woman, Makepeace straightened up and confronted Kite. 'There, Mr Kite, I don't intend to keep a dog and do all the barking, but that is how you attend to the matter. Look for a discharge, or sores...'

'Yes, sir, I understand,' said Kite, shaking himself, partly from rage, partly from his own humiliation, but his words were lost in the cheering of the men. He motioned the next woman and she turned and he touched her, briefly, with his fingertips, seeking to reassure her of his own innate kindness, shocked by the hatred in the woman's eyes, hatred that was aimed exclusively at himself. Then, in emulation of his commander, Kite stooped.

As he worked his way down the line, he heard Makepeace say, 'Put aside any with their lunar bleeding, Mr Kite,' and in this way several women were moved to one side. When he had finished, he felt no trace of the priapic urge that had quickened him at the start of his appalling task; he felt filthy, hot and begrimed, somehow paralysed by the experience and Makepeace's nastiness. He despised himself for not having remonstrated with Makepeace that the very least they could have done for the poor creatures was to carry out the examination behind a screen of canvas, but he had only thought of the notion when he had almost finished the work. Another time, perhaps, if God forbid, there ever another time.

What happened next he wrote down that night, when he could not sleep and the noises from the slave decks was not that of distress alone, but of lust and horror and degradation.

When I had Completed my Examination those Women taken by their Lunar Periods were Removed below, the Seamen handling them with a Palpable Disgust. Then our Captain came forward and Seizing Two Women he had Selected during the Examination, Withdrew to the Privacy of his Cabin. At this, as at a Signal, each of the Men who felt Inclined to Lust, took a Woman, According to the Precedence of Rank. Those Assigned to Guard, which Constituted Half of the Marines, Each Marked a Woman by placing a Hand upon her, and these were left on deck until those Occupied in Satisfying Themselves in Copulation returned to their Duty.

I noticed a Few of the Men did not Avail themselves and Submit to Temptation, though for whatever Reason was not Apparent. Molloy Abstained, which much Surprised but Gratified me, but Gerard also removed Two Women once Captain Makepeace had gone below.

This Event put me out of all Sympathy with Captn Makepeace, for where the behaviour of the Men did not Shock me, that of the Captn most assuredly did, for he speaks often of his Wife and Three Children in Liverpool and his Character as a Gentleman seemed at Variance with this Unspeakable Display of Lust...

A cry rent the hot and foetid air in the ship. It was not a scream, for there had been enough of those earlier; this was a plaintive wail of despair which was somehow the harder to bear than the shrill objections of the victimised. But it was the last noise of that noisome day. The ship became silent at last and most on board slept, the ravished and the ravishing sharing the slumber of the damned.

Kite could not sleep. Silently he went up on deck, noticing the creeping stench that now began to pervade the interior of the vessel. About the deck the handful of guards were pale shapes in the starlight. Molloy had the watch and Kite wondered if he had forborne from rape in order to keep his watch, and that by some devilish arrangement in this 'well-regulated' trade, his turn would come later.

'Not sleeping, Billy-boy?' Molloy asked wearily.

'No I am not!' Kite answered with a vehemence that surprised himself.

'Tch, tch, you *are* touchy. Gerard said you looked as if you could have murdered our gallant commander. The women upset you, eh? Well, if it's any consolation, it's always the same. When you were a little lad back in England, Englishmen were out here doing the same thing. And if it ain't Englishmen, it's Dagos, Portugooses, Frogs, Danes or square-headed Dutchmen.'

'But not Irishmen, I take it,' Kite said with a withering sarcasm.

'Oh, yes, Irishmen, Scotchmen, Welshmen,' Molloy responded quickly, 'and what difference does it make, eh?'

'Difference?' Kite spluttered. 'Why, do we treat our own women like that?' But he knew his protest was hypocritical, his mind's eye had already conjured up the dead Susie and the stabbed whore.

'B'God, Billy, you're a touchy devil. Why, certainly we may precede matters with a little flattery, or a financial agreement, but the substance is the same. And mark you, man that is made in God's image, don't forget, is prompted by ungovernable lusts at such times of extreme provocation. Think now how long it is since we saw a woman. Surely we are allowed these little moments of creation...'

'You were not so tempted,' Kite responded swiftly, 'unless you hold yourself in readiness for tomorrow.'

Molloy chuckled. 'Well, Billy, 'tis either that, or you'll think the worst of me.'

A dark and terrible thought crossed Kite's mind and he looked sharply at the ghostly figure beside him. Molloy seemed unaffected by the turmoil of the impressionable young man beside him. Kite said, 'I hope I will not have to think the worst of you...'

'Let me give you a word of advice,' Molloy

said kindly, turning towards him. 'Mark my words well, Billy. You will spend the next few weeks in an agony of temptation. Whether or not you succumb to the beast within you remains to be seen but do not, I beg you, make this an issue with Captain Make-peace. These people may seem to you to be piteous, and perhaps by our own standards they are, but ask yourself what circumstances brought them here? Why, nothing but war, war between their own chiefs and the Mandingos, or the Ashanti, or the Wolofs. These are powerful tribes who bring the spoils of their victories to trade on the coast, from Sierra Leone all along this benighted bloody country, to the Bight of Benin. If the captured blacks are not cattle themselves, then they are treated as cattle, no worse than others in other places. The Guinea coast now is no worse than the Irish coast a century ago and perhaps even the English coast before you were conquered by the Norman duke.' Molloy paused and blew the air out of his puffed cheeks. 'Pah, I sound like a damned dominie, do I not, eh? But surely it is all the work of God, Billy, foreordained and made by His Hand.'

'You are a Papist?' Kite asked.

Molloy chuckled. 'Does the notion of a Papist officer at sea surprise you?'

'No, no, I have never knowingly known one before.'

'Never known a Papist, eh? Well, well. I shan't catechise you. If it suits you to see God's Hand was providential, then so be it. You see, Billy, in company with most of my fellow creatures, Francis Molloy is incapable of untangling many mysteries, to be sure, but heed me in one thing. Do your duty by Captain Makepeace, Billy, as I have no doubt but that you will, and in due course you will earn your pay and an easy conscience.'

Kite felt a touch of kindness in Molloy's words. He had not expected such concern from so unusual a quarter. Mumbling his thanks, though unconsoled, he turned away and went below.

The next day the slaves arriving were a mixture of the sexes, clearly a sweeping-up of the emptying barracoons. Now there appeared a few older men and women and one could only guess how long they had been held prisoners before being shipped out. That afternoon a quantity of large elephant tusks and the smaller scrivelloes arrived, along with a floating raft of camwood logs which was manoeuvred alongside by half a dozen gromettoes armed with sweeps who skilfully used the river's current to assist them. More canoes arrived with woven baskets of manioc, food for the slaves during the middle passage, and Kite was compelled to remark that the trade was indeed well regulated. The enervating heat, the lack of sleep, the tormenting insects and the incessant groans and cries of the slaves, the noise of their fetters and the stink of their confinement, despite the ventilating ports purposely cut in the *Enterprize's* sides, all combined to desensitise Kite. His task became a distasteful routine. His constant proximity to the dark bodies of the slaves utterly dispelled all thoughts of sexual congress, while the stares of fear and hatred he received as the most prominent and primary agent of their distress wore down his private sympathy.

Among the slaves he found cases of medorrhoea in both men and women and these were daubed with white lead by Kerr and shunned by the men. Otherwise the slaves seemed fit and, insofar as he could tell, healthy.

As he carried out his duty on the fourth day, he was aware of Makepeace's presence on deck. At the conclusion of his examination of the last of the slaves just brought aboard, the commander called him aft.

'Well, Mr Kite, you seem to have settled to your work most commendably.' Makepeace spoke without sarcasm. Kite found it difficult to meet the captain's eyes, but he made the effort, coughing awkwardly. 'I am not indifferent to your own sensibilities, Mr Kite, but caution you not to make judgements upon others. I do not require your respect, only your obedience. You are young, and doubtless proper, but I have never asked why you were, like a fish out of water, in that filthy tavern in Liverpool. Seek not the mote in the eyes of others, Mr Kite, and miss the beam in thine own. A man's eyes are the windows into his soul. Be sure there ain't a futtock of timber or two stopping the clarity of thine own vision.'

The sarcasm inherent in the use of the Quaker form of the pronoun gave sufficient of an edge to Makepeace's statement for Kite to know the geniality had vanished from the captain's attitude. Afterwards he wrote,

Taken with Molloy's kind Caution, I Attribute Capt[n] Makepeace's Altered Attitude to a shift in Purpose now that we are to Embark on that Portion of our Voyage that we call the Middle-Passage.

Even as he waited for the ink to dry, re-reading the sentence he had just written, Kite failed to notice his own use of a significant pronoun. That he had written 'we call' signified his unconscious acceptance of his integration into a well-regulated trade.

The oppressive conditions aboard the *Enterprize* during those four days had so changed Kite that while he remained aloof from the moral turpitude of most of his fellow shipmates, he might still have followed them under the shadow of damnation and ended up indistinguishable from them. But on the last day of their loading, when the number of slaves embarked approached its final total of two hundred and eighty-five, Kite found himself staring into a face that caught his eye with a shocking intensity.

The curious, asexual propinquity that his duty had led him into seemed suddenly brought to an end by this particular confrontation. Kite had found it impossible to judge the age of the blacks, merely categorising them in his ledger as 'of about 20 y^{rs}', or 'about 25 y^{rs}', occasionally making an additional note, such as 'scarr^d, poss^{ble} warrior' or, in three cases, 'Woman with child', or to note seven females who were 'accom^{pd} by suckling child. These, unlike their menstruating sisters who were treated with a mild disgust, were almost tenderly handled by the seamen.

Such Paradoxical Behaviour, Kite noted in his journal, mitigating the conduct of his fellows with evident relief, *Argues some Influences of a Higher Civilisation amongst these Common Seamen, for here was a Manifestation of True Pity.* But his own attitude appeared to him to be less simple. Certainly he had noted some of the women possessed an attraction beyond others, just as some of the men were handsome and well set up, bearing themselves proudly. One or two of these males had imprinted their pride upon his consciousness and, in scrambling the dark and dreadful length of the slave deck, divided as it was into the male and female slave rooms, their eyes met with sparks of recognition. It was easier to accept the hatred of these young warriors than to acknowledge beauty in their women. The former was a direct consequence of the horrid confrontation brought about by the examinations, the latter was the antithesis to this intimacy, a result of luxurious con-templation and this he had been denied by the oppression and extent of his task.

But on the last afternoon, when the final canoe was awaited, Kite felt relief in the approaching end of his demeaning work and the prospect of returning to sea, clear of the green and foetid Sherbro with its insect-laden air. Perhaps, too, he had become a little blasé; nevertheless, he was sitting, sweating and uncomfortable, on the car-riage of a broadside gun as the last batch of blacks clambered down over the ship's rail, fearfully regarding their destination. It occurred to him that the *Enterprize* must seem a most strange construction, beyond even their imaginings. It was then that he saw the young woman.

She was tall and slender, and stared about her in a manner that was not without fear but was utterly without any air of submission. It was this, rather than any inherent beauty, that first attracted Kite's jaded interest and as Plantagenet began to shout his instructions, Kite was suddenly, impulsively, up on his feet.

'All right, all right, Mr Plantagenet,' Kite bellowed in so uncharacteristic an outburst that the men idling on deck, regarding this last consignment of slaves with satiated indifference, looked up and nudged each other. The linguistier turned and glared at Kite. 'Tell them quietly, man, there is no need to bellow like that, and,' Kite added sharply, 'put that damned whip away!'

'Mr Kite,' Plantagenet expostulated, tapping his breast, 'I am the man in charge of bringing aboard the blackamoors...'

'And I am the officer responsible for seeing they are in prime condition, now tell them quietly what we require them to do...' He was looking at the girl and she was looking at him as he willed himself not to lower his eyes upon her bare breasts. Then she averted her gaze, and the merest suggestion of a relieved smile nervously twitched the corners of her mouth. It was an expression of such subtle sweetness, devoid

118

of any coquetry, Kite felt, that his knees trembled and his guts churned with a powerful sensation of concupiscence. He swallowed hard and nodded at Plantagenet, who glared at Kite with hatred at his imagined loss of face.

Kite sighed, mastering himself. 'Tell them *gently*, Mr Plantagenet, like a *gentleman* would...' Plantagenet received this instruction with a kind of confused comprehension. The allusion to gentleness in such a context led him to a concept he had not previously encountered, let alone considered. His curious social pretension led him to a ridiculously exaggerated assumption of what Kite required. In any other circumstances, he would have been thought sarcastically insolent, but Plantagenet's desire for a status he did not understand but only imagined made his delivery a model of moderation at which the surrounding seamen only gaped with astonishment.

'Will you please to be taking off your garments and washing yourself, while the water is thrown over your heads,' he insisted in their native tongue. 'Then you must wash your nice clothes until they become all clean.'

The women went through the business of washing and Kite conducted his medical examination. For the most part these last groups of women had boarded the *Enter-prize* unmolested. The ship's company had slaked their sharp appetites of sexual deprivation and were, Kite learned in time, recoiling from their intimacies in a kind of disgust which was only partly directed at the slaves. As the numbers of these grew, and with the increase the risks of a rising, the seaman's duties associated with securing and tending them made them no longer objects of long-frustrated human desire, but mere parcels of cargo, representations of tasks to be done and duties to be attended. That so demanding a liability had also swiftly become a tiresome obligation distanced the white seamen from the acts of their immediate pasts.

'How could I have fucked that?' he heard Thomas say in self-disgust, though this sensation was manifested by an intimidating gesture at an adjacent male slave who barred his passage along the slave deck, seeking to shield the woman to whom Thomas referred from a further violation. The dismissal and dehumanisation implicit in Thomas's neutral pronoun, which robbed the wretched woman of gender, shocked Kite as he made his way below, following the last batch of slaves down to where Kerr and his gang were shackling them in the confined spaces allotted them.

The smell in what were now called the

slave rooms was already foul. In the five days since they began loading their human cargo there had been little effort to clean the space. With no freedom to move around and a ban on any airing or exercise on deck until the *Enterprize* was at sea, the slaves had been induced to use buckets to defecate into, but the numbers of these were limited, nor were they emptied properly. Despite a primitive attempt at sanitation by Kerr, the sharp stink of urine and the heavier odours of human excrement permeated the air. Kite had learned from Molloy and Kerr that a strict and not inconsiderate regimen would begin once they had cleared the Sherbro bar, but in the meantime the restrictions made the slave deck a terrible place.

Kite saw the girl put her hand to her mouth as she descended into the darkness from the glaring sunlight on deck. The pity he felt for all of the blacks, which he was utterly powerless to extend in any practical manner to ameliorate their condition, he now felt he should offer her. But how? Any selection of a female was clear evidence of his desire and Kite even suspected his own motives, for the strong feelings the young woman had aroused in him were unequivocally possessive.

Captain Makepeace, who had already selected a pair of female slaves to grace his bed, had so far seduced them to his purpose that they were occasionally seen in tatty gowns, thoughtfully provided by the commander. It was clear that the tide of rape had ebbed, to be replaced during the middle passage by more regular relationships between most of the men and their chosen slave.

Not merely was the trade well regulated, Kite thought bitterly, it was remarkably democratic. And, he wanted to write in his journal but could not bring himself to do so, remarkably broad in its acceptance of human lust, for he had come across one of the able seamen in the act of buggering a young black male.

On the eve of departure, Makepeace gave a dinner in his cabin. On either side of the captain sat his black mistresses, awkward in their dresses, unused to being seated on chairs and eating with their hands. They were already half-drunk, a bizarre sight in their tawdry finery, giggling, curious and uninhibited.

'I take two, Mr Kite,' said Makepeace seeing the discomfiture of his perspiring and red-faced surgeon, 'because they are company for one another.' Gerard and the other two officers round the table, sweating and stinking in the heat, slapping at the buzzing mosquitoes, drank immoderately and laughed dutifully. Kite had tried to avoid the invitation, volunteering to stand the anchor watch, but Gerard had told him his presence was insisted upon and that in any case Molloy would stand the watch with his marines.

Although Gerard had taken his pleasure of the women, he had not retained any exclusively for himself and it was only the captain who used his privilege to sport his harlots so shamelessly. The remainder of the seamen were expected to keep their selected victims shackled, except when they were required for carnal purposes. Former experiences of the slaves getting their hands on the seamen's knives prohibited too great a freedom, even for those slave women who, for whatever reason, became compliant. During the middle passage, Molloy had told Kite, he would be surprised how many of the black women acquiesced to their circumstances and could be seen squatting washing their new masters' clothing in buckets of sea- or rainwater.

'Of course,' Molloy had explained, adding detail to this picture of nautical domesticity, 'we never let them on deck without leg-irons.'

The dinner, which consisted of a deliciously baked pig, seemed set to end in riot, but Makepeace, despite appearances to the contrary, was far from being a man in the throes of unbridled lust. After about two hours, when the plates had been cleared and the company was slumped in amiable disarray, he ordered Gerard, Kite, Kerr and the gunner, a man named Mitchell, to fill their glasses. They dutifully drank a loyal toast to 'His Majesty King George' and, in view of the war, 'Damnation to His Majesty's enemies'. This done, Makepeace roused his drowsy mistresses and signalled to Gerard. Taking the hint, the first lieutenant rose and the officers clumsily and noisily withdrew.

'Until dawn, gentlemen,' Makepeace said, 'when we shall get under weigh, I wish you a good night.'

Kite did not go immediately to his cabin, but as was his habit climbed on deck. Molloy, however, was not his usual friendly self. Piqued at not being able to indulge himself at the cabin table, tortured by his own confused feelings, the second lieutenant was short-tempered and a little in liquor.

'So, you've been enjoying yourself, eh? Sporting with our gallant commander and his black whores. Now you want to come and salve your tender conscience with old Frank Molloy, the dependable bog-Irish fool who'll stand a watch while you wallow in filth...'

'That's neither true, nor just...'

'Don't speak of justice aboard here,' spat Molloy.

'Look, I volunteered to stand the anchor watch.'

'Oh, go to the devil, damn you, Kite.'

Kite stared at his friend. 'The devil,' he said quietly, 'aye, 'tis surely hell below.'

'Oh, for God's sake stop your prating, you pious bastard!' Molloy turned away, calling in a loud voice, 'Sentries report!'

Kite made for the companionway as the voices of the dutymen responded in the darkness.

'F'c'sle; all's well!'

''Tween deck forrard; all's well!'

''Tween deck aft; all's well!'

Nodding to Thomas on guard at the grating, Kite waited while the sentry unlocked and lifted the wooden lattice, then descended into the greater darkness of the cramped slave deck. This was lit by the dim gleam of lanterns set at intervals on the stanchions, but these burnt fitfully in the mephitic air, failing to penetrate the gloom to any extent. The thick atmosphere was filled with the groans, snores and miserable whimpers of the sleeping slaves; occasionally a leg-iron chinked as a slave moved in his or her restless slumber.

Kite paused, his eyes slowly adjusting. The slight high-lighting of the lamps upon a sweat-moistened shoulder, thigh, breast or buttock created the impression that he gazed out over a calm sea on a dark and impenetrable night. The occasional stirring of the slaves added to this effect, looking like the slow movement upon the black tide's surface. The sentries' cries of 'all's well' echoed ironically in his ears; how in God's name could anything be well in this hell-hole?

He moved aft a little, drawn into the dark, confined space. So, by the lights of the times in which we dwell, he thought to himself, all is well in such a well-regulated trade. God help them all. That he was responsible for these wretches appalled him. The stink of their debased state threatened to overcome him, compounding the guilt he felt after his dinner. Why had he come here, he wondered? To tend his charges? To sharpen his own sense of fear for the future? Or just upon a drunken impulse? Suddenly, utterly dejected, he wished to be out of it, free of the stench of the place. He found himself some few feet from the ladder and turned, eager for the fresh air above. The low beams kept him at a crouch as he hurried back to the short ladder, where he paused but a moment before raising his hand to bang on the underside of the grating, to stare across that black sea of limbs and bodies.

Then he felt his leg touched. It was the merest sensation, offering no threat of seizure, so brief and so light that it might have been an insect bite. Looking down he thought he saw, though he could not be sure, the face of the girl looking up at him.

Part Two

Iron

Six

The Middle Passage

During the five days they had spent embarking the slaves, Kite's duties had kept him, if not constantly busy, then constantly preoccupied. Superficial and inept though his so-called medical examinations had been, they had served to cast him more firmly in the role of the *Enterprize's* surgeon and coupled with his treatment of the Cable-Tier Rangers, established him credibly enough in his adopted profession, leaving only Captain Makepeace in possession of the truth. Moreover, while Makepeace had revealed a side of his character that Kite considered distinctly unpleasant, he had done so without lasting hostility to Kite himself. True, the captain had expressed himself with a veiled threat, but Kite found Makepeace thereafter resumed his usual smooth cordiality, even if he was accompanied by a black trull, a somewhat disconcerting sight on the quarterdeck.

Kite accepted the threat as little more than a rebuke, given like any other reprimand by the commander of a vessel maintaining his authority and the establishment of his will over that of his subordinates. If, Kite mused unhappily, there had been any real alteration in their relationship, it had been on his own part, for it was clear from the asides of Molloy and Gerard, that his own attitude had changed perceptibly: the nickname of 'Quaker' had stuck.

Oddly, Kite did not mind. In a sense it pleased him to stand against the slave trade, as a genuine Quaker would have done. Quaker opinion was not unknown in the Lakeland of Kite's boyhood; the roots of the philosophy lay in adjacent Lancashire and his father had spoken of them in admiration. But Kite could not claim any moral superiority; he was motivated less out of a general compassion for the mass of the unfortunate blacks, and more out of a specific pity for the young woman.

In the first days of the middle passage Kite found himself busy in the establishment and supervision of the regimen laid down for the slaves by Makepeace. Amid the stink of vomit and the groans of the chronically seasick, the adopted routine went some way to maintaining a semblance of cleanliness. The day began when those women who had become the concubines of the sailors, and were therefore to be trusted to a degree, went to the galley and brought the pots of manioc and rice to the slave deck where it was doled out under the watchful eye of Mr Kerr and his mates. These men were the immediate regulators of the slaves. Thereafter the deck was sluiced down and, if the weather was not too boisterous, the ventilating ports were opened. While this was in progress, the first batch of slaves were let loose and, still in leg-irons, allowed up on deck, where they walked in a circle round the waist, circling the chocked boats on the booms amidships. From the forecastle, they clinked aft along the larboard gangway, turned across the forepart of the quarter-deck and, passing the carriage gun aimed at their accommodation below, then went forward again, along the starboard gangway.

Having been specially constructed for the carriage of slaves, the *Enterprize* had a slightly elevated quarterdeck. This was raised at the hance and fenced with an athwartships rail which mounted two swivel guns. This arrangement gave a clear path across the beam of the ship to facilitate the exercise of the slaves, but, if an uprising were to occur, it provided a defensible position to be taken up aft by the ship's company. Standing at the forward end of the raised quarterdeck, his hands on the rail before him, Makepeace was able to review the condition of his cargo from a position of advantage. Makepeace undertook this duty seriously and never permitted the presence of his whores on deck at this time, which he would have considered improper. Instead he stood with his surgeon and the lieutenant of the watch, while the marines with loaded muskets, gunners manning the swivels and the midships carriage gun, and the watch on deck, all took up positions of vantage and vigilance. This show of force acted as a mild, ever-present act of passive, though potent, intimidation. Kite's dutiful attendance at these inspections filled the forenoon of every day as the *Enterprize* scudded westwards across blue seas and beneath a clear sky that sported the white and fluffy clouds of fine weather.

Each batch of slaves, their eyes downcast, shuffled four times round their circuit before passing below by way of the after companionway as the next group emerged on to the forecastle. From time to time Makepeace would stop the procession and pull a slave out of the line, concerned for the individual's condition. Commonly he bestowed this attention on a male who had been chafing his leg-iron until the man's ankles had bled. Such injuries were pointed out to Kite. A seaman named Wilson had been designated the surgeon's assistant. It was Wilson's duty to daub with white lead the right shoulder of any affected slave. After the last batch of slaves had gone below, Kite and Wilson followed them, applying tallow to their chafed ankles.

By the time this lengthy routine had been completed, it was approaching apparent noon, when the vessel's latitude was determined. At Makepeace's suggestion, Kite took upon himself the task of acting for whichever of the two lieutenants was watch below, and thus, with Makepeace and the watch-keeping officer, was party to this navigational ritual. For this the *Enterprize* was well furnished with no less than four quadrants, each of the officers being required by the owners to provide their own, while Kite was loaned an instrument that had belonged to a former, long-dead lieutenant. The man had had no relatives and therefore his belongings were not auctioned off for the benefit of his widow; instead most were given away in trading deals with the lançados who were always eager for odds and ends of apparel and artefacts with which to dignify their persons. Makepeace had withheld the quadrant on account of its value and its uselessness to the ignorant.

On the fourth morning of the passage Kite stood beside Makepeace as the slaves disconsolately circled the deck. It was a fine day, the ship was making seven knots and Makepeace was in an expansive mood.

'Well, Mr Kite,' he said waving his right hand over the passing slaves in, Kite thought, a gesture of devilish benediction. 'I think you may take some credit for the condition of these blacks.'

'Thank you,' Kite replied in a subdued tone which caused Makepeace to turn and look at him.

'Come, sir, you are still not moping over the immorality of this trade, are you? I hear you are against it, and doubt its morality. If so it is really too depressing.' Kite said nothing. The young woman had just emerged forward, where he had been watching for her, and he felt his heart quicken as she blinked in the sunshine and then stared straight at him. Though the slaves often looked about them as they came up on deck into the sunshine, by now only a few met the eyes of the white men who stood guard over them. They had long been accustomed to the presence of guards, whom they called vultures in their own tongue, and they had learned how to avoid drawing attention to themselves.

But Makepeace was unaware of Kite's preoccupation with observing the approaching woman, taking his demeanour for continuing disapproval. He let out his breath in a sigh audible above the clinking shuffle of the slaves and the moan of the wind in the rigging.

'You know, do you not, that these blacks were already prisoners long before we sought to buy them?'

The young woman had turned aft and was approaching the quarterdeck down the larboard gangway. He could not see her breasts, they were hidden by the shoulder of an older woman in front of her, but he noticed a ring was missing from her left ear.

'Their condition was abject before we took them aboard and, mark you, the women would not have been spared any horrors by the black tribes that captured them. What they are receiving now is a degree of care that they cannot have imagined possible when they were cooped up in the stockades of the King of Bulum... Why, Mr Kite, look at them; they are in the very pink!'

Kite did not hear the inept and insulting jibe, for just then the young woman turned and walked across the deck. Kite could see, so close and just below him, the glossy, upward sweep of her breasts and the slight, seductive movement of them as she walked. She had held his gaze all down the ship's side and only dropped it now, as she passed him, secure in the knowledge that he was watching her. Her long, delicate arms hung down and she lowered her head so that he saw the graceful line of her neck. She had worn a ring only in her left ear, and this was turned away from him, but as he stared down at her, he noticed the bloody graze on her ankle and, interrupting Makepeace said, 'By your leave, sir ... Wilson, daub this woman...'

Pausing, Makepeace regarded the object of Kite's solicitude. 'There, you see, that is exactly what I mean: our treatment of these wretches is humane and decent.'

Wilson quickly daubed the woman's shoulder and she passed on. Her rump moved seductively under the cotton skirt and the curve of her back and the sharp, outward jut of her hips made Kite swallow.

'Now *she'll* fetch a good price,' Makepeace remarked parenthetically before resuming his exposition. 'The canting Quakers don't comprehend the realities of existence. They seek a perfect world, where food falls like manna from heaven and each man is reasonable unto his neighbour, where love reigns in some peaceable kingdom. Pah. 'Tis all flummery imagination. Can you conceive of a world where no one loses their temper or covets another's property, where passions are roused only to worship God and never to lie with a woman except it be ordained and sanctified by the Almighty? Huh! Would that it were true! But what does the Bible give us in its opening chapters, eh? A story of disobedience followed by a story of murder, a swift descent from petty to capital crime! Remarkably soon afterwards every form of vice runs riot with mankind unchastened even by flood, earthquake, fire and plague! By Heaven, Mr Kite,' Makepeace almost roared, 'does that not fill you with a certain pride in mankind: that he can *defy Omnipotence?'* Makepeace lowered his voice. 'Why, sir, it is magnificent!'

Concluding his oration with this flourish, Makepeace turned to see the impact his manifesto had made on the young man beside him, but Kite was watching the young woman as she made her second circuit of the deck.

'So that is the way the land lies,' Makepeace muttered to himself, a sly smile playing the corners of his mouth.

Nervous of the forthcoming encounter, Kite left attending the young woman to last. Despite the quickening effect she had upon him and his growing desire for her, he was loath to commit himself and dreaded the contact he knew he would find irresistible; that much he knew about himself from his encounters with Susie. But now she was daubed and he was bound by his duty to approach her with his pot of rancid tallow, leaving Wilson to attend to the remaining male slave picked out that morning.

The young woman had seen enough of the routine to know what was required of her. Sitting quietly amid her fellow captives, she allowed Kite to ease her heavy leg-irons up her calves and to apply the sticky mess. It was odd, he thought as he knelt, that she had first touched him on the same spot. Her ankles were slim and the calves shapely. Her young skin felt smooth and cool, except where the cruel edges of the iron rings had scored and abraded her flesh. As he massaged the tallow he looked up and half-fearfully met her eyes, but there was no hatred, only the beginnings of a shy smile as she looked away. Beside her, her neighbour gave a grunt, distracting Kite so that he looked at an older woman he knew to be pregnant.

'Are you all right?' he asked, knowing the woman could not understand him, but unable to think of anything else to say.

'Aw rye, aw rye, aw rye…!' the pregnant woman exclaimed, nodding her head as tears fell from her eyes and she held her swollen belly.

Kite returned his gaze to his patient. She was staring at him again, her head slightly turned away so that the light fell upon her left ear. The gold ring had been torn out. Kite put up his hand and, though she drew back, she allowed his fingertips to touch the torn lobe. The scab was only half formed, and still oozed blood.

'It's all right,' he said again in a low, soothing voice. Then, his hand still extended, he turned and called, 'Mr Kerr?'

One of Kerr's mates, Jonas Ritchie, approached. 'Mr Kerr's on deck, Mr Kite, what d'ye want?'

'I want to know who did this?'

'What? Took the nigger's earring?'

Kite looked up at the smirking face. Many of the women wore rings in their ears, thin gold rings of little real value. Kite thought it might have been of some tribal significance, for even their black captors had left such paltry finery alone, though it was clear they had removed most valuable effects from their victims.

'Yes.'

'How should I know?'

Kite stared at Ritchie. The man was not insolent, merely indifferent. Kite turned to the woman, trying to see in her just a commercial object of flesh and blood, like a beast sent to market. Instead he saw a beautiful young woman who had begun to tremble at the presence of Ritchie and whose breathing set up a perceptible flutter about her wide, flared nostrils as if the smell of the boatswain's mate offended her.

'It's all right,' Kite repeated, touching her scabbed ear. He caught her eyes again and he wanted to read thanks and gratitude for his intervention, the social obligation laid upon her by European culture. But of course she had no notion of this sensibility, merely twitching her mouth nervously, then looking up at Ritchie as he leaned over them. In that moment, Kite sensed the enormity of what he stood upon the brink of. The nearest he could do to rescue her from her future servitude was to do what Makepeace had done with his pair of trulls, to turn them into whoring dolls and claim some sexual rights over her. Could she be one of his allowed slaves? Could he buy her and give her her freedom? The notion was immediately appealing, but the difficulties made him angry. He felt the constriction in his throat, turned away and rose to a stoop to confront Ritchie.

'Be so good as to tell your mates that these women,' Kite said, his voice cold as he gestured round at the figures lying on the deck, 'are not to be molested in this way.'

It was now that Ritchie became truly insolent, objecting to the younger man's appropriation of the tasks that were properly his and his mates.

'Very good, Mr Kite,' Ritchie said with a heavy sarcasm, 'I'll ensure that these women are only molested in the usual way.'

For a moment the two confronted each other, then Kite said, 'Stand aside, if you please,' and made for the companionway.

He did not see the parting kick Ritchie gave to the young woman, for his attention was diverted by a cry on deck and he began to run up the ladder.

'Sail ho! Broad on the windward beam, sir!'

For some time they had debated the

140

likelihood of a French frigate lying off the Guinea coast, but there had been no sign of an enemy cruiser and they had escaped to begin the middle passage, hoping to get lost in the vastness of the ocean. They would run the greatest risk, Makepeace had given his opinion, as they approached the Lesser Antilles and the French possession of Martinique and Guadeloupe. From these islands, the French naval cruisers and irregular privateers would lie in wait for the incoming slavers converging on the British possessions in the Leeward Islands. But a risk remained on the open ocean. An enemy man-of-war, either cruising opportunistically along the likely track of slavers from Guinea to the West Indies, or on her way south and bound for the Indian Ocean to prey on British Indiamen, might be encountered in these waters.

Such thoughts were uppermost in Makepeace's mind as he gave orders to clear for action and raised his glass to study the distant stranger. Hearing the order to prepare for battle, Kite turned about, his heart beating. His post was below, first seeing the slaves secured, so that no attacking enemy received a reinforcement from rebelling blacks. Ritchie was bawling out orders for the slaves to lie down, emphasising this by forcing backwards on to the deck a large Negro who had sat up. Fore and aft, additional chains were run through the wretches' leg-irons by Kerr's men, while a pair of seamen scrambled over the recumbent forms and closed the ventilating ports in the vessel's sides, shutting out a little light and seeming to seal the slaves in what might become their common, mass coffin.

It was Kite's duty to proceed below to the orlop platform once he was content with the security of the slave deck, and prepare his instruments for any surgery required on the wounded. Makepeace had presented him with an old treatise on the subject, but he had given it little attention. As he descended to the orlop, he heard the shouts of orders on deck and the rumble of the carriage guns as they were trundled out through the gunports to confront the enemy. In the semi-darkness of the lamp-lip orlop, just above the hold, he found Wilson.

The surgeon's mate was a middle-aged man whom Makepeace had appointed to the post shortly before the *Enterprize* arrived off the Sherbro. Wilson had served in the capacity on previous voyages and was familiar with the tending of the slaves, considerably easing Kite's burden as well as his conscience. Now the two of them sat in tense silence, waiting for the noise of the guns and the arrival of the first wounded to be delivered into their tender care by the fortunes of war.

The alarm proved a false one. The 'enemy frigate', converging upon them, turned out to be the ship-rigged *Marquis of Lothian*, their former companion from York Island. Relieved, the *Enterprize's* company resumed their duties, watching the other ship as she bore down towards them, British colours at her peak. But the encounter was not entirely devoid of danger, for the *Marquis of Lothian* ran close to them an hour before sunset and her commander, Captain Ross, hoisted himself up on his rail, holding on to a mizzen backstay with one hand and raising a speaking trumpet with the other.

'*Enterprize,* ahoy,' he hailed. 'Cap'n Makepeace, d'you hear me?'

Waving aside Gerard's offer of a speaking trumpet, Makepeace took up a similar position. 'Aye, I hear you, Cap'n Ross.'

'Have you any sick aboard?'

'No, sir, my slaves are all fit and well.'

'I do not mean among your slaves, sir. I mean among your crew.'

'My men are all in hearty trim, sir. What is it that concerns you?'

'Be vigilant, Cap'n Makepeace, we have the yellow jack aboard...'

'Poor devils,' said Molloy, standing close to Kite as all hands then on deck listened to the exchange and stared at the accompanying ship as if the sick would appear like a row of skulls along her rail.

'I am sorry to hear it,' shouted Makepeace, turning to Gerard who had the watch and saying, 'Keep us away, Mr Gerard, don't fall under his lee.' And Gerard ordered a slight alteration of course, keeping the *Enterprize* from running too close to the infected ship.

'Well, perhaps you will be lucky, but there were four more dead aboard the *Lutwidge* before she sailed from the Sherbro,' Ross continued.

'How many have you lost, sir?' asked Makepeace as the two vessels surged along on parallel courses, their diverging wakes slapping together in a white marbled confusion of water.

'Two yesterday, one this morning. I have seven men down with the damned fever and one on the cold threshold of eternity as we speak. Captain Makepeace…'

'What is it?'

'I should be obliged if you would keep me company… You will understand my reasoning.'

Makepeace swore, then raised his hand and cupped it about his mouth, with evident reluctance. 'I cannot well decline your request, Captain Ross, and will agree to it if you will undertake to keep a mile to loo'ard of me at all times.'

'Very well, Cap'n Makepeace. I shall keep

that station unless we are brought to action. Will you burn a lantern?'

'Aye, sir, we shall both do so.'

Ross waved his arm in agreement and jumped down from his conspicuous stance on his ship's quarterdeck rail as Makepeace regained his own deck. 'Hell and damnation,' he swore, catching Kite's eye. 'We don't want that damnable contagion aboard here. Is there any sign of the fever, Kite?'

'Not that I've seen, sir, but I'll keep my eyes open.'

'Aye,' Makepeace said and, embracing Gerard and Molloy in his remarks, added, 'and pass the word that anyone with a touch of vomiting or nausea is to report the matter at once. Old Ross is scared he'll lose half his ship's company, if not worse...'

'You mean his slaves, sir?' Kite asked, his voice edged with irony.

'No, I do not mean his slaves, Kite,' Makepeace responded sharply. Then in a reasonable tone, he went on, 'For some reason the blackamoor don't take this particular ague with the same alacrity as the white man. 'Tis said the fever comes from monkeys and, I suppose, since the Negro is relative to the monkey, has become used to it; anyway, it seems not to kill them as it does us.'

The simian comparison seemed oddly illogical to Kite, but he was thinking about how he could contain an outbreak of the Guinea marsh ague they called yellow jack. There was insufficient space to give a man quarantine in so crowded a ship as the laden *Enterprize*. God help them all if they suffered an outbreak; the white from the disease, and the blacks from the loss of the whites. Shackled in the ship with no one on deck, the miserable slaves would drift around until they all died of starvation.

Such a fate seemed too horrible to even imagine.

The first case occurred two days later, just before dark, with two seamen almost simultaneously struck down in violent shivering fits. Kite had their hammocks slung forward and by midnight both were vomiting and moaning deliriously. Makepeace immediately distanced himself, refusing Kite entrance to his cabin and ordering him to make it his business to see everything possible was done. The following morning, having the weather gauge, Makepeace ran the *Enterprize* down towards the *Marquis of Lothian* and informed Ross of the outbreak.

I am at a Loss, Kite wrote that night in his journal. *The Recurrence of the Disease may Kill us all and I, being in Close Proximity to the Infected Men, seem little likely to Avoid it.* He paused and stared into the gloomy corners of his tiny cabin. Then, in one of those rare moments a person may occasionally be vouchsafed, when a glimpse of some great purpose seems within the grasp of comprehension, and when reconciliation to fate is something to be embraced not feared, Kite suddenly began to write with rapid strokes of his scratching quill.

I cannot Pretend to see Divine Purpose in the Event. Perhaps there is Retribution in a Fever that Strikes the White Man in Preference to the Black, but it seems more likely that this Ague, with all Other Plagues and Distempers, joins with those Evils Man himself Creates, to make of this World nothing more than a Vast Game of Hazard in which the many Lose but the Few, upon occasion, most Assuredly Win. Thus was I Singled out at Random for the Cruel and Fateful Circumstance of my being Forced Hither and being Placed in this Singular Position.

He paused a moment, then dipped his quill and went on.

And if I should Doubt that I am Nothing but a Pawn to be Played at the Whim of Fate, then There is that Private Matter which beckons me on to Further Folly. But Captn Makepeace, Whom I Consider not to be a Gentleman may, in a World where a Gentlemen counts for Nought, have Struck upon something Significant in saying that Man's Greatness lies in his Defiance of Fate. If therefore Death is soon to be my Lot as it must Assuredly be Someday, may I not Seek a little Joy now?

Providence...

But providence lay unamenable, beyond his grasp. He floundered uncertainly, irresolute, for the moment of insight had gone and he knew only that he was dog-tired. His head fell forward and his mind clouded over. He felt unable to make the effort to rise and slip out of his clothes before clambering into his gentle swaying cot; instead his head dropped down upon the drying page. Suddenly the air was rent with a shriek, then another, quickly followed by a roar of rage. Kite was on his feet in an instant, and out of the cabin, fearing he knew not what. The underlying, ever-present thought of the horrors of a slave uprising quickened his heartbeat, but he moved instinctively, his perception still dopey from exhaustion.

Emerging into the gunroom he almost fell over the sprawling forms of the commander's two women, whom the crew had nicknamed Makepeace's Bedpans. They were a kicking, screaming welter of grubby petticoats, flailing limbs and flashing teeth. Makepeace had vanished, hidden behind the door of his cabin through which the two trulls had been ejected.

From a door opposite Kite's, Molloy stood yawning, staring indifferently at the two women as they fought together, crashing into the chairs set about the officers' dining table.

'Tooth and nail, Billy,' he called out wearily, 'Tooth and nail. 'Tis surgeon's business, not mine. You sort it out.' Then Molloy retreated behind his own door. Kite stared at the spread of thrashing bare legs and buttocks as one wench got the other across her waist and laid into the black flesh with a series of smacks that sounded harsh and flat in the creaking air. As he stood there stupefied, Makepeace's door opened and, obviously half-drunk and wearing only his hastily drawn-on breeches, Makepeace roared for silence. Seeing Kite, Makepeace grinned. 'You see the wisdom of keeping leg-irons on 'em now, Mr Kite, eh? Would you be a good fellow and call the after marine in.'

The two women parted and fell into an instant truce, staring up at Makepeace. It was clear they were mutually considering pleading with their master, who, for his part, ignored them. Stepping over their disarray, Kite went forward, opened the door and called the guard. The marine came aft into the gunroom and stopped, the women at his feet.

Makepeace called, 'Take these two forward, Mason, get some leg-irons on 'em and get them out of my sight. Give him a hand, Kite...' The captain stood leaning on the door frame, bracing himself against the ship's easy roll and the unbalancing effects of the wine he had consumed.

As Mason grabbed one of the women, Kite wearily stooped to take the arm of the other. Suddenly, Kite felt himself struck across the face as the woman tore free and went for Makepeace with a reel of abuse.

Makepeace straightened. In a second his right arm shot out and he took the woman's throat with such a vicious grip that her eyes started from her head. Makepeace lifted her so that her feet danced upon the deck. 'Take that bitch forward,' Makepeace said quietly to Mason, 'then come back for this one.' He looked at Kite. 'Are you all right, Mr Kite? 'Tis not always amusing to be struck by a strong black woman.'

Kite rubbed the side of his face. 'No matter, sir. May I suggest you let her throat go, sir...'

'You may suggest what you like, Kite, but let these devils once think they can strike a white man and you'll have no end of problems...' Makepeace was now regarding his victim in a matter-of-fact way. She had ceased to struggle and merely tried to take her weight on her toes. Afterwards Kite recalled that despite the gloom of the gunroom and despite the woman's dusky skin, he could see her face empurpling.

Makepeace saw this too and let her go. She dropped to the deck like a sack of grain, inert and almost completely still. Then her body heaved, drawing air into her lungs and Kite saw that she was not dead. Makepeace grunted, then stepped over her and went forward, following Mason out of the gunroom into the gloom of the 'tween deck beyond the door. Kite stared down at the gasping woman, then knelt beside her with a sigh. Putting his hand on her back, he felt the heave of her lungs as instinct grasped at the life that had hung so perilously at Makepeace's whim.

He stayed thus, stooped over the woman as her breathing became normal again, unconsciously rubbing her back, waiting for Mason to reappear and conduct her forward, wondering if she would be capable of moving herself.

'Tie her to the damned table for the night.' The commander's voice broke into Kite's thoughts and he looked up. Makepeace had re-entered the gunroom, pushing the young woman of Kite's fancy before him. His intentions were clear. Mason followed. 'Oh, take *her* out, Mason,' Makepeace ordered nodding at Kite's patient. 'Do what you like with the whore, though mind the dress...'

But Kite was not listening, he was staring at the terror in the young woman's eyes, aware that her plea could not be more eloquent than if she cried out in perfect English. What she thought of the events that had transpired in the gunroom he could only guess at, but his own complicity seemed so obvious as he squatted with his hands on the distressed and stirring female that Mason now stooped over. Kite stood up and Mason dragged his burden like a sack over the painted canvas on the deck, uncaring that her head and shoulders bumped and struck the chair legs as she passed.

Kite looked from the young woman to the leering Makepeace, then acted on an irresistible impulse to stop the captain from raping her.

He blocked the narrow space that ran down the length of the table and along which the captain and his prisoner would have to pass to reach the privacy of his cabin. 'Not her, sir!' he said, head up, his shoulders hunched, anticipating the blow and aware now of the power in the captain's hands, one of which was ominously clasping the young woman's neck.

Makepeace looked at Kite. Slowly he

turned his victim's head and regarded her. 'And why not her, Mr Kite? Do you want her for yourself? Have you developed a taste for the black wench, then? The Quaker misgivings gone at the twitch of your prick, eh?' Makepeace was chuckling. Suddenly he thrust the young woman violently forward and she cannoned into Kite, who seized her. Kite was still staring incredulously at Makepeace whom, he realised, he had mutinously defied.

'I have seen you watching her,' Makepeace said dismissively. 'Go and take your pleasure of her. That is what women are for, Mr Kite. That and the perilous business of bearing offspring.' And then Makepeace had somehow moved between them and only the bang of his cabin door marked his passing.

Kite stared at the young woman. Her face was inches from his; she was frozen in a rictus of fear.

'It's all right,' he said urgently, never recalling that he had used those very words when soothing her abraded ankles. 'It's all right,' he repeated, then, putting up his hand to stroke her face, he gently drew her into his cabin and closed the door.

'Shhhh...' He let her go, his finger to his lips, casting about him, hurriedly closing his journal and stowing it away, along with the quill and ink-well. The young woman retreated to huddle into the forward out-board corner of the cabin, from where she stared up at Kite, her beautiful dark eyes round with apprehension.

Crouched down, her vulnerability struck him with a wave of lust.

Seven

The Negress

The blaze of sudden ferocity in Kite's expression ignited a responding terror in that of the trembling, crouching Negress. She shut her eyes tight, screwing them up against his imminent assault, the only defence she could offer. It stopped Kite dead. He felt the pang of guilt as a physical wrench in his guts. Yes, he wanted the woman, as a young man wanted a woman, but not in this manner! Instead he squatted beside her and slid an arm about her shoulders, a gesture of almost fraternal concern. He felt her shudder, as the captain's half-strangled whore had shuddered, but he made no further move, sensing that inaction would the quicker console her. After a while he felt her trembling ease, and he bent and kissed the top of her head. At this she looked at him and he gently withdrew, easing himself back against the adjacent bulkhead and placing the tips of the fingers of both hands on his breast said slowly: 'Kite … I am Kite … Kite…'

She tried to enunciate the words, but her

mouth was dry and she had to swallow before she uncertainly formed his name. 'Kite…' she said.

He smiled and nodded. Then he extended his hand and without thinking, still looking into her eyes, touched her breast, raised his eyebrows questioningly and made as if to say a word. She frowned and repeated, 'Kite.'

Kite smiled again and shook his head, touched his own breast, repeated his own name, then her shoulder. She said something which he failed to catch and he quickly cupped his right ear and bent forward. She repeated the word which, if it was her name, he found himself unable to grasp. Instead he sat back on his haunches and said, 'I shall call you Puella, which is Latin for girl.' He repeated the name slowly. 'Puella.'

Since he could not discover her real name, to confer some artificial English substitute seemed but one more imposition; the Latin noun seemed a not inappropriate expedient and, he hoped, temporary substitute.

Rising, he slipped out of his cabin and reappeared with a handful of biscuits and some water from the gunroom, which he offered her. Eagerly she grabbed the carafe of water and upended it, swallowing quickly. When she had finished she gestured at her leg-irons and said something which he interpreted as a request that he should remove them.

He shrugged and shook his head. 'I cannot,' he said. Then, realising that if he said more, though she would be incapable of understanding it, she might comprehend that the matter was more complicated, he went on.

'Believe me, Puella, I would willingly remove those confounded irons if it was in my power, but they would only be replaced tomorrow.' He saw the disappointment in her eyes and it suddenly occurred to Kite that although he, along with every man aboard the *Enterprize,* knew the fate of the Negroes, they themselves would have no idea of what lay in store for them. Thus his kindness, however partial, might seem to her not a temporary amelioration of her confinement, but the end of it. He fervently wished that this was so, but knew that the morning would present him with further problems. What, he asked himself, could he do to mitigate the poor creature's distress, to show her that although she must remain shackled, he meant no harm? Impulsively, he suddenly scooped her up and laid her out in his cot, pulling a sheet over her. Touching her lightly on the cheek, he wished her good night.

Then he spread a blanket on the deck and lay down to sleep.

When he woke it was still early. The faint click of iron recalled the presence of Puella in his cot and told where she shifted uneasily in her sleep. He sighed, aware that he could do little to preserve Puella's privacy, yet dreaded her reaction to being returned to the women's room on the slave deck. He wished that there was someone on board who could translate between them, and express his intention of doing whatever he could to help her, but they had left Golden-Opportunity Plantagenet at York Island. He considered buying her himself; the notion had merit, for it offended no one and while he might be thought a damned fool, he could stomach that. But he presumed he would have to wait until the slaves were put up for sale, whenever and wherever they were landed. Then another idea struck him; so as not to wake her, he quietly slipped on his shoes and went on deck.

It was still dark and for a moment he stood in the chilly night air, staring at the first flush of the dawn to the east. Gerard had the watch and loomed up like a ghost. 'Well, Mr Kite, what a surprise, I hear you have feet of mortal clay after all.'

Kite opened his mouth to protest the innocence of his behaviour, but thought better of it, realising his continence would be as misunderstood as his own initial misunderstanding of Molloy's rectitude. It was preferable to meet his problems at a level others comprehended.

'I have taken a woman, yes. Is that so very remarkable?'

Gerard chuckled. 'In your case it's remarkable, yes. Was she good?'

'I've had better,' Kite riposted, pleased with the readiness of his glib reply.

'Have you now? Well, well. And I had you for a cock-virgin.'

'We all make mistakes, Mr Gerard. Now, perhaps you will tell me something. How do I get her made into an assistant, as the other men's women have become? She would make a good assistant to Wilson and myself.'

'Well...' Gerard appeared to consider the matter.

'Look, I understand I am entitled to profit from a slave or two. Why cannot I have this one...?'

'In lieu of payment?'

'If necessary.'

Gerard laughed. 'Are you a fool? Have you any idea what a box of problems she'll bring?'

'Then I'll sell her on,' Kite said with convincing brutality.

'Captain Makepeace doesn't favour...'

'Captain Makepeace thrust her in my face last night.' As he uttered the words Kite was seized by a sudden suspicion and immediately voiced it: 'In fact I'm not sure that he didn't intend to corrupt me by the act and prove my feet were of ordinary clay.'

Gerard chuckled beside him. 'Well, he seems to have achieved a degree of success. You now possess a zeal of the converted, Mr Kite. Only yesterday you moped about, utterly opposed to the trade, and now, here you are, up before the sun to ask me about buying a black whore.'

Kite bit his lip at the insult, then said, 'I thought perhaps you would approve. It would ease the burden on–'

'Beg pardon, sir.'

'What is it?' Gerard turned as a man approached them in the gloom. 'It's Holmes, ain't it?' Gerard peered at the figure who appeared bare legged, his shirt tails flapping in the wind. 'What are you doing on deck?'

'There's trouble below, sir–'

'What, the slaves?' broke in Gerard, suddenly tense.

'No, no, sir, not them. That's Mr Kite, ain't it? It's more fever, sir. Johnny Good is shaking in his hammock, sir, damn near threw me out, and he's started to shout about his muvver.'

'Dear God!'

'I'll go down, Mr Gerard,' Kite said. 'Take me below, Holmes.'

In the next two days eight men were taken ill, including the gunner, Mitchell, the first of the *Enterprize's* officers to be infected. The yellow jack, having lain dormant from its initial appearance among the crew of the *Enterprize,* had now incubated and struck in all its indiscriminate horror. It was only the beginning; by the end of a week one third of the ship's company were suffering, some in the preliminary stage, suffering terrible fits of uncontrollable shivering, wracked by pains in the head, the spine and the limbs, some already in the second phase, when an abatement gave the false impression of recovery before the final yellowing of skin and eyes. This was only a brief interlude, for the copious and bloody vomiting that followed was the prelude to the fatal chilling before death.

Like their consort, the *Marquis of Lothian,* aboard which the epidemic still raged, the work of the ship suffered. The morning exercise of the slaves was curtailed, then abandoned, for there were barely sufficient men fit to work the vessel. Instead, a daily burial party mustered. Makepeace, a scented handkerchief held to his face, hurriedly mumbled the Protestant rites over the corpses, which had been sewn into their hammocks and were now sent to the bottom with a cannon ball at their feet.

For Kite the outbreak was not without ironic consequence, for he had succeeded in persuading Makepeace to strike off the leg-irons from a few of the women and these included Puella. They helped nurse the dying with a tender compassion that drew from the commander the observation that, 'Such a thing seems scarcely possible and would doubtless prove so if they knew they were to be sold into a lifetime's servitude.'

But that, it seemed to Kite, was increasingly unlikely, for the mortality among the crew threatened the continuation of the voyage. This fact formed the core of a shouted debate between Makepeace and Ross at the end of the twentieth day of the passage. Although the ships' route lay within the compass of the north-east trade winds which held steady, requiring little sail trimming by day nor night, the loss of men seriously hampered the management of the slaves. That morning Molloy and Kerr were struck down.

Having compared the increasingly parlous state of his crew with that of Captain Ross, Makepeace clambered down from the rail to where Gerard and Kite waited. Kite had just reported the incapacity of Molloy, whose large frame shuddered below in the confinement of his cot.

'You know what is in my mind, Mr Gerard, if things get much worse?'

'I do, sir.'

Kite looked enquiringly from one to the other, but it was clear that the obscure reference was to be kept from him.

'How many of the blacks are affected today?' Makepeace asked.

'Only five, sir,' said Kite, 'the same number as yesterday.'

'How can this be?' Makepeace asked frowning, his expression desperate and fearful as he stared at Kite.

'They are a lower order of being,' Gerard said, 'their immunity proves it...'

'Aye, that may be true,' said Makepeace, 'but Kite here is so far unaffected and he has been in constant contact with the sick.'

'Perhaps I too am of a lower order,' Kite remarked. Black humour, he had observed, was a common means by which the seamen coped with the dread of their circumstances.

Makepeace smiled thinly. 'I think that highly possible, Kite.' He looked up at the foretopsail. 'If this wind holds we shall sight land within the sennight; it remains to be seen whether we can win this race and keep sufficient men to work the ship into port.'

'If we run into enemy men-of-war...' Gerard left the sentence incomplete, but Makepeace merely shrugged.

'Let us hope,' he said, 'we have a man left to strike the ensign.'

'Kite will do it,' said Gerard, half smiling.

I have Little Inclination to Write these Lines.

Kite dipped his quill and stared across his cabin to the rumpled cot.

We now have over Half the Ship's Company sick with the Yellow-Fever. I am Deeply Perplex'd to know where this Contagion Arises. That it Comes from the Coast of Guinea is Clear, for the Negroes have grown Accustomed to it and are hardly Affected by it, but by what means, or from what Agent the Infection Comes, the Disease remains a Great Mystery.

He paused again, recalling the Sherbro and the dense jungle that crowded its banks, hemming in the grey-green water and depositing in its stream the detritus of its endless cycle of life and death. Did the slime-laden water contain some organism that bore the fatal disease? It was not dissimilar to the fever known in England as the marsh ague, endemic, he knew, in low, boggy and foetid areas. Although the deep and flowing Sherbro seemed at first to bear little resemblance to the marshes lying in the estuaries of many English rivers, he recalled the heavy miasma which, after

164

nightfall, would descend upon the river like a thick and steaming fog. Was it this dense mist that, penetrating the opened ports and descending through the open gratings and companionways of the waist, introduced the deadly fever into the *Enterprize*.

Was it the river water, or the river-borne mist? Or both?

Then Kite remembered something with a start of horror and culpability. He himself had insisted the slaves were washed down with water from the Sherbro; had this sanitary measure actually imported the fever? 'Oh God...' he groaned, burying his head in his hands, shaking with deep sobs at his profound ignorance and the fatal events which had led to this tragedy.

'Kite ... Kite...?'

He looked up, wiping the moisture from his eyes. The Negress Puella had entered his cabin, barefoot and noiseless. She bore a bowl of steaming rice and he realised he had not eaten for hours. He nodded and expressed his thanks, taking the proffered bowl from her. She drew back to hunker down in the corner of his cabin, folding her arms on her drawn-up knees and staring up at him.

After swallowing a mouthful he said, 'You are good to me, Puella. I thank you.' He put the spoon in the bowl and extended his right hand, repeating, 'Thank you.'

She reached out and took his hand. It was the first mutual intimacy they had shared and they both smiled. 'Kite may die, Puella,' he said, 'and God knows what will become of you, but if I live, I shall not abandon you.' He cleared his throat and shook his head, adding in a firmer voice, 'No, I shall not, upon my honour.'

He knew she had no idea what he said as he made this compact with providence, but he sensed she derived some satisfaction from the sound of his voice, for she smiled again and he was beguiled by the curve of her full lips and the way a smile made her wide but not uncomely nostrils flare.

Scooping the bowl clear of rice he set it down, whereupon she rose to remove it. Standing close to him, her breasts prominent, infinitely desirable and appealing. As she took up the bowl she gently touched his cheek. He resisted an impulse to put his arm about her and in the same instant she slid her hand about his head and drew his face to her. He felt the soft firmness of her breast, the erect tissue of her nipple, against his cheek and the soft touch of her lips on the crown of his head.

'Kite,' she said slowly. Then she was gone, leaving him sitting like a loon, staring at the closed door of his cabin. He sighed, profoundly touched, then took up his quill again.

The Negresses have greatly Assisted in tending the Sick, among them a Young Woman whom we call Puella and in whom I have an Interest and Regard with Great Affection...

What did it matter what he wrote now? Who would read his journal after his death? He crossed out the dissembling *we call* and substituted *I call.*

On the following afternoon Gerard was taken ill, along with two other men, including the gunner, and while Kite almost hourly expected to begin a shuddering fit he remained strangely unaffected. Upon hearing the news of the first lieutenant's incapacity Makepeace retired to his own cabin and proceeded to render himself helplessly drunk. It was Ritchie who brought both the news that Gerard had been carried twitching from the quarterdeck to his cabin and that Makepeace had taken to the bottle. Kite was then in the 'tween deck, binding up the jaw of their most recent fatality, Francis Molloy.

Kite frowned, intent on his task, asking over his shoulder, 'Who has the deck? With Molloy dead, Captain Makepeace has no right getting drunk.'

'The steward says he's consigned the ship

to the devil, Mr Kite.'

Kite straightened up and looked at Ritchie. 'I suppose he fears that he'll be next.'

Ritchie shrugged. 'That's a risk we all run,' he observed with chilling logic, glancing at the pale form of Molloy. Then he confronted Kite with an even colder piece of logic. 'If the Cap'n goes, you'll be the last officer left. I reckon you've a touch of luck about you, Mr Kite. I've seen it before; Makepeace had it for years and maybe it ain't deserted him yet – we'll see – but you've a winning way, sir and with Mr Kerr gone... Well, sir, looks like you and Jacob Ritchie've got a leg up in life, if you know what I mean...'

Kite frowned, then the penny dropped. 'You mean you're the next senior man?'

Ritchie nodded. 'At the moment Mr Kite, it's Cap'n Makepeace, you and me...' Ritchie waved his hand at Puella and another Negress who were present, tending the sick seamen. 'Along with all this black ivory.'

Kite saw the end of Ritchie's train of thought. The system of shares upon which the rewards of the voyage rested accrued to those holding the various stations at the conclusion of the voyage. 'Yes,' he agreed hurriedly, 'I see.'

'I'm glad you do, Mr Kite. You and me

haven't always seen eye to eye, but then we can let bygones be bygones, can't we? I can work the old *Enterprize*, sir, but I'll need you to navigate, like.'

Kite nodded. The additional burden appalled him. 'I'd better go and see the Captain, just the same. We'd be desperately short-handed without him.'

Ritchie stood aside. 'Oh yes, sir, quite so, but just tell him that Jake Ritchie's now his first luff, sir.'

Kite left Ritchie laughing and made for the ladder. Ritchie watched him go, then still smiling, squeezed the buttocks of the nearer Negress.

'I Mister Thomas' woman...' she protested as she had been schooled to.

'Sure you are, sister, just as long as Mr Thomas can stand up and piss.'

Kite went aft and knocked on Makepeace's door. 'Go to the devil, whoever you are!'

'It's Kite, sir. Pray let me in...'

'To hell with you, Kite.'

Kite hesitated only an instant before forcing the flimsy door. Makepeace rose to his feet. 'Damn you!' Makepeace began, but Kite, seeing the quantity of bottle necks visible in the opened locker under the settee beneath the stern windows, over-rode him.

'Captain Makepeace, for God's sake recollect yourself. You are not sick and the ship requires you. If you submit to this meaningless debauch, do you think me capable of bringing the *Enterprize* into port?'

'I am in quarantine, Mr Kite,' Makepeace began portentously, 'to better preserve myself for precisely the purpose of bringing this brig into port...'

'And who do you expect to run the ship in the interval, sir? Are you aware that presently, with Mr Gerard like to die, your first lieutenant is Jacob Ritchie?'

Makepeace stared at Kite, frowned, then waved Kite's remark aside. 'Well, you are an officer ... haven't we taught you to take a meridian altitude?'

'I cannot tend the sick and–'

'Then give up tending the sick! The sick will die! The fever is fatal! Embrace your new opportunity with enthusiasm, Kite. It may not last long.'

Kite was appalled, he was neither surgeon nor a sea-officer, but Makepeace's remark gave him a slight opening, for the commander was not yet completely inebriated.

'D'you want to bring the ship in, sir, because if so then I will willingly stand watch-and-watch with you? We cannot have many more days to run before sighting land...'

Makepeace stared at him, then he refilled his glass. 'I shall consider your proposal,' he said and Kite knew he had lost his argument. With a look of absolute contempt for Makepeace, he left the cabin, followed by a bottle which flew through the air and smashed against the door Kite slammed behind him.

On deck Kite passed the word for Ritchie, telling him to take the watch until midnight when he himself would take over. Ritchie grinned and winked at him. 'I told you, Mr Kite.'

Kite turned away; he was desperate for some sleep. The prospect of even two or three hours away from the stench of vomit, blood and the last venting farts of the dead seemed to hold the promise of paradise.

Nothing mattered any more; the fell shadow of damnation that had fallen over his life in the Hebblewhites' barn, and against which he had struggled for so long, could no longer be opposed. He reconciled himself to death; it would come sooner or later and sooner now seemed preferable, for he lacked the will to fight the inevitable any more. Makepeace was neither a fool nor a coward, but Kite realised he had already capitulated. Makepeace had always known the enormity of the risks in his adopted trade. Perhaps these risks mitigated the cruelty of it and the mortality among the crews of the Guineamen paid in some part for those of the enslaved Negroes. Perhaps the constant presence of death prompted men of high temper and passion, such as Captain Makepeace, to take their pleasure of the black women while they still breathed...

With these dark certainties crowding his mind, Kite entered his cabin, intent only on falling fast asleep. Puella was crouching in the corner, whither she had run to escape Ritchie who, unwilling to antagonise Kite, had not followed her and had then been summoned to the quarterdeck.

'Puella...' he said thickly, swaying with fatigue. She stood hurriedly and caught him by the upper arms.

'Kite...'

Hesitantly, his hands went round her slender waist and ran down over her pert buttocks, slipping the cotton wrap from her. He felt the responsive pressure of her thighs against his and they looked at each other, she half smiling, half fearful as he bent and kissed her, losing himself in the sudden access of tremulous passion. Her nipples rasped against him as he tore at his breeches and then she was laying down before him, on the bare scrubbed planking of the deck, her knees drawn up, shielding the smooth and lovely brown expanse of her flat belly. As he exposed his throbbing and eager member she parted her legs and he tenderly knelt between them, pressing his loins down towards her black triangle of coiling pubic hair.

Woken from a deep sleep, Kite disentangled himself from Puella's deliciously wanton limbs and clambered wearily up the companionway to the quarterdeck. His mind was a turmoil of contradicting thoughts. Love and desire mixed with self-contempt and despair; hope flowed through him, to be quenched by reality, while rambling and insane thoughts of defying fate and surviving against all the odds, were brought down to sea level by a dousing of cold spray sweeping across the brig's rail as he reached the deck.

The fog of sleep cleared and he stared about him, checking the course. The man at the wheel said nothing; the death-rate aboard the *Enterprize* had so altered everything aboard the brig that it seemed no longer odd that the surgeon was also the officer of the watch. Kite stared to leeward where, just abaft the larboard beam, he could see the *Marquis of Lothian* quite clearly in the starlight, a pale ghost of a ship, her waterline delineated by the faint trace of phosphorescence.

The beauty of the sight struck him, along with the incongruity of the sentimental effect the perception had on him here, on this stinking vessel with its cargo of death and misery. The strange, contradictory thoughts made his whole being tingle, like some late extension of the shuddering orgasm he had enjoyed with Puella. He sensed something of that triumphalism touched upon by Makepeace with his theory of providential defiance; he sensed too a brief connection between the wonder of creation that united the quickening of the life forces of Puella and himself with the dreadful, bloody death of his friend Molloy.

He was recalled from this introspection by a monosyllabic protest by the man at the wheel. Turning, he saw Puella beside him. 'What are you doing here?' he began, stopping when he simultaneously realised she could neither understand him nor comprehend his hypocritical affront at the impropriety of her presence on the quarter-deck. Puella held out a twist of cloth containing something small and hard. Taking the tiny bundle, Kite thought it felt like irregular musket balls.

'Kola,' she said, pointing at her mouth. 'Good.' She hesitated, then, pointing at his own mouth, added, 'Kite... Good... Eat.'

He opened the cloth, marvelling at her slow but sure acquisition of English words. She had learnt 'eat' from the curt commands of Ritchie and his men as they compelled the seasick slaves to consume

174

their daily rations of manioc and rice. Kite recognised the nuts, which he had seen a few of the slaves eating. Makepeace had drawn his attention to them, explaining that they eased hunger and could drive away fatigue, even, it was claimed, dispel the symptoms of drunkenness and purify water. These, Kite deduced looking down at the handful he held, must have been preserved in the clothing of the blacks during their captivity in the barracoons. There could have been few left on board by now, and he assumed Puella had gone to some trouble to obtain them for his easement. He was touched by her solicitude and gratefully touched her cheek.

The man at the wheel sucked his teeth with whistling disapproval.

'Thank you,' he said tenderly to Puella and she, sensing the solitary duty to which he must attend, left him alone. As she went below, the man at the wheel muttered something. When Puella had disappeared, Kite rounded on him. 'Hold your tongue!' he snapped.

The man sniffed, but Kite let the insolence pass and, putting one of Puella's kola nuts into his mouth, he began chewing.

At dawn Kite went below and, crushing another kola nut with a pestle in his mortar, tipped the powder into a tankard and added water from the scuttlebutt. Then he went into Makepeace's cabin. The captain was in such a drunken stupor that Kite was unable to wake him. No longer tired, thanks to the masticated kola nut, Kite resumed the watch on deck, sending for the captain's steward and instructing him to give Makepeace the infusion as soon as he could.

But Makepeace made no appearance on deck during the forenoon. Kite, possessing an odd vitality and mental energy, left to his own devices, ordered all hands mustered aft at noon, when the next watch-change was due. Then, nervously giving the helm orders himself, he edged the *Enterprize* down towards the *Marquis of Lothian* and hailed Captain Ross. It was Ross's mate who made his appearance on the rail.

'Bad news, *Enterprize!* Cap'n Ross is struck with this damned plague! Where is Captain Makepeace?'

'Likewise unwell, sir,' Kite replied, unwilling to explain further with a precise definition of Makepeace's condition.

'Our fortunes are on the ebb, sir. Our only hope is that we sight land. Until tomorrow!'

'Until tomorrow,' Kite responded.

At noon, the men assembled at the break of the quarterdeck. There were sixteen of them.

'Mr Ritchie, pray take your station beside me.' Ritchie swaggered up and stood beside

Kite who turned his attention to the crew.

'Are there any among you who feel unwell?'

The men shuffled awkwardly and looked from one to another, but a negative mumble rose from them and Kite, standing behind the athwartships quarterdeck rail, nodded and cleared his throat. 'Very well. We are in a desperate plight with Mr Gerard ill and Mr Molloy dead. But we are not yet entirely destitute. Captain Makepeace is unwell, but not from the fever...'

The aside provoked a laugh from the men and one shouted, 'No sign of the yaws yet then, Mr Kite?'

Kite had no idea what the yaws were and merely smiled before resuming his address. 'As the surgeon and the only officer fit for duty, Mr Ritchie here will assist me...' Ritchie grinned at his shipmates. 'From eight bells we will take up new watches of eight men each,' Kite went on. 'For the next four hours, I want the slaves exercised and their decks mucked out.' He saw a grin pass among the men at his use of a farming expression. 'Now let's get on with it.'

By sunset Makepeace was sober and, still free of any signs of fever, somewhat contrite. Seeing Ritchie on deck he summoned Kite, who reported the events of the day.

'There's one other thing, sir,' Kite said when he had finished, regarding his commander's dissipated pallor with disgust.

'Oh?' Makepeace looked up from the compass in the binnacle as if intent on finding an error in the brig's navigation greater than that of his own dereliction of duty. 'Pray what is that?'

'We have had no new cases of yellow jack today.'

'And is that significant?'

'That is for you to decide,' said Kite, his voice coldly formal.

Makepeace stiffened and straightened up. 'Have a care, Mr Kite, that promotion don't go to your head.'

'Your solicitude is most thoughtful, Captain Makepeace.'

Makepeace regarded Kite with a jaundiced eye. 'You may go below, Mr Kite.'

Kite footed a bow and wisely held his tongue.

Later that day, when the watch changed again and Kite came on deck, Makepeace was still pacing the quarterdeck. The captain said with his charming smile, 'I have more than a reputation to maintain, Mr Kite, I have a name to keep.'

'I'm sorry, sir, I don't understand,' said Kite, frowning, still fogged by sleep.

'My name; I have to live up to it. We are at odds, Mr Kite, and I have to make peace between us. I owe you an apology; you have done a uncommonly fine job and the knowledge that you are not properly a surgeon is set aside. We are quits, Mr Kite.'

Was it that easy? That they were quits, and all dispute between them was set aside? Kite recalled the similarity of Ritchie's remark about bygones being bygones. Kite wanted to feel the weight of responsibility lifted from his shoulders, but this did not happen, though he was not one to maintain an ill-humour, even towards a man whose aberrations had for a while, threatened them all.

'It is a pity about Gerard, though,' Makepeace said.

'Yes, and Molloy.'

'Indeed yes; Molloy too, but Gerard and I had known each other a long time, and my wife is a relative of his.'

'I see, sir. I am sorry.'

'Well, we cannot weep long over the dead. Or the dying... We may yet join them in Hell.'

'That is true, sir.'

'But if our luck has improved, then we may yet turn this voyage to good account.'

Kite grinned ruefully. 'I think Mr Ritchie is somewhat sanguine on that score.'

Makepeace frowned. 'Ritchie? Oh, yes, I see, rapid promotion and an increased share. Well, much of that will be due to you.' Kite demurred. 'No, I am sincere,' Makepeace insisted. 'Mr Gerard and I had already concerted a plan if mortality had debarred the further passage of this vessel.'

'I recall hearing you speak of it,' said Kite, 'though I took no meaning from your conversation.'

'We are not yet out of trouble and it is as well if you know of it, Mr Kite. It is not unknown, in extremis, for the master of a slaver to jettison his cargo. The risk of an uprising increases with every death among the crew and it may yet be necessary.'

'I do not understand, sir. Surely, to jettison means to throw overboard. Do you mean the scrivelloes and the camwood? Surely you cannot mean...'

'Of course I mean the slaves, Mr Kite.' Makepeace looked at the young man beside him as Kite's astonishment changed to horror and outrage. 'All of them,' he added, 'your paramour included.' Then, with a sudden intensity Makepeace went on, 'Like all intelligent young men, you judge your elders. You disapproved of my whoring and drinking, but when you have survived the yellow jack, and when you have to make a decision which may account for the deaths of nearly three hundred blackamoors, then you may not view me so harshly, Mr Kite. Life walks in constant companionship with death.'

Kite considered Makepeace's strange half-apology, half-justification and, just for a second, recovered a fragment of the weird sensation he had felt that morning he had viewed the phosphor running along the waterline of the *Marquis of Lothian.*

'It is the Fates who direct us, Mr Kite,' Makepeace concluded.

For Kite, the moment of magic vanished. He was again a murderer on the run, a man drawn to the contemplation of drowning almost three hundred blackamoors. 'Of that I am only too well acquainted, Captain Makepeace.'

'Aye, sir,' Makepeace responded, his voice low. 'You are in too deep now, Mr Kite.'

Five days passed as they ran west and no further infections occurred; cautiously Kite came to believe the yellow jack had gone as mysteriously as it had arrived.

I can only Conclude, he wrote in his journal as Puella squatted in her corner and watched him,

that the Mysterious Agent of Disease Possesses a Finite Lifetime and that this is now at an End. I now Believe that the Contagion was brought aboard by the Blacks. The first Infections were Probably caught from our Initial Contact with the Negroes in the Sherbro. The later Outbreak is Likely to have come from the Slaves held on board, which Spread after we had Sailed.

181

He reread his words, wondering if he had divined the actual means by which the fever infected white men. One or two of the seamen, he had heard, had voiced the opinion that the fever was caught from the bites of mosquitoes. They argued the mosquitoes lived in the salt-marshes in the Thames estuary where the marsh ague and dengue fever were widespread. But although one man claimed the ague killed many women on the coast of Essex, the man's description of the disease's progress indicated it to be a different sickness, more like the quotidian fever of Mr Lorimoor, then the yellow jack. Moreover, for the life of him Kite could not see how a mere fly could propagate a malady vicious enough to strike a fit man down so swiftly.

The remission of the fever, coinciding as it did with Kite's initiative in re-establishing a routine aboard the *Enterprize,* gave the surviving ship's company a new lease of life. In turn this compensated for their lack of numbers in the management of the slaves. The experienced Ritchie instituted a savagely oppressive regime over the increasingly resentful male slaves, whose women urged them to rebel as the voyage dragged on and they became more and more apprehensive over their future. Many among them were not as ignorant as Kite had supposed. They understood the vastness of the ocean and that their passage was to the westward where, they had heard, there lived terrible cousins of these white men who walked the earth like great kings.

With such stories the lançados had terrorised them as they had brought them from the stockadoes and the barracoons down the Sherbro to the waiting Guineamen.

Eight

The West India Merchant

They reached Antigua four days later, dropping anchor in the harbour of St John's on the north-west coast. Here they learned the rumours of war rife on the Guinea coast were unfounded. They had been based on the assumption that the attack by a British squadron under Vice-Admiral Edward Boscawen on some French men-of-war on the Grand Banks, resulting in the capture of the *Lys* and the *Alcide*, would lead to a declaration of war from Paris. Fog had dispersed the French fleet, and Boscawen's attack, designed to prevent a large reinforcement of troops under the escort of the Comte de la Motte reaching Canada, prevented neither the new Governor of Canada, the Marquis de Vaudreuil, nor the army commander, the Marquis de Montcalm, from reaching their destination.

Nevertheless, hostilities between the two colonising powers in North America, France in Canada and Britain in the thirteen American colonies along the Atlantic coast to the south, had been

185

smouldering along the wild frontiers for some time. The first clash had come at Great Meadows on the Ohio, when a mixed force of colonial troops and Indians under a provincial major named George Washington had skirmished with French forces. But the previous summer the British had suffered disaster and humiliation when a British column under General Braddock was ambushed on the forested banks of the Monongahela. While hostilities had broken out in the backwoods, Boscawen's provocative attack on the French men-of-war failed in its objective of forcing the hand of King Louis XV into an outright declaration of war. Instead, so Makepeace and Kite now learned, a diplomatic tangle among the royal courts of Europe was embroiling the whole continent in opposing armed camps. Full-blown hostilities, it was sanguinely asserted, would come sooner or later.

But in the West Indies the remorseless workings of commerce ground on, untroubled by such considerations. Makepeace landed his slaves and they were sold at an average of nine pounds sterling, a price which furnished the *Enterprize's* commander and his reduced company with a handsome profit. As for the miserable and fearful blacks, it was only now that their future became clear. Those who had not been seasick during the middle passage now found the strange island swayed under their fettered feet and that the irons round their ankles were not to be removed. Instead they were cruelly branded by their new owners and vanished into the country, or were transhipped to other islands in the West Indies. Over a hundred were purchased by a merchant from Havana, in Cuba. Makepeace was content, though his under-manned brig was incapable for touting for cargo beyond Antigua. He was keen to refit her, recruit more hands to man her for the homeward passage from among the human flotsam that accumulated on the waterfront of St John's, and load a cargo for Liverpool before war filled the chops of the Channel with French privateers.

In the hurly-burly of discharging the slaves, who left in a mournful, iron-bound column for the mastaba in the market to be pulled and prodded by the plantation owners prior to purchase, Kite's circumstances underwent a transformation. Nor was he insensible that his own fate was in a marked contrast to that of the majority of the slaves, for he had acquired slaves of his own. When the *Enterprize* had arrived at St John's, Kite had made it clear to Makepeace his intention of securing the person of Puella and the captain had cynically charged him the exorbitant price of fifteen pounds for the privilege. On the morning that the slaves were roused for transfer to the slave market, she abandoned his cabin, and he found her cowering fearfully, her arm round a boy whose features, Kite realised, suggested he was a relative of Puella's. Kite recognised him as the victim of sodomy he had seen being abused at the beginning of the passage. Sighing, he had nodded, ordering Ritchie to release the boy's leg-irons and giving him into Puella's charge while he sought the captain.

'I am busy, Mr Kite,' Makepeace said, waving him aside as he shuffled papers in his cabin. 'You have your black whore, now indulge me and leave. I have to visit the agent and secure my homeward cargo...'

'Forgive me, Captain Makepeace, but I am determined to leave the *Enterprize*, sir. I doubt you will have need of a surgeon on the homeward voyage.'

'But I need officers. You may have Molloy's berth, Mr Kite.'

'I do not wish it, sir. Also, I wish to purchase a boy. He is, I think, Puella's brother, or perhaps cousin or nephew.'

Makepeace looked up. 'You are a bigger fool than I conceived possible.' He lay the paper he had been reading from on the table and confronted Kite, his expression hard and uncompromising. 'You may go to the devil, Kite. You will tire of the wench and the boy will only prove mischievous unless you thrash him. Sell them…'

'No, sir, that I cannot do. I intend giving them their freedom.'

'What, so that they can starve or prostitute themselves on the waterfront?' Makepeace shook his head at Kite's lack of worldliness.

'No, so that they can live under my protection.'

Makepeace shook his head. 'I will not sell you the boy. I shall save you from your own folly.'

'I am entitled to two slaves,' Kite persisted. 'I am resolved and shall buy him in the market. Surely you would rather profit directly without the auctioneer's fee.'

Makepeace shook his head and regarded Kite with sudden interest. The young man who had sewn up a harlot's arse in Liverpool had become a strong character, a man it seemed impossible to reason with, who knew his own mind. And it was odd, Makepeace thought, that the affair with the black wench had somehow strengthened this impression; quite the reverse from his intention when he had dangled her enticingly in front of Kite.

'You are incorrigible…' Makepeace's handsome face took on a harsh expression. 'Mr Kite, I had no idea, beyond serving my own ends, that taking you on board my ship would be the cause of her being saved from a plague of the yellow jack but such, I must confess, to have been the case. I – no, the whole surviving ship's company – are indebted to you. But I must warn you that within every man lie the seeds of his own destruction. You remarked my own distemper; yours is a foolish and wanton compassion. Compassion is not a vice found in the British sea services, thank God. We match our wits against a pitiless sea, against a pitiless climate and pitiless disease in a trade that better acquits itself by similarly being pitiless.

'That is why I cannot remain with you, Captain Makepeace.'

A silence fell between the two men, broken by Makepeace, who expelled air through pursed lips and shook his head. 'You are beyond me, Kite, beyond me. Whatever brought you aboard the *Enterprize* in Liverpool, I cannot think. But you may find employment here in Antigua. Do you wish me to speak to Mr Mulgrave, our agent? He is a well-known West India merchant with a large establishment here.'

'I should be obliged and most grateful.' Kite paused a moment, then said, 'I, er, I mean you will make it clear to Mr Mulgrave that I have, er, a household.'

Makepeace, who had resumed the perusal of his papers, looked up again, raising his eyebrows. 'A household? My word, Kite, you have more than that, you have delusions of grandeur!' Makepeace laughed and nodded, smiling. 'Yes, I shall speak to Mulgrave. I happen to know he is short of a clerk.'

'That is kind of you, sir.'

'We shall truly be quits, then.'

'Truly, sir.'

Makepeace suddenly held out his hand. 'I cannot think that you were preserved from the yellow jack to waste your life as a counting-house clerk, but if that is what you want... You may have the boy for the price of a man, nine pounds.'

'I agree.'

'In that case you shame me. You may have him for seven...'

'I shall pay you nine pounds, Captain Makepeace, and count myself the luckier man.'

Makepeace pulled a face. 'By Jupiter, Kite, you have the tongue of a preacher. In any case, you will have sufficient money from this voyage to subsist for a while on your own resources.' Makepeace paused, then added, 'If you keep that jade poorly shod and on short commons.'

Kite left Makepeace, uncertain of his future. The immediate responsibility of Puella and the boy had diverted his mind from the problems of his past and their long shadow on the rest of his life. The legacy of his voyage on the *Enterprize* and his brush with death and disease was to mark him for life, but when he left the Guineaman in Antigua he did so with a reputation as an extraordinary and honest, if eccentric, young man.

William Kite was fortunate in finding himself employed by Joseph Mulgrave, then the leading and most influential merchant in Antigua. Mulgrave was a tall, cadaverous man whose skin had not been burned by the tropical sun, despite thirty years in the West Indies. Mulgrave avoided exposure during daylight whenever possible, but sat at his desk in a black suit more suited to the smoke of London, venturing out only after dark when his tall figure could be seen walking through the town, looking neither to right nor left, and acknowledging no one. An unconvivial and, insofar as respectable white society was concerned, solitary bachelor, Mulgrave's sole and absorbing passion was commerce and the amassing of capital. Aloof, dispassionate and apparently devoid of any human emotion, he was spoken of in reverential tones in the ports of the Antilles; the extent of his wealth was unknown, but rumoured to be enormous. His more accountable reputation derived from his scrupulous honesty in all his business transactions.

On their first encounter, Kite thought he

had been delivered into the presence of a forbidding man of rigid views and severe habits, who would disapprove of Puella and the boy. But Mulgrave, having coldly addressed a few questions to Kite and having clearly gained from Makepeace an insight into the young man's character, proceeded to surprise him.

'You have two young blacks under your protection, I understand, Mr Kite,' Mulgrave said with dispassionate candour in a deep bass. The voice was surprising for one so slender, but was, Kite was to learn in due time, the most superficial of the surprises Mr Mulgrave would spring upon him.

'I do, sir.'

'Do you intend to live in some intimacy with the young woman?'

'If that would not offend you, sir,' Kite said cautiously, embarrassed and flushing.

The ghost of a smile flickered momentarily across Mulgrave's face and Kite saw the horizontal cicatrix of a scar that ran from the left cheekbone to the ear, the lobe of which was nicked. It added to the sinister image Makepeace presented as he formed his reply. 'Not at all, but it would be best if you were to dwell under my own roof. I have adequate accommodation and we can better teach the two of them a smattering of English sufficient for your wants.'

'That is most thoughtful of you, sir.' Kite was only half-relieved; living under the same roof as Mr Mulgrave seemed to possess little attraction.

'Do you realise that consorting with a black damns you in the eyes of many of your fellow countrymen in Antigua? The fact that they fornicate and miscegenate themselves is a measure of their hypocrisy, but that does not alter the way they will regard an open liaison such as you have adopted. Your youth and opinions are contrary to what is regarded here as acceptable; recent arrivals may be treated like lepers, so you will not find yourself in great demand at Government House, or elsewhere, for that matter.'

'I do not think that will greatly trouble me, sir.'

'Well, we shall see about that in due course. But if you intend to keep her, you will burn your boats in respect of settling here. Do you understand?' Kite nodded; the prospect of surrendering Puella at this tremulously uncertain moment in his life filled him with horror.

'Now,' went on Mulgrave, 'pray tell me the young woman's name.'

'I have called her Puella, sir.'

Mulgrave raised an eyebrow. 'And the boy?'

'I have not named him.'

'Mmm. I like the Latin tag ... Puella has a

better sound to it than Puer, but we should keep the alliteration; let us call the lad Pompey.' Again the faint trace of smile flitted across Mulgrave's face. 'They will both wear their leg-irons until they have learned sufficient English to understand their circumstances. They may find that rather hard to bear, but it is for their own good. If they run away now and are caught out in the wild country near any of the plantations, they are like to be whipped, shot or savaged by dogs long before establishing their identity.'

'I see, sir.'

'You do not see, Mr Kite,' Mulgrave said with cold finality, 'but you will, in due course. Sometimes one must be cruel to be kind. St John's has many free men and women of colour. It will be difficult for Puella and Pompey, but they will come to understand in time. When they speak enough English, we may strike off their fetters. Perhaps by then you will be settled in your own establishment. While you are under my roof, Mr Kite, I regret to inform you that you will find yourself keeping your own company, I am not a sociable man and I eat alone. You may choose to do the same or to teach Puella her table manners, but that is your affair. I hope you read; I have a fair library and you are welcome to make use of it. Now, to business. My senior clerk is a Mr Wentworth, and his assistant has lately embarked aboard the *King George* packet, intending to return to England, hence the vacant post which is now, providentially, yours. In addition to your lodging, I can defray your living expenses and provide you with a small competence. In due course other opportunities may present themselves, but that will largely depend upon your own energy.' Mulgrave's eyes remained fixed on Kite, who held their gaze steadily. 'Now, Mr Kite, in return I require absolute loyalty, perfect probity and twelve hours a day of your attention. May I assume you still wish to take up my offer?'

'You may, sir.'

And so Kite settled into the large rambling house that Joseph Mulgrave had built amid a tangle of dense thorn scrub on a hillside overlooking St John's, where Puella and Pompey began to learn English as they worked under the tutelage of Mulgrave's formidable housekeeper, a large, well-formed and handsome mulattess called Mistress Dorothea. Ignorant of the usual formalities of West Indian colonial society, yet seduced by its colourful manifestations on the waterfront that stretched along the quayside immediately outside the doors of Mulgrave's counting house, Kite fell easily into a routine. For the first time since he had stumbled into the Hebblewhites' barn, he was filled with the almost forgotten feeling of contentment. Now something like a future lay before him.

Mr Wentworth was a red-faced, perspiring, overweight and untidily dressed man whose appearance belied a keen intelligence and a considerable energy. Somewhat foppish in appearance and always a martyr to fashion in the tropical heat, he bore down upon the newcomer like a ship in full sail. An incorrigible talker, Kite soon learned that Wentworth possessed a driving ambition to rise socially. His origins were humble, for his father had been an indentured white, shipped out from England as a criminal and set to work on the plantations. His mother's origins were never referred to, so Kite assumed she had most probably been a prostitute, but the child had been seen by Mulgrave playing in the streets amid the children of free blacks, mulattoes and quadroons. Mulgrave was then a young man, newly arrived in Antigua with a livid scar on his cheek and a reputation, which was soon confirmed, as a crack shot with a pistol, suggesting a dark and, for the ladies of the island at least, a darkly romantic past. Taking the boy up, Mulgrave made the lad his servant. It was not long before Mulgrave had bought a share in an established business and was settled in St. John's. By this time he had recognised the shrewd intelligence in his youthful valet.

'One morning, to my complete astonishment,' Wentworth explained in a curious accent, 'Mr Mulgrave said that I was to accompany him and he took me to a tailor then resident in St John's and outfitted me with a gentleman's habiliments. I already knew how to read and write and I was placed directly in the counting house. Of course,' Wentworth said with a candid lack of modesty that Kite learned was a perverse copy of his benefactor's absolute honesty, 'it was not long before it was clear that I was capable of more than merely making ledger entries...'

The disparagement of Kite's own present task was not, Kite felt, meant as an insult. There was a degree of affectation in Wentworth that caused unintentional irony and it took Kite some time to realise that Wentworth's diction arose from his desire to copy Mulgrave's cool accent in what he assumed was the enunciation of the English aristocracy. Wentworth was aware that, however he got his own surname, it was that of one of England's grand families; this set his mind on ascending the social ladder. One day, he made it quite plain, when he had made his own or inherited Mulgrave's fortune, he would go to England and make his debut in what he referred to as 'polite society'. In the meantime, the lesser ladder of Antigua's colonial white establishment provided Mr Wentworth with a sufficient social challenge.

In the first few days of their acquaintance, Kite was bombarded with information about men and women of every station in the island's hierarchy. From the governor and his staff, by way of army officers, plantation owners, merchants, advocates, ship-masters, slave traders and overseers, Wentworth delivered himself of a discourse on the subtle social gradations, stressing, of course, the connections, alliances, divisions and pretensions among the white com- munity. He grew salacious when referring to these men's wives, indicating the uses of making love to Mrs This or Mrs That; that the Misses The Other were marriageable for their money, though not their looks, and that Kite, if he knew what was good for him, would make no moves to advancement without first consulting him.

'If you do that, Kite, you will not regret it,' Wentworth concluded his introductory remarks with a smile that Kite found amusing. 'Ah,' he said seriously, 'but I forgot, you co-habit openly...'

Despite the man's obsession, Kite did not dislike him. Had he personally entertained any desire for integration with Antiguan life he would have found Wentworth's patronising a mild irritant; as it was he merely recognised that Wentworth was warning a new clerk. Kite should not presume to tread on the preserves that Wentworth regarded as his own province.

'I understand,' Wentworth said with a hint of disdain, 'that you do not intend renouncing your blackamoor.'

'No, I do not.'

'I shall not hold that against you, Kite. Mr Mulgrave himself sets us an example not to be dismissed as mere licentiousness for indeed, my word, it is not in his case. For licentiousness you must look at the concubinage of Mr Lomax of the Crown Plantation! My word, sir, yes. And I feel so sorry for his wife, who is so kind a creature, or of George Radley from Willoughby... My word, they are hedonists alongside whom Mr Mulgrave is a perfect and most wonderful gentleman...'

'I am glad to hear it,' Kite replied drily.

Setting aside this torrent of obsessive social pretension, Wentworth displayed a masterly gasp of the commercial activity not merely on the island of Antigua and Guadeloupe, the adjacent French possession; of the trade in slaves with Cuba; of the export of muscovado and sugar, of rum and molasses to Liverpool, London and Bristol; and of the importance of the trans-shipment of commodities to and from the Thirteen Colonies of North America. Under this general picture of a vigorous trade, Wentworth spoke of the necessary currency transactions, of the growing importance of banking and credit, supplying asides at every opportunity to demonstrate a coup here, a timely loan there, the swift taking up of a lading and the faster settlement of an advantageous freight rate made by the House of Mulgrave. Many, though Wentworth admitted not all, were entirely due to his own acumen. He stressed that of Mulgrave in the matter of investment, of the ships in which Mulgrave had a part, but never a whole interest, 'Only a fool owns sixty-four sixty-fourths in a ship, Kite, only a fool... Oh dear, yes,' Wentworth chuckled, emphasising this recondite wisdom.

He, like the obviously much admired Mulgrave, applied only three principles to commerce; the first was to keep one's word, the second was to be inquisitive and constantly seek out new opportunities, the third was never to place too many eggs in one basket.

It took three months, much of which was spent tediously at his ledgers, for Kite to begin to truly comprehend the complexities of his new employment. He wrote and copied out letters, pasting them in the company's guard books, he learned to draft bills of lading, becoming familiar with phrases such as *Bound by God's Grace,* and *Delivered in the like Good Order* and *Well Conditioned at the Aforesaid Port, the Danger of the seas and Mortality only Excepted...* That by such documentation thousands of Africans were sent into hard labour in the sugar cane fields of the Indies and the plantations of the Carolinas faded from his perception as the middle passage of the *Enterprize* seemed more and more like a bad dream.

Wentworth patronised him, especially once he learned that Kite was from humdrum origins. It pleased him that Kite was not a name to set aside that of Wentworth or Mulgrave. But Kite found this tolerable. After the long and terrible weeks aboard the *Enterprize,* the steady routine of his life in the House of Mulgrave brought a great peace to him.

He no longer felt he was escaping, only that the dimming past was forgiven, if not forgotten. He was, of course, seduced by Puella; their relationship grew wonderfully and their self-engrossment grew daily as Puella's English improved. Mistress Dorothea proved a kind and tolerant teacher, and Kite learnt that although an Antiguan-born woman her situation was otherwise not dissimilar to Puella's. Like Wentworth, Dorothea had been picked up off the street and openly made Mulgrave's mistress. Shunned by the island's white society for this unholy admission of blatant concubinage, the naturally solitary Mulgrave had simply turned his considerable abilities to the despised opportunities offered by trade. In this he had become an institution and never, despite the disdain of formal convention, lost his romantic aura as far as the white ladies of the island were concerned. The men, many of whom overpopulated their estates with half-caste bastards, joked about Mulgrave's failure to beget 'pickaninnies' on his black mistress. The failure seemed to confirm the inadequacies of those who trafficked in mere 'goods', though there was not a man among them who would not have leapt eagerly into the beautiful Dorothea's bed had the opportunity offered. Their thin-lipped white-skinned wives, wilting in the heat or suffering vapid attacks in the heavy rains, envied Dorothea's indisputable beauty, marvelling at the uprightness of her carriage and the voluptuousness of her figure.

By the time Kite had familiarised himself with his new tasks, Puella had mastered sufficient English to exchange more than a minor daily dialogue with him. In another manifestation of his changing luck, Kite learned that Dorothea's mother had belonged to the same tribe as Puella. It took some days before Dorothea had so far recalled the tongue of her childhood that the two could gossip freely, but thereafter her coaching of Puella was swift and sure, for the common origin quickly built a bond between the two women. For all his courtesy towards her, Dorothea never felt herself even a common-law wife to the austere and remote Mulgrave. He was a man for whom intimacy was something permissible only in his bedroom. Otherwise he stood quite alone in the world and although Dorothea knew Mulgrave, better than any other person living, for a truly kind and shy man, a man who had seen her cared for and secure long before he had taken her to bed, she mourned her lack of children. That, she thought in contrast to the white planters, was a measure of his power. Withholding the potence of his copious seed convinced her that she was loved by a white spirit too powerful to conceive like a simple man. By such reasoning Dorothea could explain his fabulous wealth and the respect Mulgrave commanded, and from it too she drew the secret empowerment of herself, for hers was, she knew, a position much envied, especially by the white women.

Though Puella and her young cousin could not compensate her for her lack of children, Dorothea was overjoyed to have them in Mulgrave's huge and gloomy house. She liked Kite too, about whom she knew a great deal, thanks to Puella's confidences. Kite was a handsome contrast to the sweating Wentworth, who always treated Dorothea with a confused mixture of fascination and terror.

The swiftly burgeoning friendship between the two women soon led to Puella being freed from her odious leg-irons. Pompey was similarly freed, but his was a less happy situation. Perhaps because of the abuse to which he had been subjected aboard the *Enterprize,* or earlier in the barracoons on the banks of the Sherbro, Pompey proved a simple soul. He was destined to remain no more than a barefoot house-boy for the rest of his life, soon passing from Kite's ownership to that of Wentworth.

Kite sold him for a nominal guinea to his new acquaintance and Wentworth was pleased with the bargain. It was not long before Pompey appeared in St John's in a livery devised, Wentworth was fond of saying, by Mrs Robertson, wife to one of the garrison's officers, whom he described as 'a particular friend'. Dressed thus, Pompey was seen everywhere his master went, holding Wentworth's hat and cane until he had drunk his dish of chocolate with his hostess. Mulgrave's misanthropy encouraged Wentworth to undertake all business errands between the House of Mulgrave and its clientele, errands which Wentworth, with his talent for flattery and admiration, usually succeeded in turning to some form of personal advantage. Mulgrave did not object to this and Wentworth, having learnt much of his demeanour from his benefactor, never overstepped the limits of propriety. But his own natural sociability, a not unaffected subservience and the adroitness of his mind when considering matters of trade, made him generally welcome, for Wentworth had learned the benefits of giving disinterested advice. When this invariably proved beneficial, his stock rose and he acted as a magnet for business, a fact of which Mulgrave was not insensible.

Though Kite's work was dull, his presence and competence freed Wentworth to pursue a greater volume of business. One afternoon, after Kite had laboured at his desk for a period of some six months and the year drew to its close – when, incongruously, the community of St John's prepared to celebrate Christmas in insufferable heat – he was summoned by Mulgrave.

He was reading newspapers brought that day in the newly arrived packet and he set the broadsheet down with a rustle, to regard Kite above clasped hands. Upon these he rested his chin. It was a sign, Kite had learned, that Mulgrave was in an unbending mood. 'I wish you to dine with me this evening, Mr Kite. An hour after sunset, shall we say?'

'As you wish, sir.' Kite gave a half bow and withdrew. Shortly afterwards Wentworth returned from his daily visit to the harbour and the ships on whose behalf Mulgrave and Company acted or in which they had an interest. He too was swiftly summoned and similarly invited.

'I am to dine with Mr Mulgrave this evening,' Wentworth said when he returned from Mulgrave's private office, a satisfied smile on his face.

'So am I,' Kite countered, amused that the news put Wentworth's nose out of joint.

'That's odd...' Wentworth frowned and added, 'I've only ever known him ask us to dine before on one occasion.' Wentworth nodded. 'Oh yes, it was the night he told Cornford, your predecessor, that he had been informed that Cornford had been left three thousand pounds a year and that in view of this fact it would be in neither Cornford's nor Mulgrave and Company's interest that he should remain in the company's employment.'

'I see. Then Mulgrave knew before the beneficiary,' remarked Kite.

'Well, that's his way,' Wentworth said as if it were sufficient explanation for Mulgrave's apparent prescience. Kite saw that the single precedent was working on Wentworth's innate anxiety.

'Well, Mr Wentworth,' Kite said drily, preserving the social distinction Wentworth insisted on in the counting house, 'I am certain *I* am not to be told I have come into three thousand a year.'

'Nor me, damn it.'

'Perhaps our master is about to reveal the fact that he knows *you* to already have that sum on your own account,' Kite teased.

'Would that it was true...' Wentworth said awkwardly.

Kite laughed. 'You are colouring up, sir, I have heard it to be true.'

'Who told you?' Wentworth snapped, taking the bait.

'Miss Cunningham.'

'You do not know Miss Cunningham, Kite – do you?'

Kite shook his head. 'No, sir, I do not.'

'Then you tease me?'

'I fear I do. Will you fight me?' Kite grinned, slipping off his stool and putting up his fists. 'Come fight me, Mr Wentworth, 'tis damned tedious here today.'

Wentworth waved Kite aside. 'Get on with your work, Kite, making money is never tedious if you engage your whole intelligence upon it, to be sure.'

Kite sighed. 'That is true, Mr Wentworth.'

'I shall see you at dinner, Kite.'

On reaching the house Kite repaired at once to the wing generously set aside for his accommodation. Apprised of his arrival, Puella quickly appeared. She wore a simple gown made of scarlet cotton, such as much have been worn by the wife of a comfortable shopkeeper in Cockermouth. She ran to him, kissed him and, as he sank into a chair, knelt and removed his shoes.

'Puella, you are a wonder.'

'You like some lemonade?'

He nodded and she ran off, to return a few moments later with a glass of the cordial. He took it, leaned back and she kneeled again at his feet. Absently he tousled her hair as he drained the glass, then he smacked his lips and she took the glass from his hand and set it upon an adjacent table before sitting on his lap. After kissing, he said, 'Puella, I shall not be dining with you tonight.'

'Oh, Kite, I cannot dine with not you.'

'Without,' Kite corrected.

'Without you. What you eat tonight?'

Kite shrugged. 'I don't know what I shall eat, Puella, but I know with whom I shall eat whatever I do eat.'

She tapped the end of his nose, which she regarded as a curiously aberrant and pert proboscis. It was her way of responding when he teased her. 'Kite, you horrible!'

Kite smiled and said seriously, 'I am dining with Mr Mulgrave and, Puella, I think he has something important to say to me, and to Mr Wentworth.' He frowned. 'Has Dorothea said anything about him being unwell? I mean sick?' he added hurriedly.

Puella shook her head and lowered her eyes. 'No, Kite. Dorothea told me Mr Mulgrave was still good for her,' and she whipped up the hem of her skirt and rubbed herself with a giggle.

Kite frowned. 'Puella, you must not do that. It is not what a lady would do...'

Puella slipped from his lap and stood in front of him, her hands on her hips. 'Puella is not a lady; Puella is a black whore...'

Kite was on his feet in an instant, one arm round her waist, the other across her mouth. He was horrified. 'Puella! You are not to speak those words! Never!'

Puella smiled triumphantly up at him. 'Come then, Kite, you be good for Puella...'

An hour later Kite walked the length of the veranda, his footfalls creaking the timbers, the warm night filled with the loud chirrup of a myriad of cicadas. He found Mulgrave sitting alone in a cane chair, sipping lemonade.

'Sit down, Mr Kite.' A black servant emerged from the shadows and set down a glass alongside Kite as he lowered himself into one of Mulgrave's extraordinary wicker chaises longues. They had hardly wished each other good health when Wentworth arrived, puffing dangerously and clearly discomfited to find his junior already ensconced with their host.

Wentworth lived above the counting house and found Kite's residence under Mulgrave's private roof a touch irksome. He had, Kite thought, expected some alteration in his circumstances when he acquired a black servant in the person of Pompey, and his anxiety that Kite would replace himself in Mulgrave's plans seemed to have revived in recent weeks.

Perhaps Wentworth knew something of what was to transpire that evening. After a few moments' conversation about the affairs of the day, they went in to eat. The meal was sparse, the wine good but limited and the conversation non-existent. Mulgrave seemed unaffected, but both Wentworth and Kite felt the suspense intolerable. As the servants drew the cloth and Mulgrave selected a cigar from a humidor, he indicated they might join him in a smoke or help themselves from a decanter of rum. Wentworth accepted both, Kite neither. Mulgrave raised his eyebrow and waved the servants out. Having drawn upon his cigar and sent a feather of blue smoke across the table so that the candle flames flickered, he leaned forward on his elbows. Sitting on his left, Kite stared at the way the candlelight etched Mulgraves features. The man was handsome, in a long-faced and lugubrious fashion, his grey hair swept back over his head into a tight queue at the nape of his neck where it was severely clubbed in a ribbon as black as the suit he habitually wore.

The jagged furrow of the scar which seamed his face supported the widespread rumour that Mulgrave had fought a duel. His opponent's ball had disfigured Mulgrave's face; his own, it was said, had found a more effective target.

'Well, gentlemen,' Mulgrave said in his low bass voice, as he secured the undivided attention of his young colleagues, 'you will be wondering at the meaning of all this joyless conviviality.' He looked at the two young men and Kite thought he saw in the dark eyes a sardonic sparkle. 'From time to time in a man's life, there come moments when matters shift their ground. One such moment has come to me and therefore to you also.' He turned to Wentworth with his slight smile. 'You, Wentworth, I have always regarded as a protégé. It is true that you are a somewhat out-of-elbows fellow, always running and puffing, but you have been a faithful servant, and while I know that from time to time you have accumulated on your own account, you have never cheated me...'

Kite watched Wentworth suffer under the ruthless assessment that was, it was obvious, all too true. It made Wentworth's earlier protestations over his acquisition of capital rather amusing. At least, Kite reflected, in his own case he had neither enjoyed so long an acquaintance with Mr Mulgrave, nor had anything more than a modestly gainful employment from him.

'So, Wentworth, it is my intention to pass the whole of my business over to you once I have secured such capital as I personally required.'

Wentworth's eyes opened wide and he half-gasped, then his expression collapsed, like a man about to burst into guffaws of mirth, or howl at terrible news. With a kind of strangled cry, Wentworth buried his head in his hands, and his shoulders shook so that he seemed shaken either by great mirth or great grief. Mulgrave merely glanced at his protégé and went on steadily – like a ship dashing aside a wave, Kite thought irrelevantly.

'One does not live for ever, and I have an account elsewhere that I wish soon to settle in a private manner.' Those few words, it was clear to Kite, were all they were ever either going to have by way of explanation, but this thought had scarcely struck Kite than Mulgrave was speaking of him.

'As for you, Kite, Captain Makepeace said of you that you were an unusual young man, gifted as a surgeon and capable, he thought, of many things. Yet you remain a dilemma. You have made no effort to even promulgate the fact that you were a surgeon. I find that strange, unless you have reasons for concealing the fact.'

Kite leaned forward to speak, but Mulgrave simply raised a hand and he remained silent.

'Whatever the reason for your singular conduct in this matter, I have observed you to be the man of principle that Makepeace said you were. I have known Captain Makepeace a long time. Although given to bouts of drunkenness, in which he is in no wise unique, he is an able sea officer and was, when in command of a letter of marque in the last war, a successful privateer commander. As a slaver he is astute, taking good care of his charges, and is a man who makes his own luck. I therefore value his opinion and have decided not to wait unduly long before prosecuting my own private affairs in order to verify his judgement. In short, Mr Kite, beyond what you have already shown of yourself, I am taking you on trust.'

Kite muttered his thanks, though he was apprehensive now, certain that whatever Mulgrave was about to propose would disturb the tranquillity of his present life.

'In six months or so, I intend to return to England. War seems certain and my departure would be sooner, but matters cannot simply be dropped like a stone. In the mean time, having seen you, Wentworth, in possession of my affairs here, both as my successor and my agent, it is my intention to take passage for Carolina and afterwards Philadelphia and New York. I shall personally have relinquished my interest in all my ships and vessels in the Antilles in your favour, Wentworth, and I am moreover prejudiced against placing my person at risk at so uncertain a time. I am unwilling to sail in any vessel other than one in which I have a perfect confidence.' Mulgrave turned to Kite. 'I am therefore resolved to purchase an armed schooner in your name, Mr Kite, and, placing the vessel at least under your management if you do not feel competent to take the command, to request that you have her ready for sea by the end of January. Once purchased she will become not merely your property, but your domicile. Other details we will discuss in the coming days and I shall devote sufficient time to concert matters with each of you.' Mulgrave paused, allowing his words to sink in. Wentworth, overjoyed at his new-found wealth and already contemplating the means by which he could announce it to Antigua in general and Miss Cunningham in particular, had emerged from behind his hands, a look of stupefaction on his broad face that belied the industry of his mind.

Kite's shift in fortunes were less spectacular, though more profound. That the schooner would become his own was clear and, Kite divined, somehow congruous with the way in which Mulgrave conducted his affairs. Like Dorothea, Kite found himself bound to Mulgrave in a fashion akin in some small way to that of moral servitude. Of course, Kite could destroy that trust at his own whim, perhaps with little economic effect, but he half-guessed that in this way Mulgrave subtly secured the bonds that bound to him those people he selected as beneficiaries.

When Kite returned to Puella that night he was both elated and disturbed by the news that Mulgrave had given him. He had known that his idyllic existence would not go on for ever, but he fretted over Puella's fate, as he fretted over that of his father and sister in the distant lakes and fells of Cumbria. He was not a natural nomad, not drawn to the existence that Makepeace and others accepted as a means to a distant and uncertain end. Moreover, fate was moving him again, and this movement was inexorably towards England, where he was still regarded as a murderer.

Puella was fast asleep, replete from their

earlier lovemaking, but Kite was too stimulated by the events of the evening to lie quietly beside her. He retired to the adjacent room and, finding his long-neglected journal, he lit a candle, and found pen and ink. Opening the book he regarded the single sheet of paper that lay inside. It was a half-completed letter to his sister, Helen, and was dated some weeks earlier.

As for me, I am Well, as I Hope you and Father both are. You will Learn from this that I am in the West Indies, where Talk of War with all its Uncertainties, Prompts me to Write. I should like you to Write to me at the Address of Mulgrave & Co, St John's, Antigua, telling me the state of your Health, together with that of our Father's. I will

But he had never finished the unsatisfactory letter, unsure what to say, or whether the recipient would welcome it. With a sigh, he now lifted it up and held it in the candle flame. The paper curled then flared up, finally falling as black ash. Blowing the charred remnant on to the floor he took up his pen, dipped it in the inkwell and held it poised over his journal.

'Kite...' Puella stood in the doorway. She was naked and the candlelight fell upon the familiar curves of her beautiful brown body.

'I think I soon have pickaninny.'

Nine

The Departure

In the weeks that followed, Wentworth reminded Kite of the contented peasant in the fairy tale who, through his own endeavours and with a little help from some magic entity, succeeds in winning the king's daughter and half the kingdom. Not that Wentworth had yet won any fair hand in wedlock, but his prospects were set fair, for he had gained not half but almost the entire kingdom. Mulgrave's extraction of capital nevertheless left Wentworth in command of a substantial sum, despite the fact that the older man intended to retain an interest in the business. As for the business itself, this was to pass into Wentworth's control, Mulgrave relinquishing it with a single remark that the new owner would do well if he did not succumb to drink. Within days of Mulgrave's announcement, Kite had abandoned his desk and his indoor existence to resume his intimacy with ships. Mulgrave sent him to a seafaring man named Da Silva, a man of Portuguese blood who had served in British West Indiamen as an able seaman, as a gunner to Captain Makepeace aboard the privateer *Firedrake*, and as boatswain aboard a slaver. In his last ship, the Guineaman, Da Silva had voyaged between the Bight of Benin and Cuba, from Ngola and Ouidah to Brazil, and from Guinea to Jamaica and the Carolinas. There was little he did not know about the mariner's art.

It was Mulgrave's suggestion that Kite assumed the title and dignity of 'Captain', while he appointed Da Silva to the post of sailing master. Such an expedient would compensate for Kite's lack of experience, while not detracting from the advantages to be had from Da Silva's expertise. Da Silva accepted this arrangement with apparent contentment, unsurprisingly proving another person whose life Mulgrave had influenced. He had been paid off the slaver with nothing, the master and owner having cheated the crew and disappeared. On hearing of this infamy, Mulgrave had taken up the entire abandoned crew and found berths for them in other vessels. It was a small enough kindness, perhaps due more to preserving the people of St John's from the rapacity of two score of distressed and desperate men, but, being the man he was, it obligated Da Silva. Kite took an instant liking for the man, who was twice his age and half his height, yet possessed shoulders of an extraordinary width, a powerful chest and strong arms. Da Silva's legs were bent with rickets and his teeth were broken and caried, but his aquiline face bore a pair of fierce mustachios, which twitched when he smiled and his eyes sparkled with a relentless cheerfulness. Gold rings in his ears and a habitual bandanna gave him a piratical air.

Word soon went round St John's that this oddly assorted pair were in search of a ship, but Da Silva turned up on the second morning of their acquaintance with a pair of mules, a skin of wine and the idea that they should proceed to Willoughby, where he knew of a smart schooner with a reputation for speed and which mounted a dozen guns.

Such a diversion pleased Kite. It seemed in tune with the increasing tempo of life in Antigua, for every ship arriving from Britain brought worsening news and the outbreak of war with France was clearly imminent and preparations for the outbreak were made throughout the West Indies. The news sharpened Mulgrave's desire to be gone and, for the first time he betrayed a side of his character in contrast with his hitherto calm exterior. In traces of an irascible impatience, Kite saw signs of a man who might have been provoked to fight a duel, and might well have shot an opponent in cold blood. The thought reminded him of the accusations laid against himself; the past seemed to increasingly penetrate his consciousness as the nearness of his own departure approached.

A day or so later Kite found himself registered at the Custom House as the owner, in full, of all sixty-four parts of the Cuban-built armed schooner *Cacafuego*. On Da Silva translating the meaning from Spanish, Kite renamed her *Spitfire*. As he took possession of the vessel and they prepared to move her round to St John's, he recalled Wentworth's remark about the folly of owning a ship outright. Well, Mulgrave would underwrite the running of the vessel, Kite consoled himself, so his ownership was little more than a technicality.

Of more legal consequence was the document he had requested Mulgrave to have drawn up to free Puella as soon as he arrived back at St John's with the *Spitfire*. Freedom was conferred upon Puella a week before Kite and Da Silva considered the *Spitfire* would be ready for departure. Kite asked Dorothea to explain the meaning of freedom and to make clear to Puella that it would leave her to chose her future life. On the day appointed, Puella was dressed in a new English gown of pale blue silk. To this Dorothea added a broad-brimmed feathered hat which swept about Puella's features in a captivating aureole, throwing her striking features into sharp and distinguished relief.

Holding herself with that natural elegance that had first attracted Kite's eyes, Kite led her from Mulgrave's carriage that had brought the two black women into town. Passing through the counting house, Kite and Puella ascended the steps into Mulgrave's gloomy office, where Mulgrave and his attorney, a Mr Garvey, along with Wentworth, had the document drawn up for the principals' and the witnesses' signatures.

Dorothea had secretly coached Puella, so that when Garvey pointed to the place she should make her mark, Puella wrote in a sure, round hand, *Puella Kite-Mulgrave*. Kite could scarce hide his astonishment, both at Puella's ability to write, and to the grand name she had taken. Mulgrave's calm acceptance of the news was clear evidence that he had connived at it. Signed by Kite and Puella, witnessed by Mulgrave and Wentworth, and finally sealed by Garvey, Kite handed the instrument of manumission to Puella.

'With this, Puella, we strike the last iron fetters from you.'

Puella curtseyed as she had been taught, and said, 'I thank you.'

Kite, having bowed over her hand, pressed a kiss on her cheek. Still holding Puella's hand, Kite turned to Mulgrave. 'Sir, while it was long my intention to manumit Puella, I cannot conceive of any circumstances in which I could have done so without your assistance. We are both most grateful.'

Mulgrave smiled and shook his head dismissively. 'Mr Garvey had the burden of the task,' he said, stepping forward and taking Puella's hand from Kite. His dark eyes glittered with pleasure as he bent and kissed it. Mulgrave was followed by Wentworth and Garvey. Dorothea clasped her tribal sister, then Mulgrave led the company to a table where wine and sweetmeats were laid out. Later, as Kite followed Dorothea, Puella and Mulgrave into the carriage to return to the house, Garvey pressed into his hand a second paper with the words, 'Mr Mulgrave is a great benefactor, sir. A great benefactor.'

Settling himself in the carriage and smiling at Puella, Kite broke the wafer as the black coachman whipped up the horses and they jerked forward. When he had read the short letter, he looked up at Mulgrave sitting opposite, beside Dorothea. Mulgrave stared steadfastly out of the window and Kite felt a great affection from the graven features of this strange, aloof man.

He had settled an annuity of two hundred pounds upon Puella.

The departure of the *Spitfire* was subject to

a number of delays, but finally decided upon for Lady Day, 1756. By that time the threat of war was impinging increasingly upon trade in the West Indies, where a naval presence was increasingly felt. The passage of frigates and sloops in and out of English Harbour was no longer the desultory occasion it had been a few months earlier. Already the idlers inhabiting the waterfront of St John's, Willoughby, Falmouth and Parham had been swept up by a hot press sent in ship's boats from the naval establishment at English Harbour. Here they had been found enforced employment in the small Leeward Islands Squadron.

From the window of Mulgrave and Company's offices one morning, Kite and Mulgrave were regarding a naval sloop lying-to off St John's, her main topsail backed against the mast while she waited to escort the dozen snows, brigs and schooners just then slipping their moorings and warping out to sea. Mulgrave remarked drily, 'Now we shall see how assiduous our naval Johnnies are, Kite, for they have to choose between the lucrative pursuit of prizes and the dull, sober and routine duty of convoy escort.'

He turned to Kite. 'It is not my intention to sail in convoy, Kite, and I know Da Silva has taken aboard some powder and shot.'

'Indeed he has, sir. But he is concerned

that the, er, naval Johnnies have requisitioned the best and left us with inferior powder, of which there is little enough. I had hoped to load more.'

Mulgrave smiled. 'There is a store of it at the house, along with a quantity of small arms, which you may place on board. On an island with so many plantations there is a steady demand for powder and shot, and occasionally for muskets.'

The following morning Kite and Da Silva, with a dozen of their crew of free blacks, mulattoes and white riff-raff happily scooped up by the Portuguese sailing master before the Royal Navy's ardent young midshipmen and their gangs, followed an overgrown path up the hill behind Mulgrave's house to where a brick bomb-proof store lay hidden by thorn scrub. The unlocked door revealed a small arsenal. Sixty kegs of fine-milled black powder were carefully transferred to the *Spitfire*.

The schooner was by now lying in the harbour, her standing rigging set up a-tanto, her topsides gleaming under a fresh application of turpentine and rosin and with new canvas lying furled along her spars. Following the powder, forty stands of arms and a dozen bundles of cutlasses and boarding pikes were carried on board, so that apart from the dress of her officers and the absence of a naval pendant at her mainmast truck, there was little to distinguish the Spitfire from a man-of-war schooner.

By Lady Day, the financially significant date upon which the formalities of Mulgrave and Company's transforming itself into Mulgrave, Wentworth and Company were completed, the *Spitfire* lay ready to leave. Powder, shot and small arms had been followed on board by the packing cases, trunks and personal effects of Mulgrave, Dorothea, Puella and Kite. Late that afternoon, having gone ahead of the others, Kite welcome Mulgrave and Dorothea on board. The quayside was crowded with well-wishers and the merely curious. The brilliant colours worn by the free black women were in stark contrast to the black carriages of the island's gentry drawn up along the strand, amid which Wentworth held impatient court. A foot patrol of the garrison had been sent by Major Robertson to provide a guard of honour as Mulgrave, long an institution in Antigua, courteously raised his black tricorne as he stepped aboard the *Spitfire*. Along the waterfront a respectful cheer rippled.

The sun set as the schooner was warped out across the harbour, heading for the open sea beyond. The western sky flushed red as the halliards were manned and the sails rose up the masts, pink in the evening light. As the *Spitfire* cleared the outer limits of St John's, an unshotted gun boomed out from her bow. The concussion rolled round the bay, echoing in a long diminuendo, but this was not quite Joseph Mulgrave's final valediction to the place where he had made his name and his fortune; he had one more surprise for the Antiguans.

Amid the reverberations of the gunshot a lesser explosion went unnoticed until the first flicker of fire was seen from the quayside, prompting a gasp from the crowd. Growing indistinct in the gathering twilight against the shoulder of its hill, Mulgrave's house began to burn. It was the one thing he had denied Wentworth, though he had sold his enslaved household servants to his successor, and they now carried out their old master's last order.

As the *Spitfire* stood out to sea, her sails filling to the gentle *terral*, Mulgrave stood rigid at the taffrail, hands clasped behind his back, staring astern at the flickering light that was soon all that could be seen of the island where he had spent the greater part of his life.

The wooden structure had caught fire quickly and, long before *Spitfire* had passed beyond the horizon, the house had burned to the ground. As the last sparks faded, Mulgrave turned forward and went below.

'Good night, Captain Kite,' he said and

Kite, standing next to Da Silva at the foot of the mainmast, noticed the catch in the elderly man's voice.

'Good night, sir.'

Da Silva coughed in the darkness. 'The Senhor is tired,' he said.

Part Three

War

Ten

The Schooner

During the next year and a half, Kite and the *Spitfire* enjoyed a varied existence. For the first quarter of that period the schooner acted as Mulgrave's yacht as he coasted slowly towards New York, spending weeks at a time visiting business associates and acquaintances among the merchants and trading houses of Savannah, Charleston, Norfolk, Williamsburg, Annapolis and Philadelphia. Before their arrival in the Savannah River, *Spitfire* had passed the bastions of the Moro Castle and called at Havana before dropping her anchor in Jamaican waters off Kingston. But her visits to these ports had been brief, for Mulgrave had come down with fever, a sweating and shuddering illness accompanied by delirium that reminded Kite and Puella of the terrible plague aboard the *Enterprise*.

The cramped conditions aboard *Spitfire,* where the stern cabin had been neatly but not spaciously divided for the two establishments of Mulgrave and Kite, forced a greater intimacy between the two men. The latter learned that like Lorimoor, Mulgrave had long suffered recurrent bouts of this sweating sickness, for it was not the bloody yellow jack that laid him low. Moreover, the affliction was one of the reasons he had maintained such a private life in St John's, and its incurable nature had persuaded him to effectively adopt Wentworth as his heir. Fear of the disease explained his apparent parsimony as a host, his abstemiousness and his avoidance of the sun, when he conceived he was at most danger from suffering a feverish attack. He confided that he believed that if he returned to England, he would throw off the disease, claiming, to Kite's considerable surprise, that he believed the malady to be spread by the bites of mosquitoes.

'If the little demons bite me and bite you, they will be biting every poxed rascal in St John's,' Mulgrave gasped in a lucid moment as Kite visited him one morning. 'God knows what contagions they spread between us.' He gestured at the net that was tented above his bed and that he had ordered Kite to sleep under while in St John's. Kite had assumed the kindness to simply enable him to sleep undisturbed by the irritation of insects, whether mosquitoes or ants, or to avoid the more serious attentions of snakes and lizards. 'You must always cover yourself with such a bed-tent, Kite, while in these warm and humid latitudes,' he had insisted.

Kite stared astern through the windows at the brilliant sunlight dancing upon the blue sea. The schooner lifted easily to the waves and the coast of Cuba fell astern, misty in the heat haze. He watched a bird dip into the wake, which drew out as a thin attenuated roil of disturbed water marking the passage of *Spitfire's* hull, gradually fading as the greater power of the wind-blown waves overrode the schooner's temporary influence. Surely it was a kind of allegory of their own tiny existences, Kite thought, as Mulgrave closed his eyes; this small disturbance of the world, to be smoothed over after their passing.

Dorothea tended Mulgrave assiduously, making him concoctions which, though they could not prevent the fever, brought it swiftly to its climax and eased its passing. 'She is clever,' Puella whispered, as though in awe of Dorothea whom she loved and revered, 'she know many things and Mr Mulgrave know she know.'

'*Knows*, Puella, she knows many things and Mr Mulgrave knows she knows...'

Puella dutifully repeated Kite's correction. She never resented these and accepted them from Kite, Dorothea or Mulgrave, and all three, almost as a matter of concerted policy, corrected not merely her grammar, but her accent and diction so that she enunciated Mulgrave's title of 'mister' as if English were her native tongue, never falling into the cruder distortions of the lingua franca of the Antilles. The only occasion she complained of her tutoring was when she overheard some barbarous English used by Da Silva. Puella failed to recognise the coarse and rapid speech of the polyglot seamen as English, which in truth it scarcely resembled, but she comprehended that Kite addressed Da Silva in English, and that Da Silva responded incorrectly, mirroring her own mistakes without correction. This irritated her.

'Why do you not speak with him about his corrections, Kite?'

'About his errors, you mean, Puella... Well, it does not greatly matter that Mr Da Silva does not speak good English. I understand him, as do Mr Mulgrave and Dorothea and all the men in the crew. Besides, he will not need to learn any more now, for he is too old.'

Puella frowned. 'You confuse me, Kite.'

'No more than you do me, my Puella,' Kite laughed, caressing her swelling belly.

Puella was delivered of a son in Charleston, so the infant boy was called Charles, then Joseph William after both his benefactor and his father. The boy was the colour of creamed coffee, with his mother's dark, lustrous eyes and his father's straight nose.

'He could pass for an Italian,' Mulgrave murmured as he regarded the baby in his arms. He had asked Puella to let him hold the tiny bundle in a request that seemed so uncharacteristic that Puella looked first at Kite, before acceding. 'You must acknowledge him as your own, my boy,' Mulgrave added, looking up at Kite, who stood proudly by. Mulgrave's eyes glittered with half-suppressed tears.

'Of course, sir.'

'Good. That is as it should be. Do not be distracted by these tedious social niceties that speak against our siring sons on the country...'

They had already encountered social ostracism in Savannah, where Mulgrave was asked to leave an assembly on account of Dorothea's presence on his arm. The pretensions of English colonial society in the Carolinas, he afterwards remarked, were in odd contrast to those of the eponymous king after whom the colony was named. That the very men who asked Mulgrave to leave all had black mistresses, several of which openly paraded in grand coaches, only blackened Mulgrave's mood. The hypocrisy of Antigua was muted by contrast, an attitude fostered by a few and thus far less widespread than in Savannah. Unlike St John's, where although many of the blacks seen about the town were slaves, and though the disembarkation of slaves from the arriving Guineamen reminded everyone of the enthralment of the vast majority of the black population of enforced immigrants, the atmosphere in Savannah seemed unduly repressive. 'Here,' Mulgrave thought, voicing his observation to Kite in one of their moments of increasing friendship as the voyage advanced, 'even the slaves themselves resent Dorothea's good fortune. Is a black never to rise from the shackles of serfdom as we have done? Why, Kite, you and I know these people are capable of all that we are. That their villainous chieftains and kings sell them into our custody should enable us to liberate them by degrees. Of course there can be no swift, revolutionary change, it would invite only the most savage repression, and the white must change with the black even more profoundly, for he must give up and share his advantages...' Mulgrave trailed off and Kite suddenly saw him as an ageing man, left weakened by his last bout of fever.

'Have you always thought thus?' Kite asked.

Mulgrave gave his pallid smile and shook his head. 'No, of course not, and had Dorothea not treated my first bout of fever I doubt that I should have ever done so. But a man in exile, reduced to a sweating shadow, has to rediscover much and in doing so often finds matters are not quite as he had formerly thought them.'

'You were … exiled?' Kite tried to draw Mulgrave, but the older man divined his intention. 'You know, Kite, curiosity about many things is a great virtue, without it mankind would never have advanced, but curiosity about each other is often a great bar to advancement of any kind.'

'I beg your pardon, sir,' Kite apologised hurriedly. 'I meant no offence…'

'None was taken, I assure you.'

In the succeeding months as Charlie was weaned and began his first tentative crawls across the cabin floor encouraged by Dorothea and Puella, Kite himself learned much. Although the grander elements of society in Savannah shunned them, Mulgrave's wealth and mercantile power assured him of welcome elsewhere. Kite frequently accompanied him on his quasi-social visits as he called upon those he had traded with over the years. In this way the two men heard of the military and naval disasters befalling British arms. In the north of America, all along the border with French Canada, French troops and their Indian allies, brilliantly directed by the Marquis de Montcalm, raided and harried, shooting and burning the settlers in the backwoods, raping the women and tomahawking the men, scalping indiscriminately and carrying off children to feed their barbarous and perverse appetites in the fastnesses of their forest lodges. This frisson of fear and loathing rippled down from the dense woods of the north to the marshes and pine barrens of the south, increasing the natural apprehension of the outnumbered whites at the overwhelming numerical superiority of the natives whom their own commercial rapacity brought into their colonial economies. Between red skin and black there lay only the distinction of colour, it was argued; what a red warrior did to the whites at Oswego or Fort William Henry, a black might do to the whites of the Carolinas.

The British armies in North America proved powerless to stem this flood and seemed destined to emulate the fate of General Baddock. New York, Boston and the towns of New England were said to be overwhelmed with settlers seeking refuge from the horrors of the frontier. This situation was exacerbated by the perverse folly of the colonial assemblies, who refused to join forces in raising troops, or to cooperate in any way. Mulgrave, commenting upon this, said that if the French gained a foothold in any of the British colonies, the assembly of that colony would probably seek an accommodation with the enemy, in defiance of the legitimate right of the British Parliament in London to decide such matters. The signal failure of British arms to prevent the encroaching raids of the French and Indians, Mulgrave claimed it would be argued in the assemblies, effectively removed the right of the Houses of Parliament in London to consider themselves the superior government of the American colonies, since they could not defend their own extensive and extended borders.

In Europe the story was much the same, with Admiral Byng failing to relieve the British garrison of Minorca. This surrendered ignominiously to the French, whereupon Byng fell victim to the malice of the Duke of Newcastle's ministry, which had him shot. The charge of alleged cowardice was proved to the government's satisfaction by their own suppression of half of Byng's dispatch, which laid out his reasons for withdrawal. The execution shook British society and led to a political crisis. The outdated newspapers Kite and Mulgrave read reported defiant and scathing attacks by William Pitt, and eventually contained the news that Pitt had consented to join a ministry if the direction of the war was placed in his hands. That the King hated Pitt only seemed to the two distant observers to play into the hands of the enemy, chief among which was France, though Russia and Austria were in the field against Britain's Continental ally, Prussia.

Pitt's position was unstable and, as the French overran King George's native electorate of Hanover, Frederick II suffered a humiliating defeat in Bohemia at Kolin. The heavy subsidies Britain paid to the Prussian monarch now seemed an inordinate waste and the national debt rose accordingly.

But in this same period, Kite learned that war, though it interferes with trade, prospers traders. Prices rose and Wentworth's letters spoke of great opportunities less, and of profitable deals more often. Nor were Mulgrave and Kite detached from this profiteering. Although the *Spitfire's* voyage north was leisurely, consolidating the position of Mulgrave, Wentworth and Company as it progressed, she carried cargoes between her ports of call. These were often valuables, specie or bullion, payments placed on deposit and destined for other trading houses along the coast, or destined for the banks of Philadelphia, underwritten and guaranteed by Mulgrave's signature. Armed, fast and well manned as she was, *Spitfire* attracted this monetary traffic as merchant houses sought to salt away their gains before the impact of hostilities limited their freedom. Mulgrave's name for probity, and the fearsome appearance of the *Spitfire's* crew, added to her growing reputation, which was discreetly spread among the commercial fraternity, so that she was almost as laden as a Spanish treasure ship. Not one shipment was accepted without an agreed percentage, deductible on safe delivery, and payable to 'the Said Master and Owner, and the Said Assigns of the Schooner *Spitfire* of St John's in the Island of Antigua'.

And as Mulgrave paid his respectful farewells to men he had often previously known only by the bond inherent in their signatures, he introduced them to 'the Said Master and Owner' of the *Spitfire*. Kite's reputation was enhanced by specious rumours that he had saved an entire slaver from the yellow jack, while his vessel was known to have been a fearsome privateer. This combination seemed to promise the smile of fortune upon the handsome young man's enterprises, a perception given greater weight by the endorsement of so shrewd and respected a man as Mulgrave.

For Kite, the progress northward had a great charm. The intensity of his love affair with Puella, the birth of his son, the fruitful association with the relaxing Mulgrave and his friendship with Dorothea, indeed the entire domestic atmosphere that prevailed aboard *Spitfire* in her guise as a private yacht, conferred upon him a period of almost blissful happiness. At the time he was unaware that, in their prolonged visits, he was establishing relationships with trading houses and merchants that he would afterwards prize; but he was aware of his growing mastery of all aspects of his adopted profession of ship-master, developing what Da Silva acknowledged was a hidden ability far outweighing his former clumsy attempts at surgery. Where this aptitude had come from he could not guess, for he had never been told that his mother had been a Manx woman and her family had for generations fished the Irish Sea about the Isle of Man.

His basic understanding of navigation was brought to a practical competence by frequent practice and, unlike many masters formally but imperfectly instructed in the art, he never lost his sense of caution in conducting his ship. In mastering these skills he was helped not only by Da Silva, but by the curious loyalty of his oddly assorted crew. To man the *Spitfire,* the Portuguese sailing master had brought together some forty men whose paths had never previously crossed, other than from them being part of the casual, unemployed fraternity of the waterfront. They had never previously sailed together, nor shared a common place of origin, and this prevented them forming cliques, allowing their present common experiences to swiftly weld them together into an efficient crew. Da Silva had ensured they were well paid, and that they enjoyed a sufficiency of leisure in port so that the sight of Puella and Dorothea failed to stir them to resentment. Otherwise, Da Silva kept them hard at work. In port they toiled at cargo-handling or the general maintenance that *Spitfire* demanded and Mulgrave could underwrite; at sea, in the gruelling grind of watch-keeping. Nor was opportunity neglected to remind them frequently that it was wartime, and that their present employment might keep them from the clutches of the press gangs of the Royal Navy if they could evade trouble until they had obtained exemptions.

On their arrival at New York, Mulgrave disembarked. It had been his intention to cross the Atlantic in *Spitfire,* but at New York a number of considerations persuaded him to change his mind. The first grew out of his friendship for Kite, who proved to be a young man of great promise. Not only had Kite shown his ability as a ship-master in practical terms, but he had also demon-strated a firm grasp of the principles of commerce and, in their dealing with several American houses, had demonstrated an originality and independence of mind that suggested he would prosper on his own account. In particular, Kite had used his own money, mostly derived from his unspent pay-off from the *Enterprize*, to undertake a private speculation on a quantity of crocodile skins which he sold in Philadelphia at a profit. Mulgrave was therefore reluctant to deprive him of the opportunities thus offered by ordering the *Spitfire* to England, a reluctance that also took into consideration another factor.

One evening, on their passage from Annapolis to Philadelphia, when the *Spitfire* lay becalmed and rolling in a sluggish swell that promised a blow later, the two men had been enjoying a cigar after dinner. The women had withdrawn, as was their custom, to play with Charlie before he was settled to sleep, leaving the two men to discuss the completion of the voyage and their future plans.

'On completion of your affairs in New York,' Kite said, uneasy about his return to his native land, 'I know it to be your intention to sail for England, sir, so may I ask what port you would consider it best to make for?'

'Does it matter?' Mulgrave asked absently.

Kite shrugged, affecting a disinterest he was far from feeling. 'Only insofar as I apprehend that a passage to London is better made with a landfall to the south-ward, whereas a passage to Liverpool is otherwise, and with the probability of French ships on the lookout, I take it they will congregate in greater numbers between the Caskets and the Wight than off Malin Head.'

'You have been studying your charts, Kite. Where did you get them?'

'From a merchant in Charleston.'

'Rawlings?'

'No, sir, Bigsby, he was but newly out from Bristol, where the slave trade is much fallen off.'

'The war, I suppose...'

'Yes, and the fierce competition of Liverpool Guineamen, who run for lower wages than the Bristol ships.'

'I see.' Mulgrave paused. 'Well, then, you recommend Liverpool as entailing less risk, I assume.'

'The matter is yours to decide, sir,' Kite replied, aware that much might depend upon Mulgrave's decision. Now he had Puella and Charlie to consider and in England he was still regarded as a murderer. 'Though I should point out that despite the armament of our guns we have not fired them in anger and that one hopes it will never be necessary...'

'Amen to that,' broke in Mulgrave, 'but we cannot build assumptions on that score... That reminds me, we must obtain a letter of marque in either Philadelphia or New York.

I was intending to wait until we arrived in England, but we need its protection to avoid our crew being poached by some damned over-zealous Johnny in an under-manned frigate off the Lizard…'

'So you're for London?' Kite asked quickly, visualising a passage up the Channel.

'Or Liverpool,' countered Mulgrave swiftly. Leaning forward he ground out his cigar. As the last curl of smoke rose up from the plate, Mulgrave looked up at Kite. 'I have never asked you, Kite, for I am not curious – you know my views on personal curiosity – but you have never spoken with any enthusiasm for England. Even now, I do not detect any great eagerness in your desire to return home. Do *you* have any preference whether I should land by way of Liverpool, London, Bristol or Falmouth?' Mulgrave paused a moment and then asked, 'Tell me, would you rather perhaps remain here, on the American coast, or in the Antilles?'

Mulgrave sat back and Kite, his heart beating, responded. 'Sir, I cannot at this moment tell you what I should perhaps have told you long ago…'

Mulgrave held up his hand. 'I do not want to know anything about your personal affairs, Kite, life is too short and perilous and whatever mischief lies in the past, I have known you long enough to trust you. Only do me the honour of answering my question with an honest answer.'

'Well, sir, I should like to go home, but for the present I cannot. If, however, I could prevail upon you to undertake one small favour in my interest, that of conveying privately a letter to my sister, matters may yet resolve themselves.'

'That seems a trivial enough request, to which I can agree without reservation.'

'It would ease my mind considerably, sir.'

'Consider it done. There is, however, a favour which I must ask of you in return and which is another consideration persuading me to leave you and the schooner here, in the Americas. The present war makes a passage to England hazardous and to sail in this vessel, whether to Liverpool or London, might prove a risky or even a fatal enterprise. I am content, therefore, to take passage under convoy, perhaps in a man-of-war, if one can be found in New York. But I cannot take Dorothea. I am an old man and my health is failing; while the English air may cure my fevers, they will be otherwise to Dorothea, who frets during the rains in Antigua and complains constantly that our present northing is proving detrimental to her. Her culture and traditions belong in the tropics, don't you see, Kite; England would, I greatly fear, be fatal to her...' Mulgrave paused, then admitted frankly, 'Besides, I

249

have the impediment of another woman in England: my wife. She is still alive and I must provide for her old age. Not that I have quite failed to provide for her, despite her infidelities. Moreover, I doubt that I shall live long and leaving Dorothea on her own in England, at the mercy of rapacious relatives as well as the merciless climate, would be a cruelty I cannot contemplate.'

'What would you have me do, sir?' Kite asked, awed by the confidence and the explanation that, were it known of in St John's, would stop the speculation of a whole generation.

'Keep always your own counsel, and ally yourself with no party. Find yourself a place, Kite, and build yourself a house from where, with your youth and wealth, you can command your own destiny. There, take Dorothea under your protection, she will be a companion to Puella and an undeniable asset.' Mulgrave smiled. 'And thereby please an old man.'

Two months later, one evening some time after their arrival in New York following a passage of boisterous weather that had kept them at sea, Kite was summoned by way of a note brought by a boy from the tavern where Mulgrave had appointed their rendezvous.

Come at Once without any Mention of myself.

It is a matter of Business, the note read, *but if you are Compelled to make known your Absence, say that an Accident has Occurred to me.* Kite knew Mulgrave well enough to perceive the man did not want news of the summons getting to Dorothea and could guess its meaning. He was right. Mulgrave sat in a private room; he was dressed in travelling clothes, booted and with a new cloak on the bench beside him. On the floor stood his portmanteau.

'We must say good-bye, Kite, but you have to write a letter for me to carry and I should be obliged if you would attend to it now.' Mulgrave indicated pen, ink and paper on the table before him. His tone was as cold as when they had first met; this was indeed a business meeting, the abrupt conclusion of their partnership. Only the working of Mulgrave's face showed the emotion he was under.

Under the circumstances, Kite had some trouble writing his long-meditated but oft-postponed letter to his sister Helen. Now the time and manner of its doing were forced upon him, he made a poor job of it. Hurriedly he completed and folded it, adding the superscription and handing it to Mulgrave, who immediately stood up.

'There is a frigate leaving tonight with dispatches; the captain has kindly under-taken to gave me a passage if I serve as a volunteer. I believe,' Mulgrave added ironically, 'my status lies somewhere above a midshipman and below a lieutenant. Tell Dorothea that I have gone to visit a ship in the harbour and that the boat was upset, she will believe you, having always feared such a thing. Sometimes these women have dreams that they believe to foretell the future...' Mulgrave smiled sardonically. 'So, let matters fall out in that wise. She will not argue and there will be no corpse to bury or to grieve over. I am sorry to burden you with this piece of theatre.'

Kite shook his head. 'It is the least I can do, though I shall grieve your departure with Dorothea.'

'You have a foolishly kind heart, Kite,' Mulgrave looked at his watch and held out his hand. 'If this war goes ill, as it seems it must, you may have to come home yourself, but in the meantime, I wish you well.'

Just then a young man in naval uniform, the white patches of a midshipman on his collar, came into the room. 'Mr Mulgrave?' he asked, looking from one to another of them.

'I am he,' said Mulgrave.

'Henry Hope, at your service, sir.' The midshipman gave a clumsy bow. 'I have a boat at your disposal, but must urge you to hasten, sir. Captain Lasham is eager to get under weigh.'

Mulgrave stood up and Kite rose with him. 'Sir, you will send us word of your whereabouts?' he asked anxiously. 'If and when I come home, I should like to pay my respects.'

Mulgrave smiled and nodded. 'Of course, Kite. Wentworth is your man. He will know my whereabouts. Recall I still retain an interest in the company.'

'Of course.' Kite felt stupid; events had moved too fast. How could he tell Dorothea? She would take it extremely ill.

'Goodbye, Kite.' They shook hands.

'Goodbye, sir...' And Kite was left alone in the room as Mulgrave followed the midshipman out into the dark wintry night.

Dorothea was inconsolable and Kite sailed south for the sun and the warmth of the Antilles, bound for Antigua. The *Spitfire* bore a cargo of manufactured goods, New York gowns made 'according to the latest London fashions', wine and, despite the war, a small quantity of brandy. The schooner lay a month in St John's, a month during which Charlie first called for his mama, Wentworth bought the consignment of gowns, Da Silva bought a second schooner and Kite made plans for building a house. Between them, Kite and Wentworth debated ways of expanding their trade and, in due course, having rented a dwelling for his women and the boy, Kite sailed on the first of several voyages between Antigua, Jamaica and the Carolinas. He refused to make another Guinea voyage himself, partly from fear of contracting yellow jack and partly out of disgust for the trade, but he transhipped slaves between the islands, and bore cargoes of African manioc, camwood and scrivelloes to the American colonies.

Although French men-of-war and corsairs were at sea and active among the islands, Kite's now legendary luck held. They were chased several times, but such was the clean state of *Spitfire's* bottom and the skill of her master and crew that the schooner escaped without having to fire a gun in her defence. Privately Kite grew anxious that when his luck ran out, as he felt sure it would, he would fail to live up to the valorous expectations of others. Moreover he was plagued by fears of being found a coward in the face of the enemy.

This feeling was encouraged by a stream of tales of French successes, stories which underwrote the creeping conviction of the inevitability of defeat. Ships with which they were familiar were captured by the enemy's corsairs and carried into French ports as prizes to the privateers now operating out of Guadeloupe and Martinique to the south of them. Meanwhile the main business of the war continued badly for the British. During the succeeding summer the capture of the French naval base of Louisbourg, on Cape Breton Island, though it had been successfully carried out in the last way by a handful of American colonists, was abandoned. The British fleet bound for the Gulf of St Lawrence had been delayed by contrary winds which in turn allowed the French to slip reinforcements across the Atlantic, but this did not excuse the fact that the matter was bungled. The *New York Gazette* railed that 1757 was 'a year of the most dishonour to the Crown, of the most detriment to the subject, and of the most disgrace to the nation'.

But the patient strategies of the remarkable Pitt, now re-established in government and with the conduct of the war in his capable hands, were beginning to tell. A story circulated from the naval ships refitting in English Harbour told of an admiral who confronted Pitt with the impossibility of his instructions. Pitt, it was laughingly recounted, had discomfited the admiral. Standing up to lean on his crutches, Pitt revealed his bandaged feet, grossly swollen by gout. 'I *walk* upon impossibilities, sir,' the minister was reputed to have said, whereupon the humiliated admiral left to obey his orders. Such yarns bolstered morale, coming as they did from sea officers, of which there were an increasing number in the island. The young lieutenants of the Royal Navy seen at assemblies in St John's seemed unaffected by the disasters raining down upon their colleagues in the army. At these same assemblies, local cynics marvelled at, and repeated the accuracy of Voltaire's alleged comment upon Byng's execution. 'The English,' the Frenchman was said to have remarked, 'shoot an admiral from time to time, to encourage the others.' Whatever the truth of this reported witticism, reinforcing cruisers augmented the Leeward Islands Squadron, and word began to circulate that the French could not long be left in possession of their West Indian islands. With every man present his own master of strategy and tactics, opinions were voiced as to the best method of wresting from them Guadeloupe, Martinique, St Lucia and Marie Galante.

'By Heaven,' remarked Wentworth, rubbing his hands and discussing this matter over chocolate the following morning in the quayside office of Mulgrave, Wentworth and Company with a bunch of cronies, 'think, gentlemen, what opportunities would be laid open to us with the French trade stopped!'

Then came news, by a schooner from Barbados which had had a brush with corsairs from St Lucia, that a fleet from England had arrived in the Windward Islands. The war in the West Indies was no longer to be a matter of mosquito bites, of enemy corsairs seizing British and colonial merchant vessels, or of British privateers retaliating by snapping up French inter-island traffic. Though British naval squadrons were maintained in the Antilles to protect trade and offer convoy, a major squadron had not yet made its appearance in the Caribbean Sea. In Antigua the news spread like wildfire.

Kite heard of it shortly after *Spitfire's* anchor was dropped in the clear water of St John's and warps were run ashore. They had endured a chase for three days and he was dog-tired and wanted only to see Puella and his son before taking to his bed. Dorothea greeted him; tears poured down her cheeks and the exhausted Kite at first unkindly attributed her misery to yet another outburst of grief at the loss of Mulgrave. He had learned that the black and mulatto women set great store by what he thought of as dreams, but which they claimed to be the portentous visitations of spirits. Kite had seen them in trances and knew the contempt many of his fellow whites had for such 'primitive' behaviour, but his own intimacy with Dorothea had persuaded him that she did indeed possess powers of perception that passed his own under-standing. Now, tired yet eager to see Charlie and Puella, supposing the Dorothea had had one of her spirit-trances, but irritated by her suddenly clinging to him, Kite took her shoulders and pushed her ungently away.

'Dorothea, I beseech you...'

'Mr Kite, oh, Mr Kite, Charlie is dead.'

Eleven

The Attack

Providence reached out its Cold Hand and Grasped my Very Heart, Kite wrote of the death of Charlie, before he had to return to the affairs of men and could confide only to the blank pages of his journal. The keening and wailing of Puella and Dorothea had been terrible, their unhappiness at the Christian burial given to the little boy only compounding their grief. In his own sense of loss, Kite relived the personal horror of the death of his mother and, more shocking, felt the rebuke of fate at his former indifference to the grief of the blacks aboard the *Enterprize*. The extent to which the conditions aboard the Guineaman had hardened him, and the detachment he had felt from the Negroes as human beings, almost crushed him as he shared Puella's agony in those first few days. Though he wept when alone at night, after an exhausted Puella had fallen asleep, and though he smudged the pages of his journal with his tears, he was dry-eyed in her presence, a circumstance she failed to understand. It caused the first rift between them, for in grief Kite possessed no superiority over his dead child's mother and she beat his chest, her anger spilling from her in all the fulsome vituperation of her native tongue.

She slipped easily into this, abetted by Dorothea, who now viewed Kite with suspicion as a malign influence and not the natural heir of Joseph Mulgrave. Dorothea herself had seen things, and knew things that the white people could neither understand nor believe. That her visions and visitations were utterly convincing to her only served to underline the gulf that existed between the white man and his black mistress. Kite and Puella could never be happy, and the loss of Charlie only served to emphasise the displeasure of the spirits. Though she was a product of interbreeding, Dorothea's strong belief in the spirits had grown from the childhood spent amid the black slaves of a plantation; this had produced instincts that were only distantly comparable with Kite's vague meanderings about 'the cold grasp of providence'. Both might have arisen from primeval fears, but the former was deemed primitive while the other had the sanction of the assumption of superiority, and the demonstrable authority of overwhelming power.

Though Dorothea had submitted to her return to St John's in the train of her new protector, Captain William Kite, she had lost everything in the disappearance of Mulgrave. Her status, her house, her reason for living, had vanished in the night, caught up in the shadows of Joseph Mulgrave's cloak. She had seen that cloak only a few times aboard the *Spitfire,* for Mulgrave had bought it in Annapolis to combat the cooler air of the north, but she had seen its shadow several times since; in fact she knew now that Kite had not told her the truth, though she did not hold him a liar, for he may have himself believed what he had told her.

For her own part, Dorothea knew, like the disciples of the white man's Jesus-god, that her master and lover had not died in New York, but still lived. Or so she thought, until the night that little Charlie died. On that evening, as Kite crowded on sail to outrun a French privateer schooner from Marie Galante, Dorothea had heard the faint but memorable footfall of Mulgrave and, with a cry of joy, had leapt up expecting his embrace. So excited had she been, so certain that at last he was to return to her, that she ran quickly into the hall of the rented house, only to see the shadow of his cloak as he turned the corner of the stairs.

Dorothea rushed after him, to see the dark shape enter the bedroom in which little

Charlie's cot lay. But it was not the Mulgrave whom Dorothea loved who turned at her intrusion; it was a Mulgrave with the dead white features of a drowned corpse, and he vanished before her eyes, taking with him the last breath of the little boy.

All this Dorothea told Puella, and all this was held to be the fault of Kite. Kite was a powerful man and Dorothea knew the white men cheated each other in business. Many times Mulgrave had explained to her with a wry smile the crooked transactions of his fellow traders in the Antilles; always he outwitted them, though she rarely understood how, only that he was invariably successful. Now, she thought, Mulgrave had been in some way outwitted by Kite. She had convinced herself that Kite had managed to abandon Mulgrave in New York. Perhaps, she excitedly argued to the receptive Puella, it had been Kite who had had the house burned; it would have been quite in character for Mulgrave to have said nothing, she claimed. Now Mulgrave, bereft and left far behind without Dorothea's support, had died. Even Dorothea's long-held conviction that her benefactor would finally drown seemed quite reconcilable with this imagined but convincing scenario. The vastness of the ocean and the complex geography of New York had convinced her that drowning was a not improbable fate for a man delirious from a sudden recurrence of his malaria. But such an impressive and convincing fulfilment of her prophetic visions had little impact on Puella.

For Puella, Kite was revealed as possessing those underlying vices of all white men: an insatiable greed and an indifference to the death of others.

For a week Kite attempted to comfort the grieving Puella. To him the death was at first a mystery; he imperfectly grasped Dorothea's garbled account, only registering the extent of her ridiculous superstition that Mulgrave had taken the spirit of Charlie out of some misplaced desire for revenge. Dorothea's references to the burning of the house made no sense, and for a while Kite thought the mulatto woman was deranged. Wrapped in his own distress he was unintentionally unkind and Dorothea noted his contempt; it only fuelled her misconceptions.

Mrs Robertson, whose attempts at offering consolation were largely motivated by a desire for the handsome young sea-captain at this vulnerable and pliant moment, did explain to him that infantile asphyxia was not unknown. That she added it was particularly so among children of mixed blood was pure mischief, intended to persuade the object of her scandalous lust that consolation and a greater satisfaction lay in her own embrace. Her visit failed to reconcile Kite to the loss of his son and only hurt Puella with its sinister suggestion of infidelity, for while Kite knew nothing of either Mrs Robertson's itch or her reputation, Puella was well aware of both. As for Mrs Robertson, she took back to her teatime cronies the intelligence that Captain Kite was a most sensitive young man who was still under the spell of 'that nigger witch'. With this demeaning opprobrium the garrison wives unconsciously acknowledged the universal beauty of the young African woman and Mrs Robertson hid the extent of her private disappointment.

But Puella's appearance in some respects justified this contemptuous description. She neglected herself, she went half-naked and unkempt about the house, she crouched in dark corners as she had once quailed in Kite's cabin aboard the *Enterprize*. Kite tried to draw her out, but after the first tender and consoling embraces of his return, Dorothea's words poisoned her against him and she shunned him with mounting passion. At first he merely thought that Puella's hostility was a passing manifestation of grief. She could not, Kite reasoned with himself, understand the notion of 'infantile asphyxia' and therefore the apparently inexplicable death must, in terms that Puella understood, lie within the malicious province of her pantheistic spirit world. She would come round in due course, Kite felt sure; after all, the blacks lived close to death and had their pickaninnies by the dozen.

But Puella did not come round. Charlie had been for her something wonderful, something unique, joining her to the remarkable white man she had come close to idolising, as Dorothea had idolised Mulgrave. Bereft of children herself, Dorothea had told her the importance the white man vested in breeding a son, and that one son was better than many, for he would be a rich and powerful man, inheriting all his father's wealth. Moreover, despite the fact that the white men were indiscriminate as to where they rutted, their first wives were considered superior to all others and, even when they never shared their beds, they remained secure. The position of a first wife was assured, even when they were black. This assertion Dorothea based upon a lifetime's familiarity with the society of the Antilles and the promises made by Mulgrave. She had heard it was not the case in England, but there was no sun in England and it was a very different place to the islands.

Kite tolerated Puella's raging for a week then, one morning, he found her keening in a corner of the withdrawing room. She seemed quiescent, more as she had been on their first encounter, frightened, hurt and lonely. He knelt as he had once done aboard the slaver, and put out his hand. She bit it.

Kite recoiled with a cry of pain and astonishment. A moment later she was upon him, clawing and biting so that he had to strike her across her cheek with the flat of his hand. She reeled back and, wiping the back of one hand beneath her nose, displayed the steam of blood running down over her lips.

Kite was overwhelmed by shame and shook his head, stepping forward, his arms outstretched, uttering words of endearment. But Puella was gone, to hide behind a locked door. There she remained for two days, only taking food from Dorothea, whose expression of reproach haunted Kite like a spectre. When on the third day she refused to emerge or to speak to Kite, he resolved to return to sea without delay.

Word had come in that three ships from Falmouth and one from St John's had been taken by French corsairs. The news that several prominent St John's owners were abandoning trade, obtaining letters of marque from the governor and converting their vessels to privateers, appealed to Kite's mood. Consulting Wentworth, he put the matter in train with Garvey, the attorney. Then that same afternoon a message came overland from English Harbour. A Lieutenant Corrie of the hired cutter *Hawk* had arrived there from Guadeloupe. A British force consisting of six thousand soldiers under Major-General Thomas Hopson had some time since arrived from England. The naval squadron escorting them had combined with that of Commodore Moore at Barbados and the expedition had attacked Martinique. The attack had failed and Moore and Hopson had withdrawn to transfer their attentions to Guadeloupe. The ships' guns and the mortars of the bomb-vessels had bombarded Fort Royal on Basse Terre, silencing its guns, driving the garrison inland and setting fire to the adjacent town, where the year's harvest of sugar and rum burned furiously. Moore's ships had also bombarded and set afire Pointe-à-Pitre, the port on Grande Terre used principally by the enemy's corsairs, but by now fever and heat-stroke were seriously reducing the numbers of the unacclimatised troops. It had already killed the elderly and already ailing Hopson. The general's successor, Colonel Barrington, was now asking the colonists in Antigua to rally to the colours.

To Kite the opportunity seemed Heaven-sent. Privately, his evasion of French privateers by simply outrunning them might have enhanced his reputation and that of his speedy ship among the traders who had no wish to lose their valuable cargoes to the enemy, but not having exchanged so much as a distant shot with the French, not testing his mettle in battle, had secretly irked him. But now his son was dead and his love was repudiated. With, as he put it, the cold grasp of providence about his heart, he was indifferent to anything. He recalled Makepeace's defiant philosophy and heard it as a war cry; he was among the first to volunteer his services.

But Lieutenant Corrie brought other news and with it the whiff of disaster, for having appealed to the patriotism of the islanders, he now required preparations for the reception of six hundred sick soldiers. These, it was quickly rumoured, were but the worst afflicted; the real number approached two thousand, almost a third of the troops involved. The sick arrived in Antigua the following day, borne in two transports. Kite had spent the night aboard *Spitfire,* passing word among his crew that he wished them to muster that morning. Da Silva's ship was in port and he rejoined his old commander, 'While we settle this bloody business,' he said, shaking Kite's hand and offering Kite his condolences upon the death of Charlie.

That evening, several score of gentlemen-volunteers had mustered at Wentworth's premises where Mr Garvey appeared, offering to act as executor should any of them fall during the expedition. Though this might advance the glory of their country, several of the young bucks withdrew, declining to draw up their wills under Garvey's supervision.

'They prefer,' remarked the son of a wealthy planter named Henry Ranald, 'to stick the sword of lust into their own property, than the sword of steel into King Louis's.' The remaining men, laughing at this crude bravado, agreed to ship aboard *Spitfire* and the following morning they were at sea, stretching down towards the distant twin peaks of Guadeloupe.

The French West Indian possession of Guadeloupe consisted of two large islands so closely situated that the narrow strait between them was called merely 'the Salt River'. To the north-east lay Grande Terre, with Point-à-Pitre at the southern end of the debouchement of the Salt River into the great bay enclosed by the mountainous arms of the two islands. To the south-west lay the second island, divided into two areas by a mountainous spine running from north to south. On the eastern side of the mountains and opposite Point-à-Pitre, lay Cabes

Terre; on the western was Basse Terre, with the island's principal town of that name at its southern extremity. Offshore, a few miles to the east of Basse Terre town, lay a cluster of small islands making up Les Isles des Saintes, beyond which, further to the east, rose Marie Galante. Off the north-east coast of Grande Terre was the smaller island of La Desirade, while off its narrow eastern point, the Pointe des Châteaux, between it and Marie Galante, lay the small island of Petite Terre.

The islands of Guadeloupe came in sight two mornings later, rising from the sea in the first light of the day like a firmly delineated cloud, taking on more substance as *Spitfire* approached and the sun burned the clinging mist out of the river valleys. The gentlemen-volunteers pressed forward eager to see the goal that would soon, they felt certain, pass into the hands of the British and expose itself for exploitation by themselves, the legitimate heirs, they conceived, to the riches of the Leeward Islands. Guadeloupe they knew as far wealthier a territory than Martinique, an island from which it was said that sugar and rum worth more than the equivalent of one million pounds sterling were sent annually to France. There were, moreover, a hundred and fifty thousand slaves working on the plantations, a measure of Guadeloupe's value more readily comprehended by these young and eager men, for whom the figure of one million was beyond imagination.

Capture would divert some of this wealth their way, while the extirpation of the nests of corsairs at Point-à-Pitre and Marie Galante would release trade from the bondage of convoy. Even while they took passage in his ship and enjoyed his hospitality, many sniggered that such a change in their fortunes would 'cut the canter of Captain Kite', whose legendary luck while not sailing under convoy tended to create high freight rates for cargoes shifted by the *Spitfire*. Not that they greatly resented Kite personally, but there was an orthodox clique that suggested his taking a blackamoor woman to wife, while it might be condoned by fusty old Mulgrave, did not reflect well upon the sensibilities of younger gentlemen.

Gossiping in this wise, as the mountainous terrain of Guadeloupe grew in detail, pleasantly mantled from the sea by the brilliant green of lush tropical vegetation, they doubled Pointe des Châteaux and stood to the westward, along the southern coast of Grande Terre before a fair wind. Ahead of them rose the range of mountains bisecting Basse Terre and Cabes Terre, and tucked under the guns of Fort Louis, the toehold Barrington's reduced force had on the island, lay what appeared to be a squadron of British naval ships of war.

'So you gentlemen are from Antigua,' Colonel Barrington, temporarily a general in the field, resplendent in his scarlet coat, the gorget of his commissioned rank gleaming at his throat, sat at a table in Fort Louis with one leg propped up on a stool. It was swollen with gout, and twitched curiously, each nervous tremor sending a shadow of pain across Barrington's perspiring features. He wiped his mouth and regarded Kite and Ranald, who had been deputed to wait upon the army commander.

'Have any of you any knowledge of the interior?'

'I have, sir. Before the war I was frequently here.'

'But have you a knowledge of the *interior,* Mr Ranald? I am not interested in whether you drank tea with a French planter in Basse Terre or here, or anywhere else for that matter.' Barrington exchanged glances with the young captain of foot who had attended Kite and Ranald on their visit.

'The coastal plains where they are under cultivation, are clear, though the sugar canes can easily conceal a man. Otherwise it is rugged, sir, the higher ground split by ravines and watercourses, and covered with dense vegetation. You could hold up a column and harry troops trying to make progress through such a wilderness.'

Barrington nodded. 'So we discovered a few weeks ago,' he remarked drily.

'You would have great difficulty moving artillery,' Ranald added, to which Barrington agreed readily.

'*That* we discovered in Martinique, did we not, Goodley?' Captain Goodley agreed politely. 'Well, gentlemen,' Barrington went on, 'I thank you. I am sure we shall be able to find something useful for you to do, for I am desperately short of men and, apart from the Highlanders and marines in this place and a garrison of the 63rd Foot holding the fort at Basse Terre, the enemy is at large in the island. We can scarcely claim to have subdued him by perching on the rim of these islands. Would you wish to serve together, or as guides to my corps' commanders?'

'I doubt whether we can all acquit ourselves as competent guides,' Kite put in hurriedly, appalled at Ranald's presumption.

'But we wish to assume the character of officers,' Ranald said.

Barrington sighed and flicked an ironic glance at Goodley. 'Yes, I thought you might,' he observed. 'However, I should point out, gentlemen, that I have a thousand matters demanding my attention...'

'I have an armed schooner at your immediate disposal, General Barrington. You have only to command me,' Kite put in hurriedly, wishing to dissociate himself from the clumsy, intemperate amateurishness of Ranald.

Barrington looked from Ranald to Kite, then smiled. 'Well, perhaps before leaping so eagerly into the unknown, you should know the worst. We have had word of a French squadron off Barbados and Commodore Moore has withdrawn all the ships-of-the-line and the frigates towards Prince Rupert's Bay in the island of Dominica to cover us. Unfortunately sickness in the fleet necessitated the transfer of three hundred troops to assist the working of the ships. Apart from the transports and your own schooner, Captain... Forgive me, I have forgotten your name...'

'Kite, sir.'

'Ah, yes. Well, we are effectively cut off, Captain Kite, for as we speak the French have crept out of the forest and are breaking ground beyond the walls of this fort.' Barrington grasped a crutch and gingerly set his gouty foot down on the floor with a wince. Goodley stepped forward to help, but Barrington shook his head. His face was contorted with pain as he rose to his feet, his face glistening with sweat. He caught his breath sufficiently to resume. 'Well, we cannot sit and await an outcome dictated by the enemy; we shall have to take matters into our own hands. Do you gentlemen prepare to land with your equipment... Have you your own victuals?'

'We have brought small arms, powder and shot,' said Ranald, 'but were hoping that you would–'

'I am able to victual the party, sir,' put in Kite hurriedly, earning a relieved glance of interest from Barrington, who turned to the papers before him.

'You shall take up scouting duties ... in a body, gentlemen, skirmish ahead of our advance. I trust that will suit your character as, er, officers.'

'Splendidly, sir,' Kite said, putting up a hand on to Ranald's shoulder. 'Come Harry, the general has a great deal to attend to.'

'How long d'you give 'em, Goodley?' Barrington asked as the adjutant returned from seeing the two men back to their boat.

'Oh, just long enough to draw the French fire, sir,' Goodley laughed, adding, 'though I must say the merchant master seemed devoid of the bluster of his friend.'

'Captain Kite,' mused Barrington. 'Yes. Now pass the word for Brigadier Clavering and Colonel Crump, we must break out of this place and make the confounded French dance to *our* tune.'

Ranald's eagerness to be in action was disappointed. Barrington spent a fortnight strengthening the defences of Fort Louis, working his garrison of Highlanders and marines hard. While Ranald and his fellow gentry lounged about the decks of the *Spitfire* or took one of her two boats and went wildfowling among the islands closing off the port to the southward, Kite and Da Silva better prepared the *Spitfire* for action.

They were ordered to be ready to move, but on the due day, towards the end of March 1759, Kite received a note from Goodley instructing him to send Ranald and the majority of his volunteers aboard the transports. *Spitfire* was to remain at anchor, but ready to proceed. The order however, did not come, and to the chagrin of those left aboard the schooner they remained behind when two of the transports weighed anchor and, in company, tacked offshore and stood to the east.

Word soon passed round that they had sailed to land raiding parties at St Anne's and St François, two towns along the coast of Grande Terre to the eastwards. But shortly before sunset two days later, Barrington himself came off in a boat. He had been preceded by Goodley, who arrived with a file of kilted Highlanders of the 42nd Foot and asked Kite if he had some method of 'embarking the General'. Kite roused out the canvas chair they had used to land the ladies on their northward progress the previous year and Barrington was brought on deck, to announce the *Spitfire* to be 'my flagship'. Asking for a chair to be placed on deck, he sat down, rested his gouty foot and ordered the schooner under weigh.

'Where are we bound, sir?' Kite asked.

Goodley stepped forward with a map and pointed. 'Here, Captain, to Le Gosier, just beyond Grand Bay. There,' Goodley indicated the two adjacent transports, 'you will see the *Elizabeth Bury* and the *Orford Castle* getting under weigh. They have three hundred men embarked. We are going to attack Le Gosier–'

'I should like to serve with you, Captain Goodley,' Kite said, abruptly breaking in.

'But your schooner?'

'Mr Da Silva, my sailing master and gunner, will tend to her.'

Goodley shrugged. 'As you wish, Captain Kite, as you wish. Now, sir, we shall stand offshore and lie to until daylight. We will land at Le Gosier at dawn.'

Kite dined with Barrington and Goodley in the cabin, which had been expanded into one large stateroom after the American cruise of the previous summer. Then he went on deck, and in a state of extreme tension remained there for the rest of the

277

night, dozing in Barrington's abandoned chair while the general occupied his own bunk. It was a moonless night, but the stars were bright enough to throw faint shadows across the deck as *Spitfire* lay hove to in the light trade wind. Astern of them they could see the pale sails as the transports rode easily in the low swell. To the north the mass of the Mornes Sainte Anne, dominating the island of Grande Terre, was dark against the star-spangled sky. Kite fancied that in the dark mass of the island he could discern Puella asleep beside him. He swore under his breath and took a turn up and down the deck, impatient for the first flush of dawn.

He must have fallen into a doze leaning against the taffrail, for the helmsmen's cough woke him with a start. 'Beg pardon, Cap'n Kite, but yon transport's hauled her main yard.'

Kite shook the fog and the megrims from his brain. He could see the nearer transport, the *Orford Castle* he thought, had trimmed her sails and a pallid feather of water rose round her apple bow. Beyond her, the second transport was in the act of following suit.

Kite nodded. 'Very well; let fly heads'l sheets and up helm!'

The helmsman acknowledged his order and the watch on deck stirred themselves into action. The schooner gave up holding

278

the natural forces in balance, swung and began to make way again. A few moments later *Spitfire* was heeling to the breeze, standing after her consorts and rapidly gaining on them.

The eastern extremity of Grand Bay was separated by the inlet leading to Le Gosier by a headland called Pointe de Verdure. Further to the east, the inlet was bounded on its other side by a mass of rocks and islets which broke the surf pounding the beach. Into the gully between, the transports' boats, laden with soldiers and covered by the anchored schooner, made their way. Having dropped their anchor, a rope was hurriedly led up the *Spitfire's* starboard side and seized to the anchor cable. With the spring secured, a little more cable was veered. The effect on the wind-rode *Spitfire* was to swing her broadside round, so that Da Silva had her guns directed on the sleeping village, the houses of which were showing in the dawn's early light. Sitting in his chair, Barrington stared through a glass, but the boats, grey shapes bristling with the dull sheen of bayonets and creeping like beetles over the dull purple-coloured sea, were almost within reach of the beach before the first puff of smoke told where a disturbed sentinel had discharged his musket in alarm. More puffs from widely differing spots followed before the sound of the first discharge reached the watchers offshore. Then the beetles merged with the shore. More cracks of musketry rolled towards them.

'They've landed,' snapped Barrington, rising. 'We shan't need your guns.' Goodley and Kite saw him into his sling and then followed him over the side into the waiting boat. *Spitfire's* seamen rowed them ashore in the wake of the troops and a few minutes later Kite splashed over the side of the boat into a few inches of water and turned to help Barrington.

'Forwards! Forwards!' Barrington insisted, waving them on.

A Highlander was left to assist the general, along with a corporal and two privates as guards. Goodley, Kite and the other gentlemen volunteers ran after the file of Highlanders already tumbling ashore from *Spitfire's* second boat. Passing a few local fishing boats drawn up on the beach, they made for a lane that rose steeply towards Le Gosier. From this position, all looked different. The horizon had closed in and the grand perspective of the view from the sea vanished. Now Le Gosier was a distant hint of roofs from which small clouds of smoke, some centred with a brief and fleeting flash of fire, produced an occasional whine as a spent musket ball passed them.

A few hundred yards up the rough lane,

the intensity of the fire was focused. It seemed to have pinned down half the force of Highlanders who lay sprawled on the ground, poking their muskets forward and seeking opportunities to return fire. A young officer grinned at them, 'Lieutenant Macdonald's working round to the right, sir…'

'Very well,' Goodley nodded to the subaltern. 'Keep 'em occupied,' then he turned and, ducking down, beckoned to his own file and the volunteers. 'Follow me. Sergeant?' Goodley called to a large Scot with a tall mitre-shaped grenadier hat. The man looked up. 'Follow me with your grenadiers…'

The party moved off to the left, taking shelter behind a low bank and then, moving on, a stony wall. At first they were unobserved, but then a ball struck a rock outcrop and whined past Kite's ear. Goodley raised his hat on his sword; a fusillade of balls spun it away and then in the wake of the discharge the adjutant was over the low wall, followed by the 42nd's grenadiers. Caught up in the breathless excitement of the swiftness of events, barely understanding what was going on and regretting his almost sleepless night, Kite followed. Armed with a ship's cutlass and a pistol, he was conscious that he was the only one of the Antiguan gentry that moved forward with the soldiers.

The rest, most armed with muskets, but without bayonets, threw themselves against the wall and gave the grenadiers supporting fire by firing wildly at the wooden buildings that appeared in their front behind a few trees. Kite found himself stumbling towards these and suddenly saw a face at an open window. The soldier was taking aim at him down the foreshortened length of a musket barrel. Running forward, he raised his pistol, but the soldier fired first. The flash and bang of his discharge were translated into a loud sucking of air as the ball passed Kite. He fired his own pistol. The next moment he crashed against the wall of the house and looked back. The heads of the Antiguan gentlemen volunteers bobbed where they reloaded, but the red tide of infantrymen had passed on and he seemed quite alone, leaning, gasping for breath against this alien dwelling. Somewhere in the distance, the crackle and rattle of small-arms fire rent the air, accompanied by shouts and screams. But it all seemed strangely remote.

Although temporarily deafened by the rapid and close discharge of the French musket and his own pistol, Kite thought he detected movement within the building. It struck him as faintly ridiculous that the two of them, intent on murdering one another, were separated by only the thickness of the planking. He looked at his pistol. The means to reload it were in his pocket, but the time taken would place him and his opponent back on an equal footing. Surely, the defending Frenchman would be occupied in reloading his own weapon now? Suddenly resolute, Kite jerked into action, moving along the wall to turn the corner.

Here the noise of the fire-fight was suddenly all about him. The whine and thud of ball was accompanied by the shouts of excited men, some calling for reassurance, some blaspheming, some shouting instructions.

'Watch yer flank, Dougal laddie!'

'Oh God, ma fuckin' leig!'

'Merde!'

'Eh bien, François, eh bien!'

The door to the dwelling swung half open on Kite's right. For a split second he saw the soldier in a white linen uniform with pale yellow facings, saw the astonishment in his eyes change to anger as the long gleaming barrel of the musket again foreshortened. But they were too close, almost stumbling over each other as the soldier made to fire. Savagely Kite swept the clumsy cutlass upwards, feeling the bite of the blade as it hacked halfway through the French infantryman's extended left arm. His right hand fumbled the trigger and the flint sparked. The weapon discharged itself alongside Kite's left ear.

Kite could hear nothing, but he saw his antagonist gasp with the pain of his wound. The French soldier dropped the musket with a clatter, reeling back into the darkness. Kite followed, the impetus of the heavy cutlass swing drawing him into the house after the collapsing infantryman. As the wounded soldier fell back, his companion, sharing the same billet and still in his shirt-tails, swung his own musket towards the intruder. The gun barked and the ball stung Kite's left shoulder with the searing sensation of a burn, but then the formidable horror of the extending bayonet stabbed at him.

Kite put up his hand, uncaring if the blade severed his fingers, eager only that the evil point was deflected from his face. By the greatest good fortune, the lunge of the enemy soldier took the muzzle of the musket past Kite's extended hand, and though the point of the steel nicked his left cheek, his hand struck the barrel and parried the thrust aside. Kite dragged his right hand back, trying to raise the cutlass for a cut; instead the back of the blade, two-thirds of which was blunt, drew up between the infantryman's legs. The unfortunate wretch gasped and dropped to his knees as Kite recovered his blade and drove it forward, running the soldier through. Gasping, Kite withdrew the cutlass and swung round, half aware of a movement behind him. The man he had first wounded had fallen back on to his haunches and squatted nursing his wound, watching the outcome. Seeking an opening to kill the Englishman, the Frenchman grabbed his dropped musket, and thrust it between Kite's legs.

Kite stumbled, but now mad with blood-lust he flicked the cutlass blade by sharply pronating his wrist. The heavy blade caught the infantryman under the chin, driving his lower jaw upwards. Kite crashed into the wall as the Frenchman's head jerked violently backwards. Bracing himself against the wall, Kite swiftly extended his hand no more than an inch or two, and the cutlass point penetrated the Frenchman's neck. Blood poured from the soldier's throat as he scrabbled desperately at his punctured windpipe; Kite stepped past him and into the open air. Less than a minute had passed since he had sensed the faint movement of the enemy soldier through the wall.

Kite could see the red jackets and dark blue-black kilts of the bare-kneed High-landers as they ran about, their claymores gleaming, or fired their muskets into dwellings along the street of the village as they flushed the defenders out. A few lay inert, alongside the dead and dying enemy in their white coats, corpses prepared for death long before by their master, King Louis, and his sepulchral colours.

He ran on, spurning the horror he had left in the house, yet eager for more blood. Turning a corner, he came upon the main street of Le Gosier and his way was blocked by a line of red-coated Highlanders, their backs to him, formed up in ranks three deep. Across the entire space of a small square beyond, Kite caught a glimpse of an opposing line, the now familiar white coats topped by black tricornes. As he came up behind the Highlanders, he heard Goodley's voice barking orders, then the almost simultaneous snap of flint on frizzen. The ripple of musketry from the white-coated ranks spewed flame and smoke. The balls smacked into the adjacent walls and gaps appeared in the ranks ahead, as the Highlanders fell backwards and the men in the rear, urged by the halberds of the non-commissioned officers, moved forwards into the gaps. The Highlanders responded with rapid platoon fire, mowing down the French before they had discharged their second volley. The British musketry was relentlessly efficient, blasting the enemy line before rolling forward. Drawing their claymores as they cheered, the kilted Highlanders, grenadier and line companies, fell upon the wavering French. The white-clad infantry broke.

Kite ran with the Scots, and butchered with them, and chased the last remnants of the enemy from the square and in and out of a few houses until either they were dead, hidden, or had surrendered. Finally exhausted, Kite answered the call to re-form as Barrington hobbled into view on the arm of his attending soldier.

Goodley held out a sword taken from the dead officer commanding the French garrison. 'Le Gosier is yours, sir.'

Barrington looked about him and nodded. 'See the wounded are taken back to the ships, Mr Goodley. The rest form up in column of march with two platoons out ahead under Lieutenant Macdonald. I intend to take the French siege lines before Fort Louis in the rear. By the by, where's Captain Kite?'

'Here, sir.' Kite stepped forward.

'My God, Captain!' Barrington exclaimed, seeing the bloody state of Kite. 'You've seen some service, by the state of you. Your fellows by the wall said you'd run off! Well, well, 'tis as well you are still with us. If you'd been taken the French might have shot you as a spy.' Barrington laughed, and was joined by the officers and men round about him. 'Upon my soul, they might indeed!'

Twelve

The Widow

Although Kite returned to *Spitfire* along with the wounded, who were withdrawn to the anchored transports, Barrington's little column set out to march back to Fort Louis overland. As they approached the fort to attack the besiegers, more British troops sallied out, nipping the French between two forces. Having thus relieved his own position at Fort Louis, taking a battery of enemy 24-pounders in the process, Barrington waited for the return of Clavering and Crump from their raids on St Anne's and St François. At this time there arrived in the road the remaining transports, which had been blown to leeward of Guadeloupe, bringing welcome reinforcements to the general.

Then Barrington learned of the death of the garrison commander at Basse Terre, the only other British toehold on Guadeloupe, on the other island. An accidental magazine explosion had killed several men, while the besieging French were in the final stages of erecting a heavy battery. Barrington immediately appointed an officer to replace the garrison commander, and to expedite his arrival Kite was asked to convey this officer aboard *Spitfire*. The schooner was got under weigh and stood south for Pointe du Vieux Fort as soon as the newly appointed officer clambered aboard. Rounding the headland and hauling her foretopsail yard, *Spitfire* made up for the Rade de Basse Terre. As she coasted into the anchorage she exchanged a few shots at extreme range with a French gun, an event which was attended by hardly any danger but a great deal of self-satisfaction. Kite, however, took little further part in the action at Basse Terre beyond making a demonstration before the enemy gun battery at closer range and firing a rolling broadside ashore. De Silva and his gunners cherished the moment long afterwards, but it did little damage beyond throwing up mounds of earth and stones along the beach, holing a fishing boat and killing three goats. This diversion was carried out in support of the sally made from Basse Terre, and though its tactical significance was negligible, the breakout of the garrison drove the enemy from their lines, took their heavy artillery and raised the siege.

Kite returned to Pointe-à-Pitre and waited upon Barrington in Fort Louis with the news of success. With the town of Basse

Terre secured, Barrington went over to the offensive. Having relinquished the shoreline to the British, the French force on Guadeloupe was thinly spread and tied to the defence of strong points guarding the farms and plantations of the colonists, most of which lay in isolated valleys with rugged terrain between them. Barrington still retained a brace of bomb vessels by way of naval support and possessed the manoeuvrability conferred by the presence of the transports. He was therefore able to land his troops at will, advance into the interior and destroy the French positions at leisure.

The strongest of these lay above Mahaut Bay, where the French had been receiving supplies from the Dutch on the island of St Eustatia. Thirteen hundred men and six guns under the command of Brigadier Clavering were landed on the shores of the bay. Fighting their way through dense undergrowth and turning the French positions in rapid succession, the 4th and 42nd Foot drove after the enemy, the Highlanders wielding their claymores as they closed with their opponents, hand to hand. Clavering never gave his enemy a moment's rest, even at night, when his guns played on the French to keep them under constant pressure. Falling back, setting fire to the sugar-cane fields and breaking down bridges, the French attempted to delay

Clavering's advance as he struck south, over the narrow quasi-isthmus that lay between the twin massifs. In an energetic pursuit that brooked no obstruction, Clavering's men outflanked the French, who again retired towards another strong defensive position at Petit Bourg.

Here, however, Barrington had sent a bomb vessel from Pointe-à-Pitre, offering Kite a contract as a hired vessel if he would take *Spitfire* in support. Kite declined the offer, since he would be obliged to submit command of his beloved schooner to a naval officer, probably a superannuated lieutenant transferred from the *Orford Castle* or one of the other transports, but he volunteered *Spitfire* on exchange for a new letter of marque, to be issued in due form at Antigua on the general's written instruction. Having attracted Barrington's notice at Le Gosier, the general was delighted to reach this economic expedient and placed marines aboard *Spitfire,* making her a naval auxiliary.

Thus Kite watched through his glass as the first shells began to burst among the lines and redoubts round Petit Bourg. The bomb vessel's huge 13-inch mortar, situated amidships, boomed out every few minutes and the shells could be clearly seen, arcing up into the air with their faint trail of sparks thrown off by the fizzing fuse. At first the shells burst prematurely in the air in the last split-second of their trajectory; then they landed and there was a brief hiatus before they blew apart. But after these ranging shots the fuses were cut to the correct length and the shells landed and blew up at almost the same instant, driving the unfortunate French from their positions. Under this distant bombardment, against which they were impotent, the enemy abandoned their entrenchments before they could withdraw their cannon.

Clavering arrived shortly afterwards and cleared Petit Bourg of the last tenacious defenders of the little town. Then he rested his men during two days of torrential rain. During the downpour Crump and a further seven hundred soldiers had been on the move. Following Clavering round to Mahaut Bay, they had completed the destruction of the French depôt there before joining Clavering. Waiting at Petit Bourg for the rain to ease, the reinforced Clavering prepared to move south again, along the coast of Cabes Terre towards Sainte Marie.

By now the entire French force on Guadeloupe had rallied at Sainte Marie, where a strong position had been prepared. But the French placed too much reliance upon the impassable nature of the river and the narrow paths leading round the inland flank of the redoubt and its outlying trenches. Having suffered continually from suddenly finding the enemy's red coats flitting through the forest in their rear a moment before opening their withering and rolling musketry, the French officers' improvident neglect proved fatal.

A large party was sent to turn the French position, while the British artillery was moved up to confront the enemy lines. The guns had fired only a few rounds when the French abandoned their position as the word spread that British infantry were once more in their rear. This retreat was less precipitate than at first appeared, for a second prepared position lay on the heights above the little port. This was flanked by ravines and dense rainforest, its approach congested by undergrowth, but the British moved their guns steadily forward, while once again flanking parties advanced on either wing.

Seeing the British making yet another en-circling movement, and in an attempt to take advantage of the extended nature of Clavering's little force, the French left the shelter of their position and, covered by the fire of their own artillery, moved down the hill to engage the British centre and decide the matter. But Clavering was equal to this crisis and gathered the remnant of his troops. These were hurled against the

French and drove them back towards their entrenchments, and then in disorder from their works. The following day the local planters, fearing their rich lands would be set on fire, asked for terms. Barrington granted the French inhabitants a liberal capitulation and the wealthiest French island in the West Indies transferred its allegiance, for the time being, to Great Britain.

Hardly had the instrument of surrender been signed, than a cutter ran into the bay with the news that General Beauharnais and French reinforcements had arrived at Martinique, but this did not prevent Barrington taking Marie Galante. He then secured the new colony, appointed a government and a few days later received word at Fort Louis that a discouraged Beauharnais had sailed away. Crump was appointed as governor and the troops redeployed: three battalions were left as a garrison, the others dispersed. Barrington took a further three back to England with him and the 42nd Foot, the Black Watch, were sent on to North America.

When Barrington and the transports left for England and the Highlanders embarked for America, Kite resolved to return to Antigua. It was the end of May and before the hurricane season was upon them, he wished to decide his future. Squaring the foretopsail yard and paying out the fore- and mainsheets, *Spitfire* headed for St John's. Astern of them the island of Guadeloupe was left in the possession of the British army. The soldiers, however, were yet to suffer from their most implacable enemy; in the remaining seven months of the year, eight hundred were to die of yellow jack.

Kite spent a month in Antigua after the capture of Guadeloupe. On their return the soldiers of the 38th Foot disembarked without Major Robertson; he had been one of eleven officers killed in the capture of the island and his widow plunged into a conspicuous and affecting mourning.

But Kite also returned to bad news. Dorothea lay dying, and when Kite went to see her he was appalled. The once handsome, voluptuous and apparently age-less black woman was almost beyond recognition. Dorothea had metamorphosed into a shrivelled husk whose body hardly disturbed the clean white sheet laid over her.

Seeing her visitor, her eyes gleamed with alarm and she held out her hand for Puella. Kite regarded the two women, the one standing, the other lying inert, linked by their clasped hands. His heart filled with pity, sadness and regret.

'Dorothea...' he began, but Puella restrained his forward movement.

'She does not like you, Kite,' Puella said with a flat finality.

'What is the matter with her?' he asked, overwhelmed by a sense of desperate inadequacy.

'She is dying, Kite; she stopped eating, she does not want to live any more, now that Mr Mulgrave is dead.'

'But–' Kite began, then caught himself. For all his multiple kindnesses, Mulgrave had saddled Kite with a mighty obligation in return. He saw Dorothea watching him closely, saw the gleam of febrile intelligence in her eyes, and felt the conviction that Dorothea knew all about Mulgrave's deception. How could she then so hate him, if it was Mulgrave, her trusted and much admired lover who had, in the end, deceived her?

And then it struck Kite that, despite the protection and the advantage conferred by their association with himself and Mulgrave, these women hated their white men. He looked sharply at Puella.

'And Puella,' he asked quietly, 'do you hate me too?' Puella looked at Dorothea, as though for guidance, but the dying woman kept her eyes steadfastly upon Kite. It was clear Puella would offer him no comfort while Dorothea lived and he felt overwhelmed with weariness. 'Well, Puella,' he said, 'you are a free woman, you have a competence upon which to live. You can afford this house upon your own account and Wentworth will protect you...'

A rasping came from Dorothea and Puella bent to hear her dying friend. As she straightened up, Kite asked, 'What did she say?'

'She tells me that you will go away soon and that I may stay with you...'

'*May* stay, or *must* stay?'

'May stay, Kite.'

'And when will you choose?' he asked, his voice crackling with despair. But Puella merely shrugged.

Kite slept aboard *Spitfire* and daily attended Wentworth's premises, where the two men sought to mature their plans for the future. Every evening, Kite returned to the house to pay his respects to Dorothea, but he exchanged no more than formal remarks with Puella, and the gulf between them grew wider.

On several evenings, after these depressing visits, he dined with Wentworth and attended an assembly or two. In the aftermath of the acquisition of Guadeloupe and the return of the island's soldiery, these were gay affairs, by no means confined to the white population, but embracing the better part of the wealthier townsfolk, many of whom were mulatto or quadroon. To her regret, Mrs Robertson was prevented from attending by the conventions of widowhood, but her chagrin was increased upon learning that the handsome Captain Kite had at last abandoned his 'nigger whore' and was making his way in polite society. Anxious to secure a new protector, Mrs Robertson fell victim to panic, becoming desperate to catch the eligible bachelor before some other schemer secured his affections. To this end she browbeat Wentworth and contrived to be at his rooms one evening when Kite was known to be calling. She had removed her black lace lappets and her black dress had fallen from her splendid shoulders so that her ample bosom was indecorously exposed to view.

'Captain Kite,' she gushed, smiling and extending a hand to him, 'what a pleasure.' He bent politely over it and she seized his, drawing him down beside her, her features eager at his proximity. Despite his black servants, a sweaty and blushing Wentworth improbably pleaded a lack of lime juice to absent himself at this moment, and Mrs Robertson came swiftly to the point.

'Captain Kite,' she said, boldly placing her hand between his thighs, 'you are a most arresting man and I am deeply affected by you...' Her breath was hot on his face and the scent of her and the movement of her hand disturbed him. He felt the mounting flush of lust and twisted round. Relaxing, sure of her conquest, Mrs Robertson lay back, opening her legs and drawing up her skirt with a rustle of black silk, exposing petticoats and slender stockinged calves.

'I will do anything for you, William, anything...'

'Anything?' he whispered, stupidly wrestling with his conscience, longing to lose himself in her willing flesh and wash away the confusion in his soul. He half heard Makepeace's war cry as rising lust made him tug at himself.

'Anything,' she repeated with breathless ardour, exposing herself naked above her stockings and looking down at him as he disencumbered himself of his breeches. 'Oh, God...'

She sensed him hesitate, then quickly reassured him. 'Wentworth will not trouble us, I have seen to that...'

Kite's member sprung free and he frowned. 'What? How?'

She laughed and eased herself receptively. 'Oh, my darling don't trouble yourself, come to Kitty. Here ... here...' She reached down to guide him.

'But how,' he insisted and she saw a dangerous gleam in his eye.

'Why, silly, like this,' and she stroked his throbbing penis.

He looked at her, horrified. The extent of

her scheming struck him at the moment of entry and he recoiled, priapic, foolish and half spending in his excitement and disgust.

'You are rejecting me?' Kitty Robertson could scarce believe the fact.

Kite had stood up. He was tucking his shirt tails in and settling his breeches. 'No, I am not rejecting you,' he temporised. 'I am treating you like a whore...'

'But you like whores!' She was desperate in her disarrangement, but it was her mood that turned now. 'Or are only nigger whores to your taste?' she snarled.

Kite swiped at her, but she evaded the blow with a grin of triumph, standing up with such a sudden motion that he fell back, still adjusting his clothing. Her skirt fell to the floor and she thrust her head forward, her expression furious.

'You nigger-loving *bastard!*' she hissed.

He regretted his attempt to strike her, it cancelled out her humiliation and made her the victim, sparking her spirited riposte. 'And to think I considered you a gentleman! You are nothing but a–'

But Kite was provoked and a mounting anger overtook him. 'Be silent!' he snapped. Then recovering himself before matters flew utterly out of hand said, 'We have both behaved foolishly and impetuously...'

She was shaking her head. 'Oh, no, you shall not say so! I will not have it! I will not have *you* make a fool of me, by God!' She would submit to no soothing; she was wildly indignant, outraged, a singular contrast to her wanton eagerness of a moment before. Kite stilled his protest, letting her have her head. What did it matter? If she and Wentworth kept their mouths shut, he was not going to gain any capital from the unhappy and awkward incident. He suddenly turned and picked up his hat. The unexpected retrograde movement caught her unawares and she paused.

'For God's sake, madam, make Wentworth happy!' Kite said. 'He is rich beyond your late husband's competence and is probably sweating miserably below in an agony of disappointment that you should frig him, then offer yourself to me.'

In the brief, calculating hiatus that followed, Kite hurried from the room and down the stairs where he ran into Wentworth. 'Go to her, for God's sake, and take your pleasure; I love Puella and have no wish for her, she's as eager as an alley cat.'

The regrettable encounter with Mrs Robertson brought to an end Kite's period of irresolution. He had been half-hearted and uncertain in his dealings with Wentworth, unsure of his objectives as much as his motives. After he had drowned himself in what he privately considered to be wanton murder at La Gosier, this further disquieting evidence of his own weakness acted like a slamming door. When, ten days later, Dorothea died and Puella agreed to accompany him wherever he went, he realised that her submission was the only thing that encumbered his mind. There was nothing beyond the considerations of business to keep him in Antigua, and even these lessened when Wentworth let it be known that his proposal of marriage had been accepted by Mrs Kitty Robertson. For propriety's sake, the wedding would have to be deferred until after a year's mourning, but Mrs Robertson could not entirely hide her satisfaction: it would make her one of the richest women in the Antilles. As far as Kite was concerned, her triumph was unconcealed.

'She is a very bad woman for you, Kite,' Puella remarked one evening after they had passed her carriage when out walking along the waterfront. Kite looked at Puella. He had mooted the evening walk as a means of attempting to re-establish some contact with her, though he had not returned to sleep under her roof. He had been pleased when she accepted, for he did not want to humiliate her in front of the townsfolk of St John's after the death of Dorothea, when the excuse that she was tending the ailing mulatto was at an end. Her comment about

Mrs Robertson was the first remark she had made which showed any returning consideration for him.

'Why do you say that?' he asked.

'Because she wanted you. After the major died, she thought that you could throw over your black woman and marry her.'

'How did you know that?'

Puella shrugged. 'I know it.'

'But I did not, and now she is to marry Mr Wentworth.'

'He will make her rich and she will make him miserable.'

'Like I made you miserable?' he asked tenderly. Puella walked on saying nothing. 'Tell me something, Puella,' Kite went on, 'why did Dorothea so dislike me? Did she attribute Mr Mulgrave's disappearance to me?'

'Of course. She believed you had tricked him and that he had to go back to England.'

'I see. That is not what happened at all. Mr Mulgrave made me tell Dorothea that he had drowned. He said something about her having foretold he would drown and that it was best that she thought so.' Puella said nothing, so he went on. 'You see, Mr Mulgrave had to return to England, he went home to ease his fever and he had a wife in England. Did Dorothea know that?'

Puella shrugged again. 'Perhaps she did, I don't know.'

'The sad and stupid thing is, Puella, Mr Mulgrave is still alive…'

'No!' Puella shook her head. 'No, Mr Mulgrave is dead,' she said firmly. 'He died in the water.'

Kite held his peace. What did it matter? Dead or alive, Puella would believe what Dorothea had told her, such had been the mulatto woman's hold over her younger friend. Kite felt, with some sadness, that he had learned that whatever benefits of civilisation one conferred on these Africans, no matter how one sought to ameliorate their condition, no matter how much one was devoted to them, one could not make them anything other than Africans.

'I tell you something important, Kite.' Puella broke into his unconsciously arrogant musing. He felt her draw closer to him as they turned and began to walk back towards the house. It was already dark, the last rosy flush of sunset in the western sky was already fading and the air had assumed the first slight chill of the night. 'I am pleased that you have told me what happened to Mr Mulgrave. It is sad that Dorothea had to be left behind, but now Puella has said that she will come with you if you are going to England…'

'And if I go to America?'

'America, then, only you must take Puella.'

'Do you love me, Puella?' he asked in a low voice, leaning towards her so that a passing couple remarked on their preoccupation.

'You must come to me tonight, Kite ... but there is something important to tell you.'

Kite chuckled, his heart lifting. 'No, nothing is as important as what you have already told me.'

'Yes, something is more important. You must be careful of Mrs Robertson. She will influence Mr Wentworth, especially after you have gone. She will try and ruin your business.'

'You think she is that vindictive?'

'I do not understand "vindictive", but I know she is your enemy.'

Puella's warning crystallised Kite's intentions. The following day he called upon Wentworth and announced that he wished to realise his entire capital and that he intended to leave the island before the middle of June. Wentworth could not see Kite's logic until Kite explained there was none.

'I am resolved to leave the Antilles, my dear fellow, and not to return,' Kite explained. 'The place has too many unhappy memories.'

Wentworth thought of Kite doting upon

his late son and agreed. 'It will reduce my ability to give credit, but...'

'Banker's drafts will suffice, though a quantity of currency and bullion will be necessary for contingent expenses.'

Wentworth nodded. 'I have moidores, specie and a little bullion upon which I can readily lay my hands,' he said.

Kite smiled wryly. The 'little' bullion amused him. 'That will do very well. The rest in drafts.'

'To be drawn against Coutts' in London?'

'No,' said Kite, 'against Verhagen in New York.'

Wentworth shook his head. 'That is impossible. I have exhausted my credit with Cornelis until the next season's cane is in. He shipped me three large consignments of wine, timber, flax, notions and other fashionable fol-de-rols. The freight rates were ruinous and the underwriters' premiums exorbitant. I have yet to move much of the stuff out of my warehouse ... I'm sorry. It must be London... Does that matter?'

Slowly, Kite shook his head. So, this was how fate finally compromised him. It was funny how the fatal blow came from a quarter from which it was least expected. He recalled Julius Caesar and the death blow from Brutus. He looked at Wentworth, but Wentworth lacked the guilt of Brutus;

Wentworth was no friend turned political assassin, merely a man of commerce, venturing capital against an anticipated market. The risk made Wentworth sweat, Kite noticed, as his friend mopped his brow.

Kite wondered if he was seeing shadows, like Dorothea had; was it the vague umbral spectre of fate that, at that particular moment, lay behind Wentworth's lack of credit with the Dutch banker in New York? Kite shook his head again. 'No; I was minded to go to New York, but I can as easily change my plans.'

'You may have as much in moidores as you wish, William, I do not mean to discommode you.'

'You don't discommode me,' Kite said, smiling and rising to his feet. 'Until tomorrow, then. And have Garvey here with a bill of sale for my shares in Da Silva's schooner. I shall offer them to him.'

'No, let me buy her from you, you'll get nothing from the Portugoose.'

'In gold, then.'

'Yes,' Wentworth nodded, 'in gold. Sovereigns, if you wish.'

'As you please.' And picking up his hat, Kite left.

Part Four

Wind

Thirteen

The Hurricane

On the eve of his proposed departure for North America, Kite ran into Captain Makepeace and, inviting his old commander back to the rented house, agreed to embark a consignment of twenty slaves just then brought in by the *Enterprize* from Benin. The slaves were destined for Kingston, Jamaica, and Makepeace was not keen to delay loading molasses and rum for England, fretful that, already late in the season, he might be caught by a hurricane before he got clear of the islands.

'If you're bound for the American coast, I'd be obliged if you'd look favourably upon the task,' Makepeace pleaded, as they sat in the small courtyard set behind a high wall separating them from the hurly-burly of the St John's waterfront. The sun was setting and the sky was suffused with a rich peach hue. Kite was disposed to be cordial and laughingly agreed as the two men drank glasses of mimbo. 'You have done well, as I predicted,' Makepeace said, watching Puella as she settled quietly beside them. 'And you,

Puella, are more beautiful than I could have imagined.'

Puella lowered her eyes and remained silent; she was uneasy in Makepeace's presence, unable to adjust to the alteration in his relationship with either Kite or herself. Moreover, she did not want Kite to carry slaves in the *Spitfire*. The schooner was already loaded with a full cargo of muscovado and rum, some of which was bound for consignees in Savannah, where Kite intended replacing the discharged commodities with cotton. His returns would be modest, but with no personal contacts in Britain he did not wish to venture a speculation on a cargo which would be difficult to sell. However, despite his misgivings, he agreed to purchase a quantity of elephant's ivory from Makepeace.

'I hear you are a man of considerable substance,' Makepeace said as they concluded their transaction.

'I doubt that I could match your own substance, Captain, but you did me a considerable service when you introduced me to Mr Mulgrave. He was most generous to me as well as to Wentworth, his main protégé. I was quite undeserving.'

'I daresay you will benefit further from his munificence, then,' Makepeace remarked, helping himself to more mimbo from the jug.

Kite frowned. 'Oh. In what way?'

'Why, have you not heard? Mulgrave is dead. I would have thought his attorney, what was his name…?'

'Mr Garvey,' put in Puella, sitting up and taking more than a casual interest.

'That's it, Garvey, I'd have thought he would have let you know. Well, no matter; Mulgrave has been dead for some time. Garvey will have the details. I'm surprised you knew nothing of it.'

Kite looked at Puella. His expression was contrite; there was no need for words to pass between them. Dorothea had been right. 'Do you know the manner of his death?' Kite asked.

'Yes, he was taking passage on a wherry on the Thames when it was overset by a passing squall.'

'Then he drowned,' said Kite, and Makepeace nodded, sipping the mimbo reflectively. 'Well, I'll be damned,' Kite said and Puella stirred and silently withdrew. The sun had set and the tropical night was swiftly descending upon them; Puella habitually sought her bed early, particularly if Kite was attending to his affairs.

Kite watched her leave, her tall figure upright and walking with that peculiarly fluid grace that suggested regal ancestry. He sensed her isolation and loneliness and his heart went out to her. He was about to

313

make his excuses and hint that it was time for Makepeace to leave, when the captain poured himself another glass of mimbo and looked round the courtyard as the cool of the night eased the white men's discomfort.

'I am getting old, Kite, and am of a mind to settle soon. I have a place in Liverpool and I increasingly regret leaving it. So far I have avoided most of the plagues of Guinea, Benin and these infested islands, but a man always runs ahead of the fates. How I have avoided the yaws, I confess I don't know, but the devil, they say, looks after his own. I now own three ships besides the whole of the *Enterprize:* I acquired the *Adventure*, the *Endeavour* and the *Ambition* quite recently. The first is a fine frigate-built ship, the second a brig and the third a snow. They were all built as Bristolmen, but Liverpool has entirely eclipsed that port now, and they came cheap. They are all in good condition and now, run on Liverpool lines, are returning healthy profits. I was looking at your schooner today, she would make a small Guineaman it is true, but she would make a better privateer and I hear you already have a letter of marque and reprisal in her name.'

Kite nodded, uncertain where this rather smug catalogue of success was leading them. He was not long left in suspense. Makepeace topped up his glass.

314

'Well now, Kite, I have a proposition to make to you. With your schooner and a portion of your capital, I wish to offer you a full half-share in the ownership of this little fleet. For myself the capital will secure me some retirement with my family and the peace of mind knowing that you, as a younger man, will continue the business to the mutual benefit of us both. In particular, of course, I shall seek assurances, drawn up by due process, that the inheritance of my children will be protected; in that I trust you implicitly. For you it would be a grand opportunity...' Makepeace paused. 'Now, what do you say, eh?' Makepeace picked up his glass and drank deeply, watching Kite's reaction.

Kite nodded slowly. The news of Mulgrave's death, sad though it was, did not, he thought, have any further bearing upon his own life. If Garvey knew of it, it was certain Wentworth did. Why Wentworth had concealed it from him was a mystery, but not one that he, at this late moment, considered worth troubling himself with. He did not know how long Kitty Robertson had been intriguing with Wentworth, but he thought vaguely that she might have had something to do with the matter. It was quite possible, he thought, that she might have been manipulating the younger man for some time long before their betrothal. Wentworth was certainly not the most engaging of the island's potential lovers, but he was probably the most discreet. More certainly, he was the most liquid in terms of plunderable funds. Kite dismissed the train of thought. Despite the risks, he was wearied of St John's and felt the tug of England and the rain-swept hills of his native Cumbria. For a moment he thought of his father, and Helen, and how the letter he had written to his sister had probably never reached her, for he had received no reply, despite giving her the address of Cornelis Verhagen in New York, with whom Wentworth was in regular correspondence. But a shadow still lay over a return to Cumbria and now it confronted him.

'Well?' prompted Makepeace.

'I am attracted by your kind offer,' Kite temporised, wondering how far he could trust this man whose worst excesses he had witnessed.

'Go on, something's troubling you. Don't you trust me? I am offering you a partnership, Kite, a partnership. I am inviting you to become an inmate at my house in the knowledge that you have opinions about my conduct, even evidence of my peccadilloes, that once known in certain places could blight my life – or what's left of it.' Makepeace shifted in his chair and sat upright. He was a little drunk, but his thoughts were lucid and his voice only a trifle slurred. 'But consider, Kite, I *trust* you, upon my word I do.' Makepeace paused, letting the import of his word sink in. Then he sighed and added, 'So you may trust me and tell me what it is you fear by returning to England... Oh yes, I know of your intentions, you have touched upon the matter before, remember?'

'Well,' Kite pulled himself together, 'I should need a house in Liverpool, and it concerns me how Puella would be regarded there.'

Makepeace waved aside the problems. 'I shall see that you have a domicile befitting your standing as a wealthy sea-captain and merchant. As for Puella, if you don't become a fool and marry the girl, you may keep her as a mistress in quiet propriety in Liverpool. You have no children, so the matter may be managed, and since she is free, you will have little to concern you. I cannot speak for London, but Liverpool is a rising place and a man with money and standing is not too pressed if he is discreet and does not behave scandalously.' Makepeace smiled. 'And I have never seen you as a man likely to behave scandalously... Does that ease your mind?'

'A little...'

'There is still the matter of ... what is it that ails you, eh?' Makepeace queried.

'A murder.'

'Ahh. I see.' Makepeace nodded. He neither saw nor comprehended. 'Would you care to elaborate?' he prompted.

Kite recounted the unforgettable moments of that afternoon, omitting only his revulsion at the monstrous-headed baby that had lain between Susie's shuddering thighs. It seemed so long ago, so detached from his present existence under the velvet, star-spangled tropical sky, and he had become so different from the long-legged youth who had run in terror from the Hebblewhites' barn.

When he had finished, Makepeace asked, 'But you are in fact quite innocent?'

Kite nodded. 'Oh. Yes. Though I dream sometimes, less often than in the past but still occasionally, that I *did* kill the girl.'

'But that is merely an hallucination.'

'Yes,' Kite agreed, 'of course it is.'

'Then you have nothing to fear.'

'How so?'

'Well, you are innocent in the first place and if, in the unlikely event that you are recognised, or the brothers hear of your presence in Liverpool, the matter is brought before the justices, you are now a man of sufficient means to defend yourself.'

Kite considered the matter. 'And does this confession not tempt you to withdraw your offer?'

318

Makepeace shook his head with a smile. 'I know of few people less likely to commit murder than you, Kite. Your confession, as you call it, alters my proposal not one whit.'

Kite sighed. Makepeace had not seen him butchering French soldiers at Le Gosier. 'Very well. Though I must make plain that I shall not attempt any concealment. If my name is to be linked with yours, then I shall have perforce to take, as it were, the war into the enemy's camp and visit my father... If he still lives.'

'Of course, of course. So we may conclude that to be the principle of our partnership, then.' Makepeace held out the jug to refill Kite's glass. '"Makepeace and Kite" has a certain ring about it, don't you agree?'

Kite smiled as the mimbo ran darkly into his glass. 'Let me see how the land lies in Cumbria before we put up a shop sign in Liverpool,' he said.

'As you wish, m'dear fellow. Now to the precise nature of the sum I am asking...'

Kite called for more candles and they discussed figures until late, but when Makepeace reeled out into the night they had shaken hands, each expressing his satisfaction at the proposed new venture.

When Kite woke late next morning, Puella had been up for some time. His head was furred from the rum and the sun beat remorselessly in through the open window. Slowly the events of the previous evening trickled back into his consciousness: the news of Mulgrave's death, the knowledge that it had been concealed from him, Makepeace's proposal, his own confession, his acceptance and then the agreed figure completing the transaction. It was also, he realised with a start, the day appointed for the departure of the *Spitfire*. He had much to do and would have to call on Garvey before sailing.

'Damnation!' He leapt from the bed.

Puella came into the room silently as he threw the last of his clothes into a portmanteau, hurriedly preparing to leave the rented house.

'Kite,' she said, holding out a scrap of paper, her face a mask.

'What is it?' he asked looking up, but she merely waggled her hand impatiently, rustling the paper. The abrupt and almost monosyllabic nature of her communication with him marked the distances that remained separating them. Taking the folded note he opened it. It was written in a vaguely familiar hand that Kite could not identify; he looked at the simple date scrawled upon it.

'Where did you get this?'

'Mr Garvey.'

Of course, now he recognised the

attorney's script. 'You called on Garvey at this time of the morning?'

'It is not early,' she said flatly, waiting for the significance of the date to sink in.

Kite looked at the paper again, and then up at Puella. 'This date,' Kite began, feeling the lump in his throat, 'this date ... this is when Charlie...'

Puella nodded, her dark eyes filled with tears. 'It is also the date that Mr Mulgrave died.'

Kite recalled Dorothea's dark mutterings. 'Well, I'm damned!'

From Jamaica, *Spitfire* made for Savannah where she discharged her part-cargo of sugar and loaded cotton bales. It was the height of the hurricane season, but Kite reasoned that he was sufficiently far north to miss the worst and sailed as soon as the schooner was ready for sea.

Clear of the estuary, they headed northeast, the *Spitfire* slipping easily through the blue water. Flying fish fluttered away from her advancing shadow as it raced over the gently heaving surface of the sea, while a school of dolphins gambolled under her bowsprit, riding the invisible wave of pressure that her thrusting bow forced ahead of her hull.

Kite came below after the morning watch to break his fast to find Puella vomiting copiously. 'Ah, Puella, you were not seasick on the passage to Savannah, is the Atlantic too much for you, my love?'

Her brown skin glazed with perspiration, Puella looked up from the wooden bucket and shook her head. 'I am with child,' she said.

Three days out the steady breeze began to pick up during the early forenoon. The schooner was running with the wind and sea on her starboard quarter, the skies were untroubled, but a lumpy swell was building, running up from the south and inclining *Spitfire* to scend as she raced along. An anxiety began to gnaw at Kite. He cared little for himself or the ship and crew, they were stout enough, but Puella's condition worried him. She had carried Charlie serenely, but her present pregnancy seemed troubled. His ignorance reproached him; it seemed a lifetime ago that he had masqueraded as a surgeon and now his beloved Puella might well be in need of real help. She was the only woman on board and without Dorothea her isolation and vulnerability filled her with fear. Now the weather worsened and the battening down of the schooner only increased the staleness of the air below, trapping the sharp stink of vomit, so that both Kite and Puella were reminded of the slave deck of the *Enterprize*. Kite made Puella as comfortable as possible, but now the motion of the *Spitfire* and the mephitic air only added to the unfortunate woman's misery. It was not long before Kite was summoned on deck and compelled to leave Puella.

The *Spitfire's* mate, a tall and powerful mulatto named Christopher Jones, drew his attention to the fact that there was an edge to the wind now and a rapid darkening of the sky that presaged more than a mere gale.

'Hurricane coming, Cap'n,' Jones asserted, 'we should get all the sails down and let her run off before it.' Kite stepped forward and looked from the windward tell-tale indicating the direction of the wind to the wildly swinging compass in its bowl. While he had been below with Puella the wind had begun to shift and they were already two points off their intended course. Kite bowed to the inevitable; at least they had sea room. He looked up at Jones and nodded. The mate was already raising his voice to make himself heard above the steady thrum of the gale in the rigging. The wind was not yet so strong that they would normally take in everything, but prudence dictated they should secure the schooner before the worst was upon them.

'Leave her a scrap of canvas forrard,' Kite called in Jones's ear, 'the clew of the foretopmast staysail! We'll luff her and call all hands!'

Jones nodded agreement. 'Aye, aye, sir!'

Kite took his station beside the tiller as Jones called out the watch below. The *Spitfire's* crew was smaller than during the Guadeloupe campaign, consisting of men willing to try their fortune with a long run across the Atlantic. The promise of prize-money inherent in the well-known letter of marque that converted *Spitfire* into a privateer had proved sufficient of a lure to both the feckless and the ambitious among the unemployed seafarers who idled their lives away along the waterfront of St John's, Willoughby and Falmouth. These idlers feared the appearance of the Royal Navy's cutters and launches, sent from English Harbour in search of such likely cannon-fodder. Besides, rates of pay aboard such private ships were better by far than the risks, dangers and uncertain pay in the men-of-war of His Britannic Majesty. Now Kite watched this motley band as it assembled on deck under the direction of Jones. The mate looked aft and nodded.

'Down helm,' Kite ordered, lending his weight to the helmsman on the tiller. The *Spitfire* turned up into the wind, bucking wildly, her bowsprit stabbing first at the sky and then at the advancing walls of grey waves as they surged towards her. As they rose over the summits and the breaking crests roared and seethed past them in tumbling dissolution, they were exposed to the full strength of the wind. It tore at them with palpable force, howling in the standing rigging with a malevolent shriek as the sails flogged, rattling the swinging booms and gaffs so that the whole vessel trembled as they were lowered. Kite heard a faint scream as a terrified Puella, trapped below, thought the vessel was flying to pieces. Sheets of spray flew aboard over the bow, to be whipped aft in white streaks, so that the half-dry decks were sodden in an instant, and water streamed from every rope and spar above them. Caught in such a cascade, Kite felt his skin stung as from a lash, and he instinctively turned away.

Forward, each watch attending a mast, the gaffs came down and the reefed sails were slowly tamed by lashings as the crew bent to the task. The square topsails and the outer headsails had been taken in earlier and, after a few minutes, the schooner began to fall off the wind, rolling almost on her starboard beam ends as she swung away. Then the wind caught in the reefed staysail forward and added its power to the turning moment of the tiller. *Spitfire* crashed like a live and triumphant being over the crest and suddenly ran with the breaking sea, accelerating away from where the constraint of her master had held her for those few necessary minutes. Now, with only a scrap of canvas set over the stemhead, she tore away before the wind and Kite called for another man to be permanently stationed at the heavy tiller as it kicked in his hands.

'By Heaven, Mr Jones, she runs faster than a horse!'

'Indeed she do, sir!' Jones responded, affected by the exhilaration of the moment, with a broad grin. 'Much faster!'

By now the sky was overcast, the scud lowering like a dark mantle, closing about them in their isolation. Beneath their keel they began to feel the *Spitfire* responding to the contrary and confusing influences of a cross-swell, at variance with the seas that rolled under them. Now there was another, sideways lurch, an arrhythmic and often abrupt roll that caused the following seas to catch up and strike the stern with a hammer blow that shook the hull from stern to stem. Once such a sea boiled over the rail, pouring forward in a torrent of water that swept two men from their feet and carried them forward so that they fetched up against the foremast fiferails in a swirling welter of water.

Half an hour after they had run off before the gale, just as Kite had decided he would relinquish the deck to Jones again and go and tend to Puella, the wind suddenly veered and began to roar with a deepening tone. The change was abrupt, the increase in force incontrovertible. Kite had never heard such a noise before, even when, two years earlier, he had been in St John's as a hurricane passed to the south of the island, sweeping through the cane fields of distant Martinique with destructive effect. But this was different, the booming roar seemed to contain an unimaginable power to which the former screaming shriek was an insipid prelude.

Jones caught his eye; he was no longer exhilarated. The mulatto's face was drained of colour, eloquent evidence of his fear. Jones hauled himself aft to where Kite stood clinging to the starboard main shrouds.

'Bad!' he shouted. 'Big, big wind, Cap'n.'

'Aye,' Kite bellowed back.

'Bad hurricane, Cap'n! I'll put lifelines on the helmsmen!'

Kite nodded and let go of his handhold and plunged across the deck, fetching up against the binnacle. It took him some minutes before the spray allowed him to see clearly the relationship between the swinging card and the lubber's line, but it was obvious they were now headed north. Another such change in wind direction and they would be heading north-north-west.

He puzzled over this for some moments while Jones secured the helmsmen, but could make little sense of it. Perhaps the wind would veer when it next shifted, but something persuaded him otherwise. Fortunately they had sea room, and provided there were no other ships in the vicinity which they could run foul of, they would have an uncomfortable but not a fatal experience.

In the next quarter of an hour the wind backed another point. By now the booming roar had dulled their thoughts. Jones put the men on to the pumps to give them something to do, but Kite, as captain, could enjoy no such mind-numbing labour. He was left to try and think amid this awesome din. He became slowly aware that a subtle change was occurring. As the violence of the wind rose, the wild motion of the schooner lessened. It took Kite some time to penetrate this mystery until he realised that his vision was almost permanently obscured by the mass of water in the air. It was like a mist that moved with the speed and consistency of bird-shot, a tangible manifestation of the might of the wind. Eventually he realised that the wind in its rising had kicked up a heavy sea, but had now reached such a scale of power that it no longer did so. Now the wind simply excoriated the sea's surface, slicing it off it and carrying it to leeward. The air had become half liquid, salty, possessed of mass and density.

At first Kite thought this would ease the

burden on the *Spitfire*, for her motion was far less violent, but in this he was deceived. It took a moment to register, but now she lay down under a constant pressure, and the forces impinging upon her were no longer air but air that was sodden with a weight of water. Even as the schooner continued to run off before them, the very forces that impelled her were conniving at her destruction, pushing her myriad component parts, those hundreds of scarphs and rebated joints, those butts, tenons and knees all held together with thousands of treenails, iron bolts and copper rovings, to the limits of their individual strengths.

On deck the men huddled unhappily and Kite had to lash himself to the weather rail, the thin line of the flag halyard cutting into him as the wind tried to pluck him from his perch. Even breathing became a labour, so choked was the air with salt water, so high the pressure of the wind upon his body. The mind fumbled through this chaos, and Kite found himself a living contradiction, with every instinct in his being telling him to lie down and curl up like a wounded cat, to make himself as small and insignificant as possible, to let the great wind pass over him in the simple hope that he would survive. Against this was an instinctive urge to reason, for survival depended upon the *Spitfire* remaining undamaged, providing the means of sustaining them upon the surface of this flattened, scoured and tormented sea. To achieve this it was not enough to let her go; she required nursing, helping through her ordeal in order that she could help them.

But Kite was tired and hungry, battered by the incessant noise, soaked by the wet and driving air, buffeted and bruised by the violent assault of wind and water. As hour succeeded hour he followed the crew, and slowly slipped into a half-conscious acceptance of the inevitable. He lost interest in their compass heading, for the whole world had contracted into this small circle of white and furious water above which the once vast and over-arching sky had shrunk into a dull limit of cloud-water, as thick and circumscribing as a fog. His mind seemed capable only of asking a simple and increasingly familiar question: What did it matter? What *did* it matter?

Nor was Kite the only man upon the *Spitfire's* deck to be so afflicted. Those not hunkered down in the lee of some strong point to which they had lashed themselves stood at the tiller. The two men who struggled to keep the *Spitfire* before wind were tiring rapidly; the compass bowl was difficult to see, so they steered by the tell-tales. But their concentration lapsed, their arms ached and they received no relief.

Then a sea crashed at the stern and stove in the stern windows, canting the deck violently so that one of them lost his precarious footing. The *Spitfire* drove off to starboard with a heavy larboard lurch from which, as she broached, she did not recover.

Puella screamed as tons of water cascaded through the broken stern windows, smashing in the preventive shutters and filling the cabin with a sudden cold deluge. Perhaps it was Puella's shriek of terror, or perhaps it was the thin halyard cutting into his waist, that stirred Kite. He was vaguely troubled and roused from his catalepsy by the growing conviction that all was far from well. His mind swam, but he realised he had not heard the clunk of the pumps for some time; and then *Spitfire* protested again. The rigging to which Kite was seized suddenly jerked, and despite the roar of the wind the crack from aloft was loud enough to wake a dozing man. The maintopmast broke, snapping clean off above the doubling. The spar hung down, swaying and tugging at those ropes that still confined it. These jerked and strained under the load while the schooner fell farther over to larboard. From forward there came a report like the discharge of a gun: the shred of reefed canvas set on the forestay blew out.

Someone sent up a shout as *Spitfire* lay over on her beam ends and the deck heeled alarmingly. Kite lost his footing and hung from the weather pinrail like a sack of potatoes. The jerk finally alerted him to imminent disaster.

Kite had neither the experience nor the understanding of the great natural forces unleashed against his small schooner to comprehend that, by running off before the wind, his ignorance had contributed to their plight. Nor had Jones, notwithstanding his competence as the mate of an inter-island schooner, the faintest concept of the true nature of the hurricane. But both men, and several of the hands, knew the remedy for their present plight, and Jones's large frame was soon crouched over the weather rail, a grey silhouette against the sky forward, clinging for dear life with one hand and sawing at the rigging with the other.

The knife seemed to take an eternity to sever the first shroud, then the second was attacked. Meanwhile someone had found the axe and had jammed himself inside the main fiferails, from where he began to hack at the foot of the mainmast. Kite lugged out his own knife and turned to the tarred ropes that strained like iron bars under the load aloft, and all the while the delicate fabric of spars and rigging trembled and shook as the loose maintopmast swung wildly hither and thither in reaction to the bucking of the schooner.

But the hull lifted less readily now, sluggish with the amount of water that had been taken aboard, assaulted by the wind and laid over at such an angle that the cunning of her hull lines contributed little to her survival. The beautiful and lively schooner was rapidly disintegrating into a derelict hulk. For several long and tremulous minutes, as the men hacked and sawed, the fate of the *Spitfire* hung, quite literally, in the balance. Then, with a mighty shudder and violent windward lurch that nearly flung overboard the energetic seaman forward, the mainmast went by the board, followed by the greater portion of the foremast and the entire jib boom. The noise of this collapse was snatched away by the wind but the deck was covered by a spider's web of fallen and tangled rigging, all of it still secured or fouled in the mass of spars and wreckage now alongside. How it failed to entrap anyone was little short of miraculous.

Slowly the *Spitfire* adjusted herself to this new situation, seeking the equilibrium between the force of the wind and her own exposed surface. The drag of wreckage affected the leeward drift and slowly, as rope after rope was cut through by the labouring crew, the *Spitfire* spun round so that she stabilised with the wind on her larboard bow and the mass of spars and rigging streamed out to windward, still secured by a pair of unsevered larboard shrouds.

With this Kite bawled his relief. 'Avast there! Leave that raffle for the time being.' It was no longer banging against the hull and its drag helped hold the schooner almost head to wind, keeping her vulnerable damaged stern to leeward. Within a moment Jones had all hands turned up and the men at the pumps. The carpenter's sounding revealed four feet of water in the well. Kite swore; it was impossible that such an intake of water had not damaged the greater part of their spoilable cargo.

As if to reward them for their labour, the wind now began to drop. It died rapidly and the cloud cleared so that the sun shone and speedily dried up the deck. The sudden brightening raised spirits, and grins of relief were visible all round the deck. Kite went below to order to cook to dole out a measure of rum to everyone, then he sought to comfort Puella. He found her crouching sodden in a corner of the cabin, the deck of which was awash. Amid the water slopping up and down were personal effects; a pair of shoes, a fancy hat and a stocking belonging to Puella, some papers, a feathered quill and a shirt belonging to himself. Splintered wood from the window shutters that had been torn out of their frames, added to the mess.

Despite the water washing about her,

Puella was fast asleep. Terror and exhaustion had succeeded with her where they had failed with Kite. Bracing himself against the lurch of the schooner he tenderly lifted her and placed her, wet as she was, in the dry cot swaying above the mess on the cabin deck. Slowly the water was draining away, exposing great shards of the shattered crown glass from the windows which lay shining in the sunlight now flooding through the open frames.

Planting a kiss upon Puella's head Kite glanced out of the shattered windows as he withdrew. Conscious that the schooner was now bucking violently again he went back on deck to find the whole surface of the sea boiling. Flapping and exhausted seabirds were falling aboard, adding the quality of a nightmare to the scene. Kite noticed immediately that the wind had fallen almost dead calm and divined the reason for the chaotic state of the sea. It was liberated from the tyrannical driving of the wind and now flew first from one direction and then the other. It struck him that each incoming wave was the remnant of the wind's force, and if the waves appeared omni-directional it followed that the wind that had generated them must be omni-directional too.

How could this be? Especially as now there was little wind at all. He went aft, the deck bucking madly so that in a sense this wild and irregular motion was worse than the steady onslaught of the tempest. He managed to work aft and stood at the taffrail, and what he saw seemed like a seething madness as waves slapped into each other, sometimes throwing themselves high into the air and the *Spitfire* was tossed about betwixt summits and troughs, like a cork in a millstream.

A hint of a steady gust blew his disordered hair across his face, coinciding with a cloud crossing the sun. The passing shadow raced across the surface of the sea which had, in the sunlight, lost its grey aspect in favour of its customary blue. But he sensed no pleasure from this brief warning; he noticed that the direction of the wind was contrary to what it had been. Half understanding the mighty phenomenon, he felt the prickle of alarm. Stumbling forward he bent over the binnacle, peering at the swinging compass card to confirm his partial grasp of mighty events. Another gust of wind swept the deck and he glanced up quickly, but the tell-tale had gone with the mast. Then as if pressing its insistence upon him, the wind picked up and blew steadily. Spray lifted over the rail and pattered across the deck, laying a feather of wet planking as if to confirm its direction.

'By God,' Kite muttered to himself, 'there's more to come!'

Within the hour the sky was once more overcast and rain swept down in torrents, driving across the deck with an icy chill which was in sharp and uncomfortable contrast with the previous warm, wet salt-laden air. It was now growing dark as night fell. They had had nothing to eat since the previous day, but the wind was increasing all the time and the daylight had not quite faded behind the lowering scud, before the wind shriek had deepened to the booming roar of the returning hurricane.

They kept the pumps going all night as the *Spitfire* wallowed endlessly, her bow held off the wind by the remains of the wreckage, much of which tore free during the hours of darkness. Towards the end of the night the wind dropped, imperceptibly at first, so that it was some time before the exhausted Kite knew their ordeal was approaching its end as the hurricane finally passed them by. Dawn found the *Spitfire* left to her fate, wallowing, waterlogged in the trough of the sea.

No semblance of discipline haunted her decks. Men slumped where they fell after the toil at the pumps, or dragged themselves out of the way to lie inert, uncaring, only glad to be allowed to sleep to a gentle rocking. Dawn found them thus, and the forenoon was all but over before some, but not all, were wakened from their slumbers by a piercing shriek.

Fourteen

The Refit

It was already dark by the time they had eaten and turned-to to clear away the decks, recover from overboard what was useful, and contrive a jury rig. The *Spitfire* had been pumped out and, though she was still making water, it was not an overwhelming amount and Kite felt justified in setting half-watches and allowing the derelict schooner to drift throughout the night while below, her tired company slept.

They woke much refreshed. Although a fresh northerly wind chilled them and set up a sea that rolled the wallowing hull uncomfortably, they were spurred on by the invigoration of an urgent task. In this work Kite was ably assisted by Christopher Jones, who took upon himself much of the re-rigging. Jones proved a master of improvisation, knotting and splicing, setting up tackles and securely lashing the main boom to the stump of the mainmast. The remains of the foretopsail yard were then rigged as a boom. It was hard and tedious work, both helped and hindered by the roll of the vessel, but by nightfall two small masts were stayed rigidly and a party had begun work on roughly recutting the remaining sails. With these it was hoped that the following morning they would be under command again and heading for shelter.

For Kite the dilemma was where they should now make for. He had no idea where they were, and missed a meridian altitude at noon due to the continuing overcast. The only safe option was to return to the west and try and make an identifiable landfall on the coast of North America. In the interim he would probably be able to obtain at least one observation to determine their latitude and there was a strong likelihood that they would encounter other vessels as they drew nearer the land. But the wind was not favourable, shifting slowly in the wake of the hurricane, and having bent on their improvised suit of sails they spent another night hove-to.

Dawn the following morning found the wind settled again in its prevailing quarter of south-west and they set a course towards the north-west. For several days spirits remained optimistic, but then matters began to deteriorate as their progress remained slow and uncertain. They were already on salt provisions, but these were now unalleviated by fresh food of any kind. Their livestock had been lost in the hurricane, their bags of limes swept overboard along with their fresh yams and other vegetables. As the days dragged into weeks it was not long before one or two of the men became resentfully lethargic. This mild insubordination, Kite soon realised, came with an inflammation of the gums and, after a further week, a loosening of teeth. The first to be affected were the disreputable beachcombers among the hands, men whose bodies had been subjected to neglect and excess. Rum, that sailors' soporific, plentiful in Antigua, was a poor diet to prepare men for an ocean voyage. The outbreak of sickness coincided with two cases exhibiting the eruption of the raspberry-like pustules of the secondary stage of what was colloquially known as button-scurvy. This initially masked the outbreak of that quite different, but similarly named disease, the common scurvy.

Jones recognised the affliction of the two sailors to be yaws, an infection indistinguishable at the time from the pox, and the consequent shunning of these men by their fellows, and the general horror of contagion, made those with sore gums and loosening teeth conceal their own symptoms, ignorant that they were suffering the seaman's greater curse, the common scurvy. But the reality was unavoidable. Unused to protracted passages, Kite again confronted all the horrors of being overwhelmed by disease, a depressing repetition of the middle passage of the *Enterprize*. Neither he nor Jones knew what to do and this lack of leadership told upon the moral state of the schooner. Her sluggish progress seemed an echo of the mood on board, a lethargic indifference to everything and a slow acceptance of the inevitable. Kite abandoned all pretence at command as the first symptoms of the malaise affected him, concentrating all his energies on preserving Puella, who had hardly risen from the cot into which he had placed her at the height of the hurricane. She seemed to sink into a morass of apathy, hardly recognising him as she succumbed to the disease, and her listlessness hurt Kite, further reducing his own spirits.

In this desperate state, the *Spitfire* sailed slowly to the north-west, the last shreds of common consent seeing her steered by a tired and half-reluctant remnant of her crew. Kite and Jones clung to their duties, the habits of responsibility dying less quickly than the sense of obligation among the hands, and it was Jones who first saw the blue smudge of land on the horizon ahead of them.

It was also Jones who recognised their landfall. In later years Kite was apt to descant upon their abrupt change of luck, telling the story with a certain amount of embellishment and reducing its real impact as it assumed, for his listeners at least, the character of a *deus ex machina*. At the time, however, it moved him to revive his journal entries:

It seemed that Providence, having Passed us through the Most Extreme of Trials, had Equally Capriciously changed her Mind and, having Decided to Deliver us from the Evil of our Predicament, now Smoothed our Path. Mr Jones Recognised the Lighthouse at the Entrance to Narragansett Bay and we stood Inwards towards the Port, passing Castle Hill with our Ensign Flying.

Christopher Jones had visited Newport, Rhode Island, on several occasions when he had served in slavers, loading rum for export to the Guinea coast in exchange for imports of 'black ivory'. In the euphoria of arrival Jones took credit for having brought them into the shelter of its anchorage, to which a relieved Kite took no exception. The experience of the hurricane had reminded him of the severe limitations of his knowledge. His rise to command of the schooner had been too fast for him to acquire solid sea-sense, and too circumstantial for him to have submitted to the rigour of a real apprenticeship. Indeed so affected was he by their safe deliverance and the relief this would bring to Puella that he was content to let Jones himself act as pilot, and bring the limping, jury-rigged *Spitfire* up through the narrows between Dumpling's Rock and Brenton's Point, to the anchorage off Goat and Rose Islands. As the schooner brought up to her cable, he publicly thanked the mate and shook his hand. It was a spontaneous but inspired act; witnessed by all hands, it repaired the disintegrating morale of the crew at a stroke, reuniting them for the labour of repairing their battered vessel. In his journal, Kite briefly reflected this turn of events, generously concluding the day's entry with the remark that, *to Mr Jones goes not only the Honour of being the First to Sight Land, but of Conning the Vessel to her Anchorage off Newport.*

In the weeks that followed, *Spitfire* lay refitting in Roberts' shipyard at Newport. The men of the yard, though obliging and thorough in their work, made no attempt to offer Kite hospitality, nor a secret of their disapproval of Kite's way of life. Once Puella had been seen in town, taken by Kite to buy outer garments more suitable to a northern climate and in readiness for their eventual arrival in England, an unsubtle campaign had inveighed against them. Kite withdrew to the *Spitfire,* concerned for Puella and her unborn child. He reconciled himself to this state of affairs insofar as it relieved him of the expense of social pretension, for he was committing much of his negotiable resources on the refit, leaving him little for further expenses. High among these was the payment of his crew. Several wished to sign off and abandon the voyage, and Kite had no desire to keep unwilling hands aboard by refusing them their wages until they reached Liverpool.

In the end he was fortunate in shipping three young New Englanders for whom Rhode Island was a place of little attraction. One, a former clerk named Whisstock, claimed to nurse ambitions only satisfied by living in London, where he thought he could make his fortune. Kite nicknamed him Whittington, after the optimistic young-ster in the folk tale.

The condition of the schooner had caused Kite some anxiety but in fact she had weathered her ordeal better than he had anticipated. A portion of caulking had been dislodged by the straining of the hull, but the prompt cutting away of the vessel's top-hamper had prevented serious wracking. The *Spitfire* was first careened and the caulking renewed, after which the greater part of the work was in re-rigging her. In this Kite took the advice of the master-rigger, who suggested some modifications in tune with schooners of New England, better fitting the *Spitfire* for a winter crossing of the North Atlantic. Inviting Jones's opinion, Kite found the mate supporting the master-rigger's views and so the work was put in hand. The only other modifications were the fitting of stoves in the crew's forecastle and the cabin, where the repair work to the stern windows was extended to incorporate some additional comforts for Puella's con-venience. This latter work was done in a frosty atmosphere of severe disapproval, for Puella had nowhere to go while the carpenters laboured. Though quite indif-ferent on his own account, Kite was distressed at being unable to prevent this affecting her. She retreated into herself, and Kite, preoccupied with the affairs of the schooner, had little time for her during the day and often found her withdrawn by the evening. She would crouch silently in a corner of the cabin, sometimes muttering silently to herself, communing with the spirits and talking to Dorothea. It was a disquieting reminder of her ancestry, but Kite sensed it was her way of coping with her intense loneliness, against which he was unable to offer any comfort.

With the vessel in the hands of the shipyard, the schooner assumed the unpleasantly uncertain character of a camp on campaign. In the circumstances this was not entirely inappropriate, for during the sojourn in Rhode Island they learned the latest news of the war. The combined forces of General Sir Jeffrey Amherst and Admiral Boscawen had been successful in capturing the great French fortress at Louisbourg in July of the previous year. This was in marked contrast to the bungled attack of General Abercrombie on Fort Ticonderoga, which had been ignominiously repulsed by General Montcalm. But the French military commander was in disagreement with Governor Vaudreuil and the rumours coming down from Canada, where the British were now concentrating their effort, suggested that matters there were coming to a head. Better news from Europe was already stale; the Duke of Brunswick had won a victory at Crefeld against the Austrians, but while the work on *Spitfire* was in hand, Kite heard that Brunswick had won a second, decisive battle at Minden, on the River Weser in Hanover. Reports that the British field officer in command of the cavalry, Lord George Sackville, had disgraced himself by refusing to advance, amused the Rhode Islanders. This interest in a scandalous and gloomy addendum to the news of Minden, a battle of distant irrelevance as far as the colonists were concerned, was, Kite noted, relished largely because cheering news came from Canada. Montcalm had been killed and Quebec taken by British troops under Major General Wolfe after a night landing and a scrambling ascent of the Heights of Abraham.

The brilliant young hero of Louisbourg, Wolfe, had also been killed, but the exploit had overturned the French position and now the future of Canada as a French colony seemed at an end. There was also heartening intelligence from the distant coast of Portugal. Here, it was learned, a French squadron, on its way to join forces with the fleet at Brest, had been destroyed by Boscawen after a chase from Gibraltar.

Then, one morning, as Kite stood shivering on the deck in the frosty December air, the master-rigger climbed aboard waving a newspaper. 'See here, Cap'n, we have drubbed the French good and proper. This will sting them mightily,' he remarked gleefully. Kite took the proffered copy of the broadsheet and read of Admiral Hawke's dramatic chase of de Conflans deep into Quiberon Bay.

Apparently bad weather had driven Hawke from his blockading station of Brest and the principal French fleet had escaped to embark troops intended to invade the English coast. The French Minister, the Duc de Choiseul, had planned to seize a number of coastal towns and hold them as hostage against the return of Martinique, Guadeloupe and Quebec. This project was known of in London and on learning of the departure of Conflans from Brest, Hawke had sailed in pursuit, catching the French fleet in a rising gale off the entrance to Quiberon Bay. De Conflans hoped to slip through a narrow, rock-grit passage into the shelter of the anchorage there, confident that his local knowledge would ensure success while the onshore gale would deter Hawke's ships from closing with his fleet on a dangerous lee shore. De Conflans was wrong; Hawke's men-of-war fell upon de Conflans' in a pell-mell, running battle which continued until nightfall, as both fleets manoeuvred among the rocks. The French were overwhelmed, their fleet almost entirely annihilated in a victory which crowned a year already being described as remarkable.

'Our anxieties are at an end, it seems. Surely the French will sue for peace,' Kite said, looking up from the paper.

'Well, the luck certainly seems to be running in our favour, Cap'n, that's for sure, and with winter upon us I guess you're right. But to business, Cap'n,' the man pressed and Kite handed the newspaper back. 'See here, Cap'n, I shall complete work today and we must concert arrangements to move you from here...'

'Yes,' agreed Kite, putting the affairs of the greater world aside and returning his thoughts to the matter of the schooner. 'We shall have to reload that portion of our un-spoiled cargo which we discharged, and I have arranged a small lading from this place.'

'We will be obliged, Cap'n, if you would haul off as soon as possible.'

Kite noticed the shifting tone of the man's voice and followed his glance. Puella had come on deck, pulling a shawl tightly around her and regarding the steely cold waters of the harbour with distaste.

'As soon as possible, Cap'n,' the master-rigger repeated as he turned away.

Kite approached Puella. She looked up at him, her face troubled.

'What is the matter, my dear?' he asked, touching her gently.

'I do not like this place, Kite. It is too cold... Why do you laugh at me?'

'I am not laughing,' Kite suppressed his smile, 'but you have a talent for under-statement.'

'I have?' Puella looked doubtful, but seeing she had Kite's attention she smiled back. 'You have forgotten me, Kite. I am alone...'

'No, my darling, you are not alone, you are lonely and I am lonely and I too want to leave this place. We shall be gone soon.'

'How soon?'

Kite looked at her, then said, 'That I cannot promise, but within a week, perhaps a little less. It depends how long it takes to stow the cargo.'

'Will we be long at sea?'

'Three weeks to a month.'

'And is England as cold as this?'

'You should not be on deck. It is best that you remain in the shelter of the cabin...'

Accompanying Puella below and persuading her to remain there, Kite realised that his provisions for her were inadequate, despite the fitting of the stove. The prejudice he had encountered on their shopping expedition had shocked him, so inured had he become to the presence of black skins in the seething and vibrant waterfront of St John's. A kind of condescending tolerance existed alongside the hidebound gulfs of inequity in the Antilles. Here, in New England, the assumed equality of the northern colonies was characterised by this barrier against what he had heard euphemistically referred to as 'the race of Ham'.

For Kite, both were infinitely preferable to the stews of waterside Liverpool, where neither quality existed and dog ate dog in perpetual communal turmoil. Something of that littoral mishmash added a louche charm to St John's, set as it was amid the lush tropic vegetation, working a sinister yet

351

seductive interplay between the throbbing passions of the dominant whites and the down-trodden blacks. Here in the north, where the leaves fell from the trees in riotous colour, the austerity created a chill as penetrating as the winter frosts riming the bare black branches. Kite shuddered to be off to sea. But in the meantime he had other ideas; smiling at Puella he made his excuses and went ashore.

He walked into town, heading for a furrier's he had seen on his previous visit, intent on purchasing some adequate furs for Puella. The woods of the back-country provided an abundance of wild animals, and he was able to buy a fine fox-fur coat. He was in the act of negotiating for a large bearskin when a woman's voice overrode that of the proprietor.

'My goodness, Captain, she must be a very worthy mistress that can command so rich a wrapping.'

He turned as the proprietor, not a whit disaffected by the intrusion, bobbed a bow at the newcomer. She was young, tall and strikingly handsome in a plain grey riding habit about the shoulders of which was cast an elegant pelisse. Above dark hair a feathered hat was worn at a jaunty and improbable angle and her gloved hand held a riding crop with which she tapped her long skirt, beating quietly at the boot beneath it. Kite made a small, stiff bow. He was aware that he had coloured up, angry with himself for rising to the woman's obvious innuendo. It was quite clear that this stunning creature knew of his identity and the colour of his mistress. Having delivered her deliberate slight, she was smiling insolently at him. Her effrontery fuelled a sudden anger.

'You refer to my *wife*, madam,' he lied with such emphasis that his sincerity carried an outraged conviction which struck her like a blow from her own crop. But she was equal to the occasion and even as her cheek paled, she replied with such a cool composure that she heaped insolence upon presumption.

'Indeed,' she said, stringing out the word as though passing judgement on him. 'Your wife.'

The woman's hauteur made Kite realise that his falsehood had worsened the situation. The guilt of his own deception further infuriated him, notwithstanding the conviction of the vehement lie, for she had coolly regained the upper hand. Puella as wife was in her eyes clearly worse than Puella as whore.

'My name is William—'

'Kite,' she interrupted cuttingly. 'Yes, I know.'

'Then you have the advantage of me, madam.'

'I know that too, Captain.' She smiled victoriously. Kite felt a strong impulse to strike her, but swallowed his anger and turned to the furrier.

'We are agreed, then,' he said, ignoring the woman.

'Ten Portuguese moidores,' the man said, returning his attention to his business.

'You should pay no more than eight,' the woman's voice came from behind him.

'There, sir,' Kite said, 'are ten moidores for the bearskin and a further two for your courtesy. Pray send the goods down to my schooner before this evening.'

The astonished furrier picked up the gold coins as Kite took up his hat from the table upon which the rich fur lay spread. He turned and jammed it on his head as he confronted the woman whom he saw he had succeeded in merely amusing by his rather childish largesse. Her smile, for it was not a smirk, he was annoyed to see, tripped his restraint.

'Should you wish to learn manners, madam,' he said coldly, 'my wife would be delighted to teach–'

But he got no further. The riding crop struck his cheek and he recoiled, catching his balance and raising his hand to his face. The rising weal was already bleeding profusely as their eyes met. Behind them the furrier's sharp intake of breath seemed to have been his last conscious act before immobility seized him.

Kite's shock and the beating of his heart were as nothing, he noted with a painful smile, to hers. Regret at the impetuosity of her rash act made her first blench and then colour. She staggered a little as if resisting an impulse to faint, but then her chin went up and her challenge was irresistible.

'To teach you over a dish of tea aboard the schooner *Spitfire*, lying at Roberts' yard,' Kite finished his sentence disdainfully and stalked from the shop.

The refit of the *Spitfire* was now almost completed. As the winter afternoon drew on and the sun westered, a red ball in a cloudless sky of pale lavender, Kite was standing amidships, in final consultation with the master-rigger and Jones. The following day would see them ready to warp down to the jetty and complete their lading.

'What happened to your face, Cap'n?' Jones asked.

Instinctively Kite touched the crusty scab that marked his cheek. He looked at the master-rigger as he replied. 'Oh,' he responded, feigning indifference, 'a white lady gave it to me for sleeping with a black lady. I cannot imagine why, can you, Mr Jones?'

Jones shook his mulatto head, embarrassed in front of the master-rigger, who could scarcely contain his interest. 'Well, I'll be damned, Cap'n. They sure aren't too friendly hereabouts,' Jones said.

'You'll have noticed it too, I dare say,' Kite said pointedly.

Jones nodded. 'Aye, I have.'

The master-rigger coughed awkwardly. 'If we could just keep to the business in hand... Say, is this the lady concerned?'

Kite and Jones turned to where the master-rigger was pointing. The woman from the furrier's was stepping gingerly over the rail, her grey skirt lifted and the black leather boots gleaming in the sunset. A workman was handing her down, holding a large bundle which she had obviously passed to him for safe-keeping while she negotiated the bulwarks.

Thanking the workmen and recovering her parcel, she approached the three men. 'Captain Kite,' she said coolly meeting his eyes.

Beside Kite, Jones whistled under his breath and the master-rigger coughed again. 'Thank you, gentlemen,' said Kite, turning, raising his hat and footing a bow as the two men withdrew forward.

'Madam?'

She offered him the parcel. 'I have brought your *wife's* bearskin, Captain.'

'Thank you.' He took it and stared at her,

angry that she had chosen to invade his small kingdom, and coldly formal in the hope that she would take the hint and leave at once.

'I thought perhaps I could take tea with your wife,' she said, as if nothing unpleasant had passed between them and they had known each other for years.

'To what end, madam?' he asked with cold civility, masking his astonishment.

He saw her composure slip to the extent of her shooting a glance at Jones and the master-rigger. 'I wish to make amends, Captain,' she said, her voice low.

'And why would you wish to do that, madam? I cannot think that you act without a motive? Are you simply curious to see my wife, or are you intending to whip *her*?'

'*Please*, Captain Kite.' Her voice was little more than a whisper, her face strained. 'Do not humiliate me any more than I have already humiliated myself.'

He sighed. His cheek burned and throbbed. How could he explain to Puella what he had already explained as a flying rope's end? How could he tell her that this elegant and beautiful white woman wanted to gawp at her as a black exhibit? Knowing Puella's jealousy, how could he stop Puella from jumping to the stupid conclusion that the rich creature had designs upon Kite himself, just as Kitty Robertson had?

'I am *apologising*, Captain Kite,' the woman insisted. 'And have brought you the bearskin as an act of contrition.' She paused. 'I *would* like to meet your wife, sir, if only to explain why I struck you.'

Kite almost laughed, then he said, 'I have explained this,' he touched his cheek, 'as the result of a rope fall flying from a block.' He saw her frown with incomprehension. 'It is no matter.'

'But I should still like to meet your wife, Captain. She must be lonely cooped up aboard here.' She gestured round the deck and he suddenly wanted to be rid of her. If she wanted an olive branch then so be it.

'I owe *you* an apology,' he said, hurriedly going on to prevent interruption. 'Puella – er, that is what I call her, for it seemed cruel to give her an English name when I cannot understand her native one...' Then his courage failed him as he found her face quite enchanting.

'Go on, Captain, I understand.'

Kite swallowed. 'Well, madam, she is not my wife. In the Antilles these things are not so important...'

'Quite so,' the woman said, the hint of a self-satisfied smile playing around the corners of her mouth.

'But she is free, madam,' Kite said with as much convincing emphasis as he could muster. 'She is not a slave.'

He started to edge back towards the gangway, but the woman moved aft, towards the companionway where Puella, with that disarming intuition that she seemed to have inherited from Dorothea, stood at the top of the steps leading below.

Seeing her, the woman stepped forward, smiled and held out her hand. 'Puella,' she said, 'my name is Sarah Tyrell, I have brought you the fur Captain Kite purchased this morning. I am afraid I am also responsible for the cut on his cheek...'

Kite, trying to distinguish sincerity from condescension, wondered if she would have been so ready to make amends if Puella had been white. Confused, Puella took the proffered hand and bobbed a curtsey.

'Shall we go below?' Kite said, aware that he had been outmanoeuvred and the extraordinary tripartite encounter had brought all work to a standstill even before the sun set.

As he reached the foot of the steps and turned into the cabin, he asked coldly, 'Is it Mrs Tyrell, or Miss, madam?'

'It's Mrs, Captain. My husband is a merchant and ship-owner in this town.'

'A man of substance, I imagine,' Puella said. She had drawn herself up and stood, perfectly composed, waiting for an opening into the conversation.

Mrs Tyrell looked at Puella in surprise.

'Why … I suppose so, yes.'

'Would you care for tea or chocolate?' Puella asked courteously.

'Tea would be perfectly splendid, thank you.'

'I am afraid I shall have to attend to the matter myself,' Puella explained, 'there are no servants to wait upon us since the steward is otherwise employed at the moment.'

'Of course…' Mrs Tyrell was clearly surprised at Puella's elegance, courtesy and cool self-assurance.

'Won't you sit down, Mrs Tyrell?' Puella indicated a chair beside the repaired cabin table as she withdrew to the adjacent pantry.

'We have just suffered in a hurricane,' Kite explained awkwardly, 'hence our presence in Newport.'

'Yes,' Mrs Tyrell said, removing her gloves. 'I am, er…'

'I think it best, madam, in the circumstance, if we swiftly let bygones by bygones.'

'That is kind of you, Captain.' She paused, clearly gathering herself. 'I behaved unforgivably. I had no idea your Puella was so, so charming. Please…'

Kite capitulated and smiled sympathetically. Sarah Tyrell's fine mouth was working with some emotion and there was the faint glint of remorseful tears in her eyes.

'The matter was between us,' he said consolingly.

'You are very considerate, Captain.' Her voice was husky and there was a pregnant pause before Mrs Tyrell coughed and asked with forced interest, 'Where did you say you came from in the Antilles?'

'From St John's, in Antigua.'

'Would you have known the late Joseph Mulgrave? He was long linked with my husband in commerce...'

'We knew him well,' Puella said, bringing in a tray with cups and saucers. 'I took his name, along with Kite's, when I received my manumission.'

'I see...' said Mrs Tyrell, digesting this intelligence and further amazed at Puella's command of English.

As they waited for Puella to reappear with the teapot, Kite explained their connection with the house of Mulgrave, discovering that she knew of Wentworth and that a commercial connection still existed between her husband's enterprises and Mulgrave's successor.

'Do you trade in slaves?' Puella asked, pouring the tea.

'Well, er, yes, I'm afraid we do, Puella.'

'And are you *afraid* that you trade in sugar and rum, Sarah?' Puella asked with disarming candour, looking up and handing the elegant white woman her tea.

Kite froze, suddenly, inexplicably, outrageously and confusingly sympathetic to both victims, but Mrs Tyrell rose to the occasion. 'No, Puella, we are not apologetic about trading in sugar and rum; perhaps we should be, since they are directly linked with the trade in slaves.'

'There are some who–' Kite began, but Puella broke in.

'Kite should be. He takes me because he finds he is in love with me but he still carries slaves.'

Kite made a self-deprecating gesture. 'I annoyed Puella, by taking a few blacks from Antigua to Jamaica...'

'Love makes people do extraordinary things,' Mrs Tyrell said with sententious obscurity, sipping her tea.

'Like striking a man with a whip?' Puella asked.

'Puella!' Kite protested, astonished at how she knew. Had she overheard his remark to Jones and the master-rigger?

'No, she is right, Captain Kite, right to question me as to why I did it.' Mrs Tyrell's hand went out to restrain Kite as Puella coolly sat down with her own cup of tea. 'The trouble is, Puella, I am not certain that I can explain it. I had heard, of course, that there was a schooner at Roberts' yard and that the master had on board a Guinea woman. It is not unknown for such things to happen, even here in Rhode Island...' Mrs Tyrell paused with a sigh. 'The plain truth is that I was bored. I encountered Captain Kite in the furrier's and confronted him with ... with what I thought at the time was his outrageous behaviour. Now I feel foolish and contrite and regret what I did, the more so since making your acquaintance.'

'Well,' said Kite with relief, admiring Mrs Tyrell's considerable moral courage in confessing so handsomely, 'there's an end to the matter, then.'

'Perhaps I can make some amends,' Mrs Tyrell said, placing her drained cup on the table before her and addressing Puella. 'Tomorrow, please come and dine with us. I shall send a carriage and I shall not take a refusal. My husband will be pleased to meet you both and, Captain Kite,' she turned to Kite, 'who knows, this meeting may end happily with benefits for all of us.'

Though Kite graciously accepted the invitation, Puella resisted it. Partly through jealousy, partly through fear and largely because of being pregnant. She had no wish to embark upon a social event so ill-prepared, in conditions of such local hostility.

But Kite put up contrary arguments; Mrs Tyrell's acceptance, no matter howsoever it had been gained, cocked a snook at the prejudice of the townsfolk. It did not take much intelligence, Kite said, to see that Mrs Tyrell was a woman of influence: only a woman of influence would have sought to make a scene in the furrier's. She was also a woman of courage, for she had needed nothing less, he argued, to come aboard and apologise. Moreover, he went on, warming to the subject of acceptance, the commercial advantages that might result from any association that sprang up from a dinner were worth cultivating for their own sake. Puella rejected this as an argument for her own presence at the meal.

'If you must dine with her, dine without me,' she protested, 'if you care so much about money, leave me here. I know she has her eyes on you; her husband will be old and she will be wanting you...'

'Good heavens, Puella, she's not Kitty Robertson...'

'No!' flared Puella. 'But here you are arguing to increase trade and put money into Kitty Robertson's pocket!'

'Oh, for God's sake, Puella, if I see an advantage in trade it is to put money in *our* pockets,' an exasperated Kite protested. They fell silent, then Kite rallied. 'Look, Puella, I cannot pretend that any of this is easy for you, but when you get to England you cannot – no, by God, I *will* not let you – hide away. You will have to enter society and play your part as my ... as my wife. You are carrying my child and I shall,' he said with sudden resolution, 'make you my wife.' Then without waiting to see the impact his words had had upon her, for they had had too profound an effect upon himself, Kite blundered on. 'Look, my darling, you astonished that woman with your composure and dignity. I saw it in her eyes. You held your head up in Antigua, and you can do it here. These people here are unaffected when compared with the wives of the merchants of Liverpool and London. See this as your entrance into society, it will not be so terrible.'

'Suppose she is making some plan to, to…' Puella was weakening, Kite sensed, as she struggled to find words to express herself.

'To humiliate you?'

'Yes, to humiliate me.'

'I cannot believe that. She is not that sort of person. She is passionate and quick-tempered, but I think not ungenerous and unkind.'

'She would humiliate me if she made love to you and if she is passionate…'

'Puella,' Kite said reproachfully, embracing her, 'I love *you*. Only you.'

'She is dangerous to me, Kite,' Puella whispered. 'I feel these things. You cannot understand.'

'My darling,' Kite soothed, 'in three or

four days we shall be at sea.'

After a little they spread the bearskin on the deck.

Afterwards, Kite had to admit, the dinner was an undoubted success, and though it left him personally disturbed, it proved a triumph for Puella. Anyone who supposed the blacks ignorant and inferior to the whites would, had they known the astonishing transformation that Puella achieved, have instantly changed their mind. Puella rose from their extemporised couch transformed, invigorated and confident. Kite foolishly ascribed this to the intensity of their lovemaking on the bearskin.

When Jones informed them of the arrival of the Tyrells' carriage, Kite, who had often privately nurtured the conceit that Puella was a native princess, had no doubt of the matter as he led Puella ashore.

Puella's condition, though well into its term, was not yet obtrusive. She had readily assumed the character of the *grande dame* by hiding her burden under the ample elegance of one of Dorothea's dresses. Mulgrave had kept Dorothea expensively and, so far as Antiguan fashion allowed, fashionably dressed. Dorothea and the local dressmaker favoured the brilliant colours loved by the Africans, so Puella's skirt, while it paid due reverence to the wide mode of the day, was of a brilliant scarlet silk, which susurrated over a petticoat of yellow. Puella had cinched in the laced bodice, sufficient to both accommodate her growing belly and to expose her increasing bosom in the fashionable manner, while her ebony shoulders rose from tulle trimming of the very latest manufacture. She set off Kite's blue broadcloth coat, buff waistcoat, white breeches and hose, and silver-buckled shoes to perfection. Overall she wore the fox skin coat, while he affected a caped cloak of heavy wool worsted.

Kite had been anxious lest the Tyrells had indeed meditated some ritual humiliation, but there were no other guests present and while it was possible that none had been invited in order to save their hosts from embarrassment, Kite thought not. It was clear from the outset that Sarah Tyrell sincerely wished to make amends, or at least to signal that as her disinterested intention. Equally clearly, her husband was too much a man of commerce to be unduly troubled over superimposed conventions when they ran contrary to business opportunities. Besides, to hide the fact that they were entertaining a black woman was impossible – the servants who waited at table would carry the news about Newport within hours, though they concealed their feelings well enough at the time. Tyrell, bending over

Puella's hand as he courteously greeted her, set the tone within the hearing of his manservant by welcoming her as 'Mrs Kite'.

Tyrell was, as Puella had predicted, much older than his wife: a tall, soberly dressed man who wore a half-wig and, though far less taciturn and obscure, somewhat reminded Kite of Mulgrave. Grave in his deliberations, he had the same quality of measuring everything carefully before any commitment, knowing that once made, that commitment was permanent. Beyond the difference in their ages, he was an odd contrast to his wife; a man clearly used to being listened to and obeyed.

'Shall we go directly in to dinner?' he asked, though it was clear that he had no intention of doing anything else. It proved a shrewd move; the Tyrells were too polished to allow the conversation to become stilted. As the soup was swiftly served, Tyrell's question about the hurricane drew a general account from Kite. After this Sarah sought a few personal details of Puella's ordeal during the tempest, while Tyrell led Kite towards the subject of commerce by way of a concern for the *Spitfire's* spoilt cargo. Having drawn his young guest and made his own assessment, Tyrell asked whether Kite would carry some documents, bills of exchange and debentures to London on his behalf.

'I am not certain when I shall be in London,' Kite had said carefully, catching Sarah Tyrell's eye and colouring at her smile. 'But I am certain that I can attend to the matter.'

'I supposed, foolishly it seems, that you were making for London, but you are intending to land at Bristol, are you?' Tyrell asked.

'No, sir, it is my intention to return to Liverpool. I have an interest in a company there.'

It was clear that as soon as Kite mentioned Liverpool and his partnership with Makepeace, Tyrell showed a greater interest in cultivating a connection with him. It transpired that on his return to England Mulgrave had intended to act as agent for a number of colonial trading houses, among which was Tyrell's. Tyrell now encouraged Kite to assume the task.

'Liverpool is a growing place, Captain, and is already eclipsing Bristol...'

It occurred to Kite, as Tyrell expatiated on the mutual advantages that could arise, that Sarah Tyrell had picked up some hint of an advantage in securing the friendship of Kite early in their tea-party aboard the *Spitfire,* but he did not judge her to harshly for it. Looking across the table to where she was listening to Puella, he found it easy to forgive her. She had clearly charmed Puella, for she was speaking animatedly and, though he was attentive to Tyrell, he caught the drift of Puella's discourse, a reminiscence of her early life up to the time of her captivity. She had never spoken of it to him, and the facility with which Sarah had drawn from her the story of her youth, distracted him from Tyrell's conversation.

When the women withdrew, Kite accepted the cigar Tyrell offered him. 'Would you take a small shipment of these?' Tyrell asked, rolling the tobacco leaf alongside his ear. 'You see, Captain, I think we can do business.' Tyrell passed the decanter. 'Rhode Island is famous for its seamen and its ships, its rum and its slaves, but as it grows rich on these commodities there is a corresponding growth in demand for English manufactures. We produce much in the colonies now, but a pair of English pistols, or a fine hanger from Messrs Wilkinson, will command a higher price than a home-made article. As for London modes ... well, you are a young but not an inexperienced man in the matter of women, Captain.'

Kite seized the opportunity. It was not that he warmed to Tyrell, but he sensed the man spoke the truth as he saw it. 'You have been kind to us, sir. You will be aware that the presence of my, er, wife has caused some controversy.'

Tyrell raised an eyebrow and smiled. 'That

is true, Captain Kite, but I am not entirely immune to the lady's attractions. Don't forget that I knew Mulgrave, knew him quite well...'

'And you visited Antigua?'

Tyrell nodded, adding, 'And I knew Dorothea.' He blew cigar smoke at the ceiling. 'I also know my wife is responsible for the disfigurement of your face...'

'Please,' Kite said hurriedly, 'it is not important, Mr Tyrell. The matter is over and best forgotten.'

'That is generous of you, Captain.' Tyrell paused then, draining his glass, asked, 'So may we join hands in business?'

'I see no objection, Mr Tyrell. You are already associated with Wentworth and he with me...'

'And I know Makepeace, though I have to confess I do not much warm to him.' Tyrell smiled. 'You had better call me Arthur,' he said smiling and rising to his feet. 'Shall we join the ladies?'

Following suit, Kite felt he had been granted an honour and inclined his head. 'William Kite, at your service, Arthur.'

On that they shook hands and left the dining room.

Only when they were returning to Roberts' yard did Kite feel any disquiet. He was not quite certain how it happened, for the food

371

and wine had relaxed him, but he recalled that Tyrell had been showing Puella a small portrait of a Mohawk chieftain, which was said to be of some antiquity, when he had felt Sarah Tyrell's hand on his arm.

'Congratulations, Captain, on your good fortune,' she breathed, and Kite looked down at her fine dark eyes and red mouth. He seemed perplexed. 'Puella's anticipated confinement,' she said.

'Oh, she told you.'

'Of course not,' Sarah chuckled. 'I noticed.'

'I see...'

'No, you don't, Captain, but no matter.' She paused. 'We shall meet again, I am sure.'

'I, er, I hope so, madam...'

'Call me Sarah,' she said, her finger reaching up and touching his scabbed cheek. 'You will not forget me, I think, William.'

Kite glanced quickly at her preoccupied husband and the attentive Puella. 'No,' he replied, his heart beating foolishly, 'it would be very difficult to do that.'

She smiled and he felt his response said more than he meant, and yet paradoxically, he wanted to say more.

'Until the next time,' she whispered, drawing away from him and holding her hand out to Puella as she and Tyrell turned away from the little wooden panel that bore the image of the Mohawk sachem. 'Arthur has been showing you his great, great, oh I forget how many greats, grandfather...' It was a statement, graciously made, a rounding off of the dinner by setting a light-hearted seal upon it. Perhaps, Kite thought in the confusion of the aftermath of his moment of intimacy with Sarah Tyrell, she had meant the occasion as much for Puella as for him, and as much for him as for her husband. It had been a great making of amends. But in the carriage going back to Roberts' shipyard, as he cradled Puella under his arm, there grew a conviction that it had been chiefly for herself. The conceit tormented him as he lay awake beside the sleeping Puella, possessed of unfaithful thoughts.

'Good night, Captain,' she had said as they parted, 'it was a fair wind that blew you hither.'

Held from sleep he damned the woman who only yesterday had struck him with her riding crop, and whom he had viciously wished to strike across her lovely face. And he hoped the spirits would not be so unkind as to spoil Puella's new-found happiness.

Fifteen

The Corsair

During their last few busy days in Newport, Kite half hoped and half feared to meet Sarah Tyrell again. In the event, as Nantucket Island faded astern and resumed the blue insubstantiality that Jones had first sighted weeks earlier, he was glad that nothing further had passed between them. Arthur Tyrell had sent his clerk down with the papers he required Kite to take with him and later the same day, shortly before sailing, Kite had waited upon Tyrell in his counting house to enjoy a glass of wine and a fine view over the harbour. He had cleared *Spitfire* outwards at the Custom House and was enjoying the last moments of relaxation before he took the schooner to sea. It was Christmas Eve and a fine winter's morning. Tyrell had been in a cordial mood, solicitous that Kite would not remain in Newport over the festive season, but sympathetic to his anxiety to sail, so that Puella could be brought to bed in England, with the passage behind them.

'My wife will be disappointed,' he remarked as they took their leave, an uncomfortably enigmatic enough remark from Sarah's husband to make Kite feel a shred of guilt at the warmth Sarah had kindled in him. But it was the closest he got to Sarah, and to his relief Puella gave no further signs of jealousy. In his self-conceit, he did not realise the extent to which Puella was a prey to fear. Nearing the time of her confinement, alone and bereft of the support of Dorothea that she had enjoyed during the birth of Charlie, she was as much worried over the approaching ordeal of a long ocean passage as over the uncertainty of her future and the arrival of her quickening child.

Kite was blissfully unaware of her acute anxiety. The final arrangements about the cargo, its stowage and the necessity of attending the Custom House filled his time and thoughts. As they slipped seaward in the last of the daylight of Christmas Even, 1759, the land was already in shadow and Kite could not see the solitary horsewoman who, from the eminence of Castle Hill, watched the *Spitfire* turn east-south-east, heading south of the skein of islands beyond Buzzard's Bay.

They took their navigational departure the following day from the eastern extremity of Nantucket Island. Ahead of the *Spitfire* lay the broad expanse of the Atlantic. Taking a final glance at the low and misty shore, Kite could persuade himself that no such place as Newport existed, and no such person as Sarah Tyrell had ever smiled at him.

Only the flaking scab on his cheek reminded him otherwise.

The *Spitfire* ran east under her modified rig at a fine clip. It was cold, bitterly cold at times, and the west-north-westerly wind blew for nine days at gale force, but the schooner and her company were undeterred. The North Atlantic, even in her wintry mood, seemed disposed to treat them kindly. Those few of the hands who regretted leaving the warm climes of the tropics were seduced by Whisstock's glowing accounts of London and Liverpool, where, he affirmed, a man could live like a prince once he had made his fortune. So seductively did Whisstock descant upon the delights of these cities, so easily did he brush aside the actual mechanics of securing a fortune, that even Jones was persuaded there might be something in his claims. Consequently, one evening, as he handed over the watch to Kite, he raised the matter with him.

Kite laughed. 'He is deceived, Mr Jones. Liverpool is a foul place, though London might be well enough, I wouldn't know, I have never been there. But Liverpool...'

Kite pulled a face. 'True, there are some elegant dwellings there,' Kite went on, relying on Makepeace's assertions rather than any experience of his own, 'but without any means, and I don't suppose Whisstock has any means, he will be reduced to seeking lodgings in low alehouses where the only things he can rely upon seeking him out are the drabs and the pick-pockets.'

'It's the old choice between the pox, penury and an outward ship, then?' Jones queried with a grin.

Kite nodded. 'I fear so, Mr Jones, but he may prove useful in a counting house and so avoid the first and last. As for the pox, that depends upon his continence.'

'I supposed as much,' Jones said, embarrassed at his temporary gullibility.

They laughed and Jones, having passed over the watch and relieved himself of his ignorance, went below.

As the days passed Kite felt an increasing confidence, for the clear cold weather enabled him to verify their latitude and it held until they approached the north coast of Ireland and ran along the parallel of Malin Head, a month out of Newport, Rhode Island. He continually made plans, revised, honed and discarded them in favour of new ones; so high were his spirits that Susan Hebblewhite's murder was only a faint shadow on his horizon.

The plain truth was that the land ahead was as insubstantial as the fading blue of Nantucket astern, and the joy of sailing in this crisp, fine weather, for all the icy blow that hurled itself at them from the north-west, was unalloyed. Time enough, he thought, to worry. Makepeace was right. If not rich, Kite possessed sufficient funds to stand trial with a good defence if matters reached that extremity.

Puella grew in girth and was warm in her bearskin. The brief social encounter with Sarah had persuaded her she could hold her own among white society and Kite was too ignorant himself to disabuse her. As a country apothecary's son he was incapable of making the distinction between the easy manner of the wealthy, meritocratic colonial gentility and the rigid hierarchies of his native land. Thanks to the influence of Mulgrave and his experiences in Antigua, Kite had matured into a genteel and courteous young man. His own manner was natural and uncontrived, but as far as England was concerned he lacked the sophistication or pretension to judge how England would regard himself, let along his beautiful but black mistress. While his high mood and higher hopes were a measure of his new-found confidence, they were also a measure of his youth.

They sighted Malin Head on the horizon to the southward, and the island of Inistrahull a point or two on the starboard bow shortly before nightfall thirty-three days out from Newport. Kite bore up and hove-to for the night, unwilling to run down on so dangerous a coast in the dark. During the hours of darkness the wind dropped, and he came on deck at dawn to find them wallowing in a dense fog. What wind there was, was light and fluky, while the damp struck into their bones with far greater chill than the brisk cold wind of their passage. All about them lay a wall of damp and impenetrable vapour.

Kite swore, suddenly feeling the lonely burden of command after the jolly, light-hearted days of carefree running. He was again made abruptly and humiliatingly aware of his ignorance and lack of sea experience as the clammy fog insidiously depressed him. Lost in his thoughts he wanted to return to his cabin, to bury himself in the bearskin alongside Puella; he realised the temptation to give up and abandon matters was a strong and seductive compulsion to a man eager to conceal his inadequacy. Was this why men like Make-peace got drunk or drowned themselves in sensuality? Now vulnerable, bereft of self-confidence again, Kite felt the looming spectre of the gallows rise. He could put the future out of his mind no longer. His imagination conjured the loathsome and fearful image within the wraiths of fog, feeling again a sense of personal doom.

Fate was mocking him, chastising him for his weeks of satisfaction as *Spitfire* raced across the Western Ocean. He damned himself for his folly, for being seduced by Sarah Tyrell and agreeing to undertake her husband's commission; damned himself for listening to Makepeace and his plans for wealth and partnership. The fog was an omen, a certain portent that matters would not, *could* not, go well for him.

Kite swore again, the foul oath bursting forth with all the conviction his ardent and frustrated nature could muster. He regarded the deck ahead of him with distaste. It was now full daylight and he could see the planking sodden with condensation; every rope dripped and moisture ran in rivulets from the slatting, idle sails; even the helmsman could do little with the tiller as the rudder kicked back in the low swell. Kite fretted as the hours passed, frustrated and worried, the anxiety eating away at the pit of his stomach. He wondered whether waiting until the damned fog lifted was all he could do.

On this occasion Jones was of no use to him, for cold and fog were as unfamiliar to Jones as to Kite, and although Kite had known both since his boyhood on the fells of Cumbria, he had then borne no responsibility and he knew the country so well that he had never been lost.

Now Cumbria and its beloved fells lay not far away, beyond the narrow strait of the North Channel, through which he yet had to take the *Spitfire*. There was much yet to accomplish, and whatever happened to him, he *must* at least see his father and sister again. The decision brought him up with a round turn. This was no time for self-pity and he was suddenly contemptuous of the temptation to give in. If men like Makepeace could master situations like this, so could he. Then he suddenly recalled something Makepeace had said to him. It was almost his last remark, a friendly afterthought as he contemplated Kite's homeward passage.

'Don't forget Kite, that if you are in home waters, you have to consider the run and the set of the tide. If you are lost in fog and in soundings, you should anchor.'

He had forgotten about the tides! God, what a fool! At least he had had the forethought to put about the night before. He called forward to have a man set in the chains and to begin swinging the lead. As he waited for his order to be carried out and he leadsmen's monotonous chant to begin, he resolved that once ashore he would leave

Liverpool for Cumbria and proceed directly to his father's house. He would hire a carriage and make short work of the journey. God willing he would find his father and Helen in good health. They would take Puella in, care for her and tend her during her labour. He could then return to Liverpool, wait upon Makepeace and try his luck or take the consequences. The resolution cleared his mind. It seemed easy enough and honest enough; he had not, after all, killed Susan. A doubt crossed his mind that his father might be dead and Helen married, but then the leadsman began to call out the soundings from the starboard chains.

'By the mark thirteen!'

Kite's heart hammered; it was not a great depth of water after the bottomless Atlantic. 'Call all hands,' he bellowed, 'prepare to anchor!'

There followed half an hour of confusion as the cable was roused out and dragged forward to be bent on the starboard bower. This in turn had been released from its secure stowage, catted and prepared for dropping. By this time the leadsman was calling twenty fathoms and then twenty-five. Kite went forward and stared down into the water, telling the leadsman to leave the weight on the seabed for a moment, in order that he could estimate the speed and direction of their drift.

The line lay stubbornly against the ship's side. For a few moments Kite was deceived, then he had the lead cast again from the opposite side. The line drew rapidly away from the ship's side, out on the larboard beam. Kite hurried aft and peered into the binnacle.

'Is she steering?' he asked the helmsman.

'No, Cap'n,' the man responded, as if he had been asked if the *Spitfire* had been flying.

'Damnation!' The schooner's head lay to the north, but according to the evidence of the leadline they were drifting east. Kite was mystified, then the leadsman's voice sang out shrilly: 'By the deep four!'

'Dear Christ!'

'Let go, sir?' Jones called, his voice high pitched with fear.

'By the mark, seven!'

The temptation to relax was great. Was the depth increasing or not?

'By the mark, five!'

Then they all heard the echo, *'By the mark, five!'*

'Jeeesus Chris'!'

'Let go!' Kite shrieked, hearing the splash of the anchor, then the diminuendo of his fearful order bouncing back at them. The hairs on the nape of Kite's neck crawled as he felt the deck tremble slightly as the cable ran out through the hawsepipe. They must be close... So close.

'Nip it! Nip it!' Kite bellowed when he thought enough had run out to hold the *Spitfire*. Somewhere the unseen cliffs mocked him: *'Nip it! Nip it!'*

Kite hurried forward and peered over the side. The cable ran round the bow, rubbing against the stem, and he could see the tension in it as the anchor bit, then he felt the schooner's head snub round as the anchor brought up and spun the *Spitfire* head to tide. Now the cable ran down into the water at an angle, disappearing into the depths; the *Spitfire* was static, and not adrift on the bosom of the sea.

Kite felt the deep undulation of the incoming ocean swell and saw the velocity of the tide as it sluiced past them as if a mill-race. He felt his heartbeat subside and he swallowed, his mouth dry. Straightening up, he felt an immense relief that they were, for the moment at least, out of immediate danger.

As he composed himself, he sensed a change in the weather. The deck seemed to be less damp, the dankness of the fog diminishing, the vapour increasingly nacreous. Then, patchily at first, the limits of visibility began to extend as the fog began to thin. It took a moment to perceive anything, then slowly, with each man exclaiming at the sight, the echoes of their surprise bouncing back, the cliff reared upwards alongside them. It was huge and close, so close that the schooner was rocking to the backwash of the breaking swell as it met the vertical rock face.

'Good God!' whispered Kite to himself. He stared up at the fissured mass. The strata lay at a slight angle to the vertical. Here and there small ledges bore the stains of bird-lime, spring nesting places for guillemots, kittiwakes, razorbills and little auks. The dark purple of the striated rock reared above their mastheads and was shrouded in misty cloud and the swell broke in a ceaseless necklace of foaming water at its foot. Kite shuddered. Would the tide have swept them clear, or did sunken rocks lurk nearby, as the variability of the soundings suggested? He would never know. All that he could be certain of was that they had avoided disaster.

As the warmth of the wintry sun slowly burnt off the fog, the first whispers of a breeze began to ripple the water. Fortunately these airs came from the south-west, filling the sails so that, sheeted home, the *Spitfire* began to creep up tide, over their cable. Their situation was too precarious to tarry and Kite ordered the cable cut. They would lose an anchor but the slant of wind might be temporary and he could not wait to leave the proximity of that mighty cliff.

The *Spitfire* stood slowly to the west-north-west and the cliff disappeared astern in the mist. Kite could only suppose he had touched the coast somewhere near the Mull of Kintyre, or perhaps the coast of Islay, but he was never afterwards sure. All he knew at the time was that he must get away and stand back out into the Atlantic to wait for a final clearing of the weather before he attempted anything so foolish as to head for the North Channel and the Irish Sea.

It was two days before the visibility finally improved, and when it did, Kite saw a sail to the east. The stranger was a brig, standing close-hauled to the north-west, heading towards them.

'Outward bound,' Kite remarked to Jones, who had come on deck to relieve him. The two vessels closed on reciprocal courses, the brig flying a bright new red ensign, prompting Kite to hoist his own colours.

'I suppose,' Jones remarked, 'she could be a naval brig sloop, come to take a look at us.'

The strange vessel was edging down, and would pass close to them and Kite agreed, remarking, 'I think you're correct. She appears to have her guns run out…'

Then suddenly the two were approaching to pass close, a man standing atop the rail of the outward bound brig waving his hat and

Kite, leaping up on his own rail and hanging on to the main rigging, waved back.

'Bloody hell!' Jones yelled. 'Get down!'

The red ensign was descending in jerks to reveal the white and gold lilies of the Bourbon French. At the same instant a few puffs of grey smoke, accompanied by points of fire, rippled along the brig's gunwale. The shot tore over their heads. Holes appeared in both the main- and foresails and a ball hit the hull in a cloud of splinters which erupted with the impact. Then the brig's helm went over and her sails slammed aback. A second later first her main- and then her foreyard swung as she tacked and stood close across *Spitfire's* stern.

'He's going to rake, sir!' shouted Jones, as the horror of their predicament struck them, ending their stupefaction. Kite heard Puella screaming but thrust the intrusion aside.

'Larboard watch, run out the larboard guns! Starboard, tend the sheets! Up helm!' Kite lunged at the helmsman, helping to push the heavy wheel over to windward.

It was as well they had met the brig at the change of the watch with the entire crew on deck. Kite had no very great chance of getting off a shot at the enemy, but he could run for it, at least gaining a small lead on his opponent, whom he rightly concluded was a French corsair. By turning the same way as the enemy, Kite succeeded in buying himself a few moments' respite, avoiding the catastrophe of the brig's broadside being poured into *Spitfire's* stern where Puella was hiding.

But Puella was not hiding, she was on deck. 'What is happening?'

In the cabin she had heard the discharge of the brig's guns and felt the impact of the shot, then the heel of *Spitfire's* deck had caught her off balance as Kite turned towards the enemy. Frightened, she could remain below no longer. Kite was strangely glad to see her. She had wrapped herself in the bearskin and looked so incongruous that seeing her thus he smiled despite the circumstances.

'We are in trouble, Puella; that is a French privateer. An enemy ship. We must try and escape.'

As the brig turned, so did *Spitfire,* frustrating the French commander as he tried to place his vessel so that his guns could fire the length of the schooner's deck. Instead Kite drew away to the north and east, running before the wind, with the brig swinging in *Spitfire's* wake. Kite picked up the watch glass and levelled it on the brig. She had completed her turn in *Spitfire's* wake and although Kite had opened up a lead, she was clearly able to overhaul her quarry. That she was well manned and ably handled he had no doubt. There had been sufficient insouciance in the ruse of the waving officer, and the smart execution of her turn under their lee to convince him of that. But having turned away, Kite could think of nothing further that could be done. He looked forward. The larboard watch were laboriously loading and running out the larboard battery, but he had insufficient men to work the guns on one side of the ship, let alone two, even supposing he had a crew of competent gunners. This he had neglected, despite the letter of marque and reprisal that *Spitfire* carried. It had not been intended that she operate as a privateer until after she had fitted out properly in Liverpool. As it was, she carried scarcely sufficient powder and shot to fire off a dozen guns, let alone fight with her broadsides. Besides, Kite thought bitterly, as a privateer *Spitfire* was supposed to act offensively, not in abject self-defence.

Looking astern again he could see the brig appeared larger as she closed the gap between them. He felt a desperate and sickening sensation rising in his throat. In Newport he had heard the French were beaten, on their damned knees and reduced to suing for terms, so what in the name of Almighty God was this bastard doing chasing him in British waters?

Kite cast a wild look around the horizon,

as if his desperation would conjure up the arrival of a British cruiser, but all he could see were the distant mountains of the Scottish islands, and they were too far off to offer the slightest hope of refuge. Night too was some hours away, even in late January, and as for fog, well they had had their quota, Kite felt sure; it was not going to oblige him by shrouding them at this juncture!

'Bloody hell!' he ranted as Jones hovered anxiously.

'You'll have to strike, sir,' Jones said unhappily.

'I will lose everything... No, damn it, I shall not! Not yet anyway!'

'Our rig is cut down...'

'But we've another jib below. Get it on deck!'

The men seized the idea and went at the labour with a will. Even Jones cast aside his misgivings and was soon at the head of the crowd as another jib ran aloft. Some light-weather kites used in the West Indies appeared, straining at their bolt ropes in the breeze as Jones boomed them out like studding sails. The repaying of their hull at Newport meant they had a clean bottom, and with the extra sails their speed increased perceptibly. The schooner was racing through the water, the white bone in her teeth fanning out on either bow and, although Kite hardly dared believe it, the brig seemed not to be gaining on them so fast.

'Puella,' he said, 'be so kind as to bring me my quadrant.'

When she returned with the mahogany box, Kite removed the instrument, braced himself against the taffrail, set the index bar to zero and carefully subtended the image of the brig, measuring the angle between her plunging waterline and her main truck. Compelled to wait for some minutes before checking it again, he looked forward. Jones was adjusting sheets, carefully gauging how best to set each sail. What else could they do?

If only they could fight… But with little powder and shot, and an ineffective and small crew, Kite had little hope of anything more than discharging the guns to defend the honour of their flag before being compelled to strike it. If only…

The guns!

He could dispense with half of them without seriously prejudicing his chances of defending himself if he had to. 'Mr Jones! Jettison half the guns on each side. No, just keep three in each waist… And – and run one aft… See if you can get it into the cabin as a stern chaser!'

Kite saw Jones grin as he grasped the idea and waved his hand in acknowledgement.

The excitement between the two men was almost palpable now as Kite turned back to his pursuer and raised the quadrant again. There was a change; he bent over the arc and saw that the angle had increased. The brig was still gaining, but she surely only had a very small advantage. Perhaps when the guns went overboard...

Puella was beside him. He had almost forgotten her in his excitement. She was remarkably calm, he thought, looking at her.

'*Spitfire* is a fast schooner, Kite,' she said, her voice level.

'I hope so, my darling.'

'What do you do with the quadrant?'

He explained. 'I measure the angle...' He realised she would not understand the simple geometrical principle, so held thumb and forefinger close together, with only a small gap. Widening the gap he moved his hand closer to her face. 'If the French ship gets closer she seems to get bigger.' Then he withdrew his hand, closing the gap between the fingers again. 'If we go faster than her, she drops backwards and seems to be smaller. This,' he tapped the quadrant, 'can quickly tell me of a very, very small change, so that I can see...'

A cheer followed by a splash told where the first gun had gone overboard.

'So that I can see,' Kite resumed, 'whether we are going faster than she is, or she is going faster than we are.'

Puella crooked thumb and forefinger of her right hand together and moved her hand towards and away from her eye, nodding. 'I understand,' she said.

Kite looked at her and impulsively kissed her. Below them a widening ring of bubbling white dropped astern alongside the wake as the second gun sank to the bottom.

'Has the other ship come nearer?' she asked.

Kite raised the quadrant again, then bent over the arc. The angle was still opening, but the difference was tiny, a minute at the most. Nevertheless, the enemy was undoubtedly overhauling them. An idea occurred to Kite. 'Puella, I must teach you how to fire a pistol.'

'I know how.'

'You do?' Kite was astonished.

'Of course. Dorothea showed me.'

'Would you fight and kill Frenchmen?'

'Only if they are white,' she replied, smiling.

'Would you kill me, Puella?' he asked, only half joking.

'Only when you stop loving me,' she said, adding, 'and love Sarah Tyrell.'

'Don't be ridiculous,' he stammered. 'I will get you a pistol.'

Puella put her hand out to restrain him.

'No. I will get one myself – and Kite?'

'Yes?'

'I will not let those men in that ship take me. I will kill myself first.'

He stared at her for a moment and then said, shaking his head, 'I hope it will not come to that.'

She shrugged and went forward to the companionway. Kite watched her go: she had a damnably uncanny knack of divination, he thought uneasily. Then he picked up the quadrant. There was no doubt, the enemy brig was gaining on them, slowly but no less surely.

As another gun went overboard, Kite went forward and spoke to Jones. Then he ordered the steward to issue a tot of rum and resumed his station aft, just abaft the helmsman straining at the tiller, while Jones made the preparations Kite had ordered. It was a damned long shot, but he had little left in his locker and he guessed the Frenchman would try winging them soon.

It was another half an hour before the enemy commander felt confident enough of his greater speed to sacrifice a little of his ground, and to swing off course sufficiently to try a shot from his larboard bow chaser. The brig was slightly off on the *Spitfire's* starboard quarter, so she swung away a few degrees. The shot plunged into their wake, but it was only ten yards astern, slightly off on the larboard quarter. Another shot followed, about the same distance short, but directly astern. The wind caught the spray and carried it forward over the taffrail of the fleeing *Spitfire*.

Kite walked forward and ordered a slight alteration in course to starboard. It was just enough to bring the schooner more directly ahead of the pursuing brig and thus compel the corsair to swing even further off course for his next attempt. The enemy waited for a full twenty minutes, by which Kite no longer required his quadrant to ascertain the sober fact that they were still slowly but remorselessly losing ground. He decided he could wait no longer and went below to arm himself. He had decided to fight.

A party of seamen under Jones' direction were in the cabin, gingerly easing a four-pounder into the centre of the stern window.

'Captain Kite, I shall have to break down—'

'Yes, yes, of course; do what you must, but hurry, the sooner we can respond to his fire the better.'

A moment later an axe bit into the wooden sill across the window transom, breaking up the carpentry so recently installed at Newport after the storm damage. The crude destruction would lower the level of the woodwork so that the gun could fire over it, while the angle of traverse would be wide. Jones was extemporising train tackles and a recoil line, which if the gun were much used would probably bring down the central pillars in the structure, but it was a small price to pay if it saved the schooner.

In a corner, Puella had wound a sash about her waist and had stuffed a brace of pistols into it. 'Where did you get those?' he asked, already guessing the answer.

'From Dorothea,' she said quietly, darting a glance at the seamen. 'Mr Mulgrave let her keep a pair.'

Kite hid his surprise. As he prepared his own weapons, he told her his plan, his voice soft. At first she stared open-mouthed and then she laughed. 'If it happens, Puella,' he said, 'it will be a desperate gamble. You understand?'

'Yes, I understand. It will be all right.'

'I hope so. You must stay in the boat. I do not want you involved in the fighting.'

'I want our baby son to be born in England,' she said simply. Kite felt a wrench of remorse that he had not once considered the delicacy of Puella's condition through-out the day, let alone in contemplating the desperate measure he was about to take. He could only nod dumbly before returning to the deck.

Once Jones reported the gun in the cabin

ready, Kite called the hands aft and addressed them. They had one chance, he told them, and he had explained his intentions to the mate. It would only work if they cooperated, to which they assented.

'Very well, then. The cabin gun's crew had better be told off, Mr Jones, and we'll get to work–'

Kite never finished, for the French brig tried another shot. It passed through the starboard rail, not eight feet from where Kite was standing, and splinters sliced across the deck, catching one of the seamen in the face so that he fell back with a startled cry, blood pouring down his face.

Kite swung round. 'Steady on the helm there.'

'All steady, sir.' It was the former clerk, Whisstock, and Kite walked up to him. 'Now, Whisstock, try not to look astern.'

'Very well, Captain.'

But Kite did, just as the brig, noticeably nearer now, let fly another shot. If flew over them, so that he felt the wind of its passing suck at the air he was breathing. The ball buried itself in the larboard bulwarks with a thud. Whisstock swore and Kite remarked to no one in particular that the brig had their range. Fortunately the ball had missed the men working about the boat, set on chocks amidships between the masts.

Then there came a roar and a cloud of

smoke rose over the taffrail as the gun in the cabin below was fired. The powder smoke wafted forward, carried by the following wind. Kite missed the fall of shot, but waited for the next. As he did so, the brig fired again, but either a yaw of her own or Whisstock's momentary inattention saved them and the shot plunged alongside, level with the mainmast, but ten yards to larboard of them.

Jones fired the stern chaser a second time; again Kite missed the fall of shot but a cheer came from the window below. He doubted that they had achieved anything, beyond encouraging each other. He did not want to allow the brig to get too close before putting his madcap plan into operation, for the longer she had to wing them, the more chance she had of inflicting real damage. But he was conscious of having only the one chance and that everything depended on the hazardous plan he had put in place. He looked forward again. The cover was off the boat amidships and he saw Puella helped into it by one of the men, the pistols at her waist.

Nearby, the scratch gun crews had knocked the quoins out on the remaining trio of starboard guns and were retreating to hide under the boat. The rest of the crew had disappeared forward, crowded into the forecastle space, with only the boatswain visible, his head poking out of the forecastle companionway. He saw the man nod, his teeth bared and grinning madly.

A ball from the brig tore overhead and passed through the mainsail. The enemy were getting damned close!

Kite could wait no longer; he resolved to act the moment he next saw the tell-tale puff of smoke under the brig's bow. He turned his head, and shouted, 'Stand by the main peak halliards!' The two men posted at the mainmast threw the coiled ropes off their pins, and eased the turns belayed there.

As he saw the enemy fire again, he yelled, 'Let go the peak!'

The able seaman at the peak halyard already had the rope singled up to a turn on the belaying pin and now he threw that off. The rope snaked upwards from its carefully coiled fall, but at the same moment the enemy ball struck the stern and Kite heard from the cabin below a second wounded man scream in agony below. Everything was now happening at once and Kite fought to keep his concentration on the elements he must remain master of. Above him and winged out to larboard the main peak had dropped and the gaff swung wildly, the ensign half struck as its halyard ran slack. Beside him at the mainmast the second seaman now let go the throat halyard and the whole mainsail came down, the boom end trailing in the water. This and the loss of driving power slowed the schooner, but at this critical moment the continual screaming of the wounded man below cut into Kite's consciousness like a knife. He swore as Whisstock fought the schooner's desire to swing, the trailing main boom acting as a drag, but already the seaman who had let go the halyard was hauling on the sheet, hauling the heavy boom inboard.

He hoped the ruse had worked and the enemy thought they had shot the main halliards through, causing confusion aboard their quarry. Suddenly the brig was looming up closer. Another cloud of smoke blew over the stern and this time Kite saw their own stern chaser score a hit close to the root of the brig's bowsprit, near the gammoning. A cloud of splinters momentarily appeared and he thought he heard a shout, but he was standing close to Whisstock, his heart pumping, and he could almost sense the thundering of the helmsman's own pulse.

'Steady, my lad,' Kite said in a low voice, quite oblivious to the inappropriate use of a term for a man at least two years older than himself.

The brig was overrunning them fast now, faster perhaps than her commander wished. Kite held his course as the stern chaser barked again below him, reloaded with creditable speed. He coughed as the powder smoke blew past them and waved the cloud aside, but then the brig discharged her own gun at point-blank range. This time there was no mistake. The ball thumped into the mainmast about five feet above the deck, almost severing it at a stroke. The weight of the gear to larboard was sufficient to cause it to crack. It swayed forward, the break working right through the spar with a rending split until it parted and dropped to the deck, to lean forward at a drunken angle, restrained by the shrouds.

The brig's bow was now ranging up on the starboard quarter. Kite could see several faces peering down at him. He glanced round. His own gun's crews had hidden behind the boat amidships, and the decks looked almost deserted but for Kite himself, the helmsman and the two hands still at the main sheet. It appeared, or at least Kite hoped it appeared, as though the schooner was short-handed and had concentrated all her efforts at self-defence in the manning of her stern chaser.

Kite turned again to stare up at the brig. He could distinguish an officer from several armed ratings, and saw the former turn and shout something aft, presumably to the brig's commander. Then the man cupped his hands and shouted to Kite.

'Capitaine, do … you … strike … your … colours?'

Kite feigned incomprehension as the brig drew level, forty, thirty feet away. The larboard yardarms of her forecourse and foretopsail almost overhung the starboard quarter of *Spitfire.*

Then Jones defiantly fired the stern chaser again. He must have traversed the carriage, for the shot struck the brig amidships and Kite heard the cry of someone aboard the brig hit by a splinter. He could hear an oath, too, saw the grappling line thrown. The grapnel struck the *Spitfire's* rail and held. He drew his cutlass and cut it adrift, but another flew through the air and then the brig was ranged alongside and Kite knew they were going to be boarded before they could do any more mischief.

The sea running between the two vessels slapped back and forth, the two wakes cresting and hissing in a roil of confused water as the gap closed. On the brig the topgallant halliards were let go, the course clewgarnets were hauled up as the sheets were started and she slowed to match the speed of the disabled schooner alongside her. Kite swung round.

'Gunners! Now!' he shouted. The appointed gun crews leapt from hiding behind the boat and in an instant touched their linstocks to the breeches of three guns left in the starboard battery. At maximum elevation and double shotted, they discharged with a close sequence of booms so that Kite's ears rang. He saw the ball and langridge, composed for the most parts of carpenter's nails, rovings and scrap, tear upwards across the narrow gap. All along the brig's waist this iron hail struck indiscriminately at men, guns, ropes and the fabric of the brig's hull.

Amid the screams and shouts of fury, an order was passed and then the brig's helm went over, the yardarms loomed over the *Spitfire's* deck and she dropped alongside with a jarring crash. The next instant the enemy boarding party were jumping and flinging themselves down into the schooner's waist.

'Whisstock!' Kite bawled, discharging one pistol at an officer who had just landed and turned aft towards him. Amidships the handful of men at the three guns were driven back and Kite saw one run through. A second had got his hands on a boarding pike and parried a sword thrust before a pistol shot blew out the side of his face. But the man still thrust, impaling an enemy boarder to the rail as he fell, mortally wounded.

Kite hefted his clumsy cutlass as a French sailor struck at him. He longed for a hanger, light and handy, to fight off the assault, but he slashed wildly and yelled with all his might, 'Puella!'

Her screech was terrible; a hideous, high-pitched and attenuated shriek that tore through the air to rend the eardrums. Kite had never heard anything so dreadful as Puella rose from the boat amidships, the terrible cry ululating from her throat in a long exhalation. On her own initiative Puella had removed the shirt she had had on and emerged naked to the waist, levelling her brace of pistols at the mêlée below her.

The effect of her appearance was diabolical; the boarders paused for a vital instant, staring up at the voluptuous black manifestation which might have been from Hell itself, and then the *Spitfire's* boatswain and the bulk of the crew swept aft. Their faces were blackened with soot from the galley and they howled in pale imitation of Puella but their weapons were bright as they wielded them with telling effect. During their wait they had helped themselves to extra rum, served out by Kite's steward whose need for Dutch courage now justified itself.

As the black-faced men swept aft, Kite despatched his attacker, the crude and heavy cutlass blade raking the man's ribcage so that he fell back with a gasp. In the *Spitfire's* waist the blackguard crew were prevailing as Kite had hoped they might. Reassured, Kite looked up to the brig's quarterdeck and raised his second pistol in his left hand. Although the slightly lower freeboard of the schooner limited his view, he could see the French commander, just recovering from his surprise at Puella's appearance. Kite took careful aim and fired.

Kite's ball missed his target's head, but he caught the commander's shoulder and knocked him backwards. A moment later Kite was scrambling upwards, over the brig's rail, with the boatswain and his score of blackguards at his back, and Whisstock howling at his side. It was Guadeloupe and Le Gosier all over again. He cut and slashed with a wild kind of joy, relieved from the hours of anxiety and mad with the prospect of victory, assuaging his bloodlust and intent on putting his tormentors to the sword.

In ten bloody minutes, it was all over.

Sixteen

The Captain

If he was to be hanged, Kite thought as he paced the captured brig's quarterdeck, it might as well be as a sheep, not a lamb. Above him the Bourbon oriflamme fluttered in the breeze, superimposed by the British red ensign; astern of him the disabled *Spitfire* tugged at her tow-rope, Whisstock and two other hands left aboard to steer in the brig's wake. On their larboard side the yellow line of Formby Sands, ringed with low breakers, formed the north bank of the Mersey Estuary. Ahead of them the river was crowded with shipping, a cutter-rigged mail packet was tacking out towards them, her post-horn pendant at her single masthead, beyond her a pilot schooner was outward bound for her station off the Great Orme. Two coasters were, like themselves, inward bound, from Ireland, Man or, Kite thought with a leaping heart, Whitehaven, Silloth or Maryport on his native Cumbrian coast. Over on the Cheshire shore stood the White Rock Perch, and behind the beacon lay the low eminence of Bidston Hill, conspicuous with its windmills and the mast and spars of the lookout station. To starboard stretched the brown tidal flats of the Burbo Bank, beyond which rose the blue rounded hills of Flintshire. The dark peaks of a score of fishing boats, the paler sails of another pilot schooner and the square topsails of a cruising frigate dotted the horizon astern. It would be hard to make a more public entry on his return to Liverpool, Kite thought ruefully.

The Conspiracy of Fate, Kite had written in his journal the previous evening,

has Ensured that I shall Return in what the World Considers as Triumph. Luck Delivered into our Hands a fine French Corsair Brig, *La Malouine,* of St Malo, which having Attempted to Take us, we Boarded and carried at the Push of Pike. We found our Advantage derived from her being Short-Handed on Account of the Success of her Cruise and her having sent away the Greater Part of her Company in Prizes...

Nor had their luck ended there, Kite thought, for among those on board Jones had discovered a Liverpool pilot named Farnell, who was much relieved to be delivered from his captivity. The unfortunate man had been captured in an outward-bound snow and retained on board by the corsair's commander, Capitaine Jean-Marie Guillermic, to advise him on navigation in the North and St George's Channels. Now Farnell stood beside the helmsman and conned them up the Channel as the young flood made beneath them.

'It is a small price to pay in recompense for my freedom,' Farnell had said, waving aside any suggestion of a fee, 'though I expect my wife would have been glad to see my stern for a while,' he joked.

Below in his own cabin, Capitaine Guillermic lay a prisoner in his cot, his shoulder wound poisoning and his mind wandering in feverish distraction. In the brig's wardroom, under the guard of the boatswain whose face still bore greasy traces of his black mask, lay the rest of the wounded, including *Spitfire's* own men. Puella and the cabin steward did what they could, but four Frenchmen and five of the *Spitfire's* crew had already died of their wounds. The remainder of *La Malouine's* lay below hatches in the hold, one of their own guns loaded with langridge trained on the only access and a seaman with a lighted linstock standing guard over them.

The westerly breeze filled *La Malouine's* sails, so that she made a brave sight inward bound, a white bone in her teeth as she swept up the Formby Channel on the flood tide. The lookouts on Bidston Hill had signalled the strange brig's arrival off the Mersey bar. A crowd had gathered on the waterfront as they entered the river proper, and the Cheshire bank closed with the Lancashire coast opposite. As the spires of Liverpool drew abeam, the upper yards were dropped, the forecourse was clewed up and Farnell ordered the helm over. *La Malouine* rounded into the tide and let go her anchor, the tethered *Spitfire* following her and trailing astern on her tow-rope.

'Well, Captain Kite,' said Farnell as he confirmed the brig had brought up to her anchor, 'I am much obliged to you, and the moment my gig comes off, I shall seek your immediate accommodation in the dock.'

'That is kind of you, Mr Farnell.'

'There will be a great deal of curiosity about your arrival, Captain, but I can assure you the Liverpool underwriters will be most grateful to you. This bloody Frenchman has been making a thorough nuisance of himself for some time now, but thanks to you and your schooner, well, I at least will be able to get my anchor down in the lee of bum island, eh?' Farnell smiled and held out his hand.

The distant boom of the noon gun marked the time, but it seemed to the euphoric and tired men aboard both the brig and the schooner to be a personal salutation.

Farnell proved as good as his word. By early afternoon another pilot came aboard *La Malouine*, with a second clambering over the battered rail of *Spitfire*. As the tide slackened and approached high water, *La Malouine* weighed anchor, and crabbed across the last of the flood, to breast the dock wall and warp round into the dock. A crowd stood on the dockside as the two vessels secured in their berths, a small band had been mustered and played the topical tune 'To Glory we Steer', much popularised the previous year in celebration of British victories.

As they slowly entered the dock, drawn forward by the men walking round the capstan and heaving the dripping head warp tight, Kite regarded the waiting assembly. On the quay Kite recognised Captain Makepeace, his wife and three children by his side; Makepeace was addressing the bewigged mayor and a party of aldermen gathered behind their mace-bearer.

'We are famous, it seems, Mr Jones,' he remarked as the mate whistled his surprise.

'You're right, Captain. And to think I asked you to strike the old ensign... Deary, deary me.' Jones shook his head ruefully.

'Don't reproach yourself, Mr Jones,' Kite said cheerfully. 'No man did more to secure our success than you and I hope that, in a day or so, I shall be able to help you.'

411

Jones looked at Kite, his mouth opened in astonishment, but Kite remained studying the crowded quay. 'Ah, there's a file of soldiers...' Kite's voice trailed off as he was seized by a sudden apprehension.

'To take care of our prisoners, I suppose,' Jones offered.

Kite cleared his throat. 'Yes ... I suppose so.' Kite swept the doubt aside. 'Mr Jones?'

'Sir?'

'Be so kind as to ask Puella to come on deck.'

'There's no need, sir.'

'I'm here, Kite.'

Kite turned. Puella stood in her fox fur, which she wore over a grey silk dress, her head held high, the nostrils of her broad nose flared as she breathed the chilly air, her eyes gleaming with pride. She looked every inch an African princess and Kite felt an enormous surge of affection for her.

'I have never seen you looking so beautiful,' he said in a low voice. As *La Malouine* crept closer to her berth the crowd began to cheer. 'This is a remarkable welcome. I expected nothing like this,' he murmured.

'Captain Kite is a remarkable man,' Puella said as a gangway was run aboard.

'Captain Kite is a charlatan,' Kite muttered to himself. 'And worse ... oh, so much worse.' Then he raised his voice and said, 'I shall present you to the mayor as my wife,

Puella, and you must curtsey. It is a formality expected of us.'

'I understand,' Puella responded, nodding.

Kite hitched the surrendered sword of Captain Guillermic on his hip and eased his shoulders under his best blue broadcloth coat. He had last worn it to dine at the Tyrells' and now perhaps, with the Frenchman's sword giving him a specious claim to gentility, he was aware that such hubris preceded a fall and that file of soldiers made him sweat. But Puella was ready and the mayor was waiting. Gamely, he led Puella ashore.

Her appearance descending the gangway caused a stir, but the polyglot crew of black, mulattoes, quadroons and whites who milled in the waist watching their commander were not unfamiliar to the citizens of Liverpool.

As Kite bowed to the mayor, Jones shouted, 'Three cheers for Captain Kite of the *Spitfire!*'

The crowd joined in and it was some moments before Kite could hear the rather mumbled welcome from the mayor and accepted the dignitaries' compliments for capturing *La Malouine*. He half turned and presented Puella.

'My wife, sir, Mistress Kite.' Beside him, Puella dropped a perfect curtsey.

'Charmed, ma'am...' The mayor's tone was condescending and beside him his lady stiffened as her husband quickly reverted to Kite. 'You have been in the Antilles some time, Captain?' the mayor asked pointedly.

'I have, sir,' Kite responded coldly, adding, 'and my wife is expecting...'

Whatever further celebrations had been mediated by the mayor and corporation, these seem to have been abruptly terminated on the appearance of Puella and there was a general retrograde movement of the robed aldermen.

'Then she shall not be kept in the cold, sir. Come Captain, it is already twilight, allow me to offer my conveyance...' Captain Makepeace swept to their rescue. 'Kite, Kite,' he chuckled divertingly in a low voice, 'all this and a new brig too...'

'I have to clear inwards at the Custom House,' Kite protested mildly.

'Time enough for your jerque note tomorrow, Kite. Ride the crest of this wave while you may. Come, my coach is close by...'

'What crest?' Kite asked, a hint of bitterness in his voice as the mayor and corporation withdrew behind their mace-bearer and the band were marched off.

'The gratitude of the underwriters will, I am confident, be made manifest in due course.'

A young infantry officer suddenly barred their way. 'Captain Kite?'

Kite coloured. For one ghastly moment he thought that he confronted nemesis and that the subaltern had come to arrest him, but the young lieutenant smiled and languidly asked, 'I understand you may have some French prisoners, Captain?'

'Yes, yes, I do.' Kite turned and called out to Jones. The big mulatto ran up, a cutlass bouncing on his hip. Kite suppressed a smile at the mate's ostentation. 'Mr Jones, deliver our French prisoners to the custody of the lieutenant here.'

'Aye, aye, sir.'

'What about the wounded?' Puella interjected, attracting the lieutenant's eyes.

'I'll attend to them too, ma'am,' he said politely, staring with ill-disguised and insolent curiosity at Puella.

Kite nodded. 'Very well.'

'Come, Kite, come, Puella,' Makepeace insisted, 'it is growing cold.'

Makepeace had a comfortable house in a new terrace on the rising ground above the river. He had schooled his wife well and she gave every appearance of sincerity as she welcomed Puella into their home, expressing concern for her condition. Mrs Makepeace was a thin, plain woman, some years younger than her husband, but she was well dressed and bustling, ordering her servants to accommodate her guests and admonishing her children as they stared with ill-concealed curiosity at Puella.

'Is she a slave?' her youngest son, a boy of about eight, asked in a piping query. It was an awkward moment, but Puella smiled.

'Mrs Kite,' Mrs Makepeace explained with hurried resource, 'is a princess from Africa.'

'Does she sell slaves?' the boy went on, but Makepeace's oldest child, a girl of thirteen or fourteen, clapped her hand over her brother's mouth and said, 'You must bow to a princess, Harry,' and she dropped a respectful and diplomatic curtsey.

'Must I, Mama?' the boy Henry asked, wrenching his head out of his sister's grip.

'Most certainly, Harry,' his mother said.

Henry sighed and pouted. 'I have to bow to *every*body,' he protested, footing a jerky obeisance. Then he turned to his brother, a shy handsome boy of eleven. 'Now, Charlie, *you've* got to do it.'

Kite looked at Puella and saw the shadow cross her eyes. The coincidence of the boy's name to that of her dead child made her involuntarily lift her hand. Kite sensed she intended to distance herself from the boy, caught up perhaps by some primitive native instinct, but Charles Makepeace stepped docilely forward and taking Puella's hand, bent and kissed it.

'Your servant, ma'am,' he whispered courteously.

To Kite's relief, Puella was charmed and the awkward moment passed. Makepeace ruffled the hair of his youngest son and remarked that he was a chip off the old block.

'And spoiled to boot,' said Martha Makepeace, revealing a streak of severity that dominated her house when her indulgent husband was at sea.

Kite and Puella enjoyed a pleasant enough evening in the society of Makepeace and his wife. It did not compare for courtly elegance with the hospitality of the Tyrells on the far side of the Atlantic. Puella found Martha a cold and rather hectoring fish, but Mrs Makepeace for her part meant only kindness, informing Puella of the general state of affairs among her equals in Liverpool in a relentless manner. When the ladies had withdrawn, Martha intent on continuing her instructional monologue, Kite told Makepeace that he intended to lay his private ghosts and proceed to Cumbria at once. He hoped that there Puella would remain until she had given birth.

As for his fears, Kite explained, 'The matter must be cleared up, don't you see, before I can see my way to settling here in Liverpool.'

Makepeace nodded. 'I entirely agree. You

will suffer from too much distraction until you have discovered how the land lies and, if, God forbid, it runs ill for you, you must return here and ship out in command. God knows, you have enough vessels to choose from.'

'I had not thought that far ahead; so, you do not think I should stand trial and clear my name?'

'I see no point in courting trouble, no. As you are innocent, it is surely proper to act in an easy and open manner.'

Kite remained uncertain. 'To run away once under the impetus of youthful fear is one thing, but to slip away now would be entirely misinterpreted.'

'Ah, but if you were simply to return and go straight to sea, who would know?'

'Well, you and I...'

'Does Puella know anything of this matter?'

Kite shook his head. 'No.'

'And you do intend to marry her...'

'Yes, I do not want the child born a bastard.'

Makepeace refilled his glass. 'Kite, my dear fellow,' he said, taking a deep draught, 'you saw the interpretation put upon Puella's presence by my innocent children this evening, and you saw the, er, surprise evinced by his worship the mayor and his lady. Are you aware of the effect an extrapolation of such behaviour by society at large may have both upon you, and upon Puella?'

'And upon *you* and upon your business if it is associated with me?' Kite asked, colouring.

'Of course,' said Makepeace reasonably, draining his glass. 'Let us make no bones about it between ourselves. It is important that we understand each other perfectly, Kite. Surely you agree.' Kite nodded reluctantly. 'Very well. To Puella. She may in time be accepted, but it would be better to keep her as a mistress, if you must...'

'You have long known how I feel about Puella.'

'Aye, Kite,' Makepeace soothed, 'and I know the pleasure to be had of a blackamoor, or better still of two,' he jested, 'but she is black and black wives are too much a ... damn it, too much a novelty to be so easily shoehorned into society.'

Kite shook his head and seized the decanter, filling his own glass to mask his anger. 'Well, it is too late now. I have told her I intend to marry her and I have told the world that she is my wife. I am obliged to. Damn it, I want to!'

Makepeace sighed. 'You always were a contrary fellow...'

'Look, Makepeace, I am beholden to you; no, damn it, I am *obliged* to you, I need your assistance and we are, or are soon to be, partners – unless you want me to with-draw…?'

'No, I don't. There is a great deal to be made of our association.'

'But Puella is an embarrassment?'

Makepeace shrugged. 'Perhaps. The women do not like it. They suspect all manner of things, silly creatures, but the presence of a black woman as a legitimate, churched wife is unsettling. It uneases them to think a white man takes pleasure from lying with a blackamoor; it demeans them; it breeds jealousy and that is a contagious infection. They may take against Puella, conspire against her in some monstrous way. Damn it, Kite, the gossips will have their day. They are probably already embarked upon it as we speak, for you could scarcely have made a more public entry.'

'That thought occurred to me,' Kite agreed ruefully. 'It is scarcely without irony.'

'All will be forgiven if we prove profitable.' Makepeace raised his refilled glass. 'Let us drink to that. If you sail again and Puella sails with you, then matters will likely blow over in time. Nothing succeeds like success. If we sink, well, we sink and no one will be surprised.'

'We shall not sink,' Kite said firmly, raising his glass in response to Makepeace's toast.

'No, not if the auguries are correct. You will have added another ship to our fleet once the prize court has adjudicated, and as your letter of marque is valid they can do nothing but find in your favour. Fortunately there was no naval cruiser in sight, otherwise the Admiralty Johnnies would be claiming a share, damn them.'

'Which brings me to the vessels,' Kite said. 'After I have cleared the *Spitfire's* entry, there is the business of the deposition for the prize court.'

Makepeace held up his hand. 'For Heaven's sake relax, Kite. The prize court won't sit for weeks; as for the other matters, I offer my services as ship's husband. What, when she has been awarded to you, do you want me to do with *La Malouine?*'

Kite thought for a moment. 'It will depend upon the condemned value, but I think we should keep her, she is fast and fit for, well…' He had been about to say 'slaving', but restrained himself. 'Well, privateering, as we know. I should like her to join our fleet, though her name will need a change.'

'What shall you call her, then?' Makepeace asked.

Kite scratched his head. 'Well, to be truthful, we would not have taken her but for Puella…' Kite regaled Makepeace with an account of Puella's diabolical appearance and the affect it had on shifting the advantage to the *Spitfire's* hard-pressed crew.

Makepeace much enjoyed the yarn, nodding appreciatively. 'Then we must honour Puella's part in the action...' Makepeace paused for thought.

'*African Princess*,' Kite said in a low voice.

'What's that?' Makepeace asked.

'What about *African Princess?*'

'By God, I like that, damned if I don't!' Makepeace said enthusiastically. 'I like that and by Heaven, once the yarn of her part in the capture gets out, as it surely will, it might arouse the jealousy of the ladies, but by God she'll be popular among the men!' Makepeace slapped his thigh with glee. 'The matter's settled then: *African Princess* it shall be!'

Kite smiled. 'Good. And if you will allow her value to offset my capital stake then we may set aside the surplus for the crew, for they will have a lien against her condemned value as a legitimate prize.' Kite paused. 'If you agree, that is.'

Makepeace nodded. 'Yes. I agree. What of your mate, the mulatto fellow, Jones.'

'He's a prime seaman, but lacks schooling.'

'If you appoint him agent for the crew, would they trust him?'

'And he would have you to act on his behalf?'

Makepeace nodded.

'If I was to advise it,' Kite said, 'I think he

would accept it readily enough, as would the hands.'

'Then we shall retain him as ship-keeper and see he is put to his books. He may acquire the rudiments of navigation while we await the court's ruling. I shall inform the Admiralty marshal of the matter. As for the *Spitfire,* we shall have to take her in hand and step a new mainmast.'

'She is otherwise in excellent condition,' Kite said, telling Makepeace of his meeting with Arthur Tyrell in Rhode Island.

'And did you meet his wife?' Makepeace asked with a salacious grin.

'I did.'

'And what did you think of her?'

'Beautiful and temperamental.'

'Temperamental?' Makepeace snorted. 'Never!' He leaned forward, a little drunk, as Kite had seen him so often before. 'Now if you were to take my advice, Kite, you would bide your time before marrying and then, when old Arthur has slipped his cable and run off to Abraham's bosom, you'd secure *that* little wench. By God, but she makes a man's bowsprit into a jib boom, there's no mistake!'

'That's as maybe, but...'

'You've Puella, I know, and you love her. I know that too. Don't think I don't remember throwing her at you that night. I suppose I've only myself to blame, eh?'

'I suppose you have,' said Kite smiling wryly. 'I hadn't thought of it like that.'

'Well, 'tis pointless trying to make the world different. It tends more to profit to accept the world as it is. Now, listen, Kite, listen.' Makepeace was speaking now with some care. The hour was late and it had been a long day. They ought soon to join the ladies, who had no doubt run out of things to chatter about long ago.

'You have my absolute attention,' he said.

'Good. You, my dear fellow, must settle your mind, and then your ... oh, damn it, your wife! Take my coach and go north tomorrow, after you have been to the custom house. Then you can leave the vessels to me. Go north. See your father. Publish your banns and marry. Return when you are content. I'd be obliged for the return of my coach in the interval, but I will send it back for you if you wish. If you want to return directly, then keep my fellow and the equipage up there. You can find somewhere to stable it for a night or two, can't you?'

Kite nodded, overwhelmed at Makepeace's kindness. 'You are sure? Won't Mrs Makepeace object?'

'Of course not,' Makepeace slurred, 'of course Mrs Makepeace won't object.' He rose unsteadily. 'But come, let's go and make certain.'

Seventeen

The Return

As Makepeace's carriage rolled north, Kite tried to share Puella's wonder at the passing countryside. Fortunately it was a fine day, a late February day when the winter still occupies the high ground but there are tiny hints of the coming spring in the lower-lying land. They spent the night in Lancaster, where the shadow of the castle sent a cold shiver through Kite. His change of mood did not go unnoticed by Puella.

'What is it, Kite?'

He shook his head.

'I know something troubles you,' she insisted.

He smiled. 'We have a saying, Puella, that one shivers when a grey goose flies over one's grave. It is just a premonition, a forewarning of our mortality. A reminder that one day we will die.'

'That is like the spirit of the *obi*,' she said, and Kite gained the impression that Puella was pleased to have found some metaphysical link between her culture and his.

'It is very primitive,' Kite said without

thinking, then recalled that it was unlikely Puella understood the meaning of the word 'primitive'.

'You are primitive, Kite,' Puella said.

'Am I?' he said, unable to disguise his astonishment.

Puella nodded. 'Very primitive,' she said rubbing her enlarged belly. They rolled into the inn yard and jerked to a halt.

They crossed Westmorland next day. The long pale ruffled finger of Windermere lay between its eternal hills and Kite could scarcely believe he had been so long away and these mountains and lakes had remained as he saw them now, indifferent to him and his tribulations. They were in their stillness, he thought, as heartless as the hurricane had been in its furious, excoriating activity. His own existence was quite incidental to their own, his own concerns so petty that they had no meaning in the cold aloofness of the physical world. And yet he had a part in this physical world; he looked across the carriage to where Puella dozed. His child quickened in her brown belly and it too, God willing, would know these wild fells as its father had done. Kite found himself for the first time thinking of the child as a sentient being, individual and complete. It would have Charlie's coffee-coloured complexion, common among the children of St John's but not common here.

He recalled all Makepeace's warnings, but looking at Puella now he wondered how could one not love her. She had, after all, drawn the venom from Sarah Tyrell. Surely all would be well...

But the anxiety of his own future gnawed at him. What would become of Puella and of her child if he was arrested, flung into gaol and brought to trial? Worse, what if, for all his wealth, he was found guilty and hanged? And once the Pandora's box of worry was opened, fearful suppositions poured from it. Makepeace was but a mouthpiece! The hellish jest taunted Kite, without his protection Puella and the child would be subjected to God only knew what ignominies and humiliations. She would be seen as a nigger, her child as a pickaninny! What had he done, bringing them here, so that the unfortunate infant would see the light of day within sight of the Hebblewhites' farm?

Panic seized Kite. He broke out in a sweat. Suppose he was seen as he entered the village? The arrival of a carriage, any carriage unfamiliar to the villagers, would arouse curiosity. Within minutes the news would be carried to the Hebblewhites and they would send word to the magistrates. By the morning he would be under arrest and on his way to Carlisle to await the Assizes.

And yet he had to see his father and Helen, for with them lay the only refuge possible to Puella if the worst was to happen to him. Kite gnawed his knuckle in an agony of indecision, staring at Puella asleep on the seat opposite. Almost maddened with terror, he stared at her long black lashes lying on her dark cheeks and her slightly parted lips. Why in Heaven's name had he fallen so hopelessly in love with Puella and her black and lovely body?

And then he knew with a painful clarity, as the carriage slowed at an incline and the hummocked summit of a hill drew into view outside the window, he had turned his back on these fells; they had not driven him away, he had fled them, taking his disgust with him. For he recognised now that it had been disgust at the sight of Susie's white and quivering flesh that repelled him as much as the cretin she had born. Even as the breath left her body and she lay in so pitiful a state, Kite, her would-be lover, had experienced a powerful revulsion. Even now the thought of that moment made him sick.

Kite swore and mopped his brow. He was going mad! He let down the window and stuck his head out, gasping for air. The image of Susie, her legs apart with the monster between, slowly faded. He felt the breeze cool on his tortured face and the threatening waves of nausea subsided. The wind had got up and clouds swept in from the south-west, shrouding the summits of the old, familiar hills. Helvellyn rose to the east and the gleam of Derwent Water showed ahead as the road curved in its descent until they ran along its shore and crossed into Cumberland.

He drew back into the carriage and Puella roused herself.

'It is a small sea,' Puella said yawning and leaning half out of the window.

'It is a *lake*,' Kite explained, mastering his fears and settling back into his seat.

'Have you slept, Kite?' He shook his head. 'Have we far to go?'

'No,' he replied, wishing the drive could go on for ever.

A little later, as they came to a junction in the rough, unmade track, the coachman drew rein and asked Kite for directions. An hour later it was Kite who again leaned from the window. He recognised the spur of the mountain over the far shoulder of which he had fled the Hebblewhite brothers five years earlier. It seemed like the tensed back of an old and ossified beast, waiting to pounce upon him. Then he could see the valley opening up as the last of the daylight fell on the far side of the lake. The huge slope of broken scree still caught the sunset light as he remembered it, and the ebbing day threw the village into a premature twilight. He could see copses and farmsteads, and the tower of the church and...

He drew his head in and Puella, who had been dozing, jerked awake, staring at him. She reached out her hand and he took it, the white and brown skin almost the same tone in the gloom of the coach. We are one, he thought, she carries my child; after me, the child will live on.

'I will give you a son,' Puella said, with uncanny prescience.

'How do you know my thoughts?' he said, looking up at her, close to tears.

'I can see the spirits about you,' she said, her hand clutching his as though she also understood his fear. He turned his head aside and saw the Hebblewhites' farm roll past, its whitewash grey in the dusk.

'Dear God...' he whispered.

The coach slowed. 'Cap'n Kite, sir. Is this the place?'

Kite withdrew his hand from Puella's and dashed it across his face before peering from the window. It was almost dark, but not dark enough to obscure the sign above the door. He noted the paint was peeled and this reproached him even more than the legend: *Kite & Son.*

'Yes, stop here, if you please.'

The coach jerked to a standstill. Kite opened the door, jumped out and lowered the step. He handed Puella down as the coachman dropped from the box with a grunt and stretched with a low oath.

'I will help with the portmanteau in a moment,' Kite said. 'Allow me a moment.'

'Take yer time, sir,' the coachman said obligingly, hoping for an easy day on the morrow. 'Them nigger wimmin can't be hurried without a whip,' he added to himself, unbuttoning and urinating against the offside front carriage wheel.

'Come, my dear,' Kite said nervously, holding Puella's hand as she looked at the humble shop front. 'Let us see who is at home...'

He tugged the familiar metal rod and heard the distant jangle of the bell. No light showed from within and for a long moment the place seemed to be deserted. Then a faint light swung obliquely through the windows of the shop, as someone approached along the passageway inside. A bolt rasped and the door opened; a woman, half hidden in a mob cap peered at them, holding a candle up to Kite's face.

'Is Mr Kite within?' Kite enquired.

'Who's asking, then?'

Thankful that he was not immediately recognised, Kite had anticipated this moment. He had no wish either to startle his father, or to announce his arrival. 'I am from Liverpool and have letters for him.'

'Are you from Master Frank?' the woman asked and Kite remembered his cousin. The thought disconcerted him. Had Francis learned of the arrival of a 'Captain Kite' with a captured privateer? Had Francis been among the crowd assembled on the dockside two days previously? He had not thought of that!

'Yes,' he said hurriedly, seizing at a straw in the manner of a drowning man.

'Is that someone you have with you?' the woman peered into the darkness thrusting the candle further forward. 'God Almighty! It's the devil!'

'It's my wife,' Kite said sharply.

'Your *wife!*' The woman fell back and began to shut the door, but Kite pushed forward.

'Excuse me,' he said. 'Come, Puella.' And taking Puella's hand he entered the passage and began to mount the stairs.

Behind them the woman screeched, 'Missee! Missee! 'Tis the devil himself and his damnable missus!'

The smell of the house was exactly as he remembered, the dark stairs creaked at the fifth and the eighth step. As he reached the top of the flight and turned along the passage, the door of the small sitting room opened. The lamplight flooded out on to the bare boards, throwing out the shadow of another woman as she appeared in the doorway.

'What is it?'

'Helen?'

'Who is that?'

Kite recognised his sister's voice. 'Helen,' he said quietly, 'it's William... Your brother...'

'Oh! My God!'

Kite stepped forward as Helen fell back in a faint and then he felt himself shoved aside as the woman who had answered the door passed him, having first pushed Puella out of the way.

'Missee Helen, Missee Helen...'

Kite followed the distraught creature into the room. Helen had subsided into a chair and the mob-capped woman bent over her in a fearful fluster.

'Is she all right?' he asked, and the woman turned, her face furious.

'What business is it of yours, you damned blackguarded devil!'

Kite's jaw hung open and he felt his own knees weaken. He leant back against the wall for support.

'Susie? Susie Hebblewhite? Christ, I thought you were dead!'

The woman haranguing him stopped, her face ugly and distorted. She was far younger than the first candlelit impression had suggested. 'Who are you?' she asked. 'Who are you? I know you! You are the devil...'

'That's William,' a voice said, and Helen rose, taking Susie by the shoulders and soothing her. 'That's William, Susie. Do you remember William, Susie?'

Susan shook her head violently. 'He's a devil, Missee Helen, a devil and he's got Old Harry's wife wi' him! See! See!' Susan pointed, her stabbing finger trembling with terrified and pious indignation.

'My God!' Helen saw Puella in the doorway and Kite stepped forward to support the trembling, half-hysterical Susie in an attempt to reassure his sister.

'It's all right Helen, this is Puella, she is from Africa...'

But it was far from all right and it took some moments to calm the situation and restore a degree of equanimity to the two frightened women. But in due course Helen had ceased hugging him and had subsided to a genteel and decorous weeping while Susan, having poked Puella in passing, was finally persuaded to go down stairs and make some tea.

'I have nothing else, I'm afraid, William, we live simply.'

'It is no matter, Helen. Is... Is Father...?' He could not bring himself to finish the sentence, but left its uncertainties hanging in the close, lamplit air.

'He is out... Attending a sick woman... You will not know Mrs Sutcliffe, she is overdue and had been brought down with a fever, Old Mother Dole is with her.' Kite remembered the midwife; she had been a dark and terrible presence the night his own mother died bearing Helen. 'He may be back before long.'

'And Susie,' Kite said. 'I thought her dead!'

Helen looked at him curiously and then at Puella. 'Won't you please come in and sit down,' she said. 'I am sorry, this is all such … all so unexpected.'

Helen stared with unconcealed curiosity as Puella entered the room and sat down. She had remained passively standing quietly in the doorway throughout this extra-ordinary proceeding. Now she smiled at Helen.

'Pray do not trouble yourself,' she said, smoothing her skirt.

'She speaks…' Helen flushed and burst into a renewed flood of tears. 'Oh, William … Who is she?'

'Come, Helen,' Kite said laughing, 'Puella is … we are betrothed. She is to become my wife. She speaks perfect English. She is an African princess…'

'And you,' Helen looked up, her dark eyes sodden with apparent misery, 'by all appearances, you are a gentleman.'

'He is Captain Kite,' Puella said in-sistently.

'*Captain* Kite? I don't understand…' Helen's confusion mounted, but Kite, suffering waves of relief at the sight of Susie

Hebblewhite in the land of the living, if not quite of the wholly sane, yet still perplexed, sought to calm and question her.

'Helen, calm yourself, I beg. I shall explain everything but first tell me about Susie. I had supposed her to be dead... Did you ever get my letter? No, of course you didn't, Mulgrave died...'

'Yes, I did receive your letter. I recall it was brought me by a Midshipman Hope, who took the trouble to bring it all the way from Portsmouth.'

'Good Lord.'

'He was a pleasant man and we still correspond... Upon occasion,' Helen added wistfully.

'But you did not correspond with me,' Kite said reproachfully.

Helen shook her head and finally dried her eyes, pulling herself together with a muttered apology. 'Father would not let me. We knew you thought Susie was dead, but Father said that if you thought that, and that you had killed her, you would make your own way in the world and, since he knew no other way in which you would be stirred to do so, he would not stop you.'

'But I was innocent ... I had no hand in her murder ... I mean her injuries...'

Helen raised her hand to her lips as Susie came into the room with a tray of tea. 'Thank you, Susie,' Helen said. 'Will you wait up until the master comes home.'

'Of course, Missee Helen, I always does.'

'Helen, I have a carriage and four along with a coachman outside. Would you have room for him?'

'Mrs Ostlethwaite'll have a room, Missee Helen,' Susie said. She seemed calmer now and willing to help. 'An' I'll send him up to the farm to stable the horses.'

'That would be kind of you, Susie,' Kite said, but Susie never took her eyes off Helen and she nodded. 'If you would be so kind, Susie.'

'I'll walk up with him, then,' Susie said, throwing a quick glance at Puella. Kite heard her muttering as she left, and could hear her uttering imprecations as the eighth stair creaked under her weight.

'She doesn't appear to recognise me, or affects not to,' Kite said.

'You are much changed, Will. I hardly knew you, but for your voice; your skin is so burnt…' Helen looked nervously at Puella.

Kite expelled his breath and Helen, colouring, poured the tea. 'You know I never touched Susie, Helen,' Kite said. 'I came across her in the barn where she lay screaming and covered in blood.'

Helen nodded. 'She gave birth to a monster,' she said matter-of-factly, handing a cup to Puella. 'Philip Hebblewhite wanted people to believe you were the father and that that was why you had run away. Father was called to dress her wounds. He destroyed the still-born infant and heard her admit that she had never lain with you. 'Twas said that the child was sired by one or other of her brothers. Susie has been with us ever since but sadly the balance of her mind was disturbed and she will not recognise you, now you have changed so much.' Helen shook her head and smiled. For the first time he properly recognised his sister.

'I see,' he said, returning her smile. 'But she was terribly wounded, Helen. Forgive me, but there was blood everywhere... The pitchfork ... and,' Kite frowned, 'the child was *not* stillborn ... I am sure that the creature was living when I came upon her.'

Helen shook her head vehemently. 'Father would not lie,' she protested, 'he said the child was dead...'

'The child was dead, Helen, when I got there... But I did not tell you everything. It was not stillborn.'

Kite turned and leapt to his feet. 'Father!'

His father stood in the doorway, his old green coat about his thin shoulders, his face stubbled with his unshaven beard and furrowed with his careworn existence. 'So the prodigal returns, eh? I met his coach and four seeking lodgings at the very farm this tragedy took place in.'

'Father!' Kite repeated, nonplussed.

Mr Kite sighed. 'According to the Scripture, I am supposed to welcome the prodigal,' he said in his dry, remote tone.

'Will you not do so?' Kite asked, his voice thick with emotion as, with a delicate susurration of her grey silk dress, Puella rose with quiet dignity, her hands out-stretched towards Kite.

'Who is that black woman in my house? Is she your whore?'

Kite shook his head. 'No, Father, she is neither my whore, nor my slave. In fact, she is shortly to become my wife.'

Mr Kite's face registered no emotion. 'And what manner of man are you now, William? You look prosperous enough, but how do I know that your carriage and four is not hired?'

'If it pleases you, it is not mine. It was lent to me, Father, in order that I might come and see you...'

'That was good of you,' Mr Kite's voice was richly sarcastic. 'Five years is a long time...'

'For both of us, Father,' Kite broke in, and Kite saw his father wince at the inter-ruption.

'Well, you are here now. It is late. We shall talk of this again. I don't know where you are going to sleep, but your old room is still empty. Good night.'

'He doesn't mean it, William,' Helen

439

pleaded as Kite turned back to his sister, his face angry and hurt.

'He has no idea,' Kite said through clenched teeth. 'Good God, he has absolutely no idea!'

'He knows, Kite. But he cannot say.'

Kite rounded on Puella. 'Oh, and I suppose you can see his familiar spirits,' he said, his voice bitter with a vehement sarcasm that matched his father's.

'No,' Puella said. 'He has no spirit. He has given it all away to the woman who is having her baby.'

Kite woke in the badly made bed to a howling gale and sheets of rain flinging themselves against the window. A pallid grey daylight filtered through the small panes and he rolled over to stare up at the ceiling. The same old cracks rambled across the plaster, making a rough map of an imaginary countryside which he had once peopled with warring kings and their armies, their castles and their cities. Mountain ranges and rivers and lakes intersected this chimerical landscape.

So, he thought as a gust struck the window and Puella stirred beside him, Susie was not dead. He had lived for five years with a fear as groundless yet as real as the kings and soldiers who had warred across his ceiling in their upside down and fantastic world. How cruel fate was, he thought; how like the cold rain that drummed upon the square of glass.

Slipping from the bed he tip-toed out into the passage and then descended the stairs, remembering to step over the creaking boards, only to discover that there were more now that gave under his weight in the silence of the night.

His father was in the warm kitchen, sitting at the old square table with its rough, scrubbed surface and the three rings burnt into its surface long ago by hot pots. Kite could remember the nights his distressed and recently widowed father struggled to cook for himself and his family at the end of a long day. The older man set down a steaming tankard and rose as Kite entered the low room and, for a moment, Kite thought he was about to withdraw, but instead he leaned over and lifted the kettle off the banked fire. Kite sat on the far side of the table watching his father fill a second tankard and push it towards him. It was filled with hot toddy.

'Thank you,' Kite said as his father resumed his seat and stared into the glowing embers of the fire.

'We said the child was stillborn,' he said after a long silence, 'to still any rumours. Old Hebblewhite knew you hadn't done it, though he had seen you enter the barn. He beat his louts when they returned after chasing you and thrashed the truth out of them. I think it was Philip who gave the thing its quietus and Philip, I think, who felt he had fathered it, but who knows? It was an unpleasant business.'

'But she was...'

Mr Kite shook his head. 'Unconscious and badly injured... Very badly injured. The pitchfork... You can imagine the filth... We drew stuff from her wounds ... well, it was a nauseating business, but Old Mother Dole knew a few specifics and I was not entirely useless.' A faint smile passed over the older man's face as he looked at his son. 'She was no more badly punctured than had she been opened up for a Caesarean birth, for the pitchfork did not pass through her body. I think Philip was mad with fury; he was trying to stab the cretinous thing he had brought into the world and struck poor Susan. It was a foul affair.'

There was a long silence, as Kite digested this information. Then he said, 'Helen told me that you thought it better that I should be left to think that I had killed Susie... That even when I wrote you refused to let her reply...'

'What was the point? I could not afford to keep you.' Kite's father looked across the table. 'Well, Will, are you not twice the man now that you were then?' he asked.

'But...' Kite wanted to protest the cruelty

of leaving him ignorant.

'Besides,' his father went on, 'you had run away. I assumed you were prompted by some guilt of your own.'

Kite flushed. 'Father, I never...'

'It is of no matter now. Tell me, that black woman you have brought with you. She is with child, is she not?'

Kite nodded. 'Yes.'

'Is this the first child?'

'No. We had a son, but he died of some form of infantile asphyxia.'

'And where did this infantile asphyxia take place?'

'In Antigua.'

'Is that in the West Indies?'

'Yes.'

'And is she a slave, this black woman who is to become my daughter-in-law?'

'No. She was brought aboard the Guineaman in which I was serving, but I had her released and made free by an instrument of manumission.'

'After taking her to your bed?'

'Father, do not think of me in the same way that you think of Philip Hebblewhite. Such an irony would be too much for me.'

'But you wish me to take her into my house...'

'Only until our child is born and I have made provision for her.'

'And where will this provision be made?'

'In Liverpool, where I conduct my business.'

'In slaves and sugar, I suppose?'

'I have become a ship-master and a ship-owner, Father.'

'Like Brocklebank of Whitehaven, eh? Well, well.'

'I can much ease the circumstances of both you and Helen, Father. I can provide for your old age...'

'Do you love this black woman, Will?' Kite's father had turned towards him and Kite saw that the older man's reserve had cracked.

'I do, Father.'

'And it is not simply lust?'

'No.' Kite shook his head. Lust had inflamed him at Newport, but love for Puella had triumphed over that madness.

'And you lost a child, you said?' The import of the event seemed at last to strike his father. 'I had a grandchild without knowing it.'

'Yes, a boy,' Kite repeated, 'named Charles.'

'And what is your woman's name?'

Kite explained, prompting his father to emit a low chuckle. *'Puella*, eh? Well, well. What a strange fancy... *Girl*, eh?'

'It seemed not so strange at the time.' Kite paused, feeling the ice between them melting away. 'Now I never think of the word as anything other than her name.'

His father nodded and slowly rose to his feet. 'I am growing old, Will, but I am glad to see you hale and well.' He nodded. 'Your Puella may stay here as you wish. Let us hope she and Helen tolerate each other and that she bears you another son.' Mr Kite extended his hand and his son took it. 'So, you call yourself *Captain* Kite, no doubt. What a conceit. Well, well.'

His father went out in the direction of the latrine but paused in the doorway and turned round. His eyes twinkled and a mischievous smile played with the corners of his mouth.

'Puella, eh? Well, well. What on earth are you going to call your son?'

Kite followed his father as far as the doorway and leaned there, staring out at the dawn. The far ridge of the distant mountain's flank was as sharp as a sword-blade against the hard yellow light of the dawn. Long ago he had toiled up that steep and unforgiving slope of scree, in fear of his life with the Hebblewhite brothers in hot pursuit.

What a strange destiny had led him back. He stretched and yawned, shivering in the cold morning, the air tingling in his nostrils. The light was stronger now, sparkling on the frost riming the outbuildings, the wall and the fields beyond, yet throwing the fell into deeper shadow, its slopes, rocks, gullies and fissures hidden to him.

The freezing air invigorated him: suddenly the world seemed full of possibilities.

The publishers hope that this book has given you enjoyable reading. Large Print Books are especially designed to be as easy to see and hold as possible. If you wish a complete list of our books please ask at your local library or write directly to:

Magna Large Print Books
Magna House, Long Preston,
Skipton, North Yorkshire.
BD23 4ND

This Large Print Book for the partially sighted, who cannot read normal print, is published under the auspices of

THE ULVERSCROFT FOUNDATION